THE GIRL WHO HAD NO FEAR

MARNIE RICHES grew up on a rough estate in Manchester, aptly within sight of the dreaming spires of Strangeways Prison. Able to speak five different languages,  Modern & Medieval Dutch a University. She has been a punk artist, a property developer and

Marnie is the author of the bes of eBook thrillers, the first of which, *The Girl Who Wouldn't Die*, won The Patricia Highsmith Award for Most Exotic Location in the Dead Good Reader Awards, 2015. In 2016, the series was shortlisted for The Tess Gerritsen Award for Best Series (Dead Good Reader Awards).

By the same author:

George McKenzie series

Girl Who Wouldn't Die
The Girl Who Broke the Rules
The Girl Who Walked in the Shadows
The Girl Who Got Revenge

Manchester series

Born Bad
The Cover Up

The Girl Who Had No Fear

MARNIE RICHES

AVON
A division of HarperCollins*Publishers*
The News Building
1 London Bridge Street
London SE1 9GF

www.harpercollins.co.uk

First published in Great Britain in ebook format by HarperCollins*Publishers* 2016
This paperback edition published by HarperCollins*Publishers* 2018

1

Marnie Riches asserts the moral right to
be identified as the author of this work

A catalogue record for this book
is available from the British Library

ISBN: 9780008271473

This novel is entirely a work of fiction.
The names, characters and incidents portrayed in it are
the work of the author's imagination. Any resemblance to
actual persons, living or dead, events or localities is
entirely coincidental.

Set in Minion by Palimpsest Book Production Limited, Falkirk, Stirlingshire
Printed and bound in Great Britain by CPI Group (UK) Ltd, Croydon CR0 4YY

For Christian. May your salsa always be extra picante and your cerveza always cold.

PROLOGUE

Cambridge University Library, 30 March

When the lights went out in the University Library stacks, George held her breath. Looked around in the murk. But all she could see from the vantage point of the rickety desk where she had been reading was the glow from outside. The setting sun, pregnant with demonic menace, reflected on the Cambridge spires some way off to the east of the library, making the jagged rooftops look like the gaping, reddened maws of giant prehistoric beasts. Behind her were only the long shadows cast by the bookshelves; row after claustrophobic row, stacked to the ceiling with dusty old books. Anyone could hide among them in this twilight. The arsehole that had been following her ... could he be lying in wait?

'Who's there?' she shouted, her voice quivering. Her breath steamed on the sharp air.

No answer.

She picked up a heavy Old High German dictionary that had been left behind on the desk by some undergraduate. Held it high above her, poised to bring it crashing down on an attacker's head, should she need to.

The lights came back on suddenly, making her squint. She shrieked at the sight of a flustered-looking librarian, who in turn yelped at the spectre of a combative George, wielding the tome.

'Dr McKenzie!' the woman said, taking a step back and clasping her hand to her fleece-clad bosom. Almost tripping over her own feet, shod in the utilitarian leather flats that were popular with senior citizens and the bunion-afflicted.

Horrified, knees buckling with embarrassment and relief in equal measure, George set the dictionary down on the desk beside her. She smiled apologetically at her would-be victim. 'Mrs McMahon. I'm so sorry. The lights went out. I got spooked.' She clutched her purple mohair cardigan around her, shivering with adrenalin as much as the cold. 'You know how it is.'

The ageing librarian pursed her lips and tapped on the face of her watch. Spoke with stretched out East Anglian vowels that belied her haughty attempts at received pronunciation. 'It's 7 p.m. The library's closing in fifteen. And after all these years, a Fellow, of all people, should remember that the lights are on timers in the stacks.'

'Sorry,' George muttered, gathering her own books into a neat pile. 'It gets pretty creepy up here when the sun goes down.'

Mrs McMahon looked her up and down, eyeing George's ripped jeans and wild curls with obvious disapprobation. Clearly the type of old-timer who didn't think the University academic staff should dress like the students. But then, unexpectedly, her pruned mouth stretched into a kindly smile. 'Ah, well Spring has sprung! It's only going to get lighter of an evening.'

George nodded. 'Roll on summer, eh?' Shovelled her books into her bag. Pulled on her duffel coat and slung her bag over her shoulder, glad of the librarian's company on the long walk back down to the main entrance.

By the time she had left the imposing phallic bulk of the University Library, the glow of the sunset had been replaced by a melancholy full moon that cast an eerie glow on the car park. That feeling of being watched still hadn't abated, George acknowledged reluctantly.

Unshackling her old mountain bike, she started the cycle ride

2

back to St John's College down Burrell's Walk, feeling vulnerable as her malfunctioning bike lights flickered weakly in the darkness. No helmet, either. She was annoyed at her own negligence.

Anyone could pull me off my bike down here and not a fucking soul would be any the wiser, George thought as she pedalled hard enough to make her heart thump violently and the sweat start to roll down her back.

Scanning every dense evergreen bush for signs of the long-haired old rocker with those idiot mirror shades that covered his stalking, watchful eyes, George repeated the mantra in her head: *If I see him again, I'll kill him. Four sightings is more than just a bloody coincidence or paranoia. Nobody stalks George McKenzie and lives to tell the tale.*

Suddenly, she was blinded by a dazzling headlamp probing its way down the secluded path. A throbbing engine made the ground beneath her tremble. She felt like she was being sought out by an enemy searchlight. This was it. Whoever was after her was on a motorbike. Heading straight for her. He was going to take her out. *Fight or flight?*

Wobbling and uncertain now, she steered her mountain bike into a bush, falling over painfully into the barbs of holly leaves. The motorbike was upon her. But its rider was not the long-haired rocker George was anticipating. In the saddle was a fairly elderly woman, wearing a crash helmet covered in graffiti, whom George recognised as an eccentric engineering professor from Robinson College … or was it Girton? Not her stalker.

'Get off the path, you disease!' George shouted after the Professor.

With a defiant middle finger raised in the air, just visible in the red glow of the motorbike's tail-light, the Engineering Professor accelerated away.

George was safe, for now.

As her breathing and pulse slowed to an acceptable rate, she continued her journey with nothing more than a dented ego. She checked her watch, realising she was running late. No time to stop off at college to grab a coffee with Sally Wright in the Fellows' Drawing Room to discuss the imminent publication of their criminology tome. She'd have to make straight for the station if she were to catch the train to London. Aunty Sharon was expecting her before she went out to work. The bed in Tinesha's old room had been made up as usual, making George's regular scheduled early-morning journeys to HMP Belmarsh to conduct her research among its violent inmates that bit easier.

The cycle ride along Trumpington Street was uneventful, with the Fitzwilliam Museum, spotlit in the darkness, the only thing of note, apart from the couple making for Browns restaurant. George ploughed on to the left turn at Lensfield Road, pedalling past the three-storey Victorian houses that comprised student accommodation, mainly owned by Downing College. It was only once she had reached the junction with Hills Road, where she paused to get special fried rice from the Chinese takeaway opposite the big Catholic church, that George felt certain a car had been following her. A VW Golf that she had noticed pull in as she had pulled in.

Was that the long-haired rocker behind the wheel?

She blinked. Blinked again and peered with narrowed eyes into the darkness. Considered approaching, throwing her scalding rice into the driver's face.

But what if she was wrong, as she had been with the motorbike on Burrell's Walk? What if she was going mad and merely imagining that Bloom, the now-incarcerated transnational trafficking crime boss, known by his contemporaries as 'The Duke', had sent someone after her? As if he hadn't already tortured her enough.

'Fuck this for a game of soldiers,' she muttered under her breath.

With her foil container of food swinging in its plastic bag from her handlebar, she pedalled with as much haste as her out-of-shape legs could muster to Cambridge train station, praying the busy, brightly lit main road would afford her some safety.

Finally, leaving her bike locked in the overcrowded bike racks, she boarded the train to King's Cross. Two minutes to spare. And she even found a seat with a table.

When persistent beeping heralded departure and the doors slid shut, George's body was flooded with almost jubilant relief.

'Jesus, man. This is bullshit,' she told her laptop as she booted up. 'I've got to calm down.' She breathed in deeply; breathed out slowly. Conjured an image of her missing mother, Letitia, imagining her happily ensconced in a high-rise somewhere, maybe in Den Haag or Bruges or Southend-on-Sea, using some gigolo as a sticking plaster to nurse the wounds left by having been given a bad prognosis by that Dutch consultant. For all George knew, Letitia was bending this younger lover's ear about her 'pulmonaries' and 'sickle cell anaemics' while she pounded his body with her middle-aged bulk. George reassured herself that the enucleated eye in the gift box in Amsterdam's Vinkeles restaurant had just been a prank, care of Gordon Bloom, designed to freak her out and make her think that her mother was dead. Somehow, he'd got hold of Letitia's phone. People got mugged all the time, didn't they? She reminded herself that the emails from her father were crap, sent as a wind-up by one of Bloom's lackeys, no doubt. She hadn't genuinely heard from her father in over twenty years. Mommie Dearest, Letitia, had seen to that. Why would he start contacting her now?! This was the stance George preferred to take when she could feel herself being pulled into a downward spiral of nihilism and anxiety: Brush it under the carpet. Hope for the best.

Good. Let's crack on, you paranoid arsehole.

Clicking her emails open, chiding herself for being so foolish and uptight, George scanned the new arrivals in her inbox. But in among the late essays from second-year undergrads and correspondence from her editor about the forthcoming book and some bullshit about having to reapply to the Peterhulme Trust for research funding, there was one unread email that made her curse out loud; an email that caused the coursing, hot blood in her veins to slow to an icy trickle – another missive, ostensibly from her estranged father.

From: Michael Carlos Izquierdo Moreno (Michael.Moreno@ BritishEngineering.com)
Sent: 30 March
To: George_McKenzie@hotmail.com
Subject: I've still got my eye on you.

CHAPTER 1

Amsterdam, an apartment in Bilderdijkkade, 25 April

The naked, dark-haired man dropped the tiniest amount of liquid into the drink using a syringe. He flung the syringe down onto the granite kitchen worktop. Treated him to a smile that was loaded with promise. Lips, a little on the thin side, perhaps. But his kindly eyes were long-lashed, at odds with his almost gaunt face and bull neck. Floris tracked the thick cords of sinew that flanked the man's Adam's apple down to his collarbone, beneath which the curve of his pectoral musculature began. He had the ripped torso of a body builder. This dark-haired stranger was everything he desired at that moment, all right. Floris anticipated how he would feel inside him. Tried to remember where he had put his lube and condoms.

He took a deep breath. Was he ready for this?

He peered down at his almost painfully erect penis. Half an hour since he had taken the Viagra and he was good to go. Yes, he was ready.

The man winked. Pushed the drink into his hand.

'Go on, then. Get a little Gina down you,' he said, caressing Floris' navel hair. Starting to kiss his neck.

Floris stared into the bubbles of the now-narcotic lemonade, fizzing upwards to greet him. Rising and popping. Rising and popping. Like the men at this party. G wasn't normally his drug. Sex parties weren't normally his thing. It had been Robert's idea. Robert, who had earlier been full of assurances that he'd have his back. Now, Robert was elbow-deep inside some big blond bear, off his face on mephedrone.

'I'm not sure,' he whispered. 'I've already taken a couple of things.' He closed his eyes to savour this stranger's touch. Nagging doubt started to creep in. Should he have stayed at the club? Familiar turf. Familiar faces. Familiar routine. He could stick to his boundaries there. Now, he was in uncharted territory, wondering if he should drink from this possibly poisoned chalice.

'Go on. Everyone else has had some. It makes you horny as hell. And more relaxed.' The stranger pointed to his own sizeable engorged cock. 'You'll need it.'

Floris batted away encroaching thoughts of the end-of-term marking that was sitting on his kitchen table in his apartment. Pushed aside the stress that came with disgruntled parents who couldn't quite believe their perfect progenies could perform so badly in their tests. Nearly the holidays. Fuck them.

'Drink!' the other man said. Insistent. Excited. 'I want you.'

What the hell was his name? Hell, it didn't matter anyway. Abs. That's what he would call him, on account of the six-pack. Abs.

Floris drained the glass. Started to reciprocate the man's sexual advances, feeling suddenly bolder and wanton, though he knew it would take longer than that for the G to kick in. On the worktop were four lines of mephedrone. His new mate broke off to snort two. Gasped and grinned. Indicated that he should follow suit.

'Why not?'

Not the first time for Floris. Not with miaow miaow. That, at least, was his regular weekend treat. *Now* he was in the mood to party. He glanced over to the living area – a sickly feast for the senses. At least twenty men, maybe more, caught up in a writhing

8

tangle of tanned, toned bodies in that slick, studio apartment in Amsterdam's Oud West district. Their lascivious grunting and shouted instructions still audible above the thump, thump, thump of the sound system. The smell of aftershave, sex, poppers and lube on the air. Punctuated by laughter of those who were taking a break and having a smoke on the balcony.

'Come on,' Abs said, taking him by the hand and leading him towards the naked throng of tumescent revellers.

Abs was less skilled with his hands and mouth than anticipated, but Floris didn't care. He had promised himself he would be more daring. Had promised Robert he would try harder to be more sexually adventurous to keep their relationship fresh. And this was as good as it got, wasn't it? Being screwed roughly by a hot guy whose name he couldn't remember. Cheek by jowl with other rutting casual lovers. All of them utterly uninhibited, like something out of a gay porno flick.

Except Floris was starting to feel sleepy. And sick.

He tried to make eye contact with Robert, who was blowing his blond bear with clear enthusiasm.

'Rob,' he began. 'I don't feel good.'

Except the words hadn't come out properly. And he was struggling to catch his breath.

What was Abs doing?

Floris tried to look behind him at Abs. Make eye contact. Tell him that he was feeling weird. Tell him that he was no longer enjoying this. Was Abs even wearing a condom? Floris couldn't remember. He hadn't even asked if the man was taking PrEP or what his HIV status was. Shit. That was no good. The last thing he wanted was an unsafe encounter. He needed to extricate himself from the situation, fast. Get out of that apartment. Get some air.

But his clarity of thought was slipping away. Breath coming short, he found himself gasping for air, as if oxygen was suddenly in scant supply. His heart pounded uncomfortably in his chest; so hard that it blended with the rhythm of the thudding dance music that played on the stereo and the unforgiving rhythm of Abs as he took him roughly and remorselessly. Only dimly aware of what was happening to him, in a still-lucid corner of his mind he at least realised he had been given a dodgy dose of drugs. Was he going to be sick? The wave of nausea was suddenly intense and unbearable. Was he vomiting or just dreaming it? Fear somehow managed to reach in amongst the dull-witted drowsiness and pulled out the single, unwelcome, sharp-edged incontrovertible truth that he, Floris Engels, might die that very night.

Then, everything went blank.

CHAPTER 2

Bilderdijkgracht, 27 April

'Pull him from the water,' Van den Bergen said, standing beneath the golfing umbrella in a vain attempt to shield himself from the torrential spring rain. Shifting from one foot to another at the canal's edge, he registered that his toes were sodden where the rainwater had started to breach the stitching in his shoes. Damn. His athlete's foot would almost certainly flare up. George would be on his case. That much was certain.

'He looks rough, boss,' Elvis said at his side. Standing steadfastly just beyond the shelter of the umbrella. Water dripping off the end of his nose and coursing in rivulets from the hem of his leather jacket, the stubborn idiot.

Van den Bergen glanced down at the bloated body in the canal. Now that the frogmen had flipped him over, he could see that the white-grey skin of the man's face was stretched tight; that his eyes had taken on a ghoulish milky appearance. There were no ligature marks around his neck, just visible as its distorted, waterlogged flesh strained against the ribbed collar of his T-shirt. No facial wounds. There had been no obvious blows to the back of the head, either. The only visible damage was to the man's arm, which had been partially severed and now floated at an unlikely angle to his body. The torn flesh wafted in red fronds like some strange soft coral in the brown soup of the canal water.

'It was a bargeman that found him, wasn't it?' Van den Bergen asked, picking his glasses up at the end of the chain that hung around his neck. Perching them on his triangular nose so that he could read the neat notes in his pad. 'He was moving moorings round the corner from Bilderdijkgracht to Kostverlorenvaart, and the body emerged when he started his engine. Right?'

Elvis nodded. Rain, drip-dripping from the sorry, sodden curl of his quiff. 'Yep. That's what he said. He had pancakes at the Breakfast Café, nipped into Albert Heijn for milk and a loaf of bread—'

'I don't want to know the bargeman's bloody shopping list, Elvis,' Van den Bergen said, belching a little stomach acid silently into his mouth. 'I'm trying to work out if our dead guy's arm was severed in the water by accident by the blades on the barge's engine or as part of some fucked-up, frenzied attack by a murderous lunatic with a blunt cheese slice and an attitude problem. I've had enough nutters to last me a lifetime.'

'I know, boss.' Elvis sneezed. Blew his nose loudly. Stepped back as the frogmen heaved the waterlogged corpse onto the cobbled edge of Bijlderkade. 'This looks like it could just be some guy got drunk or stoned or both and stumbled in. Maybe he was taking a piss and got dizzy. Unlucky.' He shrugged.

Still holding the golf umbrella over him, Van den Bergen hitched up his raincoat and crouched by the body. Watched the canal water pour from the dead man's clothes back to its inky home. 'No. I don't buy it. We're not that lucky. It's the fourth floater in a month. All roughly in the same locale. We normally get ten in a *year*, maybe.' He thumbed the iron filings stubble on his chin. Was poised to run his hand through the thick thatch of his hair, but realised Marianne de Koninck would not thank him if he contaminated her corpse with white hairs. 'What do you make of this, Elvis?' he asked, staring at the dead man's distorted features. He stood, wincing as his hip cracked audibly.

But Elvis was speaking into his mobile phone. Almost shouting to make himself heard above the rain that bounced off the ground and pitted the canal water like darning needles being flung from heaven. Nodding. He peered over at the Chief Inspector. Covered the mouthpiece. 'Forensics are three minutes away,' he said. 'Marianne's with them.'

Van den Bergen nodded. 'Good. I don't believe in coincidence. Something's going on in my city. I don't like it one little bit and I've got a nasty feeling this is just the tip of the iceberg.'

CHAPTER 3

HMP Belmarsh, Thamesmead, Southeast London, 27 April

'I've already told you at least five times, I don't know where she is.' Gordon Bloom's perfectly enunciated speech sounded thick and sluggish with boredom. He rolled his functioning eye whilst the prosthetic remained unmoving in its socket. Straightening the sleeves on his crisp shirt, as though he were holding court from behind his desk in the City instead of from the other side of a scuffed table inside one of Belmarsh Prison's interview rooms. 'I've never met the woman in my life. I know nothing about your mother *or* an eyeball *or* your father *or* any of the slanderous nonsense I was convicted for.'

Studiously ignoring the photograph of Letitia that George had pushed in front of him – all sequins and cleavage, with a black marabou feather boa wrapped around her fat neck at Aunty Sharon's fortieth – he examined his diamond-studded cufflinks instead. These were the adornments of criminal royalty, appropriately worn by a minor royal. The fact that they hadn't been stolen by one of the other inmates told George exactly how 'The Duke' was regarded on the inside.

'Anyway, I thought you were interviewing me as an academic study subject,' he said. 'Not grilling me yet again about your

14

fucking mother, you tedious bitch.' He prodded at the image disdainfully. 'Why on earth would I have the first idea of the whereabouts of some low-life old has-been from the ghetto? I'm an innocent man!'

Sitting back in his chair, he flashed George with a disingenuous smile. She could see where the dental cement that plugged the hole in his incisor, once occupied by a diamond stud, had yellowed with neglect and too many cups of low-grade black tea.

'They don't let the hygienist in, I see,' she said, leaning forward in her chair; pointing to his tooth; wanting him to see that she remained unruffled by his insult.

Bloom closed his mouth abruptly. Folded his arms. 'I'm not saying another word to you. Uppity cunts like you, little Miss McKenzie, think a scroll of paper containing a qualification from a good university puts you on a par with the likes of me.' He leaned forwards, scowling. The cosmetic enhancements and adjustments to his face, which had allowed him to remain unrecognisable for so long, covering up some of the damage George had inflicted on him with her well-placed punch from a makeshift knuckle-duster, were now beginning to show signs of deterioration. His prosthetic eye was sinister and staring. 'Well, it doesn't. And you aren't.' He turned his attention defiantly to her ample bosom, though her simple black polo neck was anything but revealing. 'Your kind are only fit for one thing.'

Suppressing the urge to reach over and hit the arrogant, entitled prick yet again, George wrote the notes, 'Poor self-esteem. Possible sexual dysfunction.' on her pad, legible enough for her interviewee to read. She savoured the rancorous grimace on his face as he read it upside down.

Gordon Bloom turned around to the prison officer who stood sentry in the corner of the interview room. A mountain of a man, wearing a utility belt full of riot control knick-knacks that could stop even The Duke in his tracks.

'Get her out of here!' he yelled.

The prison officer looked quizzically at George, as though she had spoken and not his charge. 'You finished already, Dr McKenzie?' His voice was friendly. Polite.

'No, Stan. I've still got a few questions, if you don't mind,' George said. She sat tall in her seat. Took out her new tortoiseshell glasses. Watched Bloom's irritation out of the corner of her eye as she carefully, methodically, slowly polished the lenses with their special cloth and some lens cleaner. Perched them on the end of her nose. Folded the cloth neatly into perfect squares and placed it inside her case, which she snapped shut, making Bloom flinch. 'Relax, bae. I is being well gentle with you, innit?' Watched as her Southeast London street-speak visibly rankled with the toff. She shook out her curls dramatically with work-worn hands that were devoid of any adornment.

'This is ridiculous.' Bloom slapped the table top like a defiant toddler. 'I don't want to be here. My solicitor says I shouldn't speak to you. We're going to appeal, you know? And I'm going to get this absurd verdict overturned and reclaim my impeccable reputation as a pillar of the City of London's business community.'

George could see from the glint in his good eye that he believed his own hype. She fanned her hand dismissively in front of her face. 'Spare me the bravado, Lord Bloom. You wanted to be in my next book. You fancied the infamy. I could smell it on you – that desperation to fill the public with horrified awe. It's everything you ever wanted, isn't it? It's all men like you ever want.' She peered at him over the top of her glasses like an indulgent, knowing schoolmarm. Winked.

Bloom stood abruptly. Thumped his fists onto the table, making his cufflinks clink. 'If that's true, how come I kept my identity secret for decades, you presumptuous, ignorant whore? I'm not the attention-seeker you think I am, Miss McKenzie.'

'Sit down, Lord Bloom,' Stan the prison officer said, assuming the wide-legged stance of a man who was alert and ready for confrontation.

Feeling this was a wasted visit, revealing absolutely nothing new of any note, George capped her pen. The only thing she had managed to achieve during the last two sessions had been to antagonise the man who was almost certainly behind the disappearance of her mother and those infernal fucking emails. Beneath the table, she balled her fists. George, the woman, wanted to deck the mealy-mouthed upper-crust bastard. George, the professional, had learned to bite her tongue. How she needed a smoke.

'Come on. Play the game. It's *Doctor* McKenzie,' she said. 'And I think being in prison after being Mr Billionaire Hotshot at the top of the transnational trafficking heap has changed you. You've got to get the kicks where you can find them, now. What the hell do you have left apart from kudos among the inmates, who just want you to suck their cocks? The odd bit of media interest. Or me.' She closed her eyes emphatically. Arranged her full lips into a perfect pout.

When she looked up, her study subject's back was turned. Heading towards the door now with the prison officer at his side. She could see his upper body shaking in temper. Still the gentleman on the surface in his Jermyn Street City-wear, but the bloodthirsty criminal lurked just beneath the surface, she knew. Glancing over his shoulder, he shook his head damningly.

'I hope your old sow of a mother *is* dead,' he said. 'I hope she's mouldering at the bottom of a canal in Amsterdam, like I'm slowly decomposing in this dump when I should be a free man or, at least, enjoying an easy ride in an open prison in the Netherlands. All thanks to that bastard, Van den Bergen. Tell him to eat shit and die when you next see him, won't you, dear?'

'See you next week, Gordy, baby!' George retorted merrily in reply. 'Fuck you, wanker,' she said under her breath, once she was alone.

On the outside, she pulled her e-cigarette out of her bag with a shaking hand. Dragged heavily on it. Sighed heavily and thumbed a text to Aunty Sharon.

> Still no breakthrough re. Letitia. Do you
> want me to pick anything up on the way home?

The walk to the bus stop was bleak, as usual. Wind gusted across the giant Belmarsh complex, with its uniform beige brick buildings. George mused that they resembled oversized cheap motels or a 1980s commercial trading estate or perhaps a crap school – the kind where they'd invested money in a new building and nothing else, meaning it was permanently on special measures. The double-height fencing reminded her what sort of study subjects she worked with. Terrorists, murderers, violent people traffickers. Gordon Bloom. He was pretty much as bad as any other psychotic inmate the notorious Belmarsh had entertained. The only difference was, he was white, well educated and well heeled.

To her left, the modern buildings of the Woolwich Crown Court loomed, conjuring memories of a teenaged Ella, testifying against her former consorts in a closed court. George shuddered at the unwelcome flashbacks from her other life, now long gone: having to wear the ill-fitting track suits of the Victorian women's prison up north, where Letitia had left her to rot on remand; huddled in her pissy cell, fearing what the future might hold for a grass; a teenaged girl, bravely taking the punches from the other banged-up women, as they vented their frustrations on one another at a justice system that so often failed them.

As she crossed the road and ventured along a cycle path into a copse of budding trees, bus-stop-bound, she wondered why on earth she was bothering to hunt down her mother at all. Maybe the old cow had just gone AWOL of her own accord. It certainly wouldn't have been the first time.

'A year,' George whispered to the wilds of Woolwich that shot by, as the bus bounced her towards the DLR station. 'In fact, one year, one month and three days since you vanished. Where the hell are you, Letitia?' Absently taking in the rise of flashy new developments close to the riverside on her right, heralding the march of the middle class on what was traditionally an area of Southeast London on the bones of its semi-maritime arse. The low-rent, low-rise shops to her left, offering fried chicken and cheap mobile phones to the poultry- and telecoms-addicted locals. She considered the eyeball – an eyeball she had presumed to be Letitia's – which had been carefully gift-wrapped inside a fancy box, sitting on the table in Amsterdam's Vinkeles restaurant. 'The Israelites' emanating from Letitia's vibrating phone also contained within that box of delights. Now, whenever George heard Desmond Dekker, anguish tied her innards into knots.

Taking out her own phone, George thumbed out a text to Marie in Dutch. Imagined Van den Bergen's IT expert, sitting in her own cabbagey fug in the spacious IT suite that Van den Bergen had persuaded his new boss to give over to her internet research activities. Everybody had had quite enough of sharing Marie's eau-de-armpits.

```
Any news on eyeball-gate? Did some more
googling today but still nothing on my dad.
```

Trudging up the road to her aunty's place, George agonised yet again over the origins of this waking nightmare: the original out-of-the-blue email from her father, inviting her to lunch at Vinkeles, apparently as a reconciliatory gesture. His name had been used as a lure to get her to that restaurant, she felt certain.

Michael Carlos Izquierdo Moreno.

Four words that conjured in her mind's eye vivid memories of a childhood fraught with parental drama. A handsome, clever Spanish man she could now barely remember. Daddy's hairy, olive-skinned arms, swinging her high onto his shoulders. The smell of toasted tobacco and aftershave coming from his black hair and tanned neck. She had clung onto his head for dear life, thinking him so impossibly tall, though next to Van den Bergen he would in all likelihood have seemed diminutive. Speaking the Catalan Spanish to her of his native Tarragona.

Swallowing down a lump in her throat, she felt suddenly alone and vulnerable on that shabby street in Catford. Hastening past the grey-and-cream Victorian terraces towards the warmth and welcoming smells of Aunty Sharon's, paranoia started to set in. The place started to feel like an artfully constructed movie set, concealing something far more sinister behind the brick façades than the mundane workings of people's family lives. Uniform rows of houses closing in on her; stretching her route to safety indefinitely. Paranoia had been a familiar visitor in the course of the last year. She was sick of feeling that she was being watched by somebody, perhaps hiding behind some wheelie bins or over-grown hedging.

Glancing around, George sought out that long-haired old biker once again. A craggy face, partially hidden behind mirror shades, that had cropped up in her peripheral vision once too often when she had been food-shopping in Amsterdam or walking from Van den Bergen's apartment to the tram stop. Hadn't she seen him over here in the UK, too? Skulking on a platform in Lewisham when she had been waiting to catch the DLR. The sense that she was being followed now was overwhelming.

She stopped abruptly. Took her handbag-sized deodorant from her coat pocket, poised to spray any lurkers in the eyes. Gasping for air.

'Come out, you bastard!' she yelled.

CHAPTER 4

Mexico, Chiapas, 29 May

Swigging from the bottle of Dos Equis, he peered through the dusty window of the four-wheel-drive at the brothel. Bullet holes pitted the plastered outer walls, punctuating the painted sign that marked this place out as offering the average Mexican man a good time, at a price. A Corona logo had been amateurishly daubed onto a florid yellow background with black paint. The opening hours and maximum capacity had rubbed off some time ago. But he knew it was open 24/7 for a man who had the cash. This was a Chiapas town, after all. And this club was his.

Beyond the threshold, he spied a tired-looking jukebox and several cheap white plastic chairs. A young girl sat on one of them. Overweight, like most of them were. Wearing a barely-there skirt and vertiginous platform stilettos. Couldn't have been more than fourteen. Her face shone with sweat and her long black hair hung lank and greasy on her bare shoulders.

'What's the deal with her?' he asked Miguel.

At his side, Miguel leaned forwards and squinted to get a better look at the girl. 'Oh, her? She wouldn't run,' he said in English, spoken with an accent flavoured heavily with his native Spanish, with a dash of Texan twang. 'She was the only one. She was too frightened, she said. Ratted the others out, though, when we threatened to kill her mother and sisters.'

'Good. And do we know where the dumb bitches have gone?'

'Apparently they're headed towards the landing strip hidden in the mountains. Some customer with a conscience told them about it. Said they could hire a light aircraft if they clubbed together, or maybe offer the pilot their services if they couldn't.' Miguel dabbed at his forehead with a clean white handkerchief. His black hair, thick like carpet, stood to attention in sweaty spikes.

'I want you to find the chump that gave them big ideas and feed him to the crocodiles. *Comprende?*'

Miguel waggled his head in agreement. '*Naturalmente, jefe.* I'll check the CCTV. If he's local, we will find him.'

'If he's from out of town, you'll still find him.'

'*Si. Claro.*' Miguel closed his eyes. Nodding effusively.

'And put it on YouTube. Then, make sure the whole town sees what's left. Leave it in the square or something.'

'*No problemo, el cocodrilo.*'

He smiled at Miguel. Studied his pock-marked, acne-scarred face; the spare tyre that drooped over his belt and slacks. Too many cheese-laden *tostadas* and sugar-coated *churros*, no doubt. The Mexican diet was so damned greasy. He longed for the simpler fare of home but kept that thought to himself. 'Those silly whores don't realise they're running straight into the lion's den.'

The car drove on out of town and along the pitted, dusty trails that led into the mountains to the border between the Chiapas and Guatemala. Past shrines cut into the rock, containing minia-ture skeletons, adorned with flowers. Despite the vivid green forest that blanketed the mountains, this was a hellish, godfor-saken land. Even with the air-con blowing at full pelt in the Mercedes, the inferno-like heat was still stifling. And though they had left the smell of putrefaction from the ramshackle streets far behind, *el cocodrilo* nevertheless pulled the lime from the neck of his beer bottle with a determined finger and held it to his nose, enjoying the sharp, clean tang. Remembering what it was like to be permanently cool, enjoying consistently fresh air. The smell of the sea.

'We're here,' Miguel announced, as the car bounced inside a gated complex, down a rutted drive.

To one side, maize – stalks that were taller than men – grew in obedient rows on a plateau. Women, wearing colourful embroidered peasant smocks and black skirts, hacked at the ripe crop with machetes, some with babies swaddled and strapped to their backs. They froze, staring at the Mercedes with its blacked-out windows. Realising who was contained within. Deftly, they turned back to their work, keeping their heads bowed respectfully low.

'Do they work for me?' he asked.

Miguel nodded. '*Sí*. They're all trafficked Nicaraguans and Hondurans. Farming in the week. Brothels at the weekend. Every man and woman you see on the farm is yours, *jefe*.' He started to laugh. 'The farmer wasn't too pleased, but he stopped moaning once we cut his head off.'

El cocodrilo turned away from his sniggering minion. It didn't pay to be too familiar with men on the payroll. Even the ones only a rung beneath him. Rubbing his lime so that the zest left a stinging, oily slick on his fingers, he peered up at the mountains that rose in undulating green peaks on the other side of the road. Smothered in lush coffee crops. Fertile soil. Productive land. His was a diverse and lucrative business.

The white stucco hacienda appeared just ahead like a tired angel perched on a Christmas tree that had been left over from the days of colonialism – a double-storey affair with ornate arches fringing a balconied quad, topped off with a ridged terracotta roof. Small wonder the farmer had been reluctant to relinquish it. Two tattooed young men stood on the tiled veranda by the front door, holding AK-47s. Not so elegant.

The car ground to a halt in a cloud of dust.

'Where are the girls?' he asked. 'Are they inside?'

'No, *jefe*. They're lined up on the airstrip,' Miguel said. 'Awaiting your judgement.'

Ignoring the bowing sycophants and scurrying workers, he followed Miguel through the claustrophobic stalks of the maize crop for some two hundred metres. Feeling the heat strike the parched ground beneath his feet, bouncing back up into the soles of his shoes and onto his skin. Three in the afternoon. The place was an oven. And already he could hear the cicadas starting their lilting evensong. *Chapulines*, three times the size of the crickets in Europe, click-clicked their chirruping long legs together. He stood on one and committed to memory the sound of it crunching beneath his shoe. Shithole.

When the stalky growth ended in a perfect line, giving way to the giant clearing, he could breathe again. Peered out beneath the brim of his straw trilby, squinting in the sunshine to see heat rising in mesmerising waves above a perfect white airstrip cut into the scrub. At the far end of the secret runway, a light aircraft had been casually parked. His light aircraft. Purchased to carry his coke, guns and supplies. His landing strip. Silly bitches. There they were, kneeling in the flattened dirt with coffee sacking on their heads. Naked. Hands tied behind them.

Pondering how best to deal with this insurgence, he turned to Miguel. 'Bring all of the farm workers and the men here. Now.'

Walking towards the gaggle of hooded girls, he eyed the *transportistas* who guarded them warily. As arms-smuggling mercenaries, revered for their professionalism and impartiality by all the cartels, these *transportistas* were not women under his jurisdiction, despite being on his payroll. Dressed in dark utility clothing and carrying semi-automatic rifles. He recognised AK-47s, American issue AR-15s and German HK G36s. His storerooms would be replete with firepower if they had driven all the way north from Honduras with their ballistic payload.

'Ladies,' he said, tipping his hat. Making eye contact with a big bruiser of a *transportista*, wearing the skeletal figure of Santa Muerte emblazoned in white on her black T-shirt. 'Nice guns.' He winked.

The woman scowled at him. '*Hola, el cocodrilo,*' she said, re-adjusting her rifle across her hips. 'Too bad you couldn't make it to the rendezvous in Palenque in person. That little shit behind the bar needed teaching some respect. I taught him good. Okay?'

He nodded.

'Well, you've got ten cases of our finest arms in the hacienda and in Palenque. Mainly AK-47s.' She reached out to shake his hand. Her grip was like a vice, far stronger than most of the men who worked for him. He noted the tattoos, more commonly seen on the men of the mara gangs, scrolling up her inner arm, under her T-shirt sleeve, emerging at the base of her thick neck, where the ink travelled northwards over her scarred face in a demonic tapestry of blue-black. Faux-religious images of weeping women and children. Flowers and skulls of the Maya, with numbers and letters scrawled intricately across her throat in some kind of magical code that clearly meant something to the right people. 'Pleasure doing business with you. As always.'

'And you'll also take care of this problem for me?' he asked.

The farm workers and his own men had gathered along the edge of the airstrip now. Milling around awkwardly, suspecting what was about to happen, perhaps. Visibly squirming, lest the mayhem spill over from the group of absconded prostitutes, somehow tainting them.

The *transportista* nodded. '*Claro,*' she said, gabbling something to her compatriots in rapid-fire Salvadoran Spanish.

The women slung their rifles across their backs and simultaneously drew machetes in some gruesome choreographed dance. Pulled the sacks from the heads of the bewildered trafficked girls who peered around to see where they were. Wide-eyed and mouthing, '*No! No!*' when they caught sight of *el cocodrilo*. Begging for forgiveness, their pleas falling on his unsympathetic ears. Weak, corruptible bitches. Why would he ever spare them? Particularly when they were so easily replaced with the next truckload coming out of Guatemala.

There was something about the high drama of the Central Americans that appealed to him. It was amusing, all this pandemonium and Latin angst: screaming, now drowning out the high-pitched sound of the cicadas, as the girls understood the fate about to be visited upon them. Weeping from the farm workers, who grasped that this too might be their method of undoing, should they cross the mighty *el cocodrilo* and dare to take back their freedoms.

'Now,' he said.

The *transportistas* pushed the kneeling girls to the ground until they kissed the dirt with their tear-streaked faces. All bar one raised machetes in unison and, with one forceful blow, beheaded each runaway in almost perfect synchronicity. Amid the wailing of the onlookers, the girls' heads rolled away from broken bodies that pumped out their life's blood. Staring but unseeing. For them, at least, it was the end.

But as *el cocodrilo* turned to walk away from the scene of execution, he felt he was being watched.

CHAPTER 5

Amsterdam, police headquarters, then, Bouwdewijn de Groot Lyceum, Apollolaan, then, Floris Engels' apartment in Amstelveen, 28 April

'What do we know about our man in the canal?' Maarten Minks asked. Neatly folded into his chair, he sat with his pen in hand and his pad open, as though he were poised to take notes. Van den Bergen could deduce from the shine on his overenthusiastic, wrinkle-free face that he was on the cusp of getting a stiffy over the discovery of this fourth body. Waiting for his old Chief Inspector's words of wisdom, no doubt. Bloody fanboy.

'Well,' Van den Bergen began. Paused. Rearranged his long frame in his seat, grimacing as his hip clicked in protest when he tried to cross his legs. 'It's interesting, actually. His wallet and ID were still on him. No money stolen, so he couldn't have been pushed into the water after a mugging.' He took the smudged glasses from the end of the chain around his neck and perched them on his nose. Wishing now that he'd had the scratched lens replaced when George had told him to. Trying to focus on the handwriting in his notebook. Hell, maybe it wasn't the scuffing. Maybe his sight had deteriorated since the last eye test. Was it entirely unfeasible that he had glaucoma? 'Ah, his name was Floris

Engels – a maths teacher at Bouwdewijn de Groot Lyceum in the Old South part of town.'

Minks nodded. Pursed his lips. 'A teacher, eh?'

'Yes. I checked his tax records. Head of department at a posh school on the expensive side of town.' Removing his glasses, Van den Bergen stifled a belch. 'IT Marie's done some background research and revealed nothing but a photograph of him on the school's website and a Facebook account that we're waiting for permission to access. It's unlikely he was some kind of petty crook on the quiet, as far as I can make out, but I got the feeling he might have been dead before he hit the water.'

'And the number of canal deaths are stacking up,' Minks said, lacing his hands together. That fervour was still shining in his eyes.

Van den Bergen could guess exactly what he was hoping for but refused to pander to his boss' aspirations. 'I'm going out there with Elvis now to interview the Principal and some of his colleagues. We're going to check out his apartment too. Marianne's doing the postmortem this afternoon. She says, at first glance, she thinks maybe there's been some foul play.'

'Excellent!' Minks said, scribbling down a note that Van den Bergen could not read. 'Lots going on. I really do admire your old school methodical techniques, Paul.' The new Commissioner beamed at him. His cheeks flushed red and he leaned his elbow onto the desk. 'Will you be disappearing into your shed for a think?'

Is he taking the piss, Van den Bergen wondered? But then he remembered that Maarten Minks was neither Kamphuis nor Hasselblad. This smooth-skinned foetus had been fast-tracked straight out of grad school. At least Van den Bergen's long-range vision was good enough to corroborate that there was a raft of diplomas hanging above Minks on the wall behind his desk. A framed photo of him posing with the Minister for Security and Justice, the Minister of the Interior and Kingdom Relations and the bloody Prime Minister. No sign of a naked lady statue or stupid executive toys. This youthful pretender to the policing throne was all business. But he could think again if he thought Van den Bergen was going to discuss the shed. 'Do you have any suggestions regarding the shape the investigation should take? Any priorities I should know about?'

'See how the autopsy pans out. But if there are any similarities with the other floaters, I think we need to consider …'

Here it was. Van den Bergen could feel it coming. He shook his head involuntarily and popped an antacid from its blister pack onto his tongue.

'… that a serial killer is on the loose.'

When he strode out to the car park, Elvis was already waiting for him, leaning up against the BMW 7 Series he had got the new Chief of Police to cough up for when they had broken the news to him that he was going to be overlooked for the role of Commissioner, yet again. Even the top man didn't have a vehicle like Van den Bergen's. But then, nobody else had legs quite as long as his, so they could all suck it up.

'Get off the car, for God's sake,' he said. 'I've just had it valeted. I don't need your arse print on my passenger door. And don't smoke near it. The ash sticks to the paintwork.'

'Sorry, boss,' Elvis said, exhaling and stubbing his half-spent cigarette out on the ground with the heel of his cowboy boot.

Van den Bergen scrutinised his pale, blotchy face. The signs of his psoriasis flaring up again, the poor bastard. 'Are you up to this?' he asked, unlocking the car with his fob. 'You look peaky.'

'I was up all night with Mum,' Elvis said. Digging a nicotine-stained index finger into his auburn sideburns – totally at odds with the ridiculous dyed-black quiff that earned him his moniker. Even that was starting to thin a little, these days, now that he was very comfortably on the wrong side of thirty.

29

His detective opened his mouth, presumably to say more. Van den Bergen plunged into the driver's seat as quickly as his stiff hip would allow. Slammed the door shut, trapping Elvis and his earnest confessions outside. Programmed Floris Engels' address into his sat nav.

'I'm sorry,' he said quietly through recalcitrant, tight lips, when Elvis buckled in. 'I just can't—'

'It's okay, boss. I get it.'

'Just book leave when you need it.' He waved his hand dismissively, switched on the stereo and enjoyed the rather less awkward silence of Depeche Mode at a volume loud enough to drown out Elvis' attempts at conversation about his mother's condition.

'Floris Engels,' Elvis said, poking at a photograph of the dead man that he'd laid on the head teacher's desk. A flattering shot of him taken from the sideboard in his flat. Average-looking but tanned, well dressed, smiling. A shot of him dead on the canal side, his ghoulish face swollen to almost twice its normal size. He knew Van den Bergen was scrutinising his every move for signs of exhaustion. One false move and he'd be put on compassionate leave. It was the last thing he wanted. 'Tell me and the Chief Inspector here everything you know about your Head of Maths.' He crossed his right leg over his left knee, as he'd seen the boss do. Assumed the position of a relaxed and confident man with nothing to prove.

'Well, Floris is—' The head teacher was suddenly preoccupied by his hairy fingers. Frowned. 'Was a very well-respected member of my staff.' His voice shook with emotion.

Elvis tried to memorise everything about the man. Discreet gold jewellery. Expensive, pin-stitched suit befitting the head of a fee-paying school that catered for Amsterdam's *bekakte* bourgeoisie – the chattering classes – where the darling Lodewijks and Reiniers and Petronellas of wealthy parents could receive their top-drawer educations in wood-panelled, exclusive splendour.

Even the dust in the air smelled expensive at Boudewijn de Groot Lyceum. Elvis' psoriasis itched beneath his leather jacket.

'And?'

Closing his eyes, the Head pushed the photographs away. 'Floris started working here three years ago. He is …' His brow furrowed. '… was always impeccably polite, got great results from his pupils. Popular among parents. He was a model teacher.'

'What kind of man was he?' Elvis asked, wishing the Head would make eye contact with him. It irked him that he kept looking over at Van den Bergen even though it was he who was asking the questions.

The Head shrugged. 'I told you. Polite. Hard-working. Bright.'

'No,' Van den Bergen said, doodling absently in his notebook. 'That tells us what kind of employee he was.' Scratching away with his biro at a miniature sketch of his granddaughter. Finally he looked up at the Head. Put his glasses on the end of his nose and peered at the brass-embossed name plate on the desk that marked him out as Prof. Roeland Hendrix. 'Who was Floris the man, Roeland? Did you see him socially? What was his home life like? I can see from public records that he hasn't been married and that his parents are both dead. Did he have a girlfriend? Kids somewhere?'

Elvis checked his watch. Wondered if the carer was making his mother the right sort of lunch. *Carby snack with the meds. Carby snack with the meds,* he intoned, wishing his thoughts would somehow travel across town to his mother's dingy little house. He'd left all the ingredients out on the side in the kitchen. Mum kept gunning for the shitty cheap ham the carer had snuck into the fridge at her request. But he had prepared her a chickpea and bean pasta salad with rocket. *Meds three-quarters of an hour before meal.*

'Come on, Professor Hendrix,' Elvis said. 'I bet an intelligent man like you has got the measure of all his employees.'

The Head shrugged. Toyed with the silk handkerchief in his top pocket. His nails had been varnished.

Elvis touched the stiff gel of his quiff and wondered if it made him hypocritical to think ill of the Head's immaculate ponce-hands. Hid his own nicotine-stained fingers inside his pockets.

'Honestly? I know nothing about Floris at all,' the Head said. 'He was a completely private man. Kept himself to himself. An enigma, you might say. I invited him, along with other teachers, to dinner parties and soirées, but he would never come and always managed to sidestep any digging into his life outside work. And I did try. To dig, I mean.'

Van den Bergen rearranged himself in the leather armchair. His bones cracked audibly as he did so. Jesus. Is that what a lifetime of supervising door-to-doors in the rain did for a man? Elvis shuddered.

'Where did he work before here?' he asked.

'He came from the Couperus International Lyceum in Utrecht. Glowing references. He'd been there for ten years.'

The Head glanced at the grandfather clock that struck in the corner of the room. Stood abruptly. 'I'm sorry I couldn't be of more help, gentlemen.'

All the way to the unprepossessing apartment in Amstelveen's Brandwijk, Van den Bergen imagined himself shaking and shuddering his way to a premature end with Parkinson's like Elvis' mother. The bullet hole in his hip had been causing him great pain, of late, with all the damp. Were there any signs of tremors in his movement? George would be able to tell him. By the end of the week, she would be back in Amsterdam. In the meantime, he made a mental note to visit the doctor's to rule out some debilitating degenerative disease.

Curtains twitched as he parked up outside the three-storey block, with its garden view and balcony. This was perhaps the most suburban, nondescript place in the world, Van den Bergen mused. A place where nothing ever happened. Except something had happened to one of its residents.

'What do you make of this, boss?' Elvis said, running a latex-clad finger along the spines of the books on the bookshelves. Five boring-looking academic tomes about physics. *Fall of Man in Wilmslow* – a book Van den Bergen vaguely recognised as being about Alan Turing. The rest were interior design and architecture textbooks. Several British fiction titles among them that Van den Bergen had never heard of.

'He was a maths teacher, so the physics stuff fits,' he said. Casting an eye over the mid-century-style furniture in the apartment, he realised it was more Ikea repro than genuine Danish antiques. But there was a strong design element to it. That much he could see. Nothing like his thrift-shop dump, which was still reminiscent of a garage sale no matter how many times George scrubbed through. 'Somebody here knows their décor onions. No photos of women anywhere apart from this.' Using a latex-gloved hand, he picked up the portrait of a woman who was roughly in her sixties. Perhaps Engels' mother. She had the same hazel eyes, judging by the school's online profile picture of him.

Movement suddenly caught the Chief Inspector's attention. Or was it a shadow? With his heartbeat picking up pace and his policeman's instincts sharpening, he turned towards the doorway, beyond which lay the bedroom.

'Is somebody in here with us?' he whispered to Elvis. Mouthed, 'In there.' Pointed to the bedroom.

Elvis shook his head. Continued to look at the books.

Van den Bergen strode briskly into the bedroom, his plastic overshoes rustling as he crunched on the shag pile rug underfoot. Held his breath. Scanned the neat, masculine room for intruders. There was nobody there but a whiff of aftershave hung in the air. Or was he imagining things?

'I need to drink less coffee,' he muttered, running his fingers over the pistol in its holster, strapped to his torso.

He flung open the wardrobe doors to reveal immaculately

presented suiting; ties, pants and socks stowed in colour co-ordinated compartments, perhaps specifically designed for ties, pants and socks. Jumpers and tops stacked in neat piles on shelving. One set of shelves containing sombre colours. The other, less conservative combinations of teal, pink, yellow …

'Different sizes on the right side of the wardrobes to the left,' he said. 'Two men. Our victim and a lover.'

Elvis pulled open the drawer to the bedside cabinet. 'This is always the most revealing place in anyone's bedroom,' he said. 'I've got an asthma inhaler, hair putty and a men's health maga-zine from 2002. What about you?' He smirked.

'Proton pump inhibitors, floss and Tiger Balm,' Van den Bergen said, grimacing at the contents Elvis had revealed. 'Jesus. It's like the storeroom in a sex shop. Look of the size of those bloody dildos. And what the hell is *that*?' He pointed to a black rubber string of balls, growing progressively larger in size.

'Anal beads, boss.' Elvis guffawed with laughter.

'And that fucking thing?' He pointed to what appeared to be a stainless-steel egg.

'You jam it up your—'

Van den Bergen held his hand high. Thought of George's middle finger inside him and blushed. A world away from this little haul in terms of adventurousness. 'Stop. You're making my prostate twitch.' He considered his intermittent suffering with haemor-rhoids and snorted with derision at the anal beads. Appraised the carefully made bed and the dust that was beginning to settle on the bedroom furniture. 'Any sign of post addressed to somebody else? Check the kitchen. Everybody puts post in there.'

Elvis left the bedroom. Nobody had reported Floris Engels missing. There had been no evidence of a suicide note in the man's clothing. Who and where was his partner?

'Nothing,' Elvis said. 'Weird.'

'Unless he's left in a hurry and taken any documentation with him.' Van den Bergen thumbed at the jowls that were beginning to burgeon on his previously taut jawline, deep in thought. Jumped when a door slammed shut within the apartment.

'There *is* someone in here with us!' he shouted. He ran into the living room, gun in hand, trying to glimpse whoever the visitor was. 'Hello?!'

CHAPTER 6

Cambridge, Huntingdon Road, then, Stansted Airport, 29 April

'You just keep a lookout,' George told Aunty Sharon, shouting above the gusting Cambridgeshire wind. Her pulse thudded in her neck as she calculated how long it would take Sally Wright to grind and wobble her way up the hill to the student house on the Huntingdon Road. Surely a chain-smoker like her would asphyxiate before she'd be able to scale Cambridge's infamous Castle Hill on a sit-up-and-beg bicycle. *Calm down, George. Chill your boots. You get in. You get out. You get gone.* 'I'll be down in ten. I've only got a couple of bits to get. Honk if you see an angry white woman with a bad fringe. Okay? Honk!'

This was a flying visit to Cambridge, precipitated by two texts she had received the evening she had returned to Aunty Sharon's after interviewing Gordon Bloom in Belmarsh. Relieved to find that she was not, after all, being followed through the Catford backstreet by anything more sinister than an inquisitive cat and her own burgeoning paranoia, she had hastened to her aunt's house, walking straight through to the kitchen. She had put her bag squarely on a kitchen chair, so it had aligned with the edges. Rearranging it until it was just right. The routine had been like every other evening.

'All right, love,' Aunty Sharon had said. 'I've made goat curry. Fancy it?' She had lifted the lid on a simmering pan, the contents of which had smelled like heaven but had resembled diarrhoea. George had embraced her aunt, barely circling her chunky middle. Had kissed her on the cheek, feeling whiskers that hadn't been there twelve months earlier. But at least Aunty Sharon had ditched the raggedy extensions and had covered her desperately stressed natural hair with a decent wig.

Beneath her apron, Sharon had already been wearing her clothes for the club, where she served watered-down shots to the pissed denizens of Soho's *Skin Licks* titty bar.

'Oh my days, Aunty Shaz! I could eat a scabby horse on toast. I only had a bag of cheese balls all day. Bring it on. It smells bloody gorgeous.' George had flung herself onto another kitchen chair, contemplating how empty the house had felt with her cousin, Tinesha, long departed to live with her boyfriend, and Patrice who was more out than in, now that he was in the upper sixth. Once again, George – past the point where she had been the fresh young thing, out on the tiles all night long and now having reached the age where her contemporaries were married with children – had only her own company to look forward to, as the evening had stretched ahead of her. Hadn't one of the new male Fellows at college jokingly referred to George as a spinster? Some long-legged floppy-haired arsehole in a pseudo-intellectual tweed jacket, originally from Eton. Tim Hamilton. Dickhead. He'd stared at her tits when he'd said it. George had batted the thought aside. 'You go to the community centre today? Any news?'

Sharon had shaken her head and had plonked too much rice onto a plate with a giant serving spoon. 'Nah, love. Nobody's seen her. Nobody's heard nothing on the grapevine. Not a fucking sausage. Even that nosey old cow Dorothea Caines didn't have a clue, and I had to eat one of her rock-hard cupcakes to find that much out.' She had put her hand on her hip and had grimaced.

'She'd not sieved the flour. Can you get over it? I mean!' She'd made a harrumphing noise. 'Talk about taking one for the team. My God! If the Black Gang or Pecknarm Killaz or whatever the fuck those gangsta rarseclarts call themselves used her cupcakes as missiles, all there'd be left of Southeast London would be fucking craters. Craters, darling!'

Nodding, George had forked her curry into her mouth with the enthusiasm of the semi-starving. Surreptitiously grabbing at her spare tyre beneath the table, thinking it time she had a chat with Aunty Sharon about portion size, now there were fewer of them in the house.

Sharon had been unaware of George's dietary preoccupation. She had been waving the spoon at her with dangerous intent. 'I'd take that Dorothea Caines out like a fucking ninja if we was going head-to-head in a bake-off.' Droplets of curry had spattered the dated splashback tiles.

'So, still no news of Letitia. Or my dad?' George had asked, feeling irritation prickle at the roots of her hair. Same questions. Every. Single. Day.

Her aunty had fallen abruptly quiet, sniffing pointedly. Her eyes had become glassy without warning. 'Sorry, love. If anyone had seen your mum knocking around on the estate, that do-gooding righteous witch Dorothea would be the first to hear it and crow about it. Honest. Your mum's evaporated into thin air, like.' She had reached out and had grabbed George's hand, squeezing it in a show of solidarity. 'Nothing on your dad, either.'

Noticing the curry and grains of rice stuck to Sharon's index finger, George had pulled her hand away, stifling a sigh.

As she had crawled into Tinesha's old bed and had pulled the duvet up to her chin, she had thought about this impasse she had reached. An unwelcome tear had tracked along her cheekbone, running into her ear. Annoyed, she had poked at it, wondering if Letitia had been thinking about her; if she had even still been alive.

'Like fuck she is,' she had said to floral curtains, backlit by the yellow streetlight.

She had wondered yet again if there had been even the slightest possibility that her father had sent the untraceable emails, courting contact with her; saying he was watching her.

'Not after nearly twenty-five years of silence. No way,' she had told the glowing numbers on the old ticking alarm clock.

With sleep beckoning her towards yet another fitful night of tossing, turning and imagining the gruesome fate of her possibly enucleated mother, she had been jolted wide awake by her phone vibrating with two new emails. The first had been from Marie.

Police in Maastricht have found a man who may be of interest!

The second had been from Van den Bergen.

Come back to Amsterdam. I need you for something.

Now, Aunty Sharon was wedged behind the wheel of her old 53-plate Toyota Corolla, parked badly on Huntingdon Road, peering up with a puzzled look at the tired Gothic student house that loomed above them. Yellowing chintz curtains at the window and a broken pane of glass in the 1960s replacement front door.

'*You* live *here*?' she asked, curling her lip with clear disgust. 'In that dump? You having a laugh with me?'

George frowned. Shook her head dismissively and tutted. 'Save it, yeah? Beggars can't be choosers. Now remember. If you see Sally Wright—'

'What about Sally Wright?' Sally Wright asked, emerging from behind the overgrown privet that bordered the end-of-terrace. She clapped her hands together in George's face. 'Ha! Got you, you sneaky sod!'

Opening and closing her mouth, George foraged in her mental

lie-box for a good, feasible excuse as to why she had kept her flying visit to Cambridge a secret. Tried to work out how the aerobically challenged Senior Tutor had hoofed it from her office in St John's College up the road to the house inside ten minutes. Ten goddamned minutes since Aunty Shaz' car had rolled into town.

'How—?'

'Sophie Bartek,' Sally explained, marching to the taxi that George had only just clocked, parked all the while in front of Aunty Sharon. She explained to the driver that she had decided to hitch a ride back in Sharon's Toyota, paid him and sent him on his way.

'Fucking Sophie,' George said under her breath. 'Shit-stirrer owes me one.'

She forced a smile for the Professor of Criminology who ruled her academic life like a benevolent dictator; the woman she would always be indebted to for having allowed her to learn her way out of a future where petty crime or prison or stacking super-market shelves would otherwise have beckoned.

'Why haven't you been taking my calls, young lady?' Sally asked, glowering at George. Pointing with a gnarled, amber-coloured finger. 'It's our bloody book launch tomorrow evening, and Sophie tells me you're buggering back off to Amsterdam.' She folded her arms across her narrow chest, squeezing the leather of her eccentrically cut coat until she was akin to a municipal bin bag with the drawstrings pulled tight. The pruning around her mouth deepened. But that fierce gaze had lost none of its potency behind the red acetate cat's-eye glasses. 'I'll never be able to show my face in Heffers again. And all because you can't resist the pull of that old flake, Van den Bergen. The man's like a disappointing Svengali with prostate trouble. Our big night will be ruined. Now, what do you have to say for yourself?'

'You don't need me to help you blow your fucking trumpet in public, Sally. You've got that one covered all on your own, I reckon.' George didn't like being indebted. And apologies were overrated. She jammed her fist onto her hip defiantly. 'And Paul is hardly a flake, is he? He's one of the best coppers in Europe, *actually*. And if you must know, I'm going to Amsterdam because there's been a development regarding Letitia.'

'What?!' Aunty Sharon shouted from inside the Toyota.

'What?!' Sally Wright said, clutching George's arm.

George pulled herself loose from the grip of the Senior Tutor. Immediately regretted saying anything, as her aunt unbuckled and started to heave herself out of the car.

'Georgina, why on earth didn't you say anything?' Sally said, her brow furrowed, perhaps with genuine empathy.

Before George could retreat, Sharon had rounded on them both, booting Sally Wright aside unceremoniously with her ample bottom. She clasped George into a suffocating hug. The threat of tears audible in her voice.

'Is she dead?' Sharon asked. 'Has that silly cow's body been found in a wheelie bin?' She sniffed hard. 'It has, hasn't it? Oh, sweet Jesus.'

'I won't know anything until I speak to Marie, one of Paul's detectives,' George said, disengaging herself from her aunt. 'All I know is that there's a man in Maastricht. A dead guy, who's somehow connected to Letitia's disappearance. That's all she's told me so far.' She turned to the Senior Tutor, realising it would do her no favours to curry the displeasure of a woman who could have her funding rescinded at any time, leaving her broke and jobless. Sally had threatened it before, but George was older, wiser and several steps closer to having a deposit saved for her own place, now. Biting this particular gnarled proverbial hand that fed would be folly. 'That's why I can't stay for the launch, Sal.' She rearranged her features into what would pass as an apologetic smile. 'You'll be brilliant without me.'

Sally tugged at her blunt-cut fringe and scowled. Hooked her short bob behind her ear. 'But all of Dobkin's family are coming. It's a big deal, dedicating the book to his memory.'

'We robbed his research,' George said. 'I could have saved his life and I didn't. I knew Danny was up to no good and all I could think of was protecting my own arse.' George's viscera tightened at the memory of her squatting behind a car, watching her academic rival, Professor Dickwad Dobkin, succumb to the brutal intentions of her backstreet drug-dealing ex-lover. UCL's finest criminologist crumpling to the ground like a falling autumnal leaf in a quiet London WC1 square, all because he had got too close to revealing the true identities of the major players in the UK's people-trafficking rings. A bullet, punching its way into his superlative brain, that could have been avoided, had George only been quicker to punch his number into her phone. 'I don't deserve to have my name on the front of that book.'

Sally's mouth hardened to a thin line. 'We did *not* steal his research, Georgina McKenzie. Dobkin's trafficking database and the information we … *you* gathered from inmates in prison developed organically under completely separate—'

'His research made it into our book,' George said, feeling shame heat her wind-chilled cheeks from the inside. Nervously looking at Aunty Sharon, expecting a look of disapprobation but seeing only confusion in her face.

'What's some geez in Maastricht gotta do with my turd of a sister?' Sharon asked.

'It's going to be a *Sunday Times* bestseller,' Sally said, pulling a cigarette packet out of her coat pocket. She offered one to George. George shook her head but took one anyway.

Sharon, clearly unimpressed by the interloper snatching George's attention in this time of family crisis, shouted at the Senior Tutor, 'Mout a massy, yuh cyan shut yup?' Jamaican patois, delivered with such venom and speed that George was convinced the paving slabs of that genteel Cambridge road might blister at any moment. Sharon snatched the cigarette off George and lit it herself. 'Listen, Professor whatever-your name is,' she said, exhaling a cloud of blue-grey smoke in Sally's direction. 'If my niece here stands a cat in hell's chance of tracking my sister down – who's been missing for a fucking year ...' Jabbing the cigarette towards the startled Fellow. '... she's going to Amsterdam if I have to put on bloody water wings and swim her there, myself. Right? And if that means you can't roll her out at your fucking boring book launch as some novelty ghetto-fabulous lackey what serves the cooking wine and flutters her eyelashes at the dirty old codgers who pay your wages, you're just going have to suck it up, darling! Cos family comes first. Right?' She turned to George, straightening her burgundy, glossy wig. Glowing with an almost religious zeal that only Bermondsey women could really pull off when vexed. 'Get your shit together, love. We're going to the airport.' A click of the fingers meant the conversation was over.

Dropping Sally Wright off outside St John's College, leaving her open-mouthed and speechless, for once, George realised she was trembling with anticipation. Would this trip yield an answer to her questions? She covered her juddering hands with her rucksack. Not quick enough for her aunt, though.

'I see you shaking there, like you've got the DTs! It would help if you ate a proper breakfast,' she said, indicating left. Pulling up at the drop-off point at Stansted Airport, forcing the dented silver car into a bottleneck of taxis and disoriented relatives who were also dropping baggage-laden holidaymakers at Departures. Sharon reached for a cool bag at George's feet.

'Shift your feet. I made you a packed lunch,' she said. Plonked the bag onto George's lap. Grabbing her face and planting a wet kiss on her cheek, which George hastily wiped away. 'Couple of nice homemade patties and some jerk chicken. That'll keep you going for a bit.'

'Ta. I love you, Aunty Shaz.' George drank in the detail of her aunt's face, feeling suddenly melancholy. She pushed aside unexpectedly negative feelings that she couldn't quite articulate. A sense of impending loss or perhaps just separation anxiety. 'Give my love to Tin and Patrice. I'll text you.'

Aunty Sharon nodded. Her face, scrubbed of the make-up she wore to the club in the evening, seemed closer to five than forty.

'Find her, George. Find Letitia, dead or alive.'

CHAPTER 7

Amsterdam, mortuary, later

'Well, there's water in his lungs,' Marianne de Koninck said, carefully lifting the slippery-looking mass out of his chest cavity and onto the scales in the mortuary. 'That much is obvious.'

At her side, Floris Engels' milky eyes stared out from his bloated face. His scalp and legs, where Marianne's pathologist's blade had not yet got to work, were florid in places, yellowy-grey in others like bad tie-dye, the skin showing signs of wrinkling only at his extremities, as though it might shrug itself off his feet or hands. But the bloating made Van den Bergen twitch involuntarily. He hated floaters. They decomposed so bloody fast. He was glad of the clean, menthol smell of the VapoRub beneath his nostrils.

'But I'll need to test for the concentration of his serum electrolytes and examine his bones and viscera for diatoms,' she said, observing the scales' reading. 'Our canal water is quite saline in certain parts of town because of the locks at Ijmuiden letting seawater in. So, there'll be microscopic algae from the sea in his deep tissues if he's just fallen in and met a watery end in the canal. Bones are always a good indicator.' She took her scalpel and cut a sample of bone from the nub that protruded from his partially severed upper arm. Scraped the marrow into a test tube and sealed it. 'It will take a couple of days in the lab. I'm due to get his bloods back any day, though.' Pointing to his arm, she clicked her tongue against the roof of her mouth. Used her elbow to scratch at her belly beneath her scrubs. 'That has been cut cleanly with the propeller of the barge, I'd say. Definitely done postmortem. My hypothesis is that our Floris here fell or was pushed in – point of entry by the barge. He sank, got trapped under the keel of the barge until our bargeman decided he needed a change of scenery.'

Van den Bergen wondered if Marianne's muscular athlete's arms would look so alien and ugly if she too had been underwater for a period of time. 'So, he drowned, right?' he asked.

The pathologist shone a light up the dead man's nostrils and took swabs. Ever the professional, Van den Bergen wondered how she slept at night or ate after spending the working week with the dead. The last thing he needed a reminder of was his own mortality. Postmortems always left him feeling low for days.

'He's got froth in his air passages,' she said. 'Looking at his heart, I'd say it's been subject to hypoxia and pulmonary oedema, causing ventricular tachycardia and haemodilution. There's marked hyponatraemia. Everything's pointing to drowning at this stage.' Standing tall, she stretched out her back and yawned.

'Late night?' Van den Bergen asked.

'You'd only be jealous if I told you.' She winked at him. Turned her attention back to the cadaver on her stainless-steel slab.

Van den Bergen swallowed hard. Thought about the strange sexual chemistry that had historically been between them, fizzling to nothing when they had once actually found themselves in a clinch. Decided to ignore her prompt. 'Pointing to drowning. You're not sure?'

'Listen,' she said. 'Drowning in adults is rare. You guys pull a handful out of the canals in a normal year. Right? The odd drunken tourist or some idiot who thinks it's a good idea to go swimming. It's rare. So, whenever someone gets pulled out of the canal, I do two things. I test the bloods for alcohol levels and narcotics – not so easy when the body has been under water for a while, as decomp and the invasion of water in the cells makes everything so bloody difficult.' She tugged at Engels' fingernails. 'Luckily, our guy hasn't been in the water for too long. He's lost his body heat but his nails and skin haven't started to come away yet.'

'So, he can't have been in there for more than twenty-four hours,' Van den Bergen said. 'Isn't that right?'

'I'd say this guy's been in a little while longer. Thirty-six hours, maybe. Just shy of forty-eight at a push. Any longer, his nails would have started coming away.' The pathologist loped round to the far side of the body, her Crocs squeaking on the tiled floor. She pointed to his armpit. Livid purple bruises by the shoulder joint. More tricky to see on the side with the severed arm, but there, nevertheless. 'And in cases like this, I also look for bruising. Trauma signs, where somebody's hit their head on the way in or where somebody's been attacked before being pushed in. A true drowning will show hardly any signs of trauma externally. If you've had too much to drink or are stoned, you slide or roll in; you're dead inside five to ten minutes. You've inhaled a good couple of litres of water in three. But no bruising necessarily, unless you bash yourself on the way in. But here, look!'

Van den Bergen studied the small round purple bruises. Four by each armpit in total. 'He's been grabbed or lifted by someone.' Removed some photos from an A4 manila envelope that had been taken at the canal side. Sifted through them, until he found photographs of Engels' personal effects. A photograph of his shoes. 'These were expensive shoes,' he said. 'Russell & Bromley from England. Nice moccasins, but look! They're scuffed as hell at the heel and the heels themselves have been worn down.'

Marianne nodded. 'He's been dragged down to the canal by someone strong and flung in. Until I get all these results through, I'd put my money on that.' She snapped off her latex gloves and started to wash her hands at the steel sink. 'And given the other canal drownings were badly decomposed when they were discovered, who's to say similar hadn't happened to them? I didn't perform their autopsies, but Strietman said they'd all been partying too hard – drugs in the system. Who's to say they hadn't been forced into the water? He recorded an open verdict.'

'Oh shit,' Van den Bergen said. 'You really think we've got a canal killer on our hands?'

The pathologist shrugged. 'You're the Chief Inspector. You tell me.'

CHAPTER 8

Amsterdam, police headquarters, later

'When is he due back?' George asked Marie in Dutch, wrinkling her nose at the foetid smell of the IT suite. Stale sweat, with an after-kick of onions. But mainly overcooked cabbage. Even the smell of the new carpet that Van den Bergen had got funding for could not mask that distinctive bouquet.

Marie narrowed her watery blue eyes. Opened the collar of her ribbed sweater and sniffed. Shrugged absently. 'He's at the morgue.' She glanced at the clock on her computer monitor. 'He's already been gone an hour. I reckon you've got twenty minutes, tops, before he shows.'

George considered the white shards that covered the floor by Marie's feet. Eyed suspiciously the empty bag of crisps next to her keyboard. Set her bag down on the desk, rather than the floor. Yawned so that her blocked ears popped with a deafening squeak.

'Ow.' She rubbed her ears. Sniffed her fingers and was pleased to discover they smelled of the Moroccan oil she had used to tame her hair. Better than Marie's stink.

'How was your flight?' Marie asked.

'Yeah, OK. So come on, then. Tell me about this Maastricht man.' George folded her arms and studied the IT expert's face for signs of sympathy, excitement or fear that would give her an

49

inkling as to what the new lead meant for her mother. All she could see was a rash of embarrassment curling its way up Marie's neck with red tendrils.

Marie clicked her mouse several times. Brought up a photo of a corpse on screen.

George grimaced at the partially decomposed man. 'Jesus. He's no looker,' she said in English. 'What's his story?' Back to Dutch.

Marie pointed with her biro to the empty eye socket on the left-hand side of the man's face. 'They actually found him about nine months ago, buried in some heavy clay when they were doing landscaping for the new A2 Maastricht double-decker tunnel.'

'The motorway bypass?' George asked.

'Yes. Exactly. The clay had preserved his soft tissues pretty well but we don't share a database with Maastricht, so I didn't come across this record until the other day. Completely by accident and only because I was digging in the right place.' Marie blushed and hooked her lank red hair behind her ears. 'Excuse the pun.'

'And?' Wearing a scowl, George scrutinised the photo of the corpse. 'How does that relate to Letitia? I don't get it.'

'He's a DNA match.'

'Shit. Get out of town,' George said in English, standing abruptly. 'It was *his* eye? All those months ago?'

Marie nodded. She clicked up a photograph of a man who appeared altogether healthier. Alive, for a start. Dark-skinned with brown eyes and his black hair cropped brutishly. A tattoo of an indiscernible pattern on the side of his head, visible beneath the stubble on his scalp. Another tattoo of black roses scrolling around his neck.

'He wasn't bad looking,' George said, raising an eyebrow. 'What a waste.'

'Well,' Marie said, 'The eye in the gift box in Vinkeles belonged to a man, not your mother. Forensics sussed that straight away. We've known it all along. Right? So, turns out, it belonged to this poor chump.' Marie rubbed her nose, examined the inside of her empty crisp packet and tutted. 'Nasser Malik. Only twenty. Low-level Maastricht dealer, who knocked about with some really nasty types. A recent addition to the M-Boyz gang, a few of whom got busted in 2009, after a couple of kids died from a bad batch of coke that they'd cut with too much levamisole and bloody scouring powder, would you believe it? Malik had previous for dealing, burglary, GBH and car theft but had always managed to avoid prison, getting off with fines and community service. He went missing about a year ago – reported by his mother, who's a widowed dentist. Apparently, he'd had ADHD and never did particularly well at school because of it. His brother, Ahmed Malik, is a doctor in Breda but Nasser, the younger son, went off the rails after his dad died.'

George considered the handsome young fool that peered out at her from one photograph and the enucleated, ruined corpse that ogled her with one solitary half-rotted orb in the other. 'For God's sake. How tragic is that? What did the coroner say in the report? I presume you've pulled it?'

Clicking onto another tab, Marie scanned the text. 'He'd been strangled. Garrotted with soldering wire, in fact, in exactly the same manner as a couple of gang members had been killed that year, suggesting this was an organised hit.'

Pointing at the screen, George rocked back and forth in her typing chair, mulling over the information. 'A lot of planning went into that hoax lunch at Vinkeles. Somebody somewhere knew I really wanted to hear from my dad and wouldn't turn down an invitation if it came from him. Then, the whole Letitia missing bullshit. *Then*, that gift box containing my worst nightmares, waiting for me at precisely the time and place I'm supposed to be meeting my long-lost Daddy Dearest … who has also either vanished off the face of the earth or is living off-grid, without so much as an electoral registry listing online.' She inhaled deeply and rubbed her face with her hands, remembering the abject terror she had felt when she had caught sight of the brown eye, staring back at her dully from its box. She had been convinced it was Letitia's. Only Marianne de Koninck had persuaded her that the DNA had been that of a man of Asian extraction. A mystery. Now solved. George could finally let go of any nagging doubt.

Silence permeated the IT suite, leaving only the buzz of the computer terminals and the bodily funk of Marie.

'This Nasser guy was bumped to order,' George said, knocking against her full lips with a balled fist. 'Whoever is behind this wanted his eye to put the frighteners on me. A grand gesture to make me think they'd got to Letitia. Probably a shit metaphor to say I'm being watched at all times.'

'Well, some sick bastard has definitely got a hard-on for you,' Marie said, nodding. 'And it's not going to be your dad, is it? No parent would torture their child like that.' She sighed, stroking a framed photo on her desk of a pink-cheeked baby boy.

George tried to visualise her mother. The memory of that sour, over-made-up face. False-lashed eyes that were always on the lookout for slights and perceived inequities; never seeing joy in the small things or kindnesses or good intentions of the people around her. Letitia in the fur coat that made her look like a mountain lion, throwing cheap Chardonnay down her fat neck in Wetherspoons. Running her talon-tipped fingers, painted the colours of the Jamaican flag, through those caramel blonde hair extensions that she'd bought with her bingo winnings. That memory was beginning to fade, now. Gloria Gaynor at Christmas TK Maxx. That was the Letitia George remembered. That was the Letitia she wanted to remember. Not the bewildered, punctured woman who had been given the diagnosis that she had only a few years left, thanks to her sickle cell anaemia and pulmonary hypertension.

'She's out there, somewhere,' she told Marie, acknowledging a heaviness in her heart that wasn't just indigestion from eating Aunty Sharon's patties too quickly on the flight. 'Either buried in a shallow grave or chained to a radiator in some basement, annoying the shit out of her kidnapper.' She gave a chuckle, devoid of any real humour. For years, she had opted to eschew the company of Letitia the Dragon, but now, with the element of choice having been stolen from her, she felt short-changed by a family that only really consisted of her aunty and her beloved, cantankerous arsehole of a partner, Van den Bergen.

Turning her attention back to Nasser's blackened, hollow eye socket on the screen, she nodded. 'Some evil wanker has orchestrated all of this with great skill and forethought.' Sucked her teeth. 'It *must* have been The Duke. That Gordon Bloom bastard denies it every time I go to see him in Belmarsh, but, of all the people I've pissed off, who else would have had access to guys with previous, that could be just whacked to order for their eye colour?' She groaned with frustration and shouted, 'Christ on a bike!' in her native tongue.

'What about him?' A man's voice coming from the threshold to the IT suite heralded the arrival of an interloper. A familiar, deep rumble. 'Last time I heard, he'd been arrested for cycling under the influence. Gave us some bullshit about turning water into wine.'

George turned around as Marie furtively, hastily clicked her tabs shut. Van den Bergen's long frame filled the doorway, leaning against the architrave with those long legs crossed in the way that caused a knowing, wry smile to curl the edge of George's mouth upwards. 'Are you trying to make a terrible joke in my general direction, Paul van den Bergen? Because you should pack that in, right now!' She drank in the sight of him, noting the changes from the past few weeks since he had visited her in Cambridge. Looking thinner, healthy, well. Better colour from being outdoors, now the gardening season had started.

Rising to embrace her lover, she could smell on him a whiff of formalin from the mortuary and the remnants of VapoRub beneath his nose as she kissed him fleetingly on his dry, neglected lips. The difficult old bastard turned his head briskly to offer her his sharp-sand hard stubbled cheek, but in his grey hooded eyes, she spied a glint of mischief. 'What was so urgent that I had to abandon my book launch to come over?' she asked.

'This,' he said, pulling a large envelope out of his bag. Glancing over to Marie's monitor, he started to lay out photo after photo of a man who appeared to be in his early thirties. Blond, almost handsome, slender in build and very much alive in the first three. Posing on a tropical beach with another man, his arm draped casually around his shoulder and a closeness evident between them that marked them out as lovers, George was certain. In the fourth photo, he was very dead and utterly unrecognisable. A photo of some bruising around the man's armpits. Followed by further photos of three bodies in varying states of decomposition. Ragged, overblown effigies of the humans they had once been.

'Floaters?' George asked, fingering the prints and scowling at the grim portrait of a cadaver with opaque eyes and lips that had been nibbled away to reveal a deadly grin.

'Precisely,' Van den Bergen said, hanging his raincoat over the back of a chair and folding his long frame into another. 'I thought there was a link between them, but I can't work out what. We've got a twenty-year-old male – Alex Jansen.' He took out his notebook. Wedged his glasses on the end of his triangle of a nose and peered through the lenses like an overtaxed teacher. 'I've written something here and I can't bloody read it.'

He passed the book to George, who stifled a grin.

'A student vet on holiday from Utrecht University,' she read. 'Found in the Keizersgracht near Vijzelstraat. Seems to have fallen in after a party at his friend's house nearby, where he was last seen alive.'

Van den Bergen's grey eyes met hers for an instant and George felt warmed by the connection; the erotic promise that the evening might hold if he didn't get called away on police business or they didn't start arguing over something inane.

'Then, there's André van der Pol,' he continued, taking the book from her. 'Seventeen. Went to a nightclub – Church.'

'A gay club,' Marie offered, blushing. 'Pretty full on, from what I've heard.' She scratched at the angry threat of a spot on her chin. Eyes darting from her desk to the empty crisp packet. 'My neighbour goes.'

'Right,' Van den Bergen said, sighing. 'He wound up in the Singel. And finally Ed Bakker. Nineteen, from a wealthy family who were from Utrecht but who now live in Willemspark. He was out drinking with friends and seems to have gone into the Leidsegracht without leaving so much as a ripple. No witnesses for any of them. None that would come forward, anyway.'

Gazing at the photograph of what was left of the unrecognisable nineteen-year-old boy, George imagined Danny Spencer – bones she had once jumped, by now in a cemetery in Southeast London, thanks to the ruthless change in fortunes the dealer had been dealt. Letitia, possibly floating somewhere in some tributary of the North Sea, becoming food for aquatic life and passing seagulls. This was a depressing, shitty line of work to be in.

'They were all very young, apart from Floris Engels,' Van den Bergen said. 'But the three kids all had drugs and alcohol in their systems. Beer. Hash. Meth. MDMA.'

'Partying hard,' George said, closing her eyes. Remembering what it felt like to roll out of a nightclub in the small hours, full of intoxicating substances and drunk on expectation of what might yet come to pass before sun-up.

'Other than that,' Van den Bergen said, 'I can't find a connection between them. The parents all claim their dead children are angels. Their friends have got nothing but good things to say about them. No obvious commonalities, though, apart from them dying in the canals, stoned off their tits. In fact …' He stretched in his chair until his hip clicked. Grimacing, he pressed two ibuprofen out of a blister pack and swallowed them down dry. 'Maybe there isn't a bloody connection and it is just coincidence, after all. But I inherited this case off Louis Beekmans, after Minks did a reshuffle.' He rubbed at his prematurely white sideburns with a long finger.

'Who the fuck is Beekmans?' George asked.

'Sudden heart attack. He's just had a triple bypass,' Van den Bergen offered by way of explanation. Put a hand over his sternum and belched noiselessly. Clearly feeling for ventricular abnormalities. His fingers wandered southwards along his torso to his scar tissue. His hooded eyes seemed to darken. 'Anyway, his record-keeping wasn't up to much and I have a hunch there's some chicanery going on – especially now I've seen the bruises on our mysterious teacher, Mr Engels. When I get toxicology and bloods back, I'll know more. My young and shiny-faced new boss, Minks, is pushing for a serial killer, because that's what makes him feel tingly in his big-boy pants.'

'And what do you think?' George asked, surreptitiously grabbing his large hand and kissing it, as Marie reached into her desk drawer and withdrew another packet of crisps.

'I think I want a fresh pair of eyes on it,' he said, winking. 'Me, Marie, here and Elvis have run out of steam for now. Feeling up to applying your criminologist's mind to this mess, Detective Cagney?'

George thought about the tantalising opportunity to do a bit of digging on the side around the circumstances surrounding Nasser Malik's death. Spending time with her argumentative ageing lover, instead of being wheeled out on the book-signing and lecture trail by Sally Wright and marking sub-standard essays written by lazy first-year undergraduates. Then, she thought about the pot she was saving for a deposit on a flat. 'Will I get paid?' she asked.

'Maarten Minks has a fancy post-grad qualification from the London School of Economics,' he said. 'He's the polar opposite of Kamphuis. Nothing he likes more than forking out for an expert opinion to check his expert's opinion was expert enough. He can't wait to receive your invoice, Georgina.'

CHAPTER 9

Amsterdam, Van den Bergen's apartment, then, Melkweg nightclub, later

'Oh, you're not going to start going on about your bloody mother again, are you?' Van den Bergen asked over dinner. 'I thought we'd decided she'd done her usual disappearing act because the prospect of playing the second-fiddle mother figure in the drama of someone else's life didn't appeal. Isn't that Letitia all over?'

George eyed her burnt mushroom risotto. It put her in mind of cerebral matter served up in a vintage dish. She put her spoon and fork together and pushed the plate aside. 'Nice,' she said. 'I don't see you for weeks and you're on my case the minute I set foot through the door. You asked *me* over, remember?' Scraping her chair aggressively along the wooden floor, she walked into his kitchen and flung the dish on the side. 'Not the other way round. And don't give me that bullshit about you, Marie and Elvis running out of steam, because you'd only just inherited this bloody case. Face it. You've just been looking for an excuse to get me over here!'

She was aware of him moving from the dining area towards her. Kept staring at the splashback tiles, waiting to see if he was coming in to offer some placatory gesture or merely gunning for an argument at closer range. When his arms slid around her waist, she smiled. Turned around and craned her neck to look up into that familiar, handsome face. Appraising his large, hooded grey eyes, topped with those dark eyebrows. The sunken furrows either side of his mouth were back now that he had started to return to fitness. His skin, so sallow over the winter months, was now lightly tanned and reflected time spent outdoors.

'You look well. Being a grandfather agrees with you. Give us a snog, old man,' she said, smiling as she ran a finger over his stubble. 'And you'd better grow a goatee or something while I'm here, because I can't do with scouring my lips off on your five o'clock shadow.'

'Don't you like my risotto?' he asked, kissing her neck gently.

'You're a shit cook.' Stroking the soft navel hair beneath his top, she ran her fingers delicately over the long lump of his scar. 'But I missed your hot stodge so badly.' Giggling, George unzipped the fly to Van den Bergen's work trousers and dropped to her knees. Yanked down his disappointing grey jersey underpants to deal with the contents, which were wholly non-disappointing. Van den Bergen groaned as she took him into her mouth. Brought him almost to the point of no return with a tongue normally sharpened on the egos of Wormwood Scrubs wide boys, overinflated Cambridge Fellows or Peckham's finest players in their low-rise G Star Raw.

Van den Bergen buried his hands in her mass of curls, encouraging her steady rhythm. But George broke off, as he began to thrust too lustily, kissing her way up his abdomen. Teasing him with her abstemiousness so that he might afford her the same pleasure with that wry, acerbic mouth of his.

They never made it to the bedroom but they did engage in a clumsy, desire-driven tango to the sofa, where George flung her clothes on the floor, climbed astride his long, lean frame and hungrily lowered herself onto him. First, she relished his tongue on her. Then, she slid her body sinuously down towards his groin, manoeuvring him inside her. With his hands caressing her breasts, the lovers locked onto a familiar fast track that shunted and rocked them all the way to the end of their urgent thrill ride.

'Jesus. I needed that,' George said, pulling her pants and jeans back on. She clambered back onto the prone Van den Bergen and kissed him passionately.

'You're balm for the soul,' he said, wrapping his arms around her and cradling her head on his chest.

His heartbeat loped steadily along. A comforting sound. She drank in his scent of warm skin, testosterone and sport deodorant. Committed it to memory.

'I need a smoke and your hip bones are digging in me,' she said, rising. 'You're a shit mattress.'

Taking the box of tissues from the sideboard and throwing them into his lap, she stumbled to the balcony to spark her e-cigarette into life. Exhaled her smoke and what was left of her tension onto the Amsterdam night air. Listening to the animated chatter of the neighbours in adjacent apartments to the side and below. A slice of Dutch life. Those clean-living citizens knew nothing of the depravity and violence that George and Van den Bergen saw week in, week out. Good. There needed to be some innocence in the world still. And there had to be more to life than death.

'Do you know what? I fancy going dancing,' George told the full moon.

When she returned to the living room, the steady buzz of snoring coming from the sofa told her she was either going to bed or going clubbing alone.

Melkweg draped itself along the edge of the Lijnbaansgracht, like an elegant old burgher with bragging rights to its slumberous, low-rise canal-side position. Dwarfed by the outsized glazed boxes of the modern theatre that it sat next to, the five-storey town-houses behind it and the ugly apartment block in front. In the daytime, George had walked past this place and barely glanced up at it. At night, with the neon lights that shouted this was where the hip-hop, R&B and deep house happened reflected in the almost still canal water, the whole scene was transformed into something Van Gogh might have painted on acid, had he lived in modern times.

Needing to feel the bass throbbing through the soles of her feet and reminding herself that there was no shame in going clubbing alone, George pushed to the front of the queue and marched up to the door.

'Not so fast, girly!' a bouncer said, putting his beefy arm out in front of her as a barrier to entry.

George was aware of the complaints of the scantily clad teens standing behind her that she had jumped the queue. Speaking English and clearly on some sort of parent-funded mini-break, judging by the cut-crystal public school accents. Ridiculing her attire of ripped jeans, studded high-tops and the size and shape of her arse.

Turning around, George quipped, 'Have you fucking finished, children?' She sucked her teeth at them, taking in every detail of the taut white skin on their waxy faces and the glazed look in their stoned eyes. 'Or do you want me to tip off the bouncer here that yous are all underage and off your tits already?'

The group of dissenters fell silent, glancing nervously at one another. George flashed her membership card at the bouncer. Perhaps he saw some of the thunder in her expression.

'Sorry, miss. Go ahead.' Respectfully ushering her inside.

'That's more fucking like it,' George said under her breath. 'Dick.'

Inside the giant laser-lit space, the crowd heaved as one writhing organism. The smell of dry ice and alcohol was thick on the stifling, sweaty air. Music throbbing rhythmically like a beating heart. George imagined she could see sound travelling in waves from one side of the venue to the other. Losing herself in the middle of the dancefloor, she closed her eyes. Started to dance.

Tried desperately to shake the feeling that she was being watched. In here, of all places, she could hide in plain sight. Wearing an invisibility cloak of young clubbers, she could free herself from surveillance. Because surely, whoever had sent that email from her father and stolen her mother had set out with the nefarious intention of getting to her. Whether her parents were lying dead somewhere or not, she was the target. She had received the eye. The metaphor that said her every move was being scrutinised. And what she hadn't told Van den Bergen, for fear of pissing in his new-grandfather's chips, was that she had had another email, purporting to be from Michael Carlos Izquierdo Moreno. Daddy Dearest. The image of the email started to take shape in her mind's eye. Along with it, a memory of her stalker. She'd omitted to tell Van den Bergen about him, too.

Stop fucking obsessing, George told herself. *You came here to drown all that shit out and hide from the eye for a couple of hours. Listen to the music. Let the bass heal you. Nobody's watching in here.*

Trying to dispel the mounting tension, she forced herself to dance to the compulsive, lazy beat of a hip-hop track. Shaking her thang. Arms in the air. Except she couldn't relax. Her movements were out of sync with the rhythm, embarrassing the ghosts of her ancestry who almost certainly, as stereotype demanded, had had all the moves. Adrift in a sea of gyrating kids, all at least seven years younger than she was, she realised she had become stiff-arsed, like some middle-aged housewife from Staines. The music started to irritate her. Then, she got annoyed at the misogynistic lyrics.

And skanky Nasser Malik is in a fridge in a Maastricht morgue. Am I going to end up in a fridge in a morgue, with Van den Bergen grimacing at my cadaver?

Forcing her way to the bar, she decided she would get a cheap beer and just people-watch for a while. Wait for her mojo to return. But the queue for drinks was five deep and George lacked the height of the Dutch. Perching at the end of the bar, she realised a peacock of a boy in a tight T-shirt, who clearly had cash to splash, had ordered a large round of bottled Belgian beer. Waving his €50 note, he was too preoccupied with barking orders at the harried barman to notice George swipe a single bottle of Hoegaarden.

'Thanks, arsehole,' she said under her breath, grinning.

Perching upstairs on the balcony, George watched the revellers below, debating whether she should just go back to Van den Bergen's flat and admit that she was getting too old for this. Maybe Van den Bergen was making her feel prematurely too old. Fifty wasn't far away for him, after all, and then there was his granddaughter, little Eva, on the scene now.

Eyeing the younger men that buzzed nearby, all sweaty from the dancefloor with their going-out-best clobber clinging to their firm bodies, George's attention was pulled in the direction of a dealer, stealthily palming a baggie of white powder onto a boy of about eighteen. The dealer could have been a clubber. Nothing out of the ordinary, apart from the tattoo just visible in the stubble of his hair. Like Nasser Malik's tattoo. Suddenly George had become distanced enough from her own woes to really notice what was going down.

'It's snowing in Amsterdam,' she muttered.

Pushing the clubbers aside, she walked up to the dealer. He smiled down at her. A greedy, rotten-toothed smile of a seasoned junkie, earning to fund his own addiction, no doubt. Either that, or he had really shocking dental hygiene, George mused. She suppressed a full-blown grimace. Ensured there was space between them in this packed temple to hedonism.

'What you got?' she shouted above the music, careful not to come too close to his ears. They were greasy-looking with hardly any lobes, punctured by an oversized stud. She shuddered. 'You got any good coke or E?'

'Coke? No, love.' His eyes darted everywhere. Checking for the long arm of the law, no doubt. 'Crystal meth, miaow miaow, G. Might be able to get you some E by the end of the night.'

'I'll leave it thanks,' George said, backing away. Annoyed with herself, she realised she had started to lose touch. The inevitability of being closer to thirty than twenty. Too much clean living.

As George hastened out of Melkweg to wake the sleeping Van den Bergen and tell him her theory about the canal deaths, she failed to notice that she was followed home.

CHAPTER 10

Amsterdam, Melkweg nightclub, then, Leidsegracht, 30 April

It had been a long walk from the gay sauna in Nieuwezijds Armsteed to Melkweg, but Greg Patterson had agreed to hook back up with his friends for a drink and a dance before the night was out. A shame not to, since this was supposed to be Sophie's twenty-first celebration.

'I'll not be long,' he'd promised her, squeezing her hands as they all stood in the busy, cobbled square – a crossroads between the respectable Amsterdam and the red-light district. His mind had been elsewhere, contemplating the sauna and the sensual overload that awaited him in the steam of the cubicles. 'I said I'd nip to this place to get something for my mum.'

James and Poppy had exchanged a fleeting but meaningful glance with one another. Making morality judgements about him, no doubt.

'What? At nine o'clock at night?' James had asked. Nudging Poppy. Jesus. The wanker was so obvious and rude.

'You guys go!' Greg had said, ignoring the rank prejudice that had flown just beneath Sophie's radar. Typical hetties. 'I'll meet you later.' He waved dismissively. Smiling benignly. He had pulled the sleeves of his best jacket down against the chill in the evening

64

air. D&G. It had cost him all of his Christmas money off his mum and dad. 'Melkweg, right? I'll be there by midnight. I'll text so we can find each other. Okay? I promise!' He had kissed Sophie's hands, the feathers from her bright red boa tickling his nose. Perhaps he could persuade her to lend him that for Club Church, once the others had all toddled off back to the hotel. Greg had an itinerary and he had intended to stick to it. He had pecked his friend chastely on each cheek. 'Have fun, birthday girl!'

Her chubby face had been flushed pink with effervescence. Centre of attention, for once, instead of being just the dumpy girl on their languages course, whom the straight guys all ignored in favour of Giselle. Giselle was the worst person Sophie could have chosen to be BFFs with. Giselle, who was dainty like a gazelle but had all the personality of a medium-sized snail. Giselle had been hanging back, texting some beau or other, obviously. Chewing gum and smoking at the same time. Looking too cool for school, as though it had been killing her to be in Amsterdam for something as ordinary and unglamorous as fat Sophie's birthday.

'Aw, it will be rubbish without you, Greg. Come on.' Sophie had clasped at his sleeve, looking at him with undisguised adoration. 'Don't just bugger off on me.'

It wasn't the first time that this had happened. A nice girl like Sophie, falling for him. Believing that he was available and fair game because he was friendly and listened and understood. Not like the straight lads, who couldn't give a stuff. She did know he was gay. But perhaps she believed she could turn him. He had often seen the optimism shining in her eyes. He should have drawn his boundaries more clearly, but didn't want to disappoint her. And he was hardly going to ram his sexual proclivities down her throat like the cock of some guy from Grindr on a wet Saturday night in Leeds.

'See you later, Soph. Enjoy!'

And that had been that. Feeling anticipatory, he had taken

himself off to a gay bar and partaken of some traditional Dutch courage – four glasses of strong Belgian beer, though the clientele had been a little too old for him. Finally, he had meandered down to the sauna, hoping that his slightly disappointing pecs and one-pack would pass muster with the guys there who spent more hours on their bodies per week than he spent in an entire term. The drugs had helped. He had allowed one of the men to booty bump him with some crystal meth. The high had been intense. He had never felt so horny.

As the high had begun to wane, he had snorted the couple of lines of mephedrone that had been offered to him by some guy called Hank or Henk or some bloody thing beginning with an H. This was the kind of trip he had hoped for. And those were the elements of his Amsterdam adventure that he wouldn't be relaying to Sophie once they were back in halls.

Utterly fucked dry, he had traversed town, ready to drink some more and dance with the sad hetties. Just after midnight, as he entered Melkweg, his confidence was beginning to slide into the shadow of a comedown again. He needed more gear. Needed to get higher. Observing the crowd of writhing men and women, he felt out of his depth and estranged. These were not his people. But then …

'Greg!' Sophie shouted, waving avidly. Flapping her feather boa. Her polyester shift dress looking crumpled with dark rings around the armpits.

He couldn't hear her, but he could see her mouth moving. The others were with her, swaying their bodies uselessly to some R&B track. Giselle was being frotted by some local, built like a brick shithouse, by the looks. Pushing him away but enjoying every minute of the attention, no doubt.

Reluctantly, Greg started to make for their group. But then, he spotted a wraith of a man moving in amongst the clubbers. Older, dressed far better than the kids in designer casual clothes, he had the tell-tale shifty eyes and swift hands that Greg sought.

People were approaching this cuckoo in the nest, but looking the other way. Stopping. Standing. Engaging in some awkward exchange. Leaving with their hand in their pocket. A dealer.

Bypassing Sophie, he made for the wraith. He could feel the dealer weighing and getting the measure of him as though he were nothing more than a lump of raw product waiting to be graded and cut for more profitability. 'What have you got?' he asked. 'Tina? Gina? Miaow miaow?'

The wraith answered him in English, spoken with a rolling Amsterdam accent. Clearly used to dealing with tourists from across the North Sea.

Ten minutes later, Greg had downed the glass of water containing his drug of choice. Expecting to feel ready to party, as he moved back into the stifling heat of the crowded dancefloor, he started to feel like he was being watched. A wave of nausea almost knocked him to the ground.

'Are you okay?' Sophie bellowed, putting her arm around him.

He shrank from her touch. Didn't want to be that close. Nodded. His mouth prickled. Was he about to faint?

'I'm going outside,' he said.

No idea whether she had heard him or not, Greg felt panic draw him towards the exit, as though, like a bad marionette, some puppet-master controlled his movements and impulses with a yank of a string. Too many people. All watching him. Had to get away. Go where it was quiet.

Greg Patterson resolved to walk slowly down towards Club Church, hoping by the time he had got some fresh air, he would be good to go again. Six minutes, Google had told him. At this time of night, the towpath by the Leidsegracht had been clear of other pedestrians. Only the silent hulking shapes of parked cars stood between him and the gently lapping canal.

'I'm going to be sick,' he said to the streetlight, leaning against it for support. Wishing, now, that he had asked Sophie to come outside with him. Dry-heaving, he said a silent prayer that this gruesome feeling would pass; that he'd return home to see Mum and Dad and his room in halls and his gaming console and his books and Nana and the dog. *Shit. What have I done?* Memories of the sauna inserted themselves into his view of the cobbles and the notion that he might vomit on his new shoes. The laughter among strangers. The booty bump. The absurdly hot sex. So much fun that he now regretted having. *Idiot.*

There was a sound of footsteps. Good. Thank God for that. Greg was hopeful that the night-time stroller might come to his aid, should he need it.

When the still, black water rushed up to meet him, Greg was taken by surprise, not just by the freezing chill but that he had fallen in at all. Flailing his arms, trying to kick his way back up to the surface, he cried out. A muffled plea that only he heard, as the bubbles containing the last of his breath rose uselessly to the surface. His foot was snagged. His lungs were full. And then all was dark.

CHAPTER 11

Amsterdam, Sloterdijkermeer allotments, later

Sitting in a deck chair on the small decking area by his shed, Van den Bergen relished the warmth of the mid-morning sun on his face. It felt like somebody had inserted a key into the bullet hole in his hip and had tried to wind him up. But aside from the incessant, nagging ache that he had tried and failed to calm with strong ibuprofen gel, he reasoned that he was faring a damn sight better than young Greg Patterson.

Radiohead's Thom Yorke emoted out of the battery-operated CD player that George had bought him for Christmas. Wailing that the witch should be burned. The melancholy in his voice seemed fitting.

'How many's that now?' he muttered, opening a foil-wrapped pile of ham sandwiches and biting into the top one hungrily. Not bothering to sweep the crumbs off his gardening dungarees. It felt like an act of rebellion. If George saw he was eating without having washed his hands first, he would never hear the end of it. Compost beneath his fingernails from repotting his petunias into larger containers. But not all of his fingers smelled of compost and leafy growth. He sniffed his middle finger and remembered their reunion on the sofa the previous evening. Smiled. Frowned.

Remembered he was supposed to be thinking about more serious matters.

'Five,' he said to the allium globemasters that had just blossomed into giant purple balls on the end on their thick, green stems. 'Five damned floaters.'

He belched. Ham played havoc with his stomach acid. Why did he never learn? His throat had been sore of late. Maybe he had oesophageal cancer. Swallowing, he realised it was more uncomfortable than yesterday. Or perhaps he just needed a cup of coffee from his flask to wash down the sandwich.

Checking his phone for an email from Marianne de Koninck, he thought about Greg Patterson's body on the canal side at 5 a.m. that morning. Leaving George, warm in his bed, to stand in the drizzle beneath the umbrella, yet again. Next to Elvis, who had refused to share the umbrella, yet again. Marianne's number two, Daan Strietman, had found a lump of frothed mucus and vomit in the boy's throat. Later, during the preliminary examination at the morgue, he had confirmed recent rough intercourse and blistering inside the boy's rectum – apparently a common side effect of taking liquid crystal meth anally via a syringe.

Grimacing at the florid pink flesh that hung out of his sandwich, Van den Bergen folded his lunch back up, levered himself out of the chair with a grunt and flung the packet onto the deck chair.

His phone rang. Looking around the allotment, he couldn't make out where the noise was coming from. Peering inside the shed, it wasn't on the potting table. Debbie Harry hung limply on the wall, looking clueless. She was no bloody use. It wasn't in the trug of compost, with his trowel. Ringing. Ringing.

Agitated, he finally realised the phone had fallen into his oversized wellington boot.

'Yes,' he barked down the phone, wondering if his blood pressure was dangerously high. Made a mental note to switch vibrate on.

'It's Marianne,' the chief pathologist said. 'I've got the toxi-cology report back from Floris Engels. He'd taken a cocktail of drugs prior to death.'

'Oh.' Van den Bergen sat back down heavily onto his deck chair, inadvertently flattening his ham sandwiches. 'An OD?'

'Well,' she said. 'He had a lot of the drug G in his system – Gamma Hydroxybutyrate. But that wasn't what bothers me. He's also been poisoned by bad methamphetamine, commonly known as crystal meth or Tina. Acute lead poisoning, to be precise, apparently common where lead acetate has been used as a substrate in production in a bad batch.'

Van den Bergen rubbed the lengthening stubble on his chin and gazed up at the treetops contemplatively. 'What about the others? The kids?'

There was a shuffling of paper at the other end of the phone. 'I dug out the original toxicology reports from our younger floaters. There was nothing had been flagged apart from drug misuse. But then, they'd been in the water so long and were so badly decomposed, I guess it was hardly surprising the results were inconclusive. Especially given the weight of evidence that it was death by drowning, hence the open verdict. But then, when Floris Engels showed signs of having taken contaminated meth, I had the toxicology on the kids redone. And this time round, we found that they had suffered the same fate. Renal damage *was* present, consistent with severe lead poisoning. I'm sorry. I don't know how Strietman missed it. Sometimes, you just have to be looking in the right place.'

'Any other similarities starting to emerge?' he asked. Perching his glasses on the end of the nose. Unable to read the instructions on a packet of seeds, thanks to a muddy smudge on his left lens.

'Floris Engels and Greg Patterson had both had rough anal intercourse prior to death, given the abrasion. But there's nothing to say it was forced. If they'd been taking drugs …'

'It's likely they'd been partying. Right.' Fleetingly, Van den

71

Bergen tried to imagine what young gay guys might get up to in a liberal city that was full of possibilities. He grimaced as his haemorrhoids twitched involuntarily. Wondered if he was due a prostate check. 'And Ed Bakker?'

'I couldn't tell you about Ed Bakker, because of the tissue damage from being in the water so long, but witnesses say he'd been to a gay club, hadn't he?' There was a pause on the line. She was chewing something over. Something unpalatable, clearly. 'Maybe Maarten Minks is not a million miles away with his serial killer theory, Paul. What if someone is spiking gay men on purpose and then shoving them into the canals?'

'Bullshit!' Van den Bergen shouted, well aware that her theory was anything but bullshit.

'Suit yourself.' The ice in her tone of voice almost froze the line. 'You're the detective.' She hung up.

Mind whirring at how best he could step up the investigation without sparking media hysteria, he dialled George's number. She picked up on the fourth ring, sounding sleepy.

'Morning, hot stuff. What's wrong?' she asked.

'I need you to get a job.'

'A job?! What do you mean, get a job? I've got a job. I'm a criminologist, remember?' Agitation had supplanted the sleepy affection in her voice.

'You need to get a job in a nightclub. A barmaid or something. I need to find out about meth supply in the city. Urgently.' He pinched the piece of skin at the bridge of his nose, imagining her outraged expression.

'I told you this was about drugs! Didn't I say last night?' She sounded momentarily triumphant. Good. 'Hang on.' The triumph was abruptly replaced by suspicion. 'You want me to do *what*?! I don't want to work as a fucking barmaid in a club.' He could hear her sparking her e-cigarette into life.

'Don't smoke in the flat! George!'

'Yeah. Whatever.'

He imagined the fumes from the e-cigarette, lingering in his curtains. Finding their way into his lungs, causing changes in his healthy cells. An image of his father, wired up to the chemo for long afternoon sessions, hope ebbing away with every drip of poison that entered his bloodstream. Struggling to gasp his last on oxygen at the end.

Van den Bergen's own breathing quickened. 'I thought you liked clubbing! It's your chance to be like a young person.'

There was a disapproving sucking sound that almost deafened him. How could he talk her round? Marie would never be able to pull a surveillance gig like that off. 'Look, if it's any consolation, I'm going to make Elvis go undercover too.'

'As what? A shit Elvis impersonator?'

'A gay clubber.'

She started to laugh but it wasn't the sound of amusement. It was sarcastic and loaded with disappointment. 'Do you really think Elvis – the straightest man in the world – is going to abandon his terminally ill mother to twerk in chaps until some murderous homophobe tries to bump him off with an overdose and a watery end? You've lost the fucking plot, old man.'

For the second time that morning, a woman hung up on Van den Bergen, leaving him alone with a half-chewed ham sandwich and a sense that something was deeply amiss in his beloved city of Amsterdam.

CHAPTER 12

Amsterdam, Reguliersdt, 1 May

'Come on, Dirk. You can totally do this,' George told Elvis. She grabbed him by the arm and marched him towards the entrance to the Amsterdam Rainbow Cellars. Music thumped its way up and out onto the bustling Reguliersd, which thronged with clusters of men, making their way from bar to bar. A rainbow flag was suspended from the façade of the tall townhouse in which the cellars were situated, just in case the tourists hadn't worked out what sort of place this was.

Elvis swallowed hard, tugging at the uncomfortably tight white T-shirt that George had persuaded him to wear. Contemplating his burgeoning paunch, he then cast a judgemental eye over the ripped gay guys who were sitting outside a café, draped nonchalantly over their chairs like men who knew they could carry off tight clothing.

'This is ridiculous,' he said. 'This is the worst idea the boss has ever had.'

'Tell me about it,' George said. 'I've got to go and do a shift as a barmaid, now. I've only ever cleaned or danced in clubs before. What the fuck do I know about pulling pints?'

'More than I know about what to do in a gay club,' Elvis said. He followed the progress of a beautiful, leggy blonde girl, who strutted down the street in sequinned hot pants. Twenty seconds in, he realised she was holding the hand of another girl. 'I can't even dance. And I've got psoriasis.'

They stood together outside the club, staring at the two bald bouncers on the door, who were chatting animatedly to a group of bearded men wearing make-up. The taller of the two bouncers refocused his attention on Elvis. The beady-eyed stare of a man who made snap judgements about other men for a living.

Feeling stripped naked, Elvis blushed. Dropped his gaze back to his paunch and took out his phone. There was a text from the carer, marked urgent, asking where Mum's incontinence pads were hidden.

'I shouldn't be here,' he told George, texting,

```
bathroom cupboard above hot water tank
```

with a practised thumb. 'I should be at home with Mum. She's really not got long left.' He sighed heavily at the thought of having to say goodbye to the only parent he had left. A once-robust woman who had been reduced to a frail husk. Inside three months, the doctor had estimated. He would have to deal with all the admin, alone. And clear her place, alone. Oh, and bury her too. He had been able to think of nothing else for a year. Knew he should be over the moon to get away at all and spend some time as an unencumbered thirty-something man with no responsibilities. But he wasn't. 'Nightclubs aren't really my thing, either.' Touching his hair, where George had gelled it into spikes, rather than a quiff, he felt a stranger to his own skin. She had made him trim his sideburns to conform with ordinary proportions. 'Or men. Obviously.'

'Sorry, man.' Patting him on the shoulder, George offered him a cigarette, which he took gratefully. Lit her own and exhaled thoughtfully. 'You've got so much on your plate. And a needle to find in a haystack. We both have.'

'What do I even say? Or do? I don't want to …' He looked up at the rainbow flag; followed the line down to the muscular, perfectly groomed men who chatted animatedly to the bouncers beneath it. Winced.

'Look, Elv— Dirk. You're in the workplace,' George said. 'Just try to make conversation with the men in there. That's all that's expected of you, right? Ask about drugs. Dealers. Anything unusual. The sort of detective work you do every day of the week. How is this any different?'

George had the keen focus of a woman who knew better than most what to look out for on a busy street scene. Not a cop's eye, Elvis assessed. But the intuitive gaze of someone who had lived on the other side and could easily sniff out the shifty, the disingenuous and the downright illegal. 'I wish you could do this and I could be the barman in a nice, easy straight club.'

George guffawed with laughter. Pointed to her simple black jeans and T-shirt. 'I'm hardly dressed for a night on the town.' Patted her bosom. 'And I'm lacking the correct kit, let's not forget.' Checked her watch. 'Listen. I've got to go. My shift starts in five and I don't want to be late on my first night.' She squinted into the near distance. 'So, there's squad cars parked up if there's trouble?'

He nodded. 'You know the number to call.'

He didn't like the way it smelled inside. Air freshener and beer and testosterone. The stairs leading down into the club were sticky underfoot, lit with blue neon treads. Every time he passed a man, he felt certain he was being checked out. He held his stomach in, conscious of having the figure of a man who ate too many *frites* with mayonnaise, sitting for too long in the pool car on stakeouts or tending his mother and compensating for the stress with the cake he had bought to fatten her up.

At the bar, he was careful to order just a Diet Coke, though something stronger might have helped him through this hell.

Should he ask the barman about drugs? Too obvious. Was the barman giving him a funny look? Had he already sniffed him out as a straight cop? Elvis opened his mouth to ask a question but realised there were men standing behind him, clamouring to be served. He would never be heard over the din of dance music, anyway.

After twenty minutes of scanning the dancefloor to get a feel for the place, wondering why the hell middle-aged bearded men might want to drag up and wear full make-up, like bad pantomime dames, Elvis decided to be brave and head to the toilets. Remembering that his prejudices were founded only on his late father's bigotry and that nobody was likely to try to bone him unless he asked. Nobody would probably want to bone him, anyway. He found himself unexpectedly saddened at that thought.

'Oh, Olaf's such a silly bitch! Guess what? He went to the hairdresser's and asked for—'

'Fuck off, Jef. I don't need you telling everyone about my grooming disasters.'

'I don't need to tell them. They can see for themselves, you daft cow!'

Overblown gales of laughter ensued.

Standing at the urinal, Elvis listened to the inane banter of three of the most catwalk-ready handsome young men he had ever seen, gathered around the sinks where they were primping their hair. What would they be talking about had they been straight? Football. Obviously. And they wouldn't have congregated in the stinking toilets. There was a rhythmic knocking sound coming from one of the cubicles. Hastily, Elvis zipped his trousers and left without washing his hands.

Perching on a balcony above the dancefloor, he scanned the club for signs of drug use or dealing.

'Hi!' He was startled by a man's voice bellowing in his ear. 'I'm Frank. What's your name?'

Blushing in the dark, Elvis swallowed hard. Was he being hit on? Thought of a name that was neither Dirk nor that hateful damned nickname that Van den Bergen had bestowed on him, now inextricably linked with his professional persona – Elvis. 'Antoon.' He reached out to shake Frank's hand. Frank, a balding boulder of a man who clearly ate iron for breakfast, laughed nervously, raised an eyebrow and shook his hand. Firm but sweaty.

'Very formal, Antoon,' he said. 'So, what brings you here? You're new.'

Elvis opened and closed his mouth. Half-relieved that he was being hit upon. Appalled with himself that he wasn't sure where to go with this conversation. 'I'm from out of town,' he said. 'I just fancied coming out. Kicking back. You know?'

Frank started to laugh. Stroked his cheek. Elvis shrank away from his touch and folded his arms across his chest.

'I spy a man in the closet!' Frank said, smiling. 'Are you married? Fancied a walk on the wild side?'

'No, it's not like that,' Elvis said, feeling the sweat pool around his armpits and pour into the waistband of his jeans.

'Ah, shy?' Frank reached into his pocket and pulled out a baggie of white powder. 'Fancy a bit of chemical courage?'

This was more like it. 'Maybe,' Elvis said. 'Is that coke?

'Yep. I've got some meth too, if you'd prefer.'

'Cool. Where did you get it?'

'Why?' Frank's brow furrowed.

Stop acting like a cop, Elvis chastised himself. *You're undercover! This is not an interview down the station of a door-to-door. Screw this up and Van den Bergen will never respect or trust you again.* 'I hear there's a bad batch going round. You can't be too careful.'

'Oh, I think *this* is good gear,' Frank said. 'My dealer is the go-to man in chem-sex circles.'

'Chem-sex?' Elvis gulped.

Frank ran his forefinger down Elvis' sweaty chest, over his moobs and gut, which he could no longer hold in. What the fuck should he say next?

'There's been a couple of guys from the scene died lately,' he said, reasoning that if the newspaper had printed stories about the canal deaths, then it was fair game. 'Aren't you worried?'

Raising an eyebrow, Frank smiled and leaned seductively against the balcony. 'Should I be? Are you going to fuck me to death, Antoon?'

Feeling the phone vibrate in his pocket, Elvis' head started to throb with the worry that some ill-fate had befallen his mother – that was almost certainly the carer texting – and anxiety that he hadn't yet got any information of use and was now almost certainly being propositioned for sex.

'I need to know about the provenance of the gear before I … er … indulge,' he said. Thought of George and her OCD. Was she faring any better? 'I'm very uptight about these things.' He put his hand on top of Frank's. Smiled. Prayed the guy couldn't feel how dangerously fast his heart was pounding. 'My body's a temple. I'm sure you understand.'

Frank slapped him on the shoulder and threw his head back. Mirth in his opiate-glassy eyes. 'You're funny.' Grabbed at Elvis' belly. 'Temple, indeed! I like you.'

And then he said the name that would crop up in conversation time after time in every bar and club Van den Bergen sent Elvis to.

CHAPTER 13

Amsterdam, Keizer's Basement nightclub, 14 May

'Nikolay?' George asked. 'Who the hell is Nikolay?' She flipped the tap on and started to pour the first glass of beer from a new barrel. Channelling Aunty Sharon, who had spent the last two decades pulling pints in Soho. Maybe barmaiding was in the blood. The foam started to spurt, shooting up to the rim of the glass, covering George's hand and T-shirt in sticky alcoholic ejaculate. Maybe barmaiding wasn't in the blood. 'Ugh. Grim, man. I'm gonna kill Van den Bergen,' she muttered in English, wiping her hand on a bar towel.

'He's the Czech gangster I was telling you about.' At her feet, her cocktail-shaking compatriot Tom was methodically stacking a beer fridge. Whispering, lest he be overheard by the manager. 'I've heard the bouncers talking about him.'

Nikolay. Nikolay. George committed the name to memory. The first decent lead she had managed to generate in ten nights of working as a cack-handed barmaid in five different clubs across the city.

'Move aside for the expert.' Tom stood. Playfully, he pushed her out of the way and started to tinker expertly with the beer tap until it produced a steady amber stream. 'There you go,' he said. 'I've got the magic touch.' He winked at her.

George was relieved he couldn't see her blush. Eyeing his wiry, hairy forearms, she reasoned that they were the right kind of forearms. But she hated his bitten nails. Had a sudden urge to ask him why he took such good care of his hair and body and yet neglected his hands. Bitten nails made George wince inwardly. *Focus, tit! You're not here to check out some strange guy's forearms or his hand hygiene.* 'Nikolay,' she said. 'So the dealers who work in here flog his gear?'

'Oh yeah,' Tom said, grinning, as though he were pleased at having insider information with which to impress this inquisitive new barmaid. 'They used to just deliver to order outside. Turning up on mopeds like pizza guys. But they've got braver in the past year and you can spot them on the dancefloor if you know what to look for. I reckon the bouncers must be taking a cut. Nobody ever sees the man himself, though. You wouldn't catch Nikolay on house night in crappy Keizer's Basement, that's for sure. Apparently, he's the stuff of legend. Like some Scarface type, except he deals meth and other chems.'

'What? Like whizz?'

He laughed. 'Nobody takes whizz anymore.' Derision in his voice, as though George had said something preposterous, like an ageing parent trying to be cool. 'Ecstasy's popular again, but mainly it's all crystal meth and mephedrone now. Where have you been for the last couple of years?!'

'Writing my book. I told you!' she said, treating him to a winning smile; having to suppress the desperate urge to flip him the bird. *Calm down, dick. Shove your ego back in your box. It's not his fault. He doesn't know the first thing about you. He's fresh out of college and a wet-behind-the-ears middle-class kid on his gap yah.* 'I'm doing this shitty barmaiding job for research. Where else am I going to get inspiration for a novel about drug-dealing and gangs and the underworld?' She widened her eyes dramatically.

'That's *so* cool that you're a writer.' Tom leaned on the bar, as though the club was not opening in only fifteen minutes. 'I wish

I could do something arty like that.' Smiling away. Blowing smoke up her arse in a way Van den Bergen never did.

'Well, I'm pretty sure you've got some brilliant anecdotes up your sleeve. I can tell you've lived.'

He nodded enthusiastically. 'I suppose so. I've been working bars all over France, Germany and Belgium since graduation. I mean, why the hell would I wanna rush back to a job in some mind-numbing call centre in Leeds, *if* I'm lucky? I'm not ready to wear a suit and do the nine to five bollocks!'

'Hmm,' George said absently, studying Tom's white teeth for signs of food. 'Come on, then. Tell me your cool stories about this Nikolay guy.'

He leaned in conspiratorially. A little too close. The intimacy sucked the oxygen out of the air. 'I've heard his name dropped in several of the places I've worked. I like that sort of thing. You know? True life crime and dat.' He stood tall. Crossed his arms, hip-hop style.

'You didn't just say "and dat" did you?' Pushing the bar towel into his hands, George shook her head disapprovingly and started to stack clean glasses on a shelf.

An awkward silence between them descended, smothering any further conversation, until the manager strode over, giving them both instructions for the evening.

'I want you to mop the toilets through before we open,' he told George, wiping his sweaty forehead on the sleeve of his black shirt.

The pasty-faced lump was probably younger than she was, she assessed. He spoke with a strong Limburg accent. Almost certainly some southern farmer's son, who had moved to Amsterdam for a taste of life in the fast lane.

'I'm not mopping the toilets,' she said. 'I'm here as temporary bar staff.'

The manager stared at her, slack-jawed. More surprise in his expression than annoyance. 'You're a temp. And I'm your boss. You do as I say if you want to get paid.'

George was just about to tell him to go fuck himself. Remembered that Van den Bergen and the families of the floaters were relying on her. She grabbed the bucket and mop. Waited until the manager's back was turned and mouthed 'fat wanker' at the back of his head. Shook her closed fist sideways.

'You crack me up,' Tom said, a wry smile on his face.

'You'd be fit if you grew your nails and didn't have a load of tats,' George said, pointing at the inked roses and foliage that scrolled just beneath the sleeve of his T-shirt. 'And got rid of that unhygienic bloody thing in your nose.' Gesticulating with her chin towards his piercing.

'Thanks,' Tom said. 'You are fit. But you'd be fitter still, if you didn't blurt out the fucked-up contents of your head.'

George filled the bucket with soapy hot water. 'You have no idea what's going on in my head.' She eyed his crotch and grinned.

'Are you flirting with me?' he asked.

Feeling like she'd overstepped an invisible line, George looked down at the bucket. Thought about Van den Bergen, spending long days trying to chase down bad guys in some seventh level of hell that only policemen, prison workers, criminologists and forensic pathologists occupied; spending long nights next to her in the bed that they shared, trying to scorch away the stench of death and corruption in the fires of their passion … when they weren't at each other's throats. Which she perversely relished. 'No. I'm not flirting. Sorry,' she said. Looked back up and tried her damnedest to wear an expression that was encouraging and friendly only. 'But I do want to hear more about this Czech dude. He sounds nuts. What do you know about him?'

Tom shrugged. 'Like I told you. He's Nikolay. He's a Czech drug lord. He's a nutter who keeps Europe's clubland stocked with cheap meth. That's it.'

CHAPTER 14

Amsterdam, police headquarters, 15 May

As Marie trawled through the drug-user forums, searching for mention of a Czech drug lord called Nikolay, George's head started to throb. She read over her shoulder, wrinkling her nose only slightly at the smell of hair that had clearly not been washed for at least a week.

> I had outa this world hard-core porn sex with my GF on this stuff. She let me do things to her she never let me before. It was the best high ever. You gotta dissolve the meth with water and shove it up your ass for a really great high. Better than smoking.

'I can't take any more of this,' Marie said, minimising the screen.

George sat back in the chair. 'Neither can I,' she said. Yawned and stretched her arms, feeling the fatigue from night after night, working until the small hours, followed by day after day of dragging herself into the Dutch police HQ for debriefing, leaching the wellbeing and strength from her muscles. She sniffed her denim jacket and grimaced. 'I'm sick of the smell of stale beer on everything. It gets everywhere. I've had it. Van den Bergen can bugger off if he thinks I'm doing another night.'

Tearing the wrapper off a bar of Verkade milk and hazelnut

chocolate, Marie snapped off a row, offering it to George. 'Poor Elvis has got it worse. No wonder he's called in sick. I wouldn't have lasted two minutes, having to cavort and make nice with a bunch of …' She gave the impression of choosing a derogatory term from some sort of bigot's lexicon that the religious memorised from childhood. '… sodomites.' There it was.

'Seriously, Marie? That's very Dark Ages of you,' George said. 'And probably a sackable offence. Don't let Van den Bergen hear you say ignorant crap like that. And I don't want to hear it, either.'

Marie made a harrumphing noise. 'Do you want some chocolate or not?'

George eyed Marie's dirty fingernails. Shook her head emphatically.

Tutting, Marie rammed the chocolate into her own mouth. 'Suit yourself,' she said, chewing noisily.

'Any news on Floris Engels' apartment? The mystery lodger.'

'Funny you should say that.' Bringing up Facebook and logging into an account that had the anonymous blue and white silhouette of a generic man's head, Marie clicked through to the 'about' page for Floris Engels' account. 'His privacy settings were on max and he'd left no legacy information, in the event of death. That's why it's been such a pain in the backside. You ever tried to contact Facebook's admins?'

George shook her head.

'It's a nightmare,' Marie continued. 'We finally got permission to access his profile at the end of play, yesterday. And look!' She pointed to the section that revealed Floris Engels was, 'in a relationship with Robert Menck'. With one click, Menck's name led to a photo of a dark-haired man with jutting teeth that emerged from a generous smile. Smartly dressed in bright colours, he stood in his profile photo with his arm draped around a man – judging by the height of the shoulder – whose head was just out of shot. 'Van den Bergen's gone with Elvis to Menck's place of work. He lectures in architecture at Amsterdam University of the Arts.'

Eager to see what lay beyond the basic information page, George's mouse finger twitched. But she eyed Marie's sticky-looking mouse and thought better of it. 'Have you checked to see if any of the other floaters are linked to Engels?'

'Not yet,' Marie said. 'Van den Bergen asked me to prioritise our friend, Nikolay. There's only one of me, you know.' Her tone was suddenly edged with frost; her body language prickly as her shoulders narrowed and her back straightened. With a jab at the mouse, she brought up a list of the teacher's friends. 'He'd adjusted his settings so that people couldn't even view his friends list. If he was that private a person, it makes you wonder why he was on social media at all.'

'Was he on Grindr?' George asked.

'Yes. The app was on his phone. He was a frequent user.' Marie unlocked her desk drawer and pulled a package out. A slim Android phone inside an evidence bag. She set it gingerly onto the desktop. 'Some of the photos in his gallery are disgusting.' She lowered her voice. Glanced towards the door, as though the thought police lurked there, waiting to arrest not-quite-lapsed Catholics for lewd conversation. 'He had penises.'

'He had penises? How many? He must have been popular with his Grindr conquests.'

George grinned. Marie did not.

'Put Ed Bakker's name into the friends search,' George said.

Marie obliged. Sure enough, Bakker's photo emerged like a bobbing crouton from the social soup of Engels' 783 friends.

Emitting a low whistle, George tried to match the smiling face of a healthy young man with the decomposed corpse that had been pulled from the water. 'He looks in better shape on there than he does on his postmortem photos, poor bastard.'

'And he knew Engels.' Marie raised an eyebrow. Typed in the names of the other victims. 'No link to Engels,' she pronounced.

'Try Bakker's profile,' George said. 'His profile is completely public.'

When the photos of both the remaining floaters popped up in Bakker's friends list, George clapped her hands like a seal. Beaming at Marie. She reached out to pat her on the back, withdrawing only at the last minute when she remembered how much Marie's hair smelled. 'One degree of separation!' she said. 'There's a link.'

'Is there?' Marie asked. 'It's a small city.'

'Where did Engels work before Bouwdewijn de Groot Lyceum?'

Marie clicked open a spreadsheet containing row after row of information about the enigmatic maths teacher. 'Couperus International Lyceum in Utrecht,' she said. 'Another posh private school.'

As her synapses flared with inspiration, George considered the similar ages of the victims. 'I've got a theory,' she said. 'I think Engels taught all of these kids. I bet if you check the yearbook for the Couperus place, you'll find they all went there and studied under him.'

Shaking her head, Marie treated George to a disparaging smile. 'Oh, I think that's a stretch,' she said.

George took out her phone. Googled the number for the Utrecht school. Dialled, arranging Marie's elastic bands and paperclip tangle into two perfectly neat piles. An automated service picked up on the tenth ring, asking George to select from five different options. Grinding her teeth, George persisted until a woman answered. She sounded flustered, bordering on arrogant, speaking in an accent that would have been too posh even for Dutch royalty.

'My name is George McKenzie. I'm calling from the HQ of the Dutch police in Amsterdam. I need a list of your alumni from the past five years.' George's head throbbed in time with her overwrought heart. Anticipating a breakthrough. Feeling certain her hunch was correct.

'Oh, we don't give out information like that over the phone, miss,' the flustered woman said. Haughty indignation evident in her clipped consonants and impatient air. 'You'll have to request it from the head teacher.'

George ended the call. 'Shit!' Feeling choked by disappointment that this case was going nowhere fast. That her efforts in seeking her parents led her down a cul-de-sac of frustration and unanswered questions on a daily basis. 'Shit, shit, shit.' She flung her phone into her bag.

'What's eating you?' Marie asked, making a second attempt at offering her some chocolate.

This time, George accepted. Grimacing, as she used the sleeves of her hoody over her fingers to handle the packet and snap off her own row. Ignoring the fact that Marie had just mouthed 'arsehole' noiselessly at her. 'What do you think?'

'Still no news?' Marie reached out for the photo of the baby on her desk. Ran her index finger affectionately over the frame.

George shook her head. 'Nothing. Not a word about my mother. Not a trace of my father. All I have to go on is the emails. And you're sure you can't trace where they came from?'

'No. I've tried matching the email address to a bona fide account with ownership details attached to it. But BritishEngineering.com is not a genuine address. It's not a real company. It's like some weird kind of spambot or phishing thing. I just can't trace who sent it. I know it's being pinged from some server in America, but that's as far as I've got. Sorry. I've tried.'

Retrieving her phone from her bag, George reread the text of the last missive that she had received on the train to King's Cross, allegedly sent from her father.

```
You always did have my eyes, Ella. I'll
be watching you wherever you go.
   Michael (Dad) xxx
```

'I hate that whoever's sent it knows enough about my past life to call me "Ella". Gives me the creeps,' she said in English, shuddering as she filed the email away once more in a folder marked 'Eyeball', containing the original lunch invitation and an e-trail of George's investigative efforts, so far. 'Are you sure there's no trace of him online?'

Marie shook her head.

'Try Europol and Interpol again.'

'It's a waste of time. There's nothing there. I've spent hours on them over the last few days, hunting for red notices about Nikolay, our mysterious meth baron scuzzball. There's plenty of drugs forums chat about unregulated meth labs all over the Czech Republic, but there's not a shred of hard evidence online that our Nikolay exists. Certainly not on Interpol or Europol.'

'Please.'

'For heaven's sake, George! Give it up!'

Slamming her fist down onto the desk so that Marie's keyboard rattled, George shouted, 'No! Not while there's breath in my body. You of all people, Marie …' Her finger shook as she pointed, channelling the accusatory intent. 'You know what it's like to lose your family.' A meaningful glance cast in the direction of the framed photo of the baby who would never grow any older than he had been in that heart-breaking memento, taken weeks before his death.

Sighing, looking contrite, Marie turned away from George. The stiffness in her demeanour had gone now. She brought up the homepages of the Europol and Interpol websites. 'I'll see if a there's a yellow notice been issued. But it would be an unlikely feat of serendipity and that's putting it mildly.'

She plugged George's father's name into the search engines. Michael Carlos Izquierdo Moreno.

'What a mouthful.'

'Do you mind? That's my father you're talking about. It's not a mouthful if you're Spanish.'

Scrolling through links to old missing persons' notifications, Marie shook her head. 'Nothing. Sorry.'

'How far back did you search?' George asked, scrutinising the results that appeared on screen.

'Early 2015,' Marie said, scrolling, scrolling. Shrugging.

'Go further back,' George said.

Marie glanced over her shoulder. Scowling. 'There's page after page of results!'

'Please.'

Twenty fourteen yielded nothing. When Marie brought up 2013, George did not try to stifle her excited yelp.

CHAPTER 15

Mexico, Chiapas mountains, then, the border with Guatemala, 29 May

Riding the hairpin road high into the mountains made him feel a little queasy. The air was thinner at this altitude, but the heat was still unrelenting, beating down on the four-wheel-drive as though it were determined to get inside and scorch the life out of him. Bouncing up from the unyielding ground, it rose in shimmering waves.

'Is the air-con on?' he asked the driver.

'Yes, *jefe*. It's on max.' The driver looked at him through the rear-view mirror. His fear was apparent. Good.

'Get it checked when we get back in town. It's like a fucking oven in here.'

'Yes, *jefe*. Sorry.'

Stretching to the horizon, the mountainous landscape seemed to move – a stormy, undulating sea of green. He swallowed his nausea, not wanting Miguel to see any signs of weakness. It was this damned heat. And the altitude and incessant headache-inducing sunshine, where he was used to flat, grey, drab. Maybe he should eat.

As they grew closer to the Guatemalan border checkpoint, buildings started to appear by the roadside. Half-finished concrete boxes with no windows and rusting iron spires, rising from the roof. Corrugated iron shacks with Perspex roofs. Men who sat on the porch, idling the afternoon away while their wives tried to sell handicrafts to tourists from the cracked kerb. He spied a snack-shack.

'Pull over and get me an *empanada* or a *tostada* or something,' he said.

'We're supposed to meet the shipment in ten minutes, *jefe*,' Miguel said, checking the Rolex wrapped around his thick arm.

He let the silence settle in for ten, twenty, thirty seconds. Miguel snapped his fingers. 'Pull over. *El cocodrilo* needs something to eat.'

The driver pressed a number on his mobile phone, mounted on the dash. Speed dial for the driver behind him in their little convoy. A woman's voice answered in the abrupt Salvadoran Spanish of the *transportistas*. Orders barked back at her by the driver. In unison, the four-wheel-drive and ex-military truckful behind them pulled over, kicking up clouds of yellow-brown dust in their wake.

In the wing mirror, he watched a young woman emerge from the truck, her rifle slung across her front; dressed in black fatigues, sunglasses and a tight T like the others. Recognised her as the only *transportista* who hadn't beheaded one of the runaway whores. The spare. Her tattooed face seemed familiar but he couldn't place her. She strutted over to the snack bar and ordered from the proprietor – an old man with a face like a walnut. Pointed to the four-wheel-drive and then to the food. The old man stared nervously at the blacked-out windows of the Mercedes. Immediately busied himself by slapping a tortilla on his griddle. Topping it, while shooting the rear of the car with petrified glances.

The woman strode over to the car, snack in hand. The glare of the midday sun gleamed in the lenses of her sunglasses. She stood expectantly by his door. Unsmiling and looking down the road, holding the snack out. At a push of a button, the window slid down into the doorframe.

'Here,' she said.

He eyed her ample bosom, her small waist and the roundness of her hips. 'What's your name?' he asked.

'Jacinta.' Still looking into the distance.

'Named after a flower,' he said, taking the snack. 'Suits you. You're far too hot to be an ugly old *transportista*. And young. Where are you from, *chica*?' He smiled at her breasts, feeling desire stir beneath the sweaty crumpled linen of his trousers. Maybe he could get Miguel and the driver to wait while this girl blew him off in the back of the car. She had pillowy lips that were full of erotic promise, though she wore no cosmetic adornment beyond the ugly tattoos. He was the boss, after all. *El jefe*.

'Enjoy your snack.' Her face remained stern and unsmiling; her attention fixed on the empty road ahead, though it was difficult to tell with those shades.

'How about you come into the air-conditioned cool and enjoy my snack?' He grabbed his crotch. 'I'm *el cocodrilo*. But I promise not to bite.' Grinning at her, he realised his nausea had suddenly abated. He handed the *tostada* to Miguel, preparing for the girl to jump enthusiastically into the car.

Instead, she simply glanced towards his crotch, snorted disparagingly and walked back to the truck.

'Ha! Lesbian bitches, those *transportistas*,' he said to Miguel, snatching the *tostada* to his mouth, in a bid to camouflage the heat that had erupted in his cheeks.

'You want me to put a bullet in the dyke, *jefe*?' Miguel asked, smiling noncommittally, as though he was unsure as to whether he was in on a joke or had just witnessed the public ridicule of the man at the top of the slag heap and Mexico's most wanted list.

He shook his head. 'No. Leave it. Have you seen their leader, Maritza with her fat ass and that scar and the crazy tattoos on her forehead? She's the widow of one of the heads of the maras. He was iced two years ago by some rival the same day he got out of jail. She tracked down his killer and cut off his balls with a machete. Stuffed them down his throat. Those gun-smuggling whores are *loco en el coco*, but they do a damned good job for me and the boys over the border.' He slammed his palm onto the driver's seat, making him jump. 'Take us to the meet!'

Irritated and intrigued by the girl in equal measure, as the car bounced on towards the checkpoint, he barely tasted his *tostada*. There was something about the set of her jaw and the outline of her lips. A vague memory nagged at the back of his mind. He pushed it away. She was just some Salvadoran slut, after all – an offcut of the maras, no doubt, from a San Salvador slum or some shithole of a village where the police didn't dare go.

Several hundred metres from the border, he could see the green sign that declared in white letters:

Bienvenidos a la Republica de Guatemala

In smaller letters beneath, '*pais de la eternal primavera*' told him it was the country of eternal spring. He chuckled at the thought. The only thing that sprang out of Guatemala was his cargo in the back of an unmarked refrigeration truck, supposedly bound for the supermarkets of Mexico City.

Portakabins stood in rows either side of the checkpoint, where the morons working border patrol sat and played cards. Occasionally, they filled out forms or hassled locals who were crossing the border to look for work or to sell their produce at a neighbouring market. But this was a sleepy, porous entry point into Mexico.

'Have the necessary palms been greased?' he asked Miguel.

Nodding vociferously, Miguel peered through a pair of binoculars at the crossing. '*Si, jefe*. There shouldn't be any problems getting through for our men.'

'Good. Let's hope they're on time. I have a flight to catch.'

In small clusters of three and four, he watched the locals coming and going on foot across the border. Children among them. Poorly dressed in cheap jeans and brightly coloured T-shirts, shuffling along the road towards the brightly coloured Mexican roadside stalls. Though the mountains rose majestically behind them like the gateway to paradise, he knew some would almost certainly be fleeing their home on the long and dangerous journey to the US. Weren't they all? Except this lot were too stupid to find the easier route by raft across the Suchiate River. He had seen them there, carrying their worldly possessions on their heads as they waded through the water, fleeing whatever nightmare lay in their past for a future that they hoped would be better but which, he knew, would be far, far worse. Fools didn't deserve anything more.

'The trucks are coming, *jefe*!' Miguel pointed to two heavy goods vehicles that edged towards them and the checkpoint in stop/start traffic that was speed-delimited only by two armed men and two red cones.

'Have them pull into the rendezvous point straight away. Make sure Maritza's girls are ready.'

Without hindrance, the anonymous-looking juggernauts were waved through by the police. Following them for just over a mile, they turned in convoy onto a dirt track that led to a dead end in amongst the forest, the trucks parking side by side. He wiped his hands and sweaty brow on a handkerchief and stepped out of the four-wheel-drive. Already, the *transportistas* had surrounded the two trucks, weapons raised in readiness for whatever might emerge from the giant containers.

'Open them,' he told Miguel.

Miguel stepped forwards and spoke to the drivers, who tugged deferentially on their baseball caps and unlocked the doors to the cargo.

As he advanced towards the first, he scrutinised the girl in the sunglasses. Jacinta. Flint-faced Jacinta who had all the delicate subtlety of a spiny desert cactus. But what tits and what a perfect round ass. She could wait.

'Get the women out. I want to inspect them,' he told Miguel. '*Si, jefe.*'

Accompanied by a *transportista*, he retreated to the back of the first truck where the 'refrigerated' compartment was situated. Heavy duty locks were unfastened and the thick, bullet-proof door swung open slowly. From the murk emerged twenty Caucasian women. Dishevelled, wearing soiled casual clothes with lank hair and the pallor of those who had not seen daylight in a long while, they staggered into the sunshine. Barefoot. Holding their hands over their eyes, as though the bright light was more than they could withstand.

'Show me the roster,' he ordered the truck driver. 'Get the other one open.'

Looking at a list of names on the clipboard, he glanced up at the women. 'Anastasia?'

One woman with dyed black hair and fair roots nodded.

'*Da,*' she said.

'Elena?'

A blonde stepped forward. Timid in her movements, she clutched a baby pink cardigan around her shoulders. Her complexion was grey. Blue veins were visible in her jawline. He grabbed her bird-like face in his hand. Examined her bone structure.

'You have good cheekbones,' he said in Russian. Evaluated her figure. Long legs. Big tits, though they were clearly implants. Narrow in the shoulders. Typical Eastern European beauty. They all were.

A glimmer of a smile warmed the blonde girl's face. 'Thank you,' she said. 'Have we arrived in the USA?'

He shook his head. Kissed her hand gently. Stroked her breast and ignored the horrified look on her face. She tried to pull away. He clutched at her waist and pulled her to him, enjoying the feel of her jutting hipbones against his crotch. 'No, darling,' he said. Pushing her away abruptly so that she staggered back into the dust and scrub. 'You're going to do a little work for me first, to pay off some of your transportation debts.'

Anastasia, the girl with the cheap dye-job, advanced towards him. 'We were told in the Dominican Republic that we would go straight to the US to dance in your clubs. We've paid what you asked already. I take it that you are Nikolay, aren't you?' She pointed at him with a thin finger. 'You look like him. You talk Russian. So you must be him.'

'I go by many names, sugar,' he said, smiling and grabbing her roughly by the wrist until she yelped and backed away. 'Here in Mexico, you can call me *el cocodrilo*.'

'I don't want to work in Mexico! We've all paid to go to the US!' Her lips were trembling but there was a flicker of aggression in her eyes.

He turned to Maritza and snapped his fingers. The *transportista* loaded a cartridge into her rifle and pointed it at the Russian woman's head. The other gun smugglers followed suit. All weapons raised and ready to plug the dissenting women with a shower of ammo. 'Take them to Club Paraiso in Palenque,' he told the truck drivers.

As the Russian women were herded back into their refrigerated prisons, he climbed aboard the containers and inspected the huge steel barrels that were stacked behind innocuous walls built from boxes of tortilla chips. Hazard symbols were painted onto the barrels. Skulls and crossbones, leering at him like the calling cards of chemical pirates.

'Get the precursor chemicals on the plane to Yucatan,' he told Miguel. 'I'll follow them there in the morning. Make sure the *transportistas* come too. I've got another job for them. I want to inspect what's going on in the jungle before I fly to Europe.'

'Yes, *jefe*.' Miguel bowed low.

'Oh, and get me a couple of women for tonight. Get me one

with really big tits and one with a nice round ass. I need to party.'

'Do you want one of the new Russians, boss?'

He shook his head. 'No. They look like shit. They need a makeover when they get to the club. But I tell you what. Get the black-haired one with the big mouth. Anastasia.'

'Yes, *jefe*. You want to fuck her?'

'No. Feed her to the crocodiles and make the others watch.'

CHAPTER 16

Amsterdam, Academy of Architecture, Waterlooplein, then, police headquarters, 18 May

The Academy of Architecture was a grand old building with a double-fronted neo-classical façade. Cast away on its own little island of nostalgic beauty, it was surrounded by Waterlooplein's ugly, utilitarian sea of dual carriageways, cycle lanes and tram tracks.

With a heavy heart and a pocket of trapped wind that dug uncomfortably beneath his ribs, Van den Bergen spied their destination from across the road. Left his car parked outside the National Opera and Ballet building. Put up his golfing umbrella against the torrential rain that had begun to fall. It cascaded in rivulets from the canopy onto his shoes.

'Come on,' he said to Elvis, who broke into a half-jog to keep up with his long strides. 'I don't doubt for a minute that we're wasting our damned time. Getting a lead that isn't a dead end would be too much like good fortune, and that happens to other people. I hate everything about this case.'

'*You* hate it?!' Elvis said, buttoning his leather jacket uselessly against the downpour. 'I haven't been to bed before 3 a.m. in the past fortnight. The only good thing to come out of this is that I now know I can get laid every night of the week, if big hairy guys suddenly become my thing.'

Van den Bergen glanced down at his sidekick. Contemplated bollocking him for insubordination. Realised that acting under-cover as a decoy for a possible serial killer of gay men was definitely taking one for the team. 'George tells me you look very fetching in your tight T-shirt. I see you've ditched the quiff and sideburns. Maybe I'll stop calling you Elvis.'

Elvis blushed. 'Really?'

'No.'

'Look, at least we'll get a phone number for this dick or some sort of contact details.'

They marched up to the ecclesiastical splendour of Sant Egidio church, with the shabby stalls that squatted in its shadow, selling tat to students and tourists. Crossed over. Van den Bergen took the stone steps that led to the Academy's portico two at a time, over-taking the students who ambled to and from lectures. He wondered briefly if George was enjoying being among people her own age behind the bars in those nightclubs. Imagined her absconding with some handsome young waster with a tattoo and a nose-ring.

'He won't be here,' he said to Elvis, holding the door open for two young girls with stupid-coloured hair peeking beneath the hoods of their anoraks. 'This is a wild-goose chase.'

'Try to be optimistic, boss.'

'This isn't a job for brainless optimists, Elvis.'

They approached the reception desk. A stout woman with short hair greeted them.

Van den Bergen flashed her his ID. 'I'm looking for Robert Menck in connection with a murder investigation,' he said. 'I understand he works here.'

The woman opened her mouth to speak, but behind him a clatter made Van den Bergen turn around. There by the entrance stood a group of bespectacled, earnest-looking middle-aged men. In the centre of the group stood an ashen-faced dark-haired man with jutting teeth. At his feet lay scattered a layer of papers and several lever arch files. Robert Menck pushed aside his companions and shot through the front door of the Academy of Architecture like a man trying to escape his guilty conscience.

'Stop! Police!' Van den Bergen shouted, haring after him.

Almost losing his footing on the rain-slippery stairs, he hastened onto Waterlooplein. Searching desperately for his quarry. Had he already absconded around the corner into Jonas Daniël Meijerplein? Was he across the road, perhaps boarding a tram? His heart pounded inside his chest, pumping adrenalin deliciously through his body, making him feel ten years younger and stronger.

But then, as Van den Bergen stood panting in the torrential rain, he spotted Menck – running like a man who had the hounds at his feet along the middle of the road. Menck turned. Locked eyes with the Chief Inspector. Darted in front of a Volvo four-wheel-drive that was speeding recklessly through the downpour. Momentarily out of sight.

'Oh no you don't, you slippery son of a bitch!' Van den Bergen said.

Hastening after the architect, sprinting parallel to him on the opposite side of the road, he felt the thrill of gaining on his target. Knew that if he could only get across, he could intercept the bastard. At that moment, despite the fat drops of rain that bit into his skin and blinded him, he felt no pain; no anxiety; nothing but the thrill of the chase. This was police work.

But Robert Menck seemed to realise his five foot ten put him at a disadvantage next to a policeman who topped six foot five. He turned into the little marketplace by the church. Vanished.

'Bastard!' Van den Bergen shouted.

The sensible forty-eight-year-old knew he should slow down. Cross the road carefully. Or just radio for backup. But the reckless young man that still dwelled inside Van den Bergen propelled him on. He could catch this chubby arsehole. He was fit. He was determined. Sadly, his vision had not been quite as fit or determined as the rest of him for quite some time. He barely registered the oncoming tram.

'Boss!' Elvis' voice rang out just behind him.

'How did Engels know these kids?' Van den Bergen asked.

On the table in the interview room, he had laid out the harrowing photos of the young people who had been found floating in the canals before Floris Engels. Watching Menck squirm, as he absorbed the dreadful sight of those who had been submerged for too long.

'Put them away, for God's sake,' he said, holding a manicured hand over his red-rimmed eyes. 'Isn't it bad enough I've lost my partner? Why do you have to subject me to this … fucking torture?' His voice cracked. The tears rolled onto his cheeks and down the lips that were pulled tight over those jutting teeth. Robert Menck was a broken man.

'Why should I spare you the truth?' Van den Bergen asked, rubbing the lumpy scar beneath his shirt and remembering how everything had ached as he had chased this arsehole for half a mile across one of the busiest interchanges in the city, over lanes of traffic, kamikaze cyclists and unstoppable trams. 'You ran,' Van den Bergen said. 'I nearly fell under a tram because of you, you dick. You killed Floris Engels, didn't you? You killed him, and then you ran.'

'No! No! How could you say such a thing?' Menck shook his head violently and looked up at the bright lights with desperation etched into his face.

'But you admitted it was you at the flat, when me and my detective were having a look round. We were trying to work out what sort of a man your partner was, because with both parents dead and no siblings, not even Engels' own family could tell us anything of any substance about him. But you knew. And you were there. And you deliberately removed any post or documentation in the flat that would link Engels to you.'

'I was scared!'

Van den Bergen leaned forwards and scrutinised him through the smudged lenses of his glasses. Treating this calculating, selfish prick to a stern, judgemental scowl that he knew put the fear of God into most interviewees. 'You'd have packed up your clothes and shipped those out too, if you'd had the time, wouldn't you?'

'You've got it all wrong!' Menck yelled. He turned to Elvis, sitting next to Van den Bergen. Pleading in his eyes. 'Tell him! He's got the wrong end of the stick!'

'I'm sorry, Dr Menck,' Elvis said, pressing his lips together in a sympathetic smile. 'Until you explain why you ran, I'm afraid we can't do anything but assume you're involved in your late partner's death. You can see how it looks to us, can't you? Floris drowns after taking a bad batch of crystal meth. He'd had rough sex just prior to death, according to the postmortem. These other victims have died in similar circumstances and they're linked on social media. All of them.'

'Was he having affairs with them?' Van den Bergen asked. 'Did you spike the lot of them wittingly and push them into the canals as some sort of jilted lover's revenge?'

'You're insane!' Menck shouted, standing abruptly, like a tormented man trying to escape an incessant itch.

'Sit down, for Christ's sake!' Van den Bergen rose from his seat, towering above Menck. Thumped the table for good measure, knowing that the venerable Maarten Minks was watching this textbook display of good cop, bad cop through the one-way mirror. Better put on a good show. He had not yet had cause to threaten Van den Bergen with early retirement, minus pension, as had been Kamphuis' and Hasselblad's favourite trick, but didn't everyone who rose higher than Chief Inspector level always resort to that in the end? *Their default setting is bastard*, he mused. Said, 'bastard' aloud by accident.

'There's no need to be verbally abusive!' Menck said, throwing himself back down onto the chair. Sullen, now. He glared at Van den Bergen.

'You misheard me,' Van den Bergen said, glancing at the mirror. Growled almost imperceptibly, mainly annoyed at himself. He had to remember that Maarten Minks wasn't Kamphuis. Here was a Commissioner in thrall to his Chief Inspector. A chance to start over with the shiny new boss who was more like an enthusiastic sniffer dog than the arse-kissing, slippery turds Van den Bergen had grown used to. *Don't screw it up, unless you fancy spending the next fifteen years working in corporate security and having to wear a goddamned tie.* 'Now, tell us what happened the night that Floris Engels died. What's his connection to these dead kids? And why did you run?'

Robert Menck took out a packet of cigarettes. Put a cigarette in his mouth.

'Got a light?' he asked Van den Bergen.

Van den Bergen pulled the cigarette from him and snapped it in two. 'My boss likes the theory that there's a homophobic serial killer on the loose. Speak. Or you're going to jail for the multiple murder of five people.'

Staring wistfully at the broken cigarette on the table, glancing over first at Elvis and then at the recording equipment, Menck sighed. 'Floris is … was my partner.' He stopped talking abruptly. The Adam's apple in his neck pinged up and down like the ball in a bagatelle; the sclera of his eyes suddenly glassy with tears. Dimpling in his chin ushered in a bout of stuttering. 'We were together for five years. I met him through a mutual friend when he moved from Utrecht. He was a teacher and single. I was a lecturer and had just come out of a long-term relationship. We fell in love quickly and I moved into his flat after about a year when my own rental agreement came to an end.'

'So? Tell me about the night he died. The kids. The connection.' Van den Bergen established eye contact with Menck for all of fifteen seconds. Menck dropped his gaze to his cup of cold coffee.

'We had an open relationship,' he said. Looking back up at Elvis, until Elvis blushed. 'Lots of gay guys do. You're together as a couple but fuck other men. It's fine. It's commonplace. It's a blast. Mostly.'

'Was Floris into that?' Elvis asked.

Menck shook his head. 'If I'm honest, not really.' Wiping a tear from the corner of his eye. He smiled but it seemed full of anguish and regret. 'He would have preferred to be monogamous. But I was already a regular sauna and party-goer.'

'Parties?' Van den Bergen asked, thumbing his goatee.

'Sex parties,' he said. Dropping the volume of his voice so that it was almost a whisper. 'Gay saunas. It's pure hedonism. And why not?' Suddenly, he seemed confrontational and proud, sticking his chin out defiantly. 'We didn't have children. We were consenting adults. Who says you have to stay faithful to the same person? At least we weren't running around behind each other's backs like heterosexual couples, having affairs.'

Van den Bergen cleared his throat awkwardly and folded his arms. 'Tell me more about Floris and these dead kids.'

Steepling his fingers together, Menck cocked his head thoughtfully to one side. 'The night Floris died, we'd been to a chem-sex party at some guy's apartment.'

'Address,' Van den Bergen said, poised to note it down in his pad.

'Can't remember. Honestly, I was wasted. That's the trouble. We both were. The guy whose apartment it was ... we'd met him briefly at the club and he just invited us. I guess you take these things on faith. It's part of the turn-on that you never really know what you're going to get. It's exciting.'

'What had you taken?'

'Miaow miaow, G, Viagra. Floris had had crystal meth but I hadn't. I'm not keen on the stuff. It makes me aggressive.'

'Had you been drinking?'

'No. You generally don't drink on those drugs. Alcohol ruins the high. People just drink water to stay hydrated. Anyway, Floris got high. He was being fucked by some guy and seemed to be enjoying himself. I was with someone else in the same room. Next thing I know, Floris said he felt ill and was going out for a walk. That was the last I saw of him. But the guy he was with said he was going to go outside with him and make sure he was OK.'

'Why didn't you go too?' Elvis asked.

'I was busy.' Menck blushed.

'Busy in what way?'

'I was getting blown off.' He clasped his hands together. 'Hindsight's a wonderful thing.'

Frowning, Van den Bergen felt as though he was standing on the edge of a precipice, looking down into a level of hell he simply recognised nothing of. 'All the canal drowning victims showed signs of severe lead poisoning from a bad batch of crystal meth,' he said. 'How do I know you hadn't administered that to your lover? My colleagues discovered that he had taught two of the dead young men before in Utrecht. Had he had affairs with his pupils?'

'No! No way! Do you think that all gay men are paedophiles or abuse their positions of power?!' Hurt and indignation seemed to dry Menck's tears. 'Floris stayed in touch with his students because they admired him and he liked them. They became friends. And occasionally, Floris did a little dealing to supplement his income in the summer holidays.'

Slapping his pencil onto the desk, Van den Bergen scrutinised Menck's face for signs of artifice. 'He sold the dead kids meth from the same batch that killed him?'

Menck shook his head and shrugged. 'Maybe. I guess so. But he'd taken so much from different places. Meth in the club. G and mephedrone at the party.'

'So, could he have got it from this guy he was screwing? The one who took him outside for some air. Come on. There's something you're not telling me, Menck. Why did you run?'

Silence hung in the air like a brooding storm.

'Speak, for Christ's sake!' Van den Bergen yelled, slamming his hand down onto the table top so that the photographs skittered to the edges.

Menck blanched, vomiting the explanation in panicked, rapid-fire babble. 'The guy Floris had fucked came back up to the apartment in a state. He was crying and shouting. Said Floris was dead. That Floris had been stoned beyond reason and throwing up outside. There had been a struggle. Apparently, Floris kept trying to walk to the water's edge and the guy grabbed him and tried to drag him to safety. But he reckoned Floris was determined. He'd just stumbled into the canal and sank without trace. A couple of us ran outside and jumped in to try to find him. I dived down as deep as I could where this guy said he'd gone in but we couldn't for the life of us find him. And then, I guess I got cold feet because there were drugs involved and a chem-sex party and … Jesus. Can you see how bad it would be for a lecturer at the university? Can you imagine the headlines in the *Volkskrant*, if the police had come to the scene and got evidence of what we'd been doing?'

'Homosexuality isn't outlawed in Amsterdam,' Van den Bergen said. 'That's a piss-poor excuse and I don't buy it.'

'It's true!' Menck said. 'Shit sticks, even in a liberal city like ours. I lost my lover. I lost my nerve. I wasn't about to lose my career and reputation too. I'm sorry.'

'Save your apologies, you morally bankrupt piece of shit,' Van den Bergen said, leaning forwards until Menck shrank visibly in his seat. 'You've obstructed a police investigation by not coming forward and until I interview the men who were at this sex party, I still don't believe a word out of your disingenuous mouth. But tell me, who did Floris buy his meth from?'

Amid wracking sobs, Menck said something. Inaudible. Indecipherable.

'Stop simpering and speak clearly, damn it!' Van den Bergen bellowed. 'Who was Engels' dealer?'

Menck blinked tears from his red, puffy eyes. 'Nikolay.'

Van den Bergen nudged Elvis. 'Nikolay who?'

'Some Czech guy. I think his second name is Bebchuck. Yes, Nikolay Bebchuck.'

CHAPTER 17

35,000ft above Germany, 20 May

As they flew above the clouds, lulled into a wordless torpor by the thrum of the jet engines and subliminal hiss of the air-con, George thought about her father and the notification on Interpol.

'Missing,' she said, swallowing down raw, indigestible emotions. Guilt? Loss? Fear, definitely. She struggled to compartmentalise her feelings for her father in the way that she didn't with Letitia. Letitia was easy. She was a bitch. 'For years, I felt nothing for Letitia. Now, I suppose I feel a daughterly duty towards her, but sod-all else,' she told Van den Bergen, laying her head on his jumper-clad upper arm, then thinking better of it when his shoulder jutted into her ear. 'But my dad? Jesus.'

At her side, Van den Bergen was staring out of the widow at the rising sun. He turned to her. Sympathy and melancholy in those large grey eyes. He took her hand into his and kissed it, being careful to rub any excess saliva from her skin – the way she preferred. 'I'm sorry,' he said. 'Your dad was working in a really dangerous part of the world. Honduras has the highest murder rate … of anywhere. It makes Amsterdam seem like an idyllic village.'

Snatching her hand away, George glared at her lover. Suddenly irritated by his slipshod empathy and foot-in-mouth well-meaning. 'Thanks a fucking bundle. You could at least reassure me and offer me hope. For Christ's sake! My mother's buggered off to who knows where and though I've ostensibly been receiving emails from him, now I find my long-lost dad has, in fact, vanished too. In the murder capital of the world! You can be such an insensitive bastard sometimes, you know.'

'Keep your voice down!' he said, glancing nervously over the tops of the seats at the other passengers. 'It's a long way to bloody Prague. This lot don't need to hear—'

'It's all right for you,' she said, folding her arms. Lowering her voice only slightly. 'You know exactly where your nearest and dearest are.'

Van den Bergen nodded. Returned to staring out the window. 'I see,' he said. 'And when you disappear off on some ill-conceived adventure that almost gets you killed, that's all right, is it? Because I know where you are, so I couldn't possibly understand what it is to worry.'

'Twat,' George said, rummaging in her bag at her feet for the cheese sandwich she'd hastily thrown together from stale ingredients in Van den Bergen's fridge before leaving for the airport.

'Can I have some?' he asked, his attention refocused on the side of her face.

'Buy yourself some peanuts, old man. This is my sarnie. Not yours.' Taking an aggressive bite from her disappointing breakfast, she contemplated the information that Marie had finally managed to unearth. Chewing defiantly to make sure Van den Bergen knew she was annoyed.

'So, apparently my dad went out there as a contractor for a British engineering company in 2011. Aeronautical engineering, working on building a prototype for some passenger jet or other that's better equipped for landing on short runways, surrounded by mountains, like the airport in Tegucigalpa. I don't know. Some shit like that, anyway.'

Though she stared at the seat back of the passenger in front, she felt Van den Bergen watching her. Tutted and reached into her bag to bring out a second packet of sandwiches. 'Go on, then.'

He grinned. 'You made these for me?' As he opened the tinfoil, he wore an expression of pure boyish delight on his lean, ageing face.

'It's only a fucking sandwich, Paul. Not a birthday present.'

Winking. '*You* made it,' he said, biting hungrily. Speaking with his mouth full. 'I should frame it, never mind eating it.'

Narrowing her eyes to convey her discontent, she was betrayed by the smile that curled up the corners of her mouth. Nudged him, playfully. 'Anyway, I fired off this email to the place where he'd worked – Earhart Barton plc – and they said he caught a company bus to work every morning from the company's HQ in Centro Contemporáneo in Tegucigalpa to the factory in the countryside.' She tried to imagine the sort of life her father might have been living for years. Did he have a house or an apartment? Had he lived alone or had there been some woman – possibly a second family – waiting for his return at the end of the working day? Letitia had filleted him so cleanly from their lives at such an early juncture that her memory of the warm and loving Spanish man George remembered from being a small child had decayed like an old, old photograph, rendering him nothing more than hairy forearms, swinging her onto his shoulders; the smell of spicy aftershave and tobacco; an almost-faceless ghost of a family life lost.

She wiped the solitary tear that escaped the turmoil inside her head on her sleeve, turning to the aisle, lest Van den Bergen see her pain and heroically, irritatingly try to ease it with empty platitudes.

'How did he go missing, then?' he asked.

'The bus was hijacked by members of a gang, according to the local rag. They only took him. Nobody else. So, I'm guessing they wanted him for a specific skill or his perceived worth in terms of ransom.' She pictured the bus, filled with white-collar workers in their smart, short-sleeved shirts and Sta-Prest slacks, heading for a day's work at some giant, clinical facility in the middle of nowhere. Gun-toting thugs boarding the bus at a stop light. Shots fired. Shouting. Her father staring down the barrel of an Uzi, perhaps, standing with his hands in the air as some muscled brute, wearing the terrifying, dehumanising tattoos of the maras on his face like an inked balaclava, barked instructions at him to get off the bus. No struggling or else. 'Kidnapping specialists for money or services rendered is apparently a thing out there.' She held her breath. Exhaled slowly, trying to dispel the mounting anxiety in her chest. Massaged her temples. 'It's not unusual for police to discover mass graves in the country, where poor snatched bastards have been used up by the cartels, spat out and buried. The missing report was from 2013, Paul. 2013! He's not been seen since.'

Van den Bergen clasped her hand and pulled her head to his chest. She could hear the comforting loping beat of his heart. Her breathing slowed.

'Try not to think about it,' he said. 'When we get back, I'll make contact with their Chief of Police, if I can. I'll ask him to pull the missing persons file and get it translated. I'll say it's part of this tainted meth investigation. If Minks won't cough up, I'll pay for it myself.'

'Aw, you're a good man, Paul van den Bergen,' George said, stroking his goatee. 'But you wouldn't need to translate it. I've got that covered. *Hablo español.* Remember?'

Van den Bergen raised an eyebrow. Treated her to a quizzical grin. 'So that's why you learned Spanish? Because of him? I thought your dad left when you were little.'

'I guess I wanted to keep him alive in my mind,' she said. 'Get in touch with my roots, because they were mine to get in touch with. Letitia couldn't strip his genes out of my body and she never gave enough of a shit to find out what subjects I took at high school or studied on the side. So, yes.' She tapped her forehead. 'I've got Spanish installed up here instead of having photo albums full of happy family snaps.'

'How did a drop-out berk like me end up with you?' Van den Bergen chuckled. 'Any chance you've got Czech lurking in that cavernous brain of yours? Because we need to shelve your dad for now, if you don't mind, and give some thought to the legend of Nikolay Bebchuck and his apparent network of Czech meth labs.'

'I can't believe Minks is forking out for this trip,' George said, as the lights came on overhead, reminding them to fasten their seat belts. The plane jolted over a pocket of turbulence, beginning its descent in earnest. Her ears felt full. She yawned to unblock them, wincing with the pain. 'What a difference compared to that bastard Kamphuis. He still has the hots for a gay serial killer but is happy to back your hunch. Have you got a bit of a bromance going on there?'

Van den Bergen turned to her and smiled. 'Oh, I think it's you he's sweet on, Dr McKenzie!'

CHAPTER 18

Czech Republic, Prague,
Žižkov district, later

'Hurry! We've got to climb the stairs,' Roman Teminova said in perfect English with an accent that was part Czech, part pure unadulterated Tottenham. He ushered Van den Bergen and George towards the entrance of the apartment block, as though he was directing traffic in the wake of a national emergency. Slightly breathless when he spoke, the Czech detective's cheeks were flame-red, clashing with the green chequered shirt he wore beneath an ill-fitting navy suit jacket; his sandy-coloured hair dishevelled, giving him the flustered appearance of a farmer who had found himself a policeman in the city by accident, George mused. There was no doubting his sense of urgency though. 'Now! Come!'

'Hurry? Why the hell do we have to hurry?' Van den Bergen mumbled, peering up at the uppermost room in the pistachio-coloured building – six storeys above his street-level vantage point, where three silver Policie Skodas with their blue and yellow go-faster stripes were parked askew near the kerb. 'Don't you have bloody lifts in Prague?' He patted his slightly distended stomach and grimaced at George. 'I've not even digested breakfast yet.' Shook his head disapprovingly. 'Jesus. I'm getting too old for this bullshit.'

But the younger Teminova had already disappeared inside, flanked by two uniforms in riot gear, carrying guns.

Above them, burly men wearing the bulky black garb of the Policie sprinted up a vertiginous stairwell that rose to the solitary door at the top. An Escher painting come to life. Van den Bergen gripped the banister and sighed. 'I thought we were going to compare notes. Take a look around the drug hotspots in the city. I didn't expect to go on a sodding raid,' he said, belching. 'And he drives like a nutcase. I feel sick.'

'Oh, stop moaning, for God's sake!' George said, prodding him in the back. 'We've not come here to eat schnitzel and drink beer with the stag parties from Croydon.'

Shouting from above made George's pulse quicken. The rhythmic bang of a battering ram against a door drowned out Van den Bergen's complaints. Footfalls, as the police piled into the Žižkov penthouse apartment.

By the time George reached the summit of the staircase, she felt like somebody had punched her in the chest. Made a mental note to smoke less and cycle more. Van den Bergen took her by the hand and pulled her inside.

'Jesus,' she said in English, holding her nose against the sulphurous stink. 'It reeks, man!' The walls of the apartment were scuffed and filthy, covered in some dated floral wallpaper that might have been there since Communism fell. Rubbish was strewn along the skirting boards – discarded beer cans, cigarette butts and food wrappers on the uncarpeted floor.

In the living room, it was worse. A stained sofa, where a young man, whom the police had apprehended, lay face down while a uniform cuffed him. Shouting aggressively in Czech over his shoulder at his captor. Wide-eyed and clearly wired. Euro house music pounded at deafening volume from what appeared to be a high-end stereo system; jaunty pink and blue lights dancing up and down on the graphic equaliser's display. Bass, almost visibly thumping out into the foetid room from the woofers of the oversized floor-standing speakers, making the sticky wooden floor reverberate beneath George's feet and her molars ache in their dental sockets. Empty beer bottles strewn on their sides next to them, rocking gently to and fro thanks to the sound waves that issued forth. Hedonistic mayhem, juxtaposed against neat piles of cash that had been stacked carefully in a money-counter next to the arm of the sofa. 'Somebody's been using this place as party central.'

The stereo was silenced by a giant of a cop who eyed George suspiciously. She felt compelled to give him the finger, but settled instead for sucking her teeth long and low, to convey her displeasure.

'Thank God he's turned that off,' Van den Bergen said, covering his mouth and nose with the sleeve of his raincoat. 'Maybe they wouldn't screw their lives up so badly if they didn't listen to such appalling music.'

From the kitchen, Roman Teminova emerged, wearing a triumphant grin. 'Methamphetamine production,' he said, holding up a large, clear plastic bag bulging with crystals of varying sizes. He waved it towards Van den Bergen, as though showing the Dutch Chief Inspector some excellent souvenir that Prague boasted to rival anything Amsterdam could offer. 'This is only a tiny outfit, but we did a bigger bust in a nearby town yesterday and found a link to this place. Come! See for yourselves.' He handed them both gas masks and indicated that they should put them on. Pulled his own over his head, sounding suddenly tinny and muffled, as though he had been trapped inside a transistor radio. Reminiscent now of a character in a disaster movie. 'Be careful not to touch anything, of course.'

Beckoning them into the kitchen, George trod gingerly over the debris on the floor, wishing she had worn something more robust on her feet than trainers. Wellies weren't enough for this level of filth and contamination, she reflected. *Bet Van den Bergen thinks being in here is going to give him cancer. I'll not hear the end of this until he's demanded an MRI scan of his lungs and a full-throttle, five-star mole check. And for once, I can't blame the old fart.*

First, she tried to make sense of a tangle of flasks, canisters and pipes that, at a glance, looked like some kind of old-fashioned moonshine still. A burnt-out oven that might have only ever cooked up nightmares and food poisoning. The walls were dark brown with the residue of years of chemical abuse clinging to the splashbacks. Chairs, shoved beneath the small blistered kitchen table, whose upholstered backs and seat pads had almost disintegrated entirely, looking as though they had been burned in a fire.

Then, her gaze wandered downwards, past the grimy cupboards.

She gasped. Held her hand to the mouthpiece of her mask. 'Oh, Christ. You're kidding.' In the corner of the small kitchen, two kittens lay stiffly sprawled by a bowl of mould-green detritus that had once been food. Clearly dead, judging by the flies that circulated around them. 'Poor little bastards.' She needed to get out of there. Needed to get back to street level, where she could breathe the fresh air and be calmed by the sight of the stuccoed old apartment blocks in their crisp, ice-cream colours, overlooking the infamous 1960s TV tower that resembled a failed Communist experiment in building a rocket ship from concrete. Those were sights she wanted to gaze upon at 8 a.m. after a sleepless night of worrying about her parents. Touristy shit. Not this hellish scene of filth and cruelty and dead cats.

'We'd had complaints from neighbours,' Teminova said, waving his arm towards the worktop that was barely visible beneath an array of test tubes in blackened holders and boiling flasks containing unsavoury-looking amber-coloured concoctions.

On the floor, with their lids off, stood canisters, barrels and oversized bottles that had been labelled on the outside with foreboding skulls and crossbones. Large serving spoons had been shoved into the chemical contents. Most perplexingly of all, however, was the food processor sitting next to the cooker, filled with some unsightly brown goo. Unbidden and at odds with the scene before her, George was beset by a memory of Aunty Sharon's homely kitchen, with its baking equipment and spotless oven. Remembered the sweet, intoxicating smell of that place, as her aunt whipped up a rum-laced fruitcake to cheer them both on the weekends when she wasn't working a shift at Skin Licks, and Van den Bergen, Tinesha and Patrice seemed so very far away.

'It looks like this lab – if you can call it that – has been up and running for a long while,' Van den Bergen said, standing stiffly beside George, clasping his raincoat closed. 'How come you've only shut it down now?'

Uniforms, now clad in white jumpsuits, entered the claustrophobic scene, taking photographs of the makeshift equipment. Pushing them back into the living room, where Teminova removed his mask and bid that they do likewise. He ruffled his hair. Barked something at a younger-looking colleague, who nodded deferentially, then marched the complaining, cuffed dealer down the hall towards the front door.

'The problem is that we have so many of these meth labs springing up all over the country,' Teminova said, toying with the strap on the gas mask. 'Last year, the Czech police found over four hundred and sixty labs, nationally. Those are just the ones we know about. It's the tip of the iceberg, in all probability. Most are in small towns and the country, where the dealers can operate without fear of discovery. But we do get some in the city too. Žižkov has cleaned up its act over the years. But you can still get mugged after dark, coming back from having an artisan beer in a smart, hip bar. And you can always find a dealer, selling whatever your heart desires.'

'How much does a gram of meth cost?' George asked, wrinkling her nose at the coffee table that was heavily laden with overflowing ashtrays, dirty syringes, meth pipes and other drugs paraphernalia.

'Pervitin – that's what we call it. And it's relatively cheap here. About fifty dollars for a gram. Two euros for a hit. Cheaper than coke and almost acceptable in a city where smoking weed and drinking heavily is nothing out of the ordinary. We just don't have a problem with personal use, as long as people aren't flaunting it under our noses.'

'Is it not a Class A substance over here?' Van den Bergen asked, rubbing his stomach and frowning, as though everything about that place was indigestible. He glanced over to the dirty window. Glimpsing the TV tower in the near distance.

Roman Teminova shook his head. 'It's a drug that has become embedded in our culture,' he said. 'The government used to give methamphetamine to our troops after World War II to keep them alert. During the Communist era, manufacturing the chemicals used in meth was big state business. Hydrochloric acid, lithium, acetone, toluene, used in paint thinners and brake fluid! Pseudoephedrine – that's—'

'Yes, I know what that is,' George said. 'It's cold and flu meds, isn't it?'

'Yes,' Teminova said, smiling benignly, as though he was a teacher and George had said something clever in class. 'Red phosphorous – the stuff you get on match heads. Sodium hydroxide that we use to dissolve road kill.'

'My God!' Van den Bergen said, taking out his blister pack of antacids. Appraising the filthy apartment. Seemingly thinking better of swallowing anything in that foul place and shoving the pack back in his pocket. He ran his hand over his neck. 'No wonder people are getting ill and dying from this shit.'

'Anhydrous ammonia,' the Czech said, pointing to an empty canister on a windowsill behind the soiled sofa. 'Know what that's used for?' He rocked back and forth on the heels of his dated loafers. Raised an eyebrow. His florid cheeks flushed an even deeper shade of red. 'Fertiliser and strong cleaner. All, well, most of this stuff you can get hold of in DIY shops and builders' merchants. It's cheap to make and the profit margins are impressively high. Higher than coke, that's for sure. And you can control the purity and output if you cook it yourself in a dump like this, or the much bigger lab we found in the basement of a farmhouse yesterday. *Now* you can see why it's the drug of choice for our dealers.'

'But why so many labs, here in the Czech Republic in particular?' George asked. 'Not Germany. Not the Netherlands or the UK. Users on the dance and gay scene are going crazy for the stuff there, but the gear is all imported from here. I don't understand. You're talking about mass-produced chemicals under Soviet rule. It's over a decade since Communism fell.'

Teminova held his arm out to move her aside as an officer emerged from the bedroom, carrying several stacking boxes full of crystallised product. There was a gleam in the detective's sharp blue eyes that spelled out precisely how delighted he was that this raid should have taken place with his Dutch counterpart present as a witness. Perhaps he had deliberately waited to conduct the search until that morning, when they had been scheduled to arrive in Prague.

'Like I said,' he continued. 'We've lived with the drug for a long, long time. It used to be prescribed by our doctors for depression, ADHD, alcoholism, obesity … you name it. Meth was a cure-all. The only time it gets bad press is when some little turd blows their kitchen up or poisons the entire family with phosphine gas.'

'Don't you at least have some kind of regulation on the sale of pseudoephedrine?' Van den Bergen asked. 'Most countries do. We can't buy Sudafed in the Netherlands at all anymore. I wish!' He stuck the tip of his little finger inside his nostril and chuckled. 'I haven't been able to unblock my nose since a trip to the States in 1990. If I asked my pharmacist for it, she'd think I was trying to get high. You certainly can't get it in industrial quantities in most of Europe.'

'Poland,' Teminova said, walking to the window and studying the view. 'Dealers can just nip over the border and buy in bulk to their heart's content. They bring it back here and *le voilà*! It's no different from when I spent some time in the Met in the Nineties. The posh kids in Essex would drive to Hackney or Dalston to get what they wanted if they couldn't get it in their village or tinpot town. No such thing as borders or barriers where drugs are concerned.'

George spied the cats being removed from the kitchen in evidence boxes. Perhaps she had drunk too much coffee at breakfast or was simply sleep-deprived; suddenly, she felt that the air was being sucked from her lungs with a strong vacuum. 'I've got to get out of here,' she told Van den Bergen, thrusting the gas mask into the Czech detective's hands. 'And we need to talk about Nikolay Bebchuck. But somewhere nicer. With artisan coffee or some home-brewed hipster shit.'

Cradling her cold Gambrinus beer, George sat on the bench in the Letna Park beer garden, drinking in the sight of an almost sunny downtown Prague, laid out beneath them like a colourful quilted throw – terracotta rooftops, elegant spires and pastel façades of a city that had been carefully moulded and fired in the clarifying heat and passion of the Renaissance; cooled and partially buried by the ideological stodge and concrete of the Soviet era; excavated in the last twenty-five years since the Velvet Revolution by a generation that had dared to reclaim their cultural heritage and vibrant birthplace from Moscow, as an adoptive child might rediscover exotic, bohemian roots, freeing herself from a suffocating and bland guardian. It was the first time George had been to Eastern Europe. Toying with Van den Bergen's enormous foot underneath the picnic table, she was sure she could smell romance in the air.

'What do you think of Prague?' Teminova asked George.

'Your beer's shit and your sausage is too salty,' she said, clinking glasses with the detective. Grinning when he met her declaration with a confused half-smile. 'Nikolay Bebchuck. We didn't fly five hundred miles to chat about the scenery.'

At her side, Van den Bergen took out his notebook. Started to sketch the canopy of trees above them.

The smile slid from Teminova's face. 'When we've closed down meth labs, many of the dealers mention his name during questioning. Bebchuck seems to be behind much of the illegal drugs trade in the Czech Republic – at least the bigger enterprises that are well co-ordinated. You'll hear his name spoken in some of the whorehouses in Prague. Nikolay is quite the man about town when you want to shift women or product out of the country. I think he runs drugs and whores under a franchise model.'

George folded her beermat down the middle into two perfect portions. Ripped them apart with precision. 'Please don't use the word "whores" in front of me, Roman,' she said. 'It makes me a bit … stabby on account of my having a vagina.'

Van den Bergen trod heavily on her foot. Coughed uncomfortably.

'You got a frog in your throat, Chief Inspector?' she asked, turning with studied nonchalance towards her lover. 'You wanna do something about that. Maybe drink your beer.' Turned back to the Czech detective. 'Where was I? Oh, yes. Working girl or just prostitute will do fine.' She treated him to a perfect show of teeth. 'So, Bebchuck supplies chem-drugs throughout Europe? And he's into people trafficking. What do you know about him?'

Teminova said nothing. Toyed with the cuffs on his green tartan shirt. Blushing ferociously. George wondered if his flame-red cheeks might actually erupt.

'Do you even know what he looks like?' Van den Bergen asked.

'No. There's no way of knowing if he's even real. We've never found anyone in our state records who could be him. Nobody seems to know a single thing about him, apart from the dealers and brothel-keepers. And even when threatened with prison sentences, they won't talk. There's an unbreakable code of silence.'

'Europol and Interpol have no real details on the guy,' Van den Bergen said. He turned to George. 'I had Marie check. If he's travelling around the Continent or further afield, he's doing it under a completely different name with legit passport and papers.'

Sipping his beer, Teminova fell silent. George was certain he was avoiding making eye contact with her. Part of her was pleased. Part of her wished she could just make nice with strangers. It would be so much easier.

'You think one of Bebchuck's labs made the meth that's killing your kids?' he said, finally.

From his pocket, Van den Bergen pulled two specimen bags, each containing small white crystals. 'George here got this while she was undercover at an Amsterdam nightclub,' he said, poking at the first baggie with his long index finger. 'My detective, Dirk, got the other in a gay sauna.'

Teminova raised his eyebrow. 'And?'

'I was told Nikolay was the dealer's wholesale supplier,' George said, draining her glass and wondering if it would be considered unprofessional to demand a second. She bit hungrily into the sausage, almost cold now. Spoke with her mouth still partially full. Realised her manners weren't up to scratch and that Aunty Sharon would lay into her for being an uncouth pig. Covered her mouth with her hand, too desperate to get her words out to swallow. 'And Elvis – I mean, Dirk was told the same thing. Nikolay Bebchuck's name is all over town. Now, we can't work out if he's some homophobic lunatic, just out to poison and kill Dutch men who like a bit of hot cock on a Saturday night.' She studied her half-eaten sausage and set it down onto the picnic table, suddenly losing her appetite. 'Or if there's a problem with supply.'

Shaking his head, Teminova said, 'Funnily enough, we've had no reported deaths whatsoever from lead poisoning for at least five years. There haven't even been any other crystal-meth-related incidents apart from the usual petty theft by users, looking for money for their next fix. Not even the odd OD. The nearest we've got to that, like I said, is cooks poisoning themselves with phosphine gas or blowing their kitchens up. And that's not a regular occurrence. These people aren't that stupid.'

Van den Bergen dropped his biro onto the table and groaned. 'Then we've hit another dead end. Can we not arrange for an analysis of your local product and compare it to ours? Maybe this Bebchuck is deliberately shipping low-grade product outside the Czech Republic.'

Teminova took the baggies into his hands, holding them up against the sunlight, where the dull crystals started to shine like melting ice. 'I'll get our best chemists on it straight away.'

They sat on the bed in their hotel room, sipping gin from the minibar, drinking in the view of the historic rooftops and listening to the infernal bong of some irritating church or other not far away. George jumped when Van den Bergen's phone rang.

'Speak,' he said, pulling his T-shirt over his naked crotch, as though the caller could see down the phone.

'Oh. Really? I see. Yes. I'll tell her.'

Ending the call, Van den Bergen turned to George, his dark eyebrows almost arched into question marks above eyes that now sparkled with intrigue.

'Well?' George asked, setting her drink on her belly.

'Our meth does have a faulty composition, containing fatal doses of lead, but it's not from here,' he said. 'It isn't Czech at all!'

'Where the hell is it from, then?'

'Mexico.'

CHAPTER 19

Amsterdam, Keizersgracht, 21 May

Coming out of the club, arm in arm with the tall black guy he had met on the dancefloor, Jeroen Meulenbelt was feeling lucky. He. Could. Not. Wait to tell Bouvien on confectionery and nuts all about it on Monday morning. She would want details, of course. She always did. And in the relative quiet of the stockroom, disturbed only by the odd fork-lift driver, he was only too happy to fill her in and watch her jaw drop in disbelief.

'Really, Jeroen? Wow. You're so cool. That's sooooo awesome. You did what to whom? You took what? It felt like that? That sounds amazing. You know everyone. I wish I was like you.'

Poor Bouvien, with her giant arse and acne and bad pink hair. Such a nice girl otherwise. There was someone out there for everyone, even for her, he was sure. And tonight, he was strolling hand in hand along the Keizersgracht with his someone. He wondered fleetingly how big the guy's cock would be. He had never been fucked by a black dude before. Bouvien would demand to know the details, which would run as follows:

He had danced his ass off until the early hours with his friends, celebrating his twenty-first birthday in style. They had done drugs. A fuck-tonne of drugs, which was always super-fun and blocked out all the anxiety about Mum and Dad-wanker and the prats at work in the supermarket, who took the piss out of him for being camp and sweating too much. All this, after a really gorgeous Indonesian *rijsttafel* at Tempo Doeloe, which was, like, his favourite. About seven squillion different dishes, all delish, with his absolute fave being the beef rendang. He had taken all the photos and loaded them up onto Instagram, making sure he pouted and did that smouldering eye thing at the side of the table. Everybody had loved them and commented on how cool he was looking on his big day, wearing the vintage Alexander McQueen top and trousers that he'd bought with his grandmother's money, especially with his hair like that. He was, like, *totally* killing social media. Then, just at a point where he had thought he'd have to settle for going home and pulling himself off while thinking about Filip on cheese and sliced meats, he had spotted this guy. What was his name again? Wouter or Willem or something beginning with a W. Or was it Viktor? He couldn't be sure.

'What's your name again?' he asked, clasping his new lover's hand tightly.

'Roeland.'

'Oh, yes. Lovely name. You've got such incredible eyes.'

'Thanks,' Roeland said. 'I get them from my dad's side of the family, who were originally from …'

Yeah, whatever. So, then, he had captured the attention of this gorgeous creature who was definitely a nine, when he was only about a seven and a half, even though he went to the gym regularly. What more could he have hoped for? Tonight, he was going to get laid by a stunning black guy called Wouter with a giant cock and super-unusual, almost Oriental eyes from wherever the fuck he had just said. (He hadn't been listening.) Brilliant! And the guy had said he was HIV positive but undetectable and was taking PrEP. He was on Truvada, the HIV preventative drug too. They could do bareback fucking without a care in the world. Even more brilliant! Bouvien would love every last detail, apart from the sex bits.

Except the guy's phone was ringing. He was answering it. Looking all serious, like something was amiss.

'I'm so sorry, Jeroen. I'm going to have to take a rain check. My mother's ill and needs me to stop by.'

There was genuine concern in his handsome face as he glanced down at the phone's screen. Or maybe he'd had some sort of auto-call rigged up to get out of the encounter because he'd had second thoughts about boning a slightly dumpy boy from Amstelveen with a sweat problem. Maybe there was someone hotter on Grindr. Who knew? Jeroen couldn't tell.

As he disappeared into the distance beneath the streetlights, taking the hope of erotic adventure along with him, Jeroen took out his crystal meth and pipe. Sat by the canal in the relatively secluded spot by a moored motorboat and some parked cars. At gone 3 a.m., nobody would notice a young man, smoking a little more than was advisable on the occasion of his twenty-first birthday.

Forcing a grin, he took a selfie and posted it on Instagram and Twitter. Annoyed that his hair wouldn't do the right thing, flopping as it was because of the sweat and humidity from the club. And the light was terrible. Not flattering at all. He scrolled through Grindr, realising he couldn't be bothered to travel the length of the canal to find somebody to fuck. At this hour, they would almost certainly be either totally un-hot or utterly off their faces and only semi-coherent or absolutely more interested in sleep than sex. His erection had waned now, in any case, since the Viagra had worn off. He lit the crystals inside the pipe, inhaling. Feeling mellow. Wishing he was chilling with his friends. Maybe he would go to the sauna. That place was always open for business.

When the grogginess and nausea hit him, he was convinced it would pass with just a little more time in the fresh air. Perhaps he shouldn't have had alcohol with so many drugs. He had been careful not to overdo the Gina. Had the Indonesian *rijsttafel* been dodgy? Tainted chicken, perhaps. Maybe it was an idea to move away from the edge of the canal. Except, he couldn't move. Not even to grab his phone and call his mum to tell her he was feeling odd. He tried to pinpoint what had made him so abruptly unwell.

'This is the best gear you can get,' the dealer had said, as he had palmed the baggie full of crystals onto him. An older man with long grey hair, dressed like a biker, wearing mirror shades indoors. Scabs around his mouth and the worst teeth imaginable. 'You heard of Nikolay? Well, this is his gear. And it's sweet, man. Not your usual cheap Czech crap. This has come all the way from Mexico. This is some pure-as-the-driven-snow Walter White shit.'

As he took his last laboured breath on the canal's edge, Jeroen wondered how he would communicate all of this to Bouvien on Monday in the stockroom.

CHAPTER 20

Mexico, Yucatan jungle, 30 May

'When is he coming?' the man asked, wiping the sweat from his top lip. '*El cocodrilo*. When are you expecting him? Because I need more time. Another couple of days, at least.' Raising the bowl of coffee to his lips, he drank hungrily, carefully. Mustn't spill a drop, even if it was bitter and lukewarm. After yet another night of tormented half-sleep in the foetid shack that he shared with the San Diego chemist, tossing and turning on the hard, thin mattress, as much as his leg shackles would allow, feeling the moths fluttering around his face, he needed all the caffeine he could get inside him.

'You're not in a position to make demands,' the guard said.

Jorge. A short, stocky man, originally from Cozumel. A bastard of the highest order. Jorge liked to jab that rifle of his into his neck, just beneath his ear, giving him tinnitus for a week. He had to keep Jorge sweet. Couldn't face another day in solitary confinement, with blood pouring from his ear and that high-pitched buzzing.

'If he wants me to demonstrate how it works, I'll need longer.' His shirt stuck to his back like a wrinkled and peeling second skin. He wasn't as dark or hardy as these small, stocky descendants of the Maya who had evolved over generations to cope with the stifling heat. Had had to pull down the sleeves of his shirt, to avoid being baked alive by the hot branding irons of sun that seared through the leafy canopy from dawn until sundown. Trapped in the fires of hell, he knew his only hope was to appease the man they called *the crocodile*.

'You've got two hours,' Jorge said. 'Better get back to work.' He swigged from a bottle of *cerveza* that was frosty and pouring with condensation on the outside.

A jab in the ribs from the guard's rifle was all he needed to coerce him into grabbing his tools, starting the treacherous climb down into the vast cenote.

The cave was, at least, cooler than the jungle above. Swinging from the balloon basket, as Jorge lowered him, using the thick fisherman's rope, to the sparkling turquoise water, he reasoned that he had it a damn sight better than those poor bastards who laboured away in the lab, poisoning themselves slowly as they manufactured crystal meth for *el cocodrilo* and his murderous associates in the Coba cartel. The water was pure enough to drink. Not that he was allowed to fill his water bottle from it. That would be too much like indulgence, and these monsters didn't do indulgence for anyone but their own kind. He did, at least, take gulps of it while he was diving.

'Okay!' he shouted up, shielding his eyes from the sun that streamed down through the cave's almost perfectly circular entrance on the surface, some thirty or forty feet above him. His voice echoed. 'I'm down. You can leave me to it.'

Every day, he told the guard to go. Other than the experiments in the water, funded by the Coba cartel and *el cocodrilo*, this was a cave that had remained unchanged by human hand since its creation millions of years ago. No stairs carved into the rock. No ladder fixed to the opening. No way out, but for the rope and the balloon basket. Every day, the guard merely stood at the opening, holding his rifle and smoking a cigarette. A pointless scene in his own nightmarish Groundhog Day. All this time, being held in the middle of the Yucatan jungle – a setting that lent itself beautifully to disappearing into the thicket along with the buried ancient ruins and camouflaged wildlife. But never once had an opportunity to escape presented itself.

'I'm cursed,' he said as quietly as the natural echo chamber would allow. One shot to the top of his head would end him in an instant. It wouldn't do to let Jorge overhear his complaint.

Grunting, he climbed out of the basket and hauled his bag of tools with him. They clanked as he set them on the rocky cenote shore. Presently, as he laid out the things he needed for the test, and checked the efficacy of his diving mask, buoyancy control device, regulator and tank, all he could hear was the drip, drip of moisture from the curtain of green that hung in hair-like tracts from the mouth of the cenote. Lush foliage everywhere, covering the walls. The opposite of the scorched, dusty earth above that relied on the rainy season to fend off forest fires and drought. How could God be so cruel as to abandon him to a hellish life spent partly in this subterranean heaven?

Above him, he heard Jorge speaking abruptly into a walkie-talkie, his voice gravelly from too many poor-quality cigarettes. 'Hey! You'd better make it fast,' he shouted down into the cenote. '*El cocodrilo* is a half-hour ahead of schedule. If you're not ready when he arrives …' Jorge mimed a shot to the temple with his index and middle fingers.

Swallowing hard, he donned his dive gear and plopped into the cool water. Visibility was crystal-clear beneath the surface, ripples above him, radiating out like shimmering titanium. The rocky bed of the cenote was blanketed by a green fuzzy tangle of aquatic plants, suffused with darting, small fish – slivers of quicksilver that flashed in the sunlight; the long tree roots from above, dipping their tips into the pristine water for a drink. It was only testing his invention in this tranquil and secret place that had kept him from going insane.

Touching every inch of the semi-submersible with experienced, probing fingers, he checked that the Kevlar hull was strong enough to withstand the pressures of the open sea, particularly should the crew need to dive. Felt carefully along the exhaust venting pipes to reassure himself that everything was properly constructed. Examined the welding around the sizeable propellers to check no detail had been missed. His thudding heartbeat was at odds with the minimal peaceful lapping of the water against the top of the vessel, filtering down as a muffled slap, slap, slap through the body of water to his vantage point beneath the bulk of the sub.

El cocodrilo was coming. Judgement Day was upon him.

Clambering out, he stripped off his diving gear and lowered himself through the open hatch into the fibreglass helm. Immediately, he felt the temperature rise and the air quality decline. Turning the key to kick the diesel engine into action, he suddenly had light and ventilation. There had been no water ingress overnight. Good. But the quarters were cramped. He had had no option but to make the vessel slimline, so that there would be minimum wake in the open sea if it surfaced. Grunting as he bent almost double, he walked the length of the craft, inspecting every nook. It still needed toilet facilities. But *el cocodrilo* had told him to shut his trap and just build the damned thing with room for a bucket. Animal.

The propellers started to whir in the water. The sat nav was working, displaying the narco-sub's position in relation to the nearby coast clearly.

He smiled, though he felt instantly guilty for doing so. He had built this ocean-going craft, piecemeal, from composite parts that he had fashioned by hand in the jungle. And it worked. It was twelve metres of fully functioning semi-submersible. It was the only reason he was still alive.

'Hey! *Mecánico!*' came a gruff voice from above. Jorge, of course. 'Out of the sub. *El cocodrilo* is here!'

His pulse quickening and his breath coming short, he heaved

himself through the hatch. Feeling light-headed as he swapped the still, warm funk inside the vessel for the fresh, cool air of the cenote. The blistering midday sun was streaming through the yawning chasm in the roof, rendering the water a dazzling azure blue. But the light was suddenly blocked as the balloon basket started to lower. Casting enough shadow for him to see five men, standing at the mouth of the cavern, with their guns pointed at his head. Inside the basket was *el cocodrilo*. Recognisable in an instant with his distinctly un-Latin fair hair and pink skin, dressed in a loud Hawaiian shirt; he wore Ray-Ban aviator sunglasses, like a bad caricature of a 1980s Miami gangster. Standing at his side, peering directly down at him, was the odious, squat figure of his henchman, Miguel. The fat little prick who threw dissenters to the crocodiles at his boss' behest. It was unclear who was the worst out of the two.

'Ah, here he is!' *el cocodrilo* shouted. 'Our resident genius.'

He forced a smile, knowing that his life depended on maintaining a cordial relationship with the man who effectively owned him. '*Hola, jefe,*' he said. 'I explained to Jorge that I could have done with another couple of days to work on the vessel. You don't want to have spent all that money on development without having put it through rigorous testing first.'

El cocodrilo dismounted the basket, brushing down his white linen trousers carefully. He removed his sunglasses, perching them on his head. Those blue eyes with their oversized black pupils were glistening with excitement and perhaps too much of his own product. Who knew?

'I'll be the judge of that,' *el cocodrilo* said, his European origins still audible in the accent of his otherwise fluent Spanish. 'It's my two million dollars that's been spent on this narco-sub. If I say it's ready, it's ready.' He stalked down the rocky shoreline of the cenote in those ridiculous Italian leather loafers that he wore. Planted a threatening, faux-friendly hand on his shoulder. A beatified smile on his face, as he regarded the twelve metres of nautical innovation in Kevlar and fibreglass. 'The engines are running. The lights are on. All it needs is to be winched to the open sea, loaded with product and away you go.'

He didn't like *el cocodrilo*'s use of, 'away you go' but shoved the verbal anomaly to the back of his mind, dismissing it as paranoia from exhaustion and malnourishment.

'Talk me through your progress, *mecánico*. Take me on the grand tour.'

At his back, Miguel stood, revolver in hand. Pointed at him, of course. As if he would ever pick a fight with one of the most dangerous traffickers in the world in full view and within easy firing range of his gun-toting foot soldiers! He was anything but stupid.

Feeling that hand slap his shoulder, he tried to regulate his ragged breathing and started the climb back down to the hatch. Allowed the dealer to lower himself inside first. Followed him back into the stifling hull, where they stooped side by side.

'Come on, then! Impress me. What am I getting for all that cash and keeping your pathetic arse out of the ground?'

Swallowing hard, he began to explain the vessel's functions. Pointing to the glowing digital display. 'It's fully kitted out with sat nav. Runs on a two hundred and fifty kw diesel engine, with plenty of space for extra fuel in the cargo hold. I've designed it so you can have a crew of four in here, though really, *jefe*, they need a toilet.'

'And I need as much product as possible moving to the US and the Caribbean. My desire to make money is greater than your shitting needs, I'm afraid. Like I said last time. Bucket. It was good enough for the pirates. It's good enough for you. Continue.'

There is was again. The use of 'you'. He laughed nervously. Didn't intend to but couldn't stifle the impulse. 'I've used zinc bars as sacrificial anodes to reduce the corrosion of any metal parts, like the propellers, to the seawater, so this vessel should be good for multiple trips, saving you money.' He bared his teeth in a semblance of a smile. Praying that he was pleasing the nearest thing he had left to a god.

'That sounds clever. Is it clever?' *El cocodrilo* turned around to scrutinise his face. Grinning. Every bit as toothsome and dangerous as the crocodiles he was named after.

'Yes, *jefe*.'

'Have the Colombians got these anodes on their subs?'

'Yes, *jefe*. One or two.'

The smile fell from the dealer's face, replacing his boyish, breezy air with the haggard grimace of a seasoned killer. 'Then it's not that fucking clever, is it?'

Keen to placate him, he moved on to the ventilation system. 'I've had to make it quite a flat structure to sit low in the water, with plenty of ballast tanks, so that it can avoid detection by radar and sonar. It's going to be painted blue, too, so it will be very difficult to spot from the air, producing minimal wake if it's sailing just beneath or on the surface.' He slapped the fibreglass roof, hanging oppressively low. 'That means it's going to get very hot in here. So I devised a system where the hot air is run through pipes along the belly of the sub, to cool it down before it's expelled. That way, you avoid infra-red detection too.'

The reptilian grin was back again. Greedy. Almost lascivious. This was a beast of a man who feasted on triumphs and the failure of his competitors. Cold-blooded. Devoid of conscience. 'Now that's the sort of thing I like to hear!' He rubbed his pale hands together. Took a cigar from his top pocket.

'Please, *jefe*. It's unwise to smoke in here. As I said, I haven't quite finished testing all the systems and I can't guarantee the safety if you—'

But the crocodile was already flipping his lighter into life and dragging hard on the evil-smelling cigar.

'How many tonnes of gear did you say you could fit in here?' he asked.

Shaking his head slowly, he raised an eyebrow. Working out the maximum safe capacity. 'Maybe six or seven tonnes.'

'Stack it with ten.'

'No, *jefe*. Sorry. You'd need a vessel a good five or six metres longer for that.' He spread his arms wide, hoping to convince him. Imagined the crew losing their lives some twenty metres down, as the overloaded sub took on water or simply broke apart. How long did death by drowning take? Maybe a minute or two? But even one minute was a minute of blind panic and pain too long. 'The only place I could have assembled this baby, out of sight of the Federales, was in this cenote. It's perfect. A God-given workshop with a nice flat, dry shore and a deep pool for testing. But we were limited by the cave's natural proportions. If the sub was any bigger, you'd never winch it out of the hole in one piece when it's finished. It simply wouldn't have fit.'

'Ten tonnes,' *el cocodrilo* said, taking a seat in the captain's chair and swivelling around like a kid on a roundabout. Blowing his smoke dramatically in the air. 'Cut the crew down to two and you'll have space. More room in the bucket for shitting, too!' He threw his head back and laughed. 'I'm *very* excited about this!' Abruptly serious. 'But what happens if the coast guard or police spot it from the air or sea? I can't have a hundred million dollars of product getting seized.'

'This thing can dive to thirty metres inside a minute,' he said. He snapped his fingers, but no sound came, slippery as they were with sweat. 'In theory it will become immediately invisible. But that's why I need a couple more days for testing. The cenote is only five metres deep. If you want to be sure of the crew's safety and the craft's seaworthiness, the only place you can put it through its paces realistically is—'

'Miguel!' *el cocodrilo* shouted. He stood, stooping at precisely the right moment to avoid banging his head on the low ceiling. A man who was used to taking calculated risks and always coming up smelling of finest Cuban cigars and the folding stuff. Hastened to the hatch and hoisted himself out onto the flat surface of the semi-submersible, clasping the cigar between his teeth.

He followed, wondering what crazy physics-defying indulgence the monster would demand of him now.

'Miguel! Get the men to bring the sub up. I'm going to call her "Ella". Get it painted on her ass.'

Their eyes met. Mischief and menace in those dangerous blue and black wormholes that led to what might pass as this reptile's soul. He didn't understand *how* he could possibly have known, but he realised then that the name choice had been deliberate. Ella. It was suddenly clear exactly what was at stake. And it was far worse than he had anticipated.

El cocodrilo turned to him. Blew foul smoke into his face at close range. Winked. 'Jorge!' he shouted up to the opening. 'Load this lady up. And when you're done, she sets sail for the Dominican Republic. There's a cargo ship leaves the container port in Santo Domingo in eight days' time, bound for Rotterdam in the Netherlands. They're expecting my gear to be on it. Make sure that happens or I'll cut your ears off and feed them to my hungry girls.'

'But even if it's watertight and ready to sail, you won't be able to get ten tonnes on board, because you definitely will need four crew members, *jefe*,' he said, realising that if something went wrong on the voyage and there was a loss of life or destruction of the meth, his would be the neck on the line. Literally. 'It's physics. You can't fit both. It will sink.'

El cocodrilo approached him. Put his arm around him. So close, he could smell the tobacco in his hair and something distinctly more chemical on his breath. 'I'll say it one more time. Okay? Two men. That's my crew. And *mecánico*, my friend … because you're the expert and I trust you, one of them will be you.'

136

CHAPTER 21

Amsterdam, Ijselbuurt, then Keizersgracht, later, 21 May

The sound of his phone ringing woke Elvis with a jolt. Shrill and on maximum volume, he fumbled with the device, trying to silence it as quickly as possible. Dropped it between the bed and the bedside cabinet. Realised it was neither his bed nor his bedside cabinet.

'Dirk speaking,' he said, retrieving it just in time. His sluggish brain registered retrospectively that Marie's name had flashed up. 'Oh, hi, Marie.' No opportunity to ditch the call. As he spoke, only 25 per cent of his brain was dealing with speech. The rest was grappling with crippling embarrassment, some shame, a great deal of surprise and guilt at what had come to pass in the small hours.

'You sound like you've just woken up,' she said. It sounded like an accusation. Was it? Or was he just being paranoid?

'I'm working undercover, remember?' he said, pulling the duvet up to hide his nakedness from the waist down. Recognising the bitter irony but unable to enjoy the humour in it. He had crossed a line.

'Well, you'd better get your head on straight because a body has just been found by the Keizersgracht. I'm there now. Van den Bergen's on the flight back from Prague but won't be in until this afternoon. He told me to call you.' Her tone was castigatory. But then nowadays, Marie often sounded slightly like a disapproving teacher in a strict Catholic school.

'Jesus,' he said, glancing over to his bedfellow, who still slept soundly.

His phone buzzed. A text coming through. Buzzed again. Silently, he prayed it was nothing to do with his mother. Perhaps just some inane sales communication from the network provider.

'Okay. I'm not far away. I'll be there in half an hour, max.'

'You'd better make it faster than that,' Marie said. 'Marianne's coming to retrieve the body any minute and I'm struggling to take statements from witnesses and neighbours. I'm in charge of about six uniforms, who are cordoning off the scene. There's a stack of rubber-neckers, all trying to get a look at the corpse.' Her voice was becoming more high-pitched by the second. 'I can't do all this on my own!'

'I'm coming. Hang tight. I'm leaving now.'

Ringing off, Elvis checked his texts with a racing pulse. Seven of them stacked up and awaiting his attention. Three missed calls. How the hell had he not heard them? Since when had he ever slept that deeply? 'Shit!' he said aloud.

Please call. Your mother has taken a turn for the worse.

I've called an ambulance. Your mum needs to go to hospital. Think she has pneumonia.

Ambulance is here. Meet us at the hospital.

The texts continued, getting progressively worse, until the final two, which reported that his mother was hooked up to an anti-biotic drip and had been given oxygen. Her symptoms had eased. She was stable.

138

At his side, the man he had spent the night with – Arne – stirred. 'You okay?' he asked, stretching. In the almost-daylight of the bedroom, with the white blinds pulled, he looked different. More human. Less perfect. Better.

Elvis blushed, remembering the point in the club during which he had stopped being a professional and started to be a thirty-something man who was so tired of juggling, so tired of putting everybody else first, so tired of running the other way whenever the opportunity for adventure or fun presented itself. He'd had enough of being scared to live. And when the nice man with the kind face and mesmerising eyes had leaned in to kiss him, unexpectedly, Elvis' brain and body had been flooded with endorphins and adrenalin and a desperate hankering for something beyond policing and the part-time palliative care of his mother.

'I've got to go,' he said, springing from the bed. Scanning the room for the trail of clothes that had been successively abandoned in the heat of the moment. 'There's an emergency with my mother and I've just had an urgent callout from work.' He could feel the anxiety mounting, replacing the scorching embarrassment that was leaching heat from every pore in his body.

'Oh,' Arne said. Disappointment evident. Surprisingly.

Turning back to him as he pulled on his pants, Elvis frowned. 'You're sad that I'm going?' he asked.

Arne sprang out of bed. Struggling to look at his nakedness now that morning had arrived, bringing with it the usual limitations, expectations and pressures that shaped Elvis' mundane existence, he focused on his socks. Hopping on his left foot, as he pulled one onto the right.

'Wait!' Arne said.

He placed a hand on Elvis' shoulder, so that Elvis had no option but to stand and face him. Confronted by those huge eyes, easily as beautiful as any girl's he'd ever seen. They kissed. Elvis felt the memories of the previous night register in his groin. Lust that he'd never thought himself capable of. Passion that he had never quite achieved with women. It had felt right. Arne's body somehow seemed to fit him properly – a sensation that had always eluded him in the handful of abortive sexual encounters he'd had over the years. And yet, the sharp scratch of his stubble made him break off.

'Seriously. I'm sorry, but I have to go.' He pushed his one-night stand away, wondering how to end this awkward parting, beyond simply walking out. 'It's absolutely nothing personal.'

'Last night was your first time, wasn't it?' Arne asked, taking Elvis' hand and placing it on his chest. Stroking his cheek.

Reaching out for his T-shirt, Elvis felt tears threaten. Torn between wanting to undo the past twelve hours and wanting to experience them all over again; needing to rush to the hospital to his mother's bedside but not wanting to. Not again. He could barely face being taunted by the prospect of her end once more, only to find she would be patched up and sent home for more months of her suffering and his servitude. He was so utterly worn down by having to grieve on a fortnightly basis. And should she survive, he dreaded her seeing his guilty secret laid bare, as though an account of last night were written on his forehead – she had always been too astute, and he had never been able to ring-fence a part of his life that she couldn't scrutinise and pronounce judgement upon, apart from work. He wished he could stay with this affectionate and beautiful stranger but knew he had to show up to the canal-side or face the wrath of the boss on his return.

'Can I see you again, Dirk?' Arne said, leaning in for another kiss.

Elvis backed away. Startled by the proposition. 'Really?' Saw the earnest intentions in the man's face. Felt hope and something resembling happiness stir within him, like long-lost emotions buried beneath the strata of despair and responsibility that had settled over the years; suddenly excavated by a gay man he would never have believed he'd be attracted to and whom he knew absolutely nothing about. 'Er … I've got to go.'

'How is she?'

The first question he asked as he walked briskly in the direction of the Victorieplein stop for the tram into town. Paying no attention to the faceless, almost suburban surrounds of Arne's neighbourhood in Ijselbuurt. Only thinking of his mother.

'You should be here,' the carer said. 'This is really above and beyond duty, you know.'

'I'm sorry. Look, you said she was stable. Can you put the doctor or a nurse on? Please. I've got an emergency at work and it's not like the first time she's been shipped off to hospital, is it? Obviously, if Mum's on death's—'

But Mevrouw van Lennep wasn't listening. Had she cut him off, the sour-faced old trout? No. There was the sound of rustling at the other end. A younger woman's voice. Kindly.

'Hello, Dirk. May I call you Dirk? I'm Dr Mehmood. I understand that you're Femke's son and next of kin. Is that correct?'

'Yes. Please, how is she?'

'She's not very well, I'm afraid. We've got her breathing under control, but the problem is that she has aspiration pneumonia because of her swallowing difficulties. It's common in cases of advanced Parkinson's.' There was a flick and rustle of paperwork, just audible above the jaunty, tinkling bell of the tram. 'I see she's been admitted three times when she's suffered this build-up in her lungs due to the dysphagia.'

'Yes. Is she awake? Can I speak to her?'

'Well, wouldn't you rather come to see her?' Disbelief and judgement in the doctor's voice.

'I'm a policeman. I've got to attend a murder scene.' Checking around the tram to see if anybody was eavesdropping on the conversation, Elvis wondered what these people, going about their daily business, would make of him, if they knew the other end of the conversation. He cringed inwardly. Knew exactly how it seemed. He was a first-rate shit and a terrible son.

'I see.'

Judging by the tone of her voice, this doctor really didn't see at all. 'Well, like I say, we've got everything in hand for now. But your mother is very frail. Very frail indeed, Dirk. Things can change quickly, I'm afraid.'

There was a pregnant silence, during which Elvis could hear hospital noises in the background. Beeping. Telephones ringing. Nurses' chatter. Tannoy announcements.

'I'll be over as soon as I can. Maybe in as little as an hour, if I can manage to hand over to my colleague. I've been working on surveillance all night. I didn't get—'

'If there are changes, we'll call.'

As his cheeks caught fire, broadcasting to the whole of Amsterdam that he was morally bankrupt, selfish, bordering on sociopathic and the worst child in the world, who had in fact been luxuriating in all sorts of hedonistic self-indulgence for the greater part of the night, rather than working on 'surveillance', the doctor was abruptly replaced by Mevrouw van Lennep again.

'You've got a bloody cheek, Dirk. I'll stay here another hour and then I'm off. I've got my cats to feed. My shift finished twenty minutes ago! You were supposed to be back to take over! You promised. I don't get paid enough for this and I've got my own life, you know. I live to work. I don't work to live. It's fine for you with your respectable job and your government pay and pension and paid holidays. But I rely on you! I said I'd look after your mum nights, when you're working on whatever it is you're working on. And *you* said you'd pay me double my hourly rate. And *you* said you'd not let me down. Well, you're letting me down, Dirk. And you're letting your mother down!'

Silence. She had hung up.

Sighing, he visualised his mother, hooked up to all of those machines. A diminutive figure, growing weaker by the day. But tenacious in spirit. What would she say, if she knew what he'd done? She'd slap his face and tell him his father and grandparents would be spinning in their graves, in all likelihood.

He ignored the text from Arne. Sweet nothings, glowing on his screen. Jesus. What had he started?

'That was a bloody long twenty minutes,' Marie said, staring pointedly at her watch. Squatting by the body, with her digital camera hanging around her neck.

'Mum's taken a turn for the worse,' he said, digging his hands deep into his new leather jacket. At his feet, a young man, already grey and ghoulish-looking, was sitting stiffly against the side of a car by the canal's edge. Staring blankly at the opposite bank of the Keizersgracht. A pool of vomit beside him. 'Bet she looks better than this poor sod, though.'

'You should be with your mum. Go to her! Go on. I'll cope.'

'She's fine for now. I'll go in a minute.' The guilt pushed down on his shoulders, forcing his hands even further into his pockets.

In his peripheral vision, beyond the fluttering police tape and uniforms trying desperately to keep the overzealous pedestrians away from the scene, he recognised Marianne de Koninck's white forensics van approaching. Good. As soon as the body was carted off, he could probably make a case for slipping away to the hospital for a bit.

'How long have you been here?' he asked, yawning.

Marie snapped a close-up of the dead man's face. The flash highlighted the purple-blue cyanosis on his lips and earlobes. 'I'd only just arrived when I called you.' She changed position and snapped again. 'A dog-walker called him in. People have been trudging past all morning, but you know what it's like. If you see someone slumped against a car and a pool of sick on the floor, the last thing you're going to do is start poking around.'

'Good Samaritans are hard come by in the city.'

'I'll say.'

Squatting beside her to get a better look, he grimaced and

143

winced. Feeling his acrobatic debut performance in the bedroom with another man register just about everywhere below the waist. 'I'm stiff as a board,' he said. 'This undercover shit is killing me. Too many late nights. Too much sodding dancing.'

Chuckling, Marie nudged him in the ribs. 'And to think you've been bragging for years about how you've got two left feet and hate nightclubs. Van den Bergen knew exactly which buttons to push! Ha. You can't fault the old bastard for having a perverse sense of humour.' Narrowing her watery blue eyes, she paused. 'You've changed,' she said.

Elvis blushed. 'No I haven't. What makes you say that?'

'You've lost weight. Your hair's trendy, all of a sudden. You used to look like a Nineties throwback who had been shrunk in the wash. Now you've got new cool clothes – I hope you're putting the receipts in as expenses.'

'You bet, I will.'

'My God. I'm not sure we could even legitimately call you Elvis anymore.' She tugged at her greasy red hair. Her face crumpled into full-blown mirth.

'Laughing at the dead?' Marianne de Koninck's voice resounded behind them. Business-like. Almost manly. Unforgiving.

He turned around, feeling too small and naff and parochial for his stylish leather jacket and new designer sneakers. Caught sight of the chief of Forensic Pathology's solemn po-face and almost saw a disapproving Van den Bergen in those hollow runner's cheeks and that over-worked-out neck.

'No, Marianne. It's—. We've—. Tell her, Marie.'

Marie ogled her scuffed green suede boots studiously. 'Jeroen Meulenbelt. Just turned twenty-one yesterday. His ID is still on him. Nothing has been stolen. His vomit reeks of chemicals and I found this –' she waved a baggie of crystals in the air '– on his person.'

'Definitely not a robbery,' Elvis said, wanting desperately to contribute something. 'Sounds like an OD of sorts, like the others.'

Marianne de Koninck held her hand out for the baggie. 'I'll have it analysed. If it turns out this poor kid had lead poisoning like the others, we'll soon see if it's the same batch. Van den Bergen called me last night to say this meth is coming from Mexico. The experts in Prague were able to pinpoint it precisely as the work of the Coba cartel that operates out of the Yucatan Peninsula.'

'Coba?' Elvis asked. 'Mexico? But every dealer I've managed to chat up has been banging on about some Czech called Nikolay.'

'Speak to Van den Bergen,' de Koninck said, unceremoniously shooing them both out of the way.

'And the only other name I've heard dropped – and this was from one of my informants who approached me while I was undercover,' Dirk said, 'has been Stijn Pietersen.'

De Koninck rounded on him, pushing him up against the side of her white van. 'You what?' Her sharp gaze almost filleted the details from him before he could speak. 'Say that again.'

'Stijn Pietersen.'

'The Rotterdam Silencer? The bastard who planted a bullet in Van den Bergen's hip and ran Europe's underworld?'

'Well, I guess so,' he croaked. 'But that was over a decade ago, wasn't it?'

She removed her muscled forearm from his throat. 'I thought he was in prison.'

'So did I,' Marie said.

CHAPTER 22

Amsterdam, police headquarters, later

'How did we miss this?!' Maarten Minks said, speaking in a quiet voice that was almost more menacing than Kamphuis' and Hasselblad's propensity for bawling Van den Bergen out. Not that it would have even the slightest effect on him. Not at his age. No way. He knew all the psychological tricks in the book and none of them had ever worked on him.

Van den Bergen sighed deeply. Gazed through the smudged lenses of his glasses at the printout of the report from the Prague police. 'Ask our guys at the lab,' he said. Appraising the pink in Minks' cheeks over the top of his glasses.

'You can't know what you don't know,' George said, carefully tweaking her sheaf of papers into perfect alignment with one another with tight, precise fingers. 'And the funding cuts don't help. You can't expect five-star accuracy on a two-star budget, can you?'

The tone of her voice was disparaging. No surprises there. But he could feel the tension radiating from her body. Minks made her uncomfortable. It was the first time Van den Bergen's new boss had ever lost it. Normally, his default setting seemed to be boundless enthusiasm. He bandied about phrases like 'can-do attitude' and was unstinting in his praise of Van den Bergen and his team – especially George. But this morning, it felt rather like the sun had gone behind thick cloud and a chill wind had started to blow. Minks was an unknown quantity, and George clearly wasn't coping well with that.

Beneath the table, Van den Bergen put a comforting hand on her thigh. She swiped him away. Shot him a venomous glance. He was tempted to smile but resisted. Started to sketch his grand-daughter's face into the margin of his notepad.

'The Czech authorities have really got their hands full, thanks to what appears to be an insatiable national appetite for the drug,' he said, delicately cross-hatching baby Eva's cheeks to accentuate their chubbiness. 'Its market over here and in the UK is more niche and restricted to the odd hard-core clubber but mainly gay men on the scene. My detective, Dirk, saw an eye-watering amount of drug use on the gay scene, where it seems they're heavily into what's called "chem-sex", I believe.' Feeling his haemorrhoids involuntarily twitching, he shifted his position in his seat. 'It's a new cultural phenomenon, closely linked to the advent of dating apps like Grindr. Guys arrange hook-ups – often with multiple willing partners. Men bring the drugs in. They're crazy for meth, apparently because it makes them …' He abandoned his sketch to scan his notes for Elvis' observations, written in a scrawling, childlike hand. '"*Horny as hell so they can't get enough*", he says here.' Blinked hard, watching Minks' mouth prune. 'But Dr McKenzie, here, operated undercover mainly at straight clubs and saw relatively little, didn't you?'

He turned to George, but she was intent only on staring out Minks. No doubt trying to bore a hole in the side of his face with indignation. The muscles in her jaw flickered up and down. Grinding her molars again. He wondered fleetingly if she would expend so much energy needlessly when she got to his age, once he was either drooling in an old people's home or scattered in the North Sea.

'There are a lot of dealers on mopeds who service the straight clubs,' she said. 'Like in London, I guess. Kids place orders with them like calling for take-out pizza. They park up outside to dole out coke and ecstasy. But there's definitely quite a bit of mephedrone and meth around too. The bouncers superficially go through the motions of keeping the clubs dealer-free, but that's all for show. You don't get to be a successful dealer by taking no for an answer. Know what I mean?' She grinned and winked. Scowled when she was met by Minks' deadpan expression. 'Everyone's heard of Nikolay, though. He's like some kind of Scarface larger-than-life character.'

Van den Bergen steepled his fingers together, mindful of the fact that the meeting had already overrun. 'But even in Prague, where he's supposed to live, the police haven't got a clue to his whereabouts. Nobody's ever seen him in the flesh. Or at least they're keeping shtum if they have.' He was due his new herbal meds for the acid reflux. Twenty minutes before eating, the herbalist had said. One tablespoon of apple cider vinegar in a glass of water with half a dissolved teaspoon of Manuka honey. He had to stick to the regime rigidly. Aloe vera juice too. Avoiding trigger foods like caffeine and tomatoes, which he was trying and failing to do. Tamara had insisted he try to put fewer chemicals into his body now that he was 'Opa'. Or Grumpy Gramps, as George preferred to call him. *Hurry up, Minks, for Christ's sake. Stop swinging your dick and just transfer this case to that new narcotics hump you brought in from Utrecht, André Vorenveld.* 'Nikolay Bebchuck could be a myth, for all we know, created on purpose by his dealers to protect his identity. Or maybe even a front for an organised trafficking ring – not one individual. I'd say that's more likely. In my considerable experience.'

'But there's nothing to say it's not a serial killer, singling out gay men, is there?' Minks tapped defiantly on the polished surface of his new oak desk. 'Five out of six of our victims were gay men. They all died in the same manner. That can't be a coincidence, can it?'

Rocking back on his chair and hooking his hands behind his neck, Van den Bergen tried to sigh but instead emitted only a low growl. He had promised George he would stop doing that with this new boss, if only to preserve everyone else's sanity. 'Look! With all due respect, Maarten, I think you're forcing two and two together and making five. This isn't about a serial killer. It's about a drugs trafficker. A nasty one. The Czechs have expert analysts. They picked up immediately that the gear killing our kids is Mexican.'

Minks raised his hands in the air, his normally pale skin colouring up yet again. Van den Bergen had never seen him this agitated before. Perhaps because he could see the sexy newspaper headlines of NEW COMMISSIONER COCKBLOCKS GAY-SLAYER evaporating as the investigation progressed.

'They all died in or by the bloody canals, for God's sake! Someone had dragged Floris Engels by his underarms.'

'You don't get it, do you?' George shouted. 'Even the kindest-hearted soul wouldn't necessarily fancy being implicated in the death of a friend or fuck-buddy. Who wants to get a criminal record and ruin their life just because somebody else overdid it?'

'Well, I would!' Minks said.

'So would I,' Van den Bergen said. 'But that's why we're police officers and not criminals.'

Sucking her teeth and treating Van den Bergen to an icy stare, George paused just long enough to let him know that she didn't appreciate the implicit criticism of her past. Not that he meant it. But she wouldn't see it that way, of course.

'Meth turns these men into cold and clinical fuck-bots,' she said. 'I've heard about it from interviewees in prison.'

She fluffed out her hair dramatically. Dr McKenzie in the house, taking absolutely zero shit from Minks, who knew far less about the subject than she did. *That's my girl*, Van den Bergen thought.

'Plenty of guys inside for sexual assault and petty theft when they've been high on meth, in particular,' she continued. 'Floris' partner tried to save him and then clearly thought better of it once he realised he wasn't going to find him easily in that canal. He was high. He made the decision to flee the scene when he was off his cake on a cocktail of party drugs. Simple. There's no damned serial killer. There's just a shitty cultural phenomenon which has sprung up and some morally bankrupt scuzzball in the Americas who's smuggling poison into Europe.' She rapped on the table with her index finger. 'That's your killer! We need to go to Mexico and find this "Nikolay". You want a multiple murderer? He's your man!'

'No!' Van den Bergen said, surprising himself with the ferocity of his outburst. Fixed his attention on Minks. 'Pass it on to André and his new narco-team.' He looked at George askance, noticing that she had the glimmer of a smile tugging at the corner of her lips. 'I can't go haring off to bloody Mexico. I've got a grand-daughter and responsibilities in Amsterdam. There are leads I need to pursue here, anyway. Unanticipated developments.'

Minks folded his arms, never taking his eyes from George, who had started to make a perfectly round ball out of elastic bands.

'Can you stop that, please?' he asked, pointing to the ball.

'No.'

Attention moving back to Van den Bergen. 'Hang on. What unanticipated developments?'

Saying the name over and over in his head, he acknowledged the pain flooding through his hip from the old bullet wound. 'The Rotterdam Silencer,' he said out loud. 'Stijn Pietersen.'

Minks' impassive face was devoid of understanding. Too bloody young to remember, Van den Bergen mused. *This kid was still in rookie college when I was working my arse off to bring Stijn Bastard Pietersen down.*

Reaching over, George placed an understanding hand on his forearm. Stroking his skin gently with her thumb. He patted her hand. Knew that she, above anyone else, understood the anguish that had caused him to buckle at the knees when Marianne de Koninck had called him as soon as their flight had come to a standstill at Schiphol. Far more of a nemesis than Kamphuis had ever been, the mention of Stijn Pietersen's name had almost triggered a full-on panic attack as they were disembarking the aircraft. He could feel the prickling at his extremities even now, as he recalled the crowded aisle, full of stag-party-goers and business folk returning home from Prague, hoisting their rucksacks and briefcases to their chests defensively. All wanting to be first off. And the brusque Dutchman with the Breda accent telling him to move his fucking arse. But all he had been able to do was shallow-breathe through gritted teeth.

Stijn Pietersen was out. Worse still, Stijn Pietersen was at large. Again. How the hell had that happened without him knowing? He was losing his touch.

'If Elvis' informant is right, and the Rotterdam Silencer is getting his feet back under the table in the Netherlands, we've got a lot more to worry about than bad meth.'

Minks rose from his desk. A trim man in quiet, quality suiting. One of the new poster-boys of the Dutch police now that the old guard had gone. Better than Kamphuis, no doubt. But still gunning for the big brass ring, rather than doing the police work and keeping the streets safe. Van den Bergen could smell the future politician in Minks. It was a sour, curdling scent of ambition, at odds with the whiff of expensive aftershave and the cracked leather of his vintage old boys' desk chair.

Staring out of the window at the car park below, Minks said, 'If the results of the meth found on Jeroen Meulenbelt come back saying it's Mexican, let me know. I'll make my decision on our next step then. In the meantime, prepare a press release, telling the gay community that there's a killer out there. We cannot afford to sacrifice their safety on your hunch and some blast from the past, Van den Bergen.'

He turned on his heel, locking eyes with George. Transferring his scrutiny to Van den Bergen, as if daring him to disagree. The worm had suddenly turned.

With every fibre in his being, Van den Bergen fought the urge to stand and give this arrogant upstart a mouthful. He could feel the acid spraying into his gullet. 'We'll see about that,' he said.

Minks approached the desk. Smiled at George. Glowered at the Chief Inspector. 'I've just told you to prepare a press release, Van den Bergen. That's a direct order. Do I make myself understood?'

CHAPTER 23

Amsterdam, Van den Bergen's apartment, 22 May

With Van den Bergen over at Tamara's, shoehorning in a visit to little Eva before her bath and bedtime routine kicked in, George sat in her lover's apartment, staring at the screen on her laptop. Feeling more alone than she had ever felt in her life.

'Where the fuck are you?' she asked, reading the words from the latest email over and over, as if some meaning behind them would somehow present itself.

From: Michael Carlos Izquierdo Moreno (Michael.Moreno@BritishEngineering.com)
Sent: 12 April
To: George_McKenzie@hotmail.com
Subject: Checking in

Dear George,

Just sending you another little note to say I'm watching over you, like a good dad. You take too many risks, you know. A job like yours could get you into a lot of deep water. Send my love to your mother.

Oh wait. You can't!

Love Dad x

'Taunting arsehole,' she shouted, slamming the lid of the laptop shut.

Marching to the kitchen, she opened the cupboard above the kettle, where she knew Van den Bergen hid the junk for those days when he couldn't abide his stupid alkaline diet any longer. She pulled out the Thai sweet chilli-flavoured Kettle Chips she had brought from England, stuffed a handful into her mouth and thought about her situation.

Both her parents were missing. Somebody kept sending her menacing notes, pretending to be her dad. She was certain they weren't from him and there had only been four in total in the space of a year. Each time, the message had been the same: *I'm watching you.*

'What bastard is watching me?' she shouted, peering out of the kitchen window onto the small clump of trees below. Scanning the empty street and the parked cars that sat in a neat row, looking innocent enough. 'Are you out there, you fucker?' Imagining whoever had written the emails could hear her. Wanting to show she wasn't afraid. 'Why me? Why is it always me?!' she asked the photo of Letitia that she had pinned to Van den Bergen's cork noticeboard. It was a snap of her mother at one of Aunty Sharon's birthday parties some years ago, uncharactegrinning at whoever had been behind the camera, with her arm around her sister, the birthday girl, as though they were friends. Resplendent in a low-cut silver lamé top that George had no memory of. 'Wilderness years,' she said aloud. The time when she had eschewed all contact with Letitia the Dragon, choosing to pursue a brand-new life on her own. She shook her head at the image, knowing instinctively that her mother had just said something cutting to Aunty Sharon prior to the photo opportunity, given the younger sister's downturned mouth and the hurt in her eyes.

Feeling frustration and fear overwhelm her, George stuffed yet more Kettle Chips into her mouth. Grinding them down, since punishing the crisps was the only power she had left.

'Where are you, you horrible cow?'

A year since her mother had slept on Van den Bergen's sofa, bemoaning her 'pulmonaries' and refusing to go into temporary accommodation with Aunty Sharon, Tinesha and Patrice. A year since George had woken to find her gone. No note. No phone. Her coat still hanging on the peg in the hall.

And now, Dad. As if he hadn't already been torn from her life too soon by the Dragon, who couldn't abide giving an inch but who had always excelled in taking a mile.

'How could you leave me?' George's voice was now a whisper. She padded through to the living room, opening her laptop to the tab that was now permanently loaded. An employee listing for the engineering company that had contracted her father to work in Honduras. Not the bogus British Engineering domain that the emails purported to be from, but a company called Earhart Barton. The photo was perhaps no more than a couple of years old and the image showed he had barely aged, though that thick, black Spanish hair had receded right back, necessitating a short crop. But the eyes were still the same. Large, intelligent, kind brown eyes topped by brows like fat slugs. Long lashes that gave his otherwise serious expression an almost childlike appearance. All those years, she had been unable to recollect his features in any detail – the product of Letitia having thrown every last photo of him onto a bonfire in the shitty back yard of George's childhood home. Setting fire to them with lighter fuel and a discarded cigarette butt inside George's Barbie bedroom bin. George had cried as much for the loss of the bin as she had for the photos but, at six, she had not understood the emotional consequences of losing all mementos of the man she had adored. Papa. She could still recall his smell of tobacco and spicy after-shave. Could still remember the way his hair sprouted around his neck when he hadn't been to the barber's in a while, encroached upon by curling black back hairs that she had liked to tug as a toddler, whenever he put her on his shoulders. Furry Papa.

'Jesus! Why are you doing this to yourself, you fucking

masochist?' she shouted, heading away from the image on the laptop and over to the patio doors. 'Letitia brainwashed you into never giving a shit if he lived or died, and *now* you're bothered that he's gone?'

As she sparked her e-cigarette into life on the balcony, tears came suddenly and in torrents like a spring downpour. For the first time in years, perhaps since she had been rejected in a hospital side-room by her first love, Ad, George felt sorry for herself.

Taking out her phone, she sat on Van den Bergen's rattan patio chair and put her slipper-clad feet up on a large planter containing a passion-flower climber. Dialled her aunt's number. Sharon answered on the fourth ring, the sound of Radio 4 in the background.

'All right, love?' Aunty Sharon said. Her voice was supercharged with faux cheeriness. Clearly still hating not having the kids at home often. 'What a lovely surprise. I was just doing my cleaning and thinking of you. There's this new limescale remover in Tesco—'

'Oh fuck the limescale remover,' George said, feeling sadness and impotence engulf her. 'I can't ... I can't ...' She let everything out on a deafening wail. Spotted one of the neighbours walking too slowly along the pavement below, gawping up at her – a snotty, weeping black girl on the grumpy old detective's balcony. Perhaps the interfering geriatric fart would spread gossip that Van den Bergen had been hitting her. George stood. 'You seen enough, you nosey old bastard?' she yelled in English down at the old man. 'Not you,' she clarified for Aunty Sharon's benefit.

'What the hell has got into you?' her aunt asked. 'What's the matter, darling? Tell your Aunty Shaz.'

Through hiccups, sobs and then sniffles, George explained how the latest piece of information unearthed by Marie – that her father had disappeared in the most dangerous country in the world – had filled her with dread.

'I'm sure this has got something to do with me,' she said.

'Again! Like I haven't already had enough of this "past coming back to bite me on the arse" nonsense.'

'Oh, George, love. You've got yourself a stalker, is all,' Sharon said. 'You don't half attract them, babe. You're like some kind of pervert magnet. That's my theory, anyway.'

Toeing the passion-flower plant, George wiped her face with the sleeve of her hoody and nodded. 'I guess. Maybe.'

'Maybe nothing! You're in that line of business. You spend all your days interviewing murderers and sex pests in prison. You think some of them don't get out eventually and come looking for the pretty girl with the big tits and stinking attitude, who asked too many questions?' On the other end of the phone, Aunty Sharon started to laugh heartily. 'You want your old cleaning job back at Skin Licks? You'll only get groped by the punters in there!'

Inhaling deeply on her e-cigarette, George forced a hollow chuckle. 'No ta. But it's obviously not just some perv with a hard-on for English girls, is it? It's only just over twelve months since I had a human eyeball sent to me. I know it turned out to be some bloke with a shady past and some bad connections, and not Letitia at all, but there's a murderous nutcase out there, Aunty Shaz. Somebody who knows my email address and keeps reminding me that I'm on their radar. They're using Dad's name to contact me. However infrequently, it's still freaky as shit. And fact is, my dad's reported missing on Interpol. Fucking Interpol! I didn't make it up. Both parents. Gone.' Once more, George found herself overwhelmed by sorrow. 'I can't take it anymore! The not knowing.' She failed to mention the ageing biker she had seen in her peripheral vision on more than one occasion.

'Aw, take a deep breath, love,' her aunt said. 'I wish I was there to give you a big hug. But listen, if you think it would help with closure and that, we could hold a funeral for your mum. Bury an empty coffin, like. When I lost little D and Derek, I felt different after the send-off.'

'We don't know she's dead!'

'Come on, George. How long's it been now?'

Shaking her head, George started to regret having called her aunt. Usually her unconditional ally, today Sharon wasn't getting her at all. 'I don't want a fake funeral. It's not right. And if it does turn out that she's just buggered off with some toy boy, I'd look a bit of a twat, burying an empty coffin and putting up a headstone for her.'

'Oh, she'd fucking love that!' Sharon guffawed down the phone. 'Then she would be centre of attention. Knowing that cheeky cow, my sister, she'd turn up incognito and sit on the back pew of the church just to see who showed up! She'd lap every tear up!'

There was a pause. George knew she ought to ask Aunty Sharon how she was doing and whether there was any news from London, but the reason behind the phone call forced its way out of her mouth before she had time to self-censor.

'I'm working on this drugs thing over here. I've got the chance to go to Mexico. At the Dutch police's expense. What do you think?' She dug her thumbnail into the weave of her jeans, trying to expunge dirt that simply wasn't there.

'What do I think what? Mexico? I've heard Cancun's nice. Why? Are you thinking of squeezing a freebie holiday out of them? Nipping off for the three S's with old lanky bollocks?'

'No. I want to find Dad.' There. She had said it.

'Are you fucking mental?!' Aunty Sharon shouted at such volume that George had to hold the phone away from her ear. 'For Christ's sake, girl. Listen to my wisdom, yeah? If your dad was so keen on hearing from you, he'd have been in touch donkey's years ago, whether that cow my sister had told him to do one or not.'

Standing to lean over the balcony, George weighed those stinging words carefully. Their implication punctured a soft spot deep within her – the part she had fortified over the years with an almost impenetrable wall of ballsy bluster. But Aunty Sharon had just pierced through to the sacred space that contained the battered remnants of George's childish optimism and nostalgic longing for her early years.

'He loved me. There's no way of knowing if he sent letters or tried to make contact.'

'Stop kidding yourself, love.' The sympathy in her aunt's voice was audible but the bitter, unpalatable message was unsugared. 'Listen, you imagine life with Letitia. Seriously.'

'I did spend my first sixteen years with her!'

'And you couldn't wait to beat a shitty path out of that nightmare, could you? And I don't blame you. Cos my sister's poison. So, imagine you're some random geezer she met at a nightclub, what knocks her up. Even if you love the bones of your kid, would you really hang around for a lifetime of torture with that fruit and nutcase? Cos I fucking wouldn't.'

Silently, George shook her head. 'And I didn't, did I?'

'You listen to your Aunty Shaz,' Sharon said. 'Don't go to Mexico. Right? Don't do it, George. Don't go looking for trouble. Having Letitia going AWOL is bad enough. But if you get on a plane to some shithole what's notorious for drug smuggling and that, hoping to look for Daddy Dearest after all these years – Daddy who's already been topped by some cartel arsehole, in all likelihood – you're sticking your hand in the hornet's nest. Don't expect not to get stung. Do you get me?'

'Yes,' George said, already thinking ahead to the conversation she needed to have next. No longer paying any heed to her well-meaning aunt.

'Cos I seen that *Breaking Bad* on the telly, and you don't wanna be messing with those Latino types. It ain't all guacamole and fucking mojitos, love. And let's face it, you've got a bit of a track record for getting into hot water, what with your—'

'Okay. Cheers. Speak soon, Aunty Shaz.' Without further warning or explanation, George hung up.

Hot water. Deep water, the email had said. The canals of Amsterdam were deep water. Could there be some kind of a connection or message in the email's words? With a thudding heart, George retreated to the living room, closed the patio doors and drew the curtains. Maybe somebody was watching her, right at that moment. Someone she couldn't spot with her naked eye. Someone with a long-range lens. A man who knew she was helping with the investigation of the canal deaths. The biker with the long hair, perhaps.

'Shit!' Flashbacks to living in the bedsit in the Cracked Pot Coffee Shop, George felt strongly like somebody was making themselves familiar with her routine, her past, her heart's desires. 'Calm down, you idiot,' she counselled herself.

Perching on the edge of Van den Bergen's sofa, George dialled Marie's number. Realised she would probably be working over-time, even though it was after 5 p.m.

'Come on! Pick up!' she said, drumming the fingers of her left hand on Van den Bergen's battered old coffee table. Frowning at the cup ring his coffee had left last week. She'd have to sand that out. Scuffs were one thing. Cup rings were forbidden.

'Marie speaking.' George could hear irritation in her voice. Perhaps it was catching.

'Hey. It's me. I don't suppose you've had those results of the meth test back from Marianne de Koninck, have you?'

There was the sound of mouse-clicking and Marie's deep sighing. 'The Jeroen Meulenbelt scene?'

'Yep. The latest canal guy, the one where Elvis found a dry stash in his jacket.'

'Here we go,' Marie said. 'It's just come in.'

'And?' George held her breath, running her index finger round and around the cup ring.

'Mexican. Same chemical composition as the other stuff. Contains super-high levels of lead.'

Allowing herself the beginnings of a furtive smile, George glanced over at the photo of her father on the Earhart Barton website. 'Van den Bergen know about this yet?'

'No,' Marie said. 'He's been out all afternoon. But you'd know that, wouldn't you? I thought he'd gone to visit—'

'Can you put me through to Maarten Minks?' George asked. Her furtive smile transformed into a broad, scheming grin. She pulled her sheaf of Spanish crib sheets from under her laptop. Those months spent brushing up might not be wasted after all.

CHAPTER 24

Mexico, Cancun airport, 26 May

'Take your bloody raincoat off, Paul. You look like you're about to have an apoplexy.' George stood by the baggage carousel in the marble-tiled airport, watching the pasty-faced British tourists take out their petty pent-up irritation with one another through the medium of their suitcases – the women, chastising the men for allowing them to go past without interception; the men, marching the length of the baggage reclaim hall to heave them passive-aggressively onto poorly behaved trolleys which rammed only slightly into the women's knees.

That's what an eight-hour flight will do to you, George thought.

'I'll wear my raincoat if I want to,' Van den Bergen said, mopping at his shining brow with a tissue. Red in the face already. 'I never wanted to come on this ridiculous wild-goose chase. I've got a family to think about back home.'

Staring at him in disbelief, George sucked her teeth. 'Please your fucking self. Go on, then. Melt, you cantankerous old bastard!'

He tutted. 'You're obsessed!' he said. 'This was never within our remit. Trekking to bloody Cancun via Gatwick. You only got Maarten to agree to fund this fool's errand because you flirted with him.'

George glanced at her watch. Noticed that time was running out. Caught sight of the departures board. She had only twenty minutes before her window of opportunity closed. Her heart was pounding in her chest at the thought of what she was about to do. Did he suspect? Had Marie ratted her out? Was his grumpiness on the flight an indication that he knew exactly what she was planning.

'George!' he said. 'Your case.'

She jumped. It had sounded more like a command than anything else. But then her every sense was on fire.

'I've got eyes, thanks,' she said.

Her red suitcase moved towards her slowly. *Come on! Hurry up!* When Van den Bergen stepped in to pull it from the carousel, she elbowed him out of the way and lugged it off herself. Pulled the handle upright. Ignored the disappointment that was etched into his flushed face.

'I was only trying to be helpful,' he said. 'I don't know what's got into you. I don't know why we're arguing in Cancun airport when we could be arguing in bed at home. Mexican food plays havoc with my stomach.' He touched his abdomen, as if to illustrate his point better. 'And I hate that guacamole crap. Avocado tastes like soap.'

As if plugging the flow of complaint from his mouth, George clamped his face between her hot hands, pulling his head down to meet her and planting a passionate kiss on his lips. 'Be good, old man. Say, "*Hola!*" to the Federales. Don't run off with a señorita, or you'll wake up with a *piñata*'s head in your bed when we get back. *Hasta luego, mi amor!*'

'What?' Van den Bergen said, touching his lips. He raised an eyebrow, clearly perplexed.

But George didn't have time to explain. 'I'll call. I promise.'

When he reached out to pull her back, he grabbed at empty air. George ran as fast as possible across the shining marble hall, following arrows for international transfers on the overhead signs.

'George! Come back! I'm sorry!' Van den Bergen's voice rang out behind her, but the ticket in her pocket was like a magnet, drawing her to the departure gate where the connecting flight to Tegucigalpa in Honduras would soon be closing its doors for take-off.

CHAPTER 25

Honduras, Tegucigalpa, later

'Oh Jesus, I'm going to die,' George muttered beneath her breath.

The jet had descended lower, lower, lower over the mountains that surrounded the Honduran capital of Tegucigalpa. Trees were scudding beneath the aircraft's belly. Disconcerting enough, even for someone like her, used to flying regularly into Schiphol, where the flights were practically skimming the North Sea before touchdown. But this?

George studied the other passengers. In her immediate vicinity, a mixture of Mexican business people and what appeared to be Honduran students. All clearly shitting their pants. When the jet banked sharp to the right, she let out a yelp.

'Fuck me!' She prayed to a God she wished she believed in that they'd make it down in one piece. Clutched the printout of the photo of her father in her clammy hand. 'I'd better find you after going through this bullshit, Papa.'

The corrugated iron and clapboard shanty towns – the *barrios* – passed beneath them like whitewashed Lego bricks. The plane banked again, steering against the pull of a strong crosswind. In unison, her fellow passengers groaned. She could see both women and men making the sign of the cross. George clenched her eyes shut. Couldn't bear not knowing what was going on. Opened them again, resolving to face death with dignity and bravery, if it was coming prematurely in this old flying tin can.

Through the window on the other side of the aisle, she spotted the runway. It was at an unachievable angle in relation to the plane. They were definitely going to crash. The wing on the right dipped abruptly and the plane dropped further from the sky, looking as though it was going to land on the corrugated roof of a *barrio* shack at any moment.

'How the actual f …?'

But George's mutterings went unanswered as the aircraft lunged ever downwards, hitting Toncontín International Airport's notoriously short runway with a squeal of overtaxed tyres and the whine of brakes that were surely working too hard. A round of applause burst out around her.

You're shitting me, George thought, clapping along. She had arrived.

Having cleared customs and immigration, she ran through the plan in her head. Get a taxi. Go to her father's former place of employment. That was it. At that moment, she wondered fleetingly if she had been a little overimpulsive in her decision to come here. But there was no time for pointless regret. Considering how meagre her means were, she had been lucky to get the bulk of her journey there funded by the Dutch police. The rest she owed to Marie, who had lent her the money for the plane ticket as a gesture of sisterly solidarity. Anything else would go on George's credit card. She would worry about it later.

She emerged from the sanitised cool of the airport terminal to be confronted by a queue of taxis.

'Where to?' a taxi driver asked her in English, clearly judging her to be an American tourist.

She answered him in Spanish, giving the address of Earhart Barton's corporate HQ in the commercial district of downtown Tegucigalpa, or Tegus, as the locals called it. Noticed the driver's raised eyebrow. Had nine long months of covertly brushing up on her language skills and watching snippets of El Salvadoran telenovelas on YouTube failed her? George was nothing if not a conscientious student and she already had had a thorough grounding in the language, good enough to bag her a Spanish degree, after all. *He'll smell the fear on you if you don't believe in yourself.*

He opened the door to the white cab with the yellow number emblazoned on the side. Gave her a price that sounded realistic for a local to pay. George allowed herself a satisfied smile. Her hard work had paid off.

Inside, the car smelled of hot faux-leather upholstery and stale cigarettes, masked by a pine air freshener. George was horrified by crumbs that had settled into the stitching on the back seat. *You can't exactly get out and walk, you berk. You're in the murder capital of the world. Take a deep breath and stop being a dick. Maybe they're really clean crumbs. Maybe they weren't inside somebody's mouth first.*

'You come from El Salvador?' the taxi driver asked, studying her through his rear-view mirror with weary-looking eyes. 'I can hear it in your accent.'

'Yes. Originally. But I live here now.' Was she convincing? Had she used the proper grammar? Would he be able to pick her out as a fake?

No reprisal. Perhaps he was keeping his suspicions to himself and already wondering how to rip her off.

Glancing down at the crumbs, she started to count slowly to twenty, breathing in. Breathing out. Mindful of her surroundings. The sound of the beeping car horns. The stink of the car. The trash that was strewn along the edges of the road. *Stop panicking. You can totally pull this off. Languages have always been your thing.*

But the traffic had ground to a halt. Fanning herself against the oppressive Central American heat that rose in rippling waves from the cars in front, George pondered whether she should talk to this stranger. Was it safe? He was about 50. Wore a clean, pressed white shirt and slacks. He didn't look like trouble. He was almost certainly somebody's father.

'Where do you live?' he asked, pre-empting her. Raising his voice to be heard over the Latin music that played on the car's stereo. A statue of the Virgin Mary dangled from the rear-view mirror, swinging to and fro as the car inched forwards.

'I bet working as a taxi driver in this city is the most interesting job in the world,' she said, sidestepping his question. Treating him to her killer smile when he glanced at her through the mirror.

'Oh, I don't know about that,' he said, laughing. 'It's stressful.'

'Why?'

George could see the man start to blink repeatedly. Saw his shoulders stiffening. 'Go on,' she said. 'I'm just a boring old city worker. You can tell me. I don't know anyone scary!' Smiled again, trying to look as winsome as possible.

'The war tax,' he said after a period of silence that lasted for almost half a song. 'Having to give those pricks a big chunk of my earnings just to park outside the airport.'

'What, the police?' she asked.

Through the mirror he gave her a disbelieving look. 'No. They're thieving bastards, but they're not as bad as the gangs. The gangs have even started taking "war tax" from parents whose kids go to school. Did you know that? My sister-in-law can't afford to give her son a packed lunch because she's handed over his dinner money to some robbing bastard with an AK-47. This place has gone to hell.'

'Which gangs?' George asked.

The driver's stare in the mirror became suddenly hard and hostile. 'Even a posh girl from out of town like you should know what I'm talking about,' he said. 'You're a reporter, aren't you?'

'No!' George said, shaking her head vigorously, realising she had aroused his suspicion. Asking the wrong person too many questions in a place like Tegucigalpa got you shot. This wasn't Southeast London where she could blend in. One of the locals. This was …

The driver abruptly applied the handbrake and turned round, peering beyond George, through the back window.

'Oh, Jesus,' he said. 'This doesn't look good.'

He applied the central locking. George's breath came short. She gripped the seat belt that didn't quite work, wondering what the hell was going on. On the outside lane, mopeds cruised past, carrying shirtless young men, covered in tattoos. George blinked hard. The tattoos covered their heads and necks as well as their torsos. Peering into each car. As they approached the taxi, she shrank towards the driver's side window. *Look the other way*, she told herself. But as the men on the final moped slowed and pulled up alongside them, she couldn't help but meet the gaze of the man on the back, who ducked to peer into the taxi. The features of his face were barely discernible beneath the heavy patterning of symbols, skulls and numbers in dark blue-grey ink on his brown skin. But his eyes shone with youth, focus and mischievous intent.

This was no Danny Spencer. This guy was in a different league. Barely into manhood, this moron on the moped would eat five Dannys for breakfast and still be hungry for more.

Turning away, finally, George sensed that they had moved on. She looked up. The mopeds were some way ahead now.

'The maras,' she said, exhaling gratefully.

'Don't even say their names,' the driver said. 'Just thank God they weren't coming for either of us.'

Leaning forwards in her seat, George watched the men's progress further down the traffic queue. About two hundred metres in front, they stopped – one moped pulling in front of and the other alongside a people carrier. Drew their guns.

'Here we go,' the taxi driver said. 'Look away, miss. You don't need to see this. And get down.' He ducked over his handbrake and rested his head on the passenger seat.

But George was still watching, open-mouthed, as the gang-members pulled a middle-aged man from the people carrier and shot him in the head several times. They sped off on the mopeds, leaving the dead body of their unfortunate target in the middle of the road.

'Jesus Christ on a bike!' George shouted in English. 'I don't fucking believe what I just saw.' Then she remembered she was meant to be from El Salvador and repeated similar sentiments in Spanish. But it was too late.

'You lied,' the taxi driver said. He turned around to size her up properly. He was still speaking in Spanish, at least. 'You're American. You *are* a reporter.'

George sighed heavily. Shook her head. 'No. British.' She bit her lip sheepishly, still speaking in the El Salvadoran Spanish, though the game was now up. 'I work at a university in England. I'm trying to find my father.' Feeling honesty was the only route available to her, she pulled the photograph of her father from her rucksack. Showed it to the driver. 'Michael Carlos Izquierdo Moreno,' she said. 'He was Spanish but working for the engineering firm where you're taking me. They've also got a big facility up in the hills somewhere.'

Taking the photo from her, the driver studied her father's earnest-looking face and shook his head. 'Don't recognise him. Sorry,' he said. Turning back to the road ahead and gripping his steering wheel, they moved off slowly, drawing closer to the dead man in the middle of the road, who was now surrounded by five or six passers-by. 'What happened to your father?'

George told him the story of how he had been abducted at gunpoint from a corporate minibus, destined for the rural outpost of his employer. Explained that he hadn't been seen since.

The driver shrugged. 'As you can see,' he said, steering his taxi slowly around the body in the middle of the almost gridlocked street. 'That sort of thing happens all the time, here. Unless you can afford to live behind high walls and barbed wire and get yourself a bodyguard, you're at the mercy of the gangs from the moment you get up to the moment you go to sleep, and every goddamned minute in between. And, more often than not, the police either turn a blind eye or don't have the capacity to solve crimes. I get robbed. My son gets robbed. You don't walk through the parks at night, here. You don't walk through the parks during the day! This is Honduras!' Honking his horn and carving up a yellow school bus, he was finally free of the traffic and picked up pace.

'I might be wasting my time. Maybe he's dead …' George said, peering at the buildings that now appeared more robustly built as they neared the commercial centre. In the distance, the Bank of Honduras loomed. It was as though some big gleaming corporate block of glass and concrete had been shipped in from the City of London and simply plonked in the middle of a down-at-heel Central American capital. Thick cables spanned the length of the street overhead, weeds grew from the central reservation and verdant mountains provided an unlikely backdrop. The sort of country where the rich got richer and there was zero trickle-down effect. A broken country. The ultimate banana republic.

'Lady, if he's dead, he'd have been found in the middle of the street, like that poor bastard back there.' He gesticulated towards the scene of the carjacking with his thumb. Took a cigarette from the packet in his shirt pocket and lit up. 'You smoke?'

George took one of the loosely packed cigarettes and lit up. Offered thanks, mulling over the opportunity that had suddenly presented itself.

'What's your name?' she asked, studying the back of the driver's head.

'Javier,' he said. 'But I'm not telling you my family name!' He grinned, showing off a mouth full of nicotine-stained teeth in the mirror. Indicated and pulled into a parking bay by a medium-sized concrete block. The head office of her father's employer, Earhart Barton.

Reaching into her handbag, George pulled out a sheaf of US dollars. 'Wait for me while I'm in there,' she said. 'And then, I've got a proposition for you.'

CHAPTER 26

Mexico, a Cancun police station, 27 May

'These are the photos of the kids that were found dead in New York,' John Baldini told Van den Bergen. He laid fourteen photographs onto the table in the stiflingly hot office of the police station. 'This is what *mi amigo* Gonzales here asked me to come down to Cancun to talk to you about.' He tapped the corner of one of the photos with a meaty finger. A rippling mass of testosterone and policing enthusiasm, representing God's own country, apparently – the US of freaking A.

The DEA officer had been a surprise introduction to Van den Bergen's itinerary. Met at the airport by his Mexican counterpart, Juan Felipe Gonzales himself, Van den Bergen had been transported to the local police station in a Policía Federal black-and-white pick-up truck. In a cage of sorts in the loading area behind the cab, three helmeted, Kevlar-clad members of the Gendarmería had been standing to attention, clutching what appeared to be army-issue rifles.

'You didn't have to go to all this trouble,' Van den Bergen had said absently, forcing a smile, thinking all the while about George's sudden disappearance into the crowds at the airport, bound, no doubt, for one of the onward destinations that flashed up on the departures board. He had swallowed down a lump of fear, relieved that Gonzales had no inkling as to how a Dutch Chief Inspector normally looked. For all the Mexican had known, panic-stricken might have been Van den Bergen's default expression. 'Is this how you normally travel?'

'This is Mexico, my friend,' Gonzales had said, keen eyes on the taxi drivers and tourists that swarmed around them. He had gestured that Van den Bergen should get in the vehicle promptly. 'Welcome, Paul!'

Inside the truck, Van den Bergen's jet-lagged mind had been so overtaxed with lack of sleep and worry about his lover, he had barely taken in the new, colourful world that flashed by, brightly lit by strong Caribbean sunshine. Lush and unfamiliar trees had studded the main boulevard that led from the airport. Modern buildings were square, flat-roofed in the main and cheaply constructed, with every wall stuccoed and painted either white, yellow or some other ice-cream shade. On the highway, which had been little more than a dual carriageway, battered trucks, mopeds and the odd gleaming people carrier or SUV from the States had weaved from lane to lane haphazardly. American-style school buses painted all over with startling Mayan designs had crawled along the slow lane, advertising some aquatic theme park called Xel-Ha. The route had hosted checkpoints of armed police every so often and had been peppered every now and then by the grand, manned entrances to holiday resorts and the high walls that surrounded them. He had been treated to glimpses of the perfect azure Caribbean Sea in the distance. These had been sights that should have refreshed a jaded brain that had grown accustomed only to the grind of work and the grey skies of Northern or Eastern Europe for decades. But Van den Bergen's party of two had been one member short, so he had been unable to concentrate on anything else.

'Where is Dr McKenzie?' Gonzales had asked, pausing in his ad hoc guided tour of the outskirts of Cancun, as if he had read Van den Bergen's mind. He had scratched at hairless cheeks that were pocked with acne scarring, giving him the appearance of a much younger man. Not a single grey hair among the black.

'Oh, she wasn't feeling well,' Van den Bergen had said, wondering why his mouth had spat out such a blatant lie while his brain had been diligently trying to work out a justifiable excuse as to why his criminology expert had absconded. 'Her suitcase turned up before mine, so she's gone straight to the hotel. Upset stomach.' He had tried to wince convincingly, patting his own stomach, which had concealed an inferno of stress-induced acid that could have engulfed the entire dense jungle of the Yucatan Peninsula in flames. Where the hell was George?

He had spent his first exhausting day sweating profusely in an office at the back of the police station, where the air conditioning had broken, learning about the difficulties faced by the Mexican Federales in policing a country on its knees.

'The cartels are entrenched,' Gonzales had told him in perfect English spoken with a Mexican accent that had a Texan tang to it. 'People are so poor and the politicians have failed them so often that gangs have gotten a foothold in small towns and villages.' He had run through a slide show of photos taken in rural locations where shirtless gang members had been arrested and lined up against graffitied walls, their hands cuffed behind them. Pictures of broken bodies, deep red blood pooling beneath them in the dazzling sunshine of bleached-out, dusty streets. Several shots of homespun meth labs that had been raided, set up in shabby kitchens or shacks built in the seclusion of thick jungle. Basic equipment stacked on picnic tables. Buckets and hoses and Bunsen burners connected to huge butane canisters. 'This is what we're up against,' he had said. 'If you're starving and can't get a job, and some scary, badass gang guy comes to you and offers you hard cash to get involved in this kind of thing or says he's going to kill you and your children if you don't keep your mouth shut, what are you going to do?'

Van den Bergen had shaken his head. Staring at a slide of a

tiny woman, standing by a shack that had been constructed from little more than sticks, with a thatched roof. Clutching a baby, with two other small children at her feet, the camera had caught her weeping as members of the Gendarmería had led a young man away in cuffs. 'Poverty. I get it. Not everybody can work in the hotel trade or get a job in a supermarket.'

'We're a transit country,' Gonzales had said. 'It's a simple matter of supply and demand. Colombian coke needs to find its way north to the USA. Central American countries are the only way through. While there's a culture of corruption in government and a desperate underclass that can barely feed itself, those cartel boys know they've got the entire country in the palm of their hands. That's where all the money and the power is. They're the real kings of Mexico and they're brutal. They kill with impunity. They traffic coke, people, guns ... whatever they can turn a profit from. Life is *worthless*. The law means *nothing* to them. They are afraid of *nobody*.' Gonzales had punctuated his points with a dismissive slice of his hand through the air. His lips had pursed. 'And the worst thing is, as the DEA and the Mexican police have clamped down on the coca coming in from South America, these clever sons of bitches worked out they can make meth on their own turf instead and make even more money. The entire world is their market.' He had thumped the table that had held the projector. 'Crystal methamphetamine is gonna be the death of this country if we're not careful. And it's already killing our kids.'

'And that's why I'm here,' Van den Bergen had said, nodding and wishing George was with him. He had pulled the files on the canal deaths from his bag and passed them to his Mexican counterpart.

'Tomorrow,' Gonzales had said, leafing through the notes on Floris Engels. 'You're gonna meet a friend of mine from the DEA. All the way from New York City. John Baldini. You'll like him. He's one of the good guys. And he's got information you're gonna be very interested in.'

And so it was that. Van den Bergen watched as John Baldini arranged the fourteen photos of seven dead kids on the table in the roasting hot office. A set of two photos for each victim – one taken while they had still been alive and the second, a forensics snap of their corpse.

The place was perfused with the smell of cheap disinfectant and too much deodorant that failed to mask a lingering undertone of stale sweat.

Van den Bergen surreptitiously sniffed his armpits. Regarded the images in front of him.

'They came to me from homicide because they were all poisoned by the same bad batch of crystal methamphetamine,' Baldini said. 'Same shit as you got over there in Amsterdam, Holland.'

'Lead poisoning?' Van den Bergen asked.

'Yes siree. Lucky for us, because they didn't see death coming for them, they didn't throw the meth down some storm drain or flush it in case they got picked up by the cops. All but one of them still had crystals on their person. Mainly, we found them collapsed on the street in the Meatpacking District, downtown, and they all died in the small hours. It's real busy round there, but under cover of darkness – I guess a guy could still pass out and just be taken for some bum who liked his liquor too much. It's New York City. You know? Ain't it the same in Amsterdam?'

Van den Bergen contemplated the comparison. Hadn't his victims been abandoned? Not quite. They had in the main disappeared into the water. Alone. 'No,' he said. 'We have a population of less than a million. I like to think it's nothing like New York. In London, maybe, you could die in a crowd and not be noticed. Bigger cities. But not Amsterdam.' He thumbed his goatee, feeling the sweat moisten his fingertips. Resolved to shave it off once he got back to the hotel. He was just too damned hot for an extra layer. 'If a body lies undiscovered in my city, it's generally because somebody wanted to hide it.'

Baldini and Gonzales exchanged a look that Van den Bergen couldn't be bothered to interpret. He tugged at his trousers that stuck to his thighs unpleasantly, mulling over the text he had received from George around 5 p.m. the previous evening.

```
I am alive. I love you.
```

That had been it. Nothing more. No detail of where she had gone, though he had asked Marie to find out what flight she had taken. Marie was taking a suspiciously long time coming back to him with the information, though. Bloody women, ganging together!

Feeling jet lag and anxiety tugging his attention span out of the room and away from the voices of the DEA agent and the Federale, he pinched himself on the back of the hand. Zoned back into the New Yorker's presentation.

'My guys in homicide … they figured these kids felt a little queasy, came out of a club. Badabing badaboom. The bad meth had gotten into their bloodstream. They were dead pretty damn quick.'

'Lucky they weren't robbed,' Gonzales said, raising an eyebrow.

'I know, right?' Baldini bumped fists with the Mexican detective. 'Sometimes you get lucky, you get a piece of the puzzle you'd been missing. That's what makes our job the greatest. Am I right?' He turned to Gonzales and grinned.

'*Exactamente*, bro!'

Sipping from a plastic cup of coffee that was too strong and which was wreaking havoc with his stomach, Van den Bergen clicked his tongue on the roof of his mouth. Popped a paracetamol from a blister pack and swallowed it with the bitter drink. Fixed Gonzales with a questioning stare. 'Why am I only hearing about this match now? How can you be sure?'

Before Gonzales could answer, Baldini leaned forwards, balancing both elbows on the table which made his overdeveloped biceps look like thick, gnarled branches on a tree. 'My *hombre*

177

Gonzales here forwarded me the email you sent to him, containing the chemical composition of the meth you found on your latest dead guy. You gotta interpret the data like analysing a fingerprint. And our lab guy found it's an exact match.'

'My people in the Mexican Polícia Federal Ministerial narrowed it down to having been manufactured near here,' Gonzales said. 'I would make an educated guess that there's some meth lab in the Yucatan jungle churning this crap out. We will find it.' He smiled and nodded sagely.

Picking up two of the photos, Van den Bergen pushed his glasses onto his nose and contemplated the faces – a young man of about 20 and a girl of no more than 18. Scabbing around their mouths and dead eyes. All of the seven victims appeared far older than the ages shown in their case files.

'Meth plays havoc with dental health,' Van den Bergen said, tutting as he scrutinised the photos where the victims were smiling; scowling at the rotten, blackened stumps that counted for teeth, barely embedded in receding, florid gums. 'These are almost as horrible as the postmortem photos.' He touched his own carefully tended teeth. Grimaced. 'Christ! That must have been very painful. Didn't these kids see your anti-drugs poster campaigns with the dried-up old junkies? Even I've seen them!'

Both his American and Mexican counterparts laughed dryly, making Van den Bergen feel like he was missing some kind of joke. Were they laughing at him, he wondered? If George was here, she'd be able to pick up any sarcasm in their English that he might otherwise miss. Or irony. Except he probably did irony better than them. And why weren't they bothered by the insane heat and humidity? He watched them, patting nonchalantly at their glistening foreheads with folded tissues as if it wasn't thirty-seven degrees outside. As if he wasn't a wringing wet spectacle, wearing suiting that was designed for the distinctly non-balmy climes of Bijlmer, where it was a steady twelve degrees with a stiff wind coming off the North Sea, all summer long. And how much of a freak did he feel, towering over Gonzales – a tiny barrel-chested descendant of the Maya – with his six feet five of white hairy limbs like some ludicrous albino spider? Where the hell was George to tell him that he was a passable-looking human being?

Juan Felipe Gonzales held up one of the photos of a young man. Clearly a mugshot that had been taken in some police station in downtown NYC. 'Kids like this don't pay attention to advertising campaigns, my friend,' he told Van den Bergen. 'Maybe kids who go to college and have parents who care. They're the kind that listen to good advice and act on it. Not these kids.' There was sadness in his half-smile.

Gonzales' gold tooth and slicked-back black hair glinted under the fluorescent lighting, giving him the look of a tubby 1980s porn star, Van den Bergen imagined. George would say he was being uncharitable. But then George wasn't bloody well there. Acid erupted along his gullet at the thought of her gallivanting on her own on some wild-goose chase in a gang-ravaged shithole … Best not to think about it.

'They're no different from our boys and girls who get sucked into the cartels as street dealers, lookouts, informants, muscle … By the time kids like this wind up dead, they've usually got rap sheets as long as their arms. Am I right, John?' Gonzales turned to the stocky American.

'You sure are, buddy,' Baldini said, patting at his shaved head with the tissue paper. 'These kids get sucked in young – usually through peer pressure and lack of opportunity.' He thumped himself on the chest. Van den Bergen was just about to offer him an antacid when he started to speak again. 'New York's a fucking great city and I'm proud to live there …' Not acid reflux. It had just been some overly dramatic show of civic pride. 'But there are still some tough neighbourhoods. There's just too many damn kids using drugs to deal with the boredom or dull the pain of a shitty home life. Some of them just wanna get laid easy.' The muscles in his bull neck flinched.

John Baldini picked up a plastic glass of water and held it with a degree of swagger. Made a smacking sound with his lips as he sated his thirst. Van den Bergen noted how he sat with his legs slightly apart. Was this the sort of alpha male who never doubted his place in the world or that his life was evolving exactly as he would wish it to? He brought his own bony knees together and resolved never to sit with his legs astride like that again.

'Anyway, the reason we're here today, gentlemen,' Baldini said, holding those meaty arms aloft like a pontificating, pumped-up Jesus, 'is that Gonzales here has got a problem with some douche in his jurisdiction supplying toxic waste that's infesting the whole fucking world. And you, Van den Bergen … you and me got the same pain in the ass. We both got tax-paying citizens dying on the back of this shit. Gentlemen, we got work to do in Cancun.'

'Well said, bro,' Gonzales said, glancing at his watch. He slapped his paunch. 'But first, lunch.' Turned to Van den Bergen. 'How about I take you for some traditional Mexican food?'

'Like last night?' Van den Bergen asked, scowling. 'That chicken?'

Gonzales nodded. 'Sure. I know a place does the best *burritos* and *churros* in town. Or you wanna *quesadilla*? They got refried beans, fresh salsa, guacamole, cheese …' He kissed the tips of his fingers.

Shit, Van den Bergen thought. *More of that spicy salsa crap.* The raw onions and garlic had played havoc with his digestion all night long. 'Can I get a ham sandwich?' he asked, removing his glasses and letting them hang at the end of their chain.

For the second time, Gonzales and Baldini exchanged a knowing look.

CHAPTER 27

Honduras, a barrio in the mountains above Tegucigalpa, at the same time

'Get up!' the woman said, kicking the metal frame of George's bed.

Opening her eyes, George caught sight of her roommate. A dark-skinned woman who was perhaps in her mid-twenties. Her long black hair was tied back in a utilitarian ponytail. Like the others, she wore black combat trousers and a simple black vest.

'Paola, isn't it?' she said in Spanish.

'You want something to eat?' Paola folded her arms, partially obscuring the delicate artistry of her tattoos that scrolled from her wrists to her shoulders, disappearing beneath the sleeves of her vest where the ink reappeared on her neck, winding up onto her cheeks. The girl threw a bottle of water to George.

Sitting up, George rubbed her face and unscrewed the lid of the bottle. Her stomach churned at the thought of drinking from a receptacle that somebody else had drunk from. She didn't dare look down at the thin camp bed she had spent the night on. Memories of the cockroaches that had scattered in the dead of the night when Paola had switched the naked bulb on almost took George's breath away. But she knew she had to keep cool.

'Thanks. Yes. That would be great.'

Paola picked up a rucksack that hung from a hook above her own cot. Rummaged inside. Reached up to a shelf that contained a bible and two photos of an old woman cuddling a grinning toddler and grabbed a box. 'Maritza will sort you out with some ammo and your own gun once you've eaten. Make it snappy though. We've got to be in the truck and ready to go in twenty minutes. Okay?' She stuffed the box into her bag. George caught sight of it – rounds of bullets. Then the girl reached under her cot and retrieved what George guessed to be a semi-automatic rifle, the kind she had only ever seen in films before. 'You know how to handle one of these?' Paola asked?

'Naturally,' George lied, trying to look as hard and as knowledgeable as possible under the circumstances.

Once her roommate had left the shack, George bent double on her mattress, dry-heaving from the stink of refuse coming from outside. She batted fat black flies away that darted around her head, on the brink of tears. Suddenly, the dark days of her girlhood seemed like playtime compared to this hell on earth. And she knew it would get worse.

'What have I done?' she asked under her breath. 'I must be fucking mental.'

What time was it? She peered through the open hole in the corrugated sheeting that served as a window. The sun was already up, but not high. Surreptitiously, she sneaked a peak at her Longines watch that Van den Bergen had bought her for her twenty-fifth birthday. Only 6 a.m. and the sweat was already pouring down her back and trickling in rivulets from beneath her breasts.

'Shit. The tats.' Holding her breath, she slid her boots onto her bare feet and padded to the window, holding her left arm aloft to examine it in the daylight; peering down at her chest. Exhaled heavily when she saw that they had not smudged in the night. She padded back to her cot to check that they had not rubbed off onto the sheets either. No sign of the ink having transferred onto the greying bedlinen.

But the ink had dulled somewhat, having soaked into her skin. Taking the black permanent felt tip with a shaking hand and a thudding heart, she carefully started to retrace the pen over the intricate patterns of the giant, stick-on tattoos she had pre-ordered from the internet. They weren't a million miles away from the ink sported by gang members of an El Salvadoran mara and the temporary tattoos had promised to be wash-proof for up to a fortnight.

'Oh, shit, shit, shit!' she said, trying and failing to be neat but swift. 'Why the fuck didn't I pay more attention in art? Come on, you bungling turd. Fuck it!' She stopped. Inhaled deeply and spoke to the bare bulb that hung from a cable suspended on a hook in the shack's ceiling. 'I bet Van den Bergen would do a brilliant job of this.'

In the late afternoon of the previous day, in the relative safety and calm of the taxi driver's modest three-roomed house in a poor suburb of Tegucigalpa in the hills, George had begun her transformation with the temporary tattoos, watched by the driver's children. They had been fascinated by her, but his wife had expressed her misgivings with undisguised hostility.

'If they discover she is a fraud,' the wife had said, speaking through gritted teeth as she kneaded dough at the kitchen table, 'and they trace it back to you, they'll find you, you idiot! They're going to come to our house and kill the lot of us. You, me, the kids. Finished. They'll dump our bodies in the street to set an example.'

'You're overreacting,' he had said. 'She's not going to lie … much, are you?' He had turned to George and had nodded encouragingly at her.

George had paused in her tattooing exercise and had turned to the four small children who had been watching her so intently. The youngest – perhaps 3 years old – had been sucking her thumb, tugging at the hem of her food-stained dress. Big brown eyes watching George's every move. The child had treated her to a coy smile when she had paused her careful application to survey her audience.

Swallowing hard, George had realised that a fistful of dollars wasn't enough to compensate the taxi driver for the enormous risk he was taking on her behalf. 'I'm very good at this,' she had said, trying to calm the agitated wife. 'I've done this before. I've been in a gang back home. I know how to make them think I'm one of them. Honestly, you've got to trust me. Your husband trusts me.'

'It's the only way she stands a chance of finding her father,' the driver had said.

His wife had treated him to a sceptical glare, uttering something so quickly in some Tegucigalpan dialect that George failed to follow her retort. In response, he had waved the roll of money George had given him. 'We can't afford to turn this down, my love.'

Knowing that she wore an expensive Longines watch on her wrist that would probably keep this family fed for several months, George had almost been tempted to give that to them in addition to the dollars. But sentimentality had stayed her tongue. She had remembered Van den Bergen presenting her with the box on her birthday, fastening the leather strap around her wrist with gentle fingers. Giving away something with such sentimental value would hurt, she had known, and later in her quest, if she made it that far, she had reasoned that the Swiss watch might well serve as currency that might spare her life in a world where money spoke the loudest.

'What in God's name are you going to do with her?' the wife had asked.

'I need to get to the Chiapas,' George had said, trying to engage with the woman who could end her Central American venture and her life simply by leaving her house and waiting for a member of one of the maras to walk by.

'Guatemala?' the woman had asked. 'I thought you said he was taken by a local gang.'

George had nodded. 'Yes. But my father's last boss introduced me to one of the other employees who had been on the work's shuttle bus the day it got held up. He had a theory ...'

Her memory of visiting the corporate HQ of Earhart Barton had still been fresh enough for George to recollect the pitch of the man's voice and the bone structure of his face that marked him out as having a mix of both Spanish and native Honduran ancestry. Her father's colleague, Diego, had been dressed in smart trousers and a crisp shirt. He had had a gentle voice that she had strained to hear above the whir of the air conditioning.

'Kidnappings happen all the time in Tegus,' he had said. 'The gangs make sizeable amounts of money from them. I have a guard outside my house. The firm had provided Michael with one too, I believe. He got perks as an overseas worker. They must have been paying him damned well to lure him over here.' He had examined his almost delicate draughtsman's hands and sighed. 'When my contract ends in two months, I'm going to the United States. I've been offered a job – it's the opportunity I've been praying for for years. I can't wait to get me and my family out of this hellhole.' George had been able to see desperation and guilt in his eyes in equal measure.

'So what do you think happened to my father?' she had asked. 'Your boss told me the police had investigated it for two days and then dropped it, saying the trail went cold.'

Diego had folded his arms. Adjusted his glasses. Sighed contemplatively. 'Michael was my friend. I still miss him. He was a good guy. When he was taken, I read the newspapers avidly for weeks to see if any other professionals had been kidnapped. I watched news and those shitty reality TV shows that cover the "murders as they happen". You seen them?'

George had nodded. 'I've seen clips on YouTube.'

'Well, I pieced the information together and from what I could gather, the maras snatch targeted individuals to order.'

'What do you mean? Who orders it?'

'The Mexican cartels, usually. There have been quite a few skilled engineers and scientists taken over the last few years. Just disappeared.' He had mimed a puff of smoke erupting with those delicate fingers. 'If you look at old news reports online, you can see some have been found dead as far north as Tijuana.'

'Did they find any alive?' George had asked, inadvertently placing a hand over her heart and recalling the sight of her father's black hair and hairy forearms as she had sat on his shoulders.

Shaking his head, Diego had glanced furtively towards the window. 'I don't know. But basically, the dead guys were engineers, architects, scientists ... skilled men and women. They had been trafficked north from other Central American countries by the cartels to design and supervise the build of more sophisticated tunnels through to San Diego or better meth labs in the jungle or ...' He had leaned forwards, staring at George's chin with something bordering on enthusiasm. 'I even heard of them being forced to design semi-submersibles for smuggling drugs along the coast.'

'So your theory is that the maras stole my father to sell to a Mexican cartel.'

Diego had nodded energetically. 'Definitely. If they had only wanted ransom, they would have come to our boss with their guns held high and their hands out. Your dad was testing a prototype for a new airline jet engine at our facility in the mountains. Anybody with a laptop could find out he had experience in working on aeronautical projects and that he had worked for the Armada Española too – the Spanish navy.'

George acknowledged the pain of a fleeting pang of guilt that she had never once tried to Google her father, despite her fond memories of her infancy. Too busy wallowing in her own melodrama and emotionally stunted by some perverse loyalty to Letitia.

'If I was a cartel boss and I wanted to build, say, one of these semi-submersibles or some kind of transportation for my drugs and trafficked people,' Diego continued, 'I'd want to recruit a man like Michael. Or me! Or any of the other hundred-plus engineers who work here.'

'But they picked on my father, didn't they?' George had raised an eyebrow. A nasty, sneaking suspicion crawling along her every synapse that the phenomena of disappearing Daddy Dearest, absconded Letitia the Dragon and the bogus emails, sent to her from some server in the Americas, were almost certainly linked. 'If my dad had been trafficked north to the Mexican cartels, where would they do the handover, do you think?' she had asked …

'*Chiapas?*' the taxi driver's wife had said. 'She wants to get to Chiapas? Why doesn't she get a bus or the train north like a normal person? Why take her to meet *them*? Are you mad?'

'It's what she wants,' the driver had said, shrugging. 'And I know where they hang out.'

George had nodded eagerly, willing the woman to collude. 'It's the only way,' she had said. 'If the cops want to brush my father's disappearance under the carpet and if his ex-colleague was right about cartel involvement, I need to get on the inside.' She had held her hands aloft in a gesture of surrender. 'All I need is to hitch a ride to the right part of town and for your husband to point me in the direction of their safe house. I won't mention your names. Nobody will ever know about your involvement, señora. I promise.'

The journey to the *barrio* had taken them further up into the mountains. At dusk, they had snaked through winding roads that had been little more than shack-lined dirt tracks. With the sun setting, enshrouding the city in an incredible orange-pink light, the distant views had been spectacular from the passenger seat of the white taxi on those stretches of road that took them over open ground, unobscured by dwellings. But close up, George had been appalled by landslides of trash that seemed to pour down the upper slopes in 200-metre tracts, as though a volcano had erupted over Tegucigalpa, spewing used water bottles and filthy nappies instead of molten lava on the hillside occupants. The smell of putrefying effluent and food waste had started to come through the air-conditioning, filling the taxi with a choking stink.

'Jesus,' she had said to the driver. 'Doesn't the city council collect the rubbish? This is appalling.'

He had merely laughed in response.

As they had travelled deeper into the sprawling, ramshackle *barrios*, George had started to question to wisdom of her chosen route to Guatemala. But it had been too late.

'We are deep in gang territory now,' her companion had said. 'Look!'

He had gesticulated with his chin towards a makeshift bar, which had been little more than a shack, containing a fat woman who had been sitting beside a plastic table, selling bottles of beer from a barrel full of ice. Outside, a group of about ten young men had gathered in the satanic-looking red light of the sunset. They had been drinking beer and laughing at each other's jokes. Nothing unusual there, in a warm place where beer was in ready supply at sundown. But George had toyed nervously with the strap of her rucksack and had removed her watch when she had caught sight of the bodies of these men.

They had all worn the same kind of baggy jeans, low-slung at the waist, showing the tops of their pants above the waistline – the same style that George had seen every day of the week gracing the bottom half of wide boys on the streets of London. But on their naked top halves, they had all been covered in the same kind of tribal tattoos that she had seen sported by the guys on the mopeds, hours earlier on her journey from the airport to her father's place of employment. Blue-black or black ink covering every inch of their skin, from their waistlines upwards. All had either shaved heads or close crops. In many of the men, the tattoos had ended at the neckline and their heads were clear of markings, but there had been a frightening few who had been inked all over with carefully crafted skulls, numbers, words, flowers and the faces, presumably, of loved ones or the fallen. George had found them, in equal parts, mesmerising and terrifying.

'You're in the lion's den, now,' her driver had said. 'Are you armed?'

'No,' George had said, gulping and wondering if Van den Bergen would ever forgive her for being so utterly stupid. Would he refuse to mourn her on principle for leaving him alone? *Pull yourself together, you weak-as-piss, wimpy cow*, she had chided herself silently. *You made a decision to leave the safety of Cancun for a damned good reason. See this through. You'd regret it for the rest of your life if you don't.* 'I'll be fine. I'm pretty handy with a rucksack and my fists.' She had glanced over at him, giving a weak and unconvincing smile.

The driver had tutted and slowed. Reached over to open his glove compartment and had pulled out a large hunting knife in a sheath. 'Here,' he had said. 'Take this. A good-looking young girl like you will attract the wrong attention out here.'

'But where you're taking me, I'll be safe from those guys, won't I?' she had asked, taking a lingering look at the gang members as the taxi sped off up the dirt track.

'Once you're out of my car, you're on your own,' he had said. 'They might reject you. If that happens ...' He had drawn a line across his neck with his index finger.

'We'll see,' George had said, the sensible academic in her still wondering if she could ask the driver simply to take her back to the airport, saying it had all been a terrible mistake.

'Here we are,' he had said.

Darkness had fallen in earnest. They had pulled up outside a shack that was lit by bare bulbs strung from the ceiling; moths fluttering to and fro past the yellow light, battering themselves against the bulb's glass. Inside, she had glimpsed three women, sitting on a dilapidated sofa, cleaning rifle parts as they had watched some glitzy show on a small TV set.

'I wish you the best of luck,' the driver had said, clasping her hands inside his. 'May God watch over you.' He had crossed himself and patted her on her cheek. 'Go! Find your father.'

As the taxi had turned back towards the safer suburbs, its red tail-lights glowing in the distance and becoming ever smaller, George had taken a deep breath.

'Come on, Dr McKenzie. It's showtime.'

Rifles had clicked into action the moment she had set foot inside that sweaty shack. George had been faced with the women she had seen through the window on approach, plus about eight more who had appeared from another room at the back of the shack.

'Who the fuck are you?' a middle-aged woman had asked, stalking towards George and poking the butt of her rifle into George's newly inked shoulder. She had had the same Salvadoran accent that George had tried to perfect; covered in similar tattoos to the ones George had seen on male gang members, winding their way out from the collar and sleeves of a black T-shirt that sported a faded print of the skeletal yet beautiful figure of Santa Muerte. A deep scar that bubbled up along the woman's left cheekbone had left George in no doubt that this was not someone to trifle with. She had appraised George with all the analytic skill of a scanner. 'What are you doing here?'

'Who the fuck are you?' George had asked, hoisting her bag high on her shoulder so that her convincing temporary tattoos had been clearly on show. 'I was told by Nikolay that I'd find you here.'

All eyes had been trained on her. All rifles had been pointed at her head, poised to end her relatively short life in as long as it took to pull a trigger.

'Nikolay?' the woman had asked, her thick black eyebrows

190

drawing together to make her one of the hardest-looking individuals George had ever met.

Her heart had beat so fast and so loudly, George had been certain the woman would be able to hear it or, at least, sense her mortal fear. 'Nikolay Bebchuck. I got into trouble back home with the police, so I went over to work in Europe,' she had said. 'First for The Duke in London, doing a bit of dealing and minding his girls who work in his clubs, until he got sent down. Then, for Nikolay in Amsterdam. He said you'd be able to fix me up with work.'

'Where are you from? You're not one of us but you look like one of us and sound familiar but not quite right. Are you a cop?' There had been fury in the woman's eyes at the mere possibility. She had widened her aggressor's stance and had moved the barrel of the rifle up to George's throat.

Unrest had erupted suddenly in that foetid-smelling claustrophobic metal box, with the younger women registering their mistrust of George at the tops of their voices. What had followed had been a fast and brutal-sounding exchange of words between the women. Then, silence as the rest of the group had clearly deferred to the frightening woman in the Santa Muerte T-shirt.

At that moment, George had been sure that she was about to be killed. There had not even been space in her head for thoughts of Van den Bergen. Only the basic survival instinct that she should keep her breathing even and maintain eye contact with her inquisitor at all costs.

'You're a cop,' the woman had repeated.

'I'm not a cop. Do I look like a fucking cop?' George had laughed, whilst rifling through her mental files of all the things she had researched before embarking on this trip that, at that moment, felt tantamount to a suicide mission. Finally, a useful detail had presented itself and she had made a hand sign of a Salvadoran mara. Another long shot. But the body language of the women in the room had seemed to soften slightly and George had noticed the odd nod and wry smile. 'I'm originally from San Salvador,' she had said, manufacturing an air of confidence by carefully controlling her breathing and projecting her speech. 'Salvadoran father and a black British mother. That's why I sound a bit different. That's how I came to spend time in Europe for a few years. But now I'm back and I'm here, hoping you can use my experience and another pair of big cojones – the kind only a woman has!'

The rifle's position had not moved. The other women had clearly been put at their ease by the gang hand sign but their leader had been no such pushover.

'How come you're in Honduras, looking for work with the *transportistas*?' she had asked. 'We've got all the girls we need. And we don't need drug dealers. We're gun smugglers and hired muscle.'

'I'm on the trail of someone who owes me money,' she had said. 'A Spaniard named Michael Carlos Izquierdo Moreno. You heard of him?'

'No.'

'Someone told me he was taken off a bus in Tegus a while ago and shipped north by the maras to work for a Mexican cartel. An engineer. But this bastard owes me three thousand dollars and when I find him …' In a move that had been so deft that the other women in the room had gasped audibly, George had reached into the waistband at the back of her jeans and whipped out the hunting knife that the taxi driver had given her. She had brandished it beneath the lightbulb so that it glinted menacingly; pointing it towards her opponent as though she feared nothing and was as loco in the coco as her alleged gang member status had suggested. 'If he's not got my money, I'm going to cut him from here …' She had almost touched the carotid artery of the *transportista* with the tip of the blade. 'To here.' Moving the blade down towards the woman's groin. 'But Nikolay sent me to Tegus with a message for one of his business associates. He said, once

I'd delivered it, if I wanted to earn some money and to track down this Moreno son of a bitch, you would be the women to go to. You could help me get to Chiapas.'

Engaged in a stand-off of sorts, the woman had held George's gaze for at least a full minute without speaking, as though she had been calculating whether this interloper constituted a risk worth taking.

Had they even heard of the mysterious Nikolay, the Eastern European drugs baron? It had been a long shot that his name might have travelled across the Atlantic, despite it being ubiquitous in Europe and there being a clear link through the drugs to Mexico.

'You'll sleep with Paola,' the woman had said, finally, lowering her rifle.

George had nodded solemnly, sliding her hunting knife back into its sheath. Inside she had been grinning like a demented hyena and mentally twerking her way around the shack but she had resolved it would be deadly to let her hard-woman mask slip for even a second. She had remembered how the toughest women had behaved and held themselves in prison. They had never revealed the slightest weakness and neither would she.

'My name's Maritza,' the woman had said.

'My name's Jacinta.' George had held out her hand, and Maritza had pre-empted her handshake with the gang sign.

'You answer to me,' she had said. 'Tomorrow, we set off for Nikolay's brothel in Palenque. I've got a truck full of AKs that I need to get to the boys up there. Maybe you'll get to see Nikolay himself. You can ask him about your guy, Izquierdo Moreno.' Maritza had pulled out a cigarette and lit it, blowing smoke into George's face. She had held out the packet as some gesture of solidarity, perhaps. 'And by the way …' She had curled her lip, making her scar deepen. 'Did you get your tattoos done by a blind man? They're terrible!'

Amid gales of laughter, George hadn't been able to move her hands momentarily. She had felt the blood freezing into ice crystals inside her veins. 'Hang on. Are you saying Nikolay's here? In Central America?'

'Oh yes,' Maritza had said, foisting the cigarette on her. 'He has several names. Over here, we call him *el cocodrilo*.'

And so it was, the following morning, George put the freshening touches to her tattoos under the light of the bare bulb, knowing that by sundown, she might meet Nikolay Bebchuck face to face: the man whom she was supposed to work for and be on good terms with.

'Come on, Jacinta,' Paola said, standing at the doorway as George slid her felt-tip pen into her bag.

'How long have you been there?' George asked. Had she witnessed George drawing on her arm and chest?

But Paola didn't answer. 'The truck's ready,' she said, staring at the ink on George's collarbone. 'Get your things. We're leaving.'

CHAPTER 28

Amsterdam, Onze Lieve Vrouw Hospital, 28 May

'You might be leaving today,' Elvis said, keeping his disingenuous voice as bright as possible. 'Once we get you home, I'll get you nice and comfortable in front of the television. Would you like that? I've ordered you a box set of an American TV series called *Atlantic Boardwalk*. It should be delivered tomorrow, with any luck, so there's plenty to watch. And I think you'll like it, Mum. It's all about the Prohibition era. You love that historical stuff, don't you?' Elvis stroked his mother's hand, making a conscious effort not to look directly into her eyes, lest he see the end in hers and she see his secret in his.

The medical equipment that was sustaining her life hissed and bleeped industriously. But those reassuring sounds were all but drowned out by the rattling noise coming from her chest and the laboured sound of her breathing into the monstrosity of a mask that the doctors had put on her to get oxygen into her bloodstream. Glancing at it, he shuddered. It was more of a cage than a mask, with its metal head-straps and tubing, reminding him vaguely of a tie-fighter pilot from *Star Wars*. His mother had always hated *Star Wars*.

'I've got to go in a minute, Mum,' he said, finally steeling himself to look at her properly.

It was a terrible sight. His once robustly built, pink-cheeked mother was unrecognisable; wasting and wan in a hospital bed with just one skeletally thin arm visible above the bedding, plugged with cannulas, the skin wrinkled with malnutrition.

The dragging sensation that seemed to stretch his heart was a mixture of sorrow and guilt, he realised. He was certain that the end was near and yet, hadn't they both been here several times before, only to have been duped by antibiotics and fate? In truth, he wanted it over with, so that she would stop suffering and he could move on with his life instead of being trapped in this exhausting cycle of juggling work with caring and hospital visits. Part of him just wanted to be happy and experience the lighter side to life, like other men in their thirties did. Look forward with optimism. Enjoy the moment. Make plans.

But Elvis felt like the antithesis of a man in his prime at that moment. His epiphany with Arne, which promised much and gave him a tantalising glimpse of what could be, only served to make him feel distinctly sub-prime.

The dying are the most selfish people in the world, he thought. *Let go, Mum. Let's get this over with.*

While his mother was still alive, she was involuntarily sucking from him every ounce of energy and every minute of non-work time that he had. His mother would never ever sanction a relationship between two men, either. She was stealing his future and he was sick of it. Worse still, Elvis was wracked with crippling guilt for acknowledging such deep-seated resentment.

'I'm sorry, Mum,' he said, leaning over to kiss her forehead. She smelled of decaying skin and medicinal alcohol. He took the clean, small sponge the nurse had given him and moistened it in iced water. Lifted the mask momentarily so that the oxygen machine's reading plummeted abruptly, reducing the apparatus to a riot of alarm bells and flashing warning lights. He wiped his mother's mouth gently. Responding to his touch, she smacked her lips and stuck her tongue out to receive the moisture. 'I'm a shit son,' he said. Replacing the mask, waiting until the oxygen levels had risen again. Leaving.

Outside, his phone pinged with a text from Van den Bergen.

```
Can't get hold of Marie. Get her to text
me with George's location. I know she
knows. Tell her she's fired if she doesn't
tell me everything. And what's new on that
bastard Stijn Pietersen? The food here is
crap. It's too hot. I've got the shits.
VdB.
```

He was about to respond when he felt a tap on his shoulder.

'Hello, Detective,' a man said. 'I heard you're looking for information on the Rotterdam Silencer.'

With his fist drawn back, anticipating attack, Elvis spun around to see a grubby-looking man in his fifties, who wore yellowing jeans and a beat-up biker's jacket. His long grey hair hung about his shoulders in greasy tracts and was topped off with a bandana, giving him the air of an old Guns N' Roses roadie whom the years hadn't been kind to. Elvis knew exactly what sort of raddled eyes were behind the mirror shades.

'You?' he said, lowering his fist and laying his palm over his chest. He realised that the man must have been following him on a regular basis to have worked out that he would be visiting the hospital on his own at this time of day. 'I called you last week and you gave me an earful of bullshit about how you'd gone straight and didn't want to speak to the cops anymore. What the hell have you got to say that I'd want to hear?'

The man's scabbed lips peeled back to reveal a cartoon villain's grin of florid, receding gums and blackened stumps. 'For the right price, I'll tell you.'

CHAPTER 29

Mexico, Yucatan jungle, 30 May

'I want you to pilot the sub eastwards across the Caribbean Sea until you reach the Cayman Islands,' *el cocodrilo* said with a feverish excitement clearly audible in his voice. 'Then, you'll head past Cuba and Jamaica and skirt around to the Dominican Republic, where you'll be met at a secluded rendezvous point just off the coast, near Santo Domingo. Jorge will be given the co-ordinates for the sat nav, but you will be in charge of the vessel.'

Kneeling on the jungle floor by entrance to the cenote, the man held his hands behind his head, cowed by the sight of the pistol in *el cocodrilo*'s hand. Satisfied that the vessel was water-tight and functioning, his captor had decided that the semi-submersible should be brought up from its hiding place, at last, loaded with contraband and launched on its maiden voyage with him in it.

'You're making a mistake, *jefe*,' he said, squeezing his eyes shut to block out the sight of the weapon. 'I'm no sailor. I might have built the thing, but I'm the last man you should have piloting it on the high seas. Honestly.'

The impact of the pistol against his temple stung, whipping his head off to the side at an awkward angle; the vertebrae in his neck responding with a nauseating crack. Knocking his glasses to the dusty ground. Suddenly, *el cocodrilo* was kneeling beside him. He could smell his breath – stale beer, cigars and the sweet, fatty smell of cured meat.

'Listen, *mecánico*,' he said. 'It's my fucking millions of dollars have gone into building this tub ...'

In his peripheral vision, he could just about make out his captor's mouth – a cruel, mean mouth with no discernible lips. His mahogany-tanned European skin, deeply etched with crow's-feet, was blotched with deeper brown melanin spots on his cheekbones and forehead, testifying to too many years spent living in a climate to which he was genetically not well suited. *El cocodrilo* was an interloper, he reflected, and yet he had successfully embroidered himself in the fabric of the infamous Coba cartel. A successful schemer. A masterful manipulator. His realm was not just a few meth labs in the dense, sweaty tangle of the Yucatan jungle. This son of a bitch had the four corners of the world as his playground. So why was a cold-blooded monster with the international pretensions of a modern-day conquistador so hell-bent on prolonging his agony, when he could find much bigger, more entertaining sport elsewhere, he wondered?

'So, if I say *my mecánico* will captain *my* sub's maiden voyage, you'll do it, or I'll put a bullet in you – or worse.'

'You couldn't do worse. I'm your slave. And this is lunacy!' he said. 'You're planning to overload it, so it's going to sink anyway and kill everyone on board. That's physics, *jefe*. And I don't know how to chart the high seas.' He shook his head vigorously, imagining being shut into the belly of the vessel he had designed and built by hand over a period of years. Already gripped by claustrophobia, he found he was gasping for breath in the searing heat like a drowning fish. 'I know nothing about currents and tides or weather reports. Haven't I done everything you asked?' he asked, dimly aware of blood dripping from his temple to the jungle floor. 'I built you a semi-submersible that works. But I wanted you to let me test it at depth. It's still an unknown quantity beyond a few metres.'

El cocodrilo grabbed his chin and yanked his face upwards so that he was forced to look into those piercing blue eyes. Without the aid of the varifocal lenses in his spectacles, they were slightly fuzzy but no less terrifying. Eyes that delighted in the sight of human beings being eaten by the crocodiles he kept as pets.

'You've done everything I've told you to,' *el cocodrilo* said, 'because if you hadn't, I'd have killed you. And now, I'm telling you to pilot that fucking sub to the Dominican, so my meth can be loaded onto the cargo ship bound for Rotterdam in four days' time.'

A thick forearm reached forwards and plucked his glasses from the ground, handing them back to him.

'You'll need these,' Miguel said. Standing with his feet together, almost to attention, like a tubby, poorly trained soldier, *el cocodrilo*'s sidekick pointed to the crane that was perched by the entrance to the cenote. 'Here she comes, *jefe.*'

El cocodrilo was on his feet, watching, as the twelve-metre-long semi-submersible was winched clear of the cenote entrance and hoisted into the air. The surrounding jungle swallowed the sound of the men shouting instructions to one another. This way. Take it higher. Left a bit.

Silently, he sent a prayer skywards beyond the green canopy to the perfect cobalt-blue of the cloudless Mexican sky that he be forgiven for the part he had been forced to play in the inevitable demise and even deaths of those innocents who succumbed to the lure of whatever poison *el cocodrilo*'s men brewed in the jungle. It had never been his intention to collaborate with murderous traffickers, but he was just one of hundreds of scientists who were eking out miserable half-lives in the jungles, deserts and mountains of Central America, having been kidnapped by gangs and forced into professional servitude in aid of the cartels' drugs trade. There had only ever been one thought that had kept him going. Just the one precious thought of the one precious being, whose photo was concealed behind the back of his watch. He meditated on that photo now as the sub was lowered onto a trailer and towed into a road of sorts that had been hacked into the thicket.

A rifle in his back compelled him to stand.

'Move it,' Jorge said, kicking him in the ankles with heavy, dusty boots.

The musky smell of Jorge's sweat was overpowering. He was a stocky barrel of a man with bulging upper arms covered in the obligatory tattoos and cropped black hair that was thick and perfectly straight like carpet. Quintessentially gang material. They all dressed the same in low-slung jeans and vests. They all acted the same, like cloned Rottweilers on steroids. The thought of being trapped below the sea for three days in a vessel that was effectively a floating sarcophagus with this stinking, hostile brute was unbearable. He said nothing, however.

'And if you think you can take the easy way out of this by sinking that sub or trying to get us spotted by the coast guard in the hope that they'll rescue your sorry ass,' Jorge continued, 'I'll kill you with my own bare hands.'

'Thanks for the handy suggestion,' he said, quiet enough to go unheard.

Now, as they followed the sub's trailer, pulled by mules across the rutted land, under cover of the jungle's dense canopy, he contemplated how he might do exactly as Jorge had suggested. Get caught. It was the only way. Until now, he had had no opportunity whatsoever to contemplate escape. They had been watching him continually and he had had nothing but uninhabited wilderness and no water supply for miles around. But now … The risk of Jorge putting a bullet in him was high, but it was a calculated risk. How likely was it that one of these guys, when faced with the possibility of being caught red-handed by the Federales or coast guard, manning a sub that contained tonnes and tonnes of meth, would think first of saving his own skin and abandon that million-dollar tub before you could count *uno, dos, tres*? He allowed himself an almost imperceptible smile.

'What are you so damned happy about?' Jorge asked, poking him in the back with the sight of the rifle. Perhaps escaping this particular guard's beady-eyed stare was going to prove more difficult than anticipated.

'Nothing,' he said. 'I'm not happy. I'm looking forward to a change of scenery. That's all.'

Beyond the trees, he knew there was a glorious Caribbean sunset. The jungle was suffused with a pink glow. But as the daylight started to fail, the mosquitoes buzzed and whined around him, landing on his sweat-slick skin where it was exposed. Lightning-quick will-o'-the-wisps that he could never slap away before they had already drunk their fill of his blood. The itching would be unbearable later. At least in the cartel's secret compound, where he shared a shack with a kidnapped American chemist from San Diego, mosquito nets were provided for when darkness fell.

Three days in a boiling hot, poorly ventilated, overloaded sub with Jorge and arms and legs covered in mosquito bites, he thought. *I must have been some son of a bitch in a previous life to deserve this torture.* He wondered briefly if there was any mileage in praying to the skeletal figure of Santa Muerte, as the Mexican gang members did. Would she look kindly on him and help him to derail his journey along this particular route to the afterlife? Was that how these things worked?

Too bad he was no longer a religious man.

Even amid the cacophony of noise from the nocturnal jungle creatures as they came out to play and hunt, the growling of his empty stomach was audible. With sweat rolling off his emaciated frame at an unsustainable rate, his mouth had been dry and cracked at the edges for hours.

'Drink,' he said, his voice now little more than a croak.

'Sure. Share mine.' Jorge cracked open a new bottle of mineral water and drank thirstily until there were only one or two mouthfuls in the bottom. He grinned nastily. 'Don't take it all or I'll cut your greedy tongue out.'

Being careful to take only one swig, his concentration lapsed momentarily. He tripped on the root of a wild tamarind tree. Landed heavily on his knees, yelping. Insects scuttled away into the undergrowth. He imagined that he saw the spotted pelt of a muscular jaguar, moving stealthily in the tropical thicket, only metres away. He envied it its power and liberty.

'Get up, you useless piece of shit,' Jorge said, thumping him in the shoulder with the butt of the rifle. 'You want me to tell *el cocodrilo* that you'd sooner be pet food than captain his submarine?'

Shaking his head, he willed himself to stand tall, not wanting to show any emotional weakness. His pride and dignity were all he had left, after all. Though having shared a bucket as a latrine for years with the Texan chemist, there wasn't even much left of that.

The procession presently started to head down a slope that had been cut into the otherwise flat terrain of the jungle. The rumble of traffic was audible some way off. He calculated that it must be highway 307 that ran the length of the coast. Naturally, they would have to cross that somehow to get from the jungle interior to the sea.

Deeper and deeper they went, until walls of soil and tree roots rose above them on either side. In the twilight, he could make out an arch – the entrance to a tunnel, jet-black where the remaining light of the day could not penetrate. The rumble of traffic grew progressively louder, shaking the excavated ground. He could hear miniature landslides of sandy soil hitting the ground as it was dislodged by the weight of some heavy goods vehicle, thundering its way along the highway from the south up to Cancun with its delivery of bananas or trafficked and desperate

Mexicans and Guatemalans, hiding among produce, hoping to head across the Gulf of Mexico and into Florida under cover of darkness.

'Is the tunnel safe?' he asked Jorge. The scouts that led the group shone torches inside the underground path that danced in beams on the makeshift walls. 'Every time a truck goes over, that's a lot of weight to bear.'

'How the fuck should I know, *mecánico*?' Even in the murk of dusk, at least four metres below the floor of the jungle, he could see his guard's disparaging sneer. 'They've got plenty of dorks like you working for them. Maybe they got a tunnel genius or some shit to make it. You spend a couple of million dollars on a sub, you're not going to take a chance on a tunnel collapsing on your head are you?' He tutted. 'And stop fucking asking questions or I'll shove a snake in your pants when you're sleeping, you smart ass.'

Contemplating their journey to the Dominican Republic, he wondered if Jorge slept deeply. Even a drug-fuelled pig like him would have to sleep at some point during the course of three days. Having designed the sub to evade radar, sonar and infrared detection, he would have to come up with some cunning way of scuppering the vessel's invisibility, sabotaging the voyage by alerting the coast guard to their presence. It was the only way. Providing the damned thing didn't take water on board first.

In the tunnel, he could barely see. Jorge took a torch out from the back pocket of his jeans and shone the harsh light into his face.

'Don't think you're going to slip away while we're down here. There's nowhere to go, and Jorge's got his eye on you.' Jorge shone the torch onto his own face from his chin upwards, giving himself a ghoulish appearance, drawing attention to the black teardrops that had been tattooed on his lower eyelids. A card-carrying killer. Though he was already well aware of that. There were entry-level expectations when it came to the upper echelons of the Coba cartel.

Down there, the air smelled of soil, rotten foliage and decaying excreta from the animals who had instinctively worked out that this was a safe route to the other side of the highway. Water from the recent tropical rains had accumulated and now pooled at their feet, seeping into his ramshackle boots. Looking behind him, he did wonder if he could somehow backtrack and bolt for the jungle. But the excavated path was so narrow and enclosed by the high walls of earth that Jorge would have no trouble in picking him off with a well-aimed shot. Dust fell from the unsupported roof above. No props. Nothing to stop the entire thing from caving in. No engineer had cast an eye over this tunnel's construction.

The falling dust turned to clumps of earth dropping onto his head as they reached what he guessed was the midway-point of the tunnel. The rumble of a truck in the distance grew louder, reverberating around the inexpertly dug thoroughfare.

'Christ! It's going to cave in,' he shouted, realising that if the tunnel collapsed, it would cause a sinkhole in the highway. They would be crushed beneath an inevitable multiple pile-up of cars and trucks. 'We need to run!'

'Don't talk crap,' Jorge said.

His voice was all but drowned out by the deafening thunder of the truck directly above them. Earth and rocks started to fall in earnest as deadly hard rain.

CHAPTER 30

Mexico, Hotel Bahia Maya, Cancun, then, the Yucatan jungle, 30 May

The insistent knocking at the door of his hotel room jolted Van den Bergen awake.

'Where am I?' he said, wiping the string of drool from his jaw and staring at the ceiling fan that spun above him. Then he remembered. 'Shit.' Glanced at his alarm clock that said 11 p.m. Still jet-lagged and exhausted from being dragged to a bodega where his stomach acid had consumed nearly everything in the place, he had made his excuses and passed out on his bed by 9.30 p.m. So, who the hell was this?

He padded to the door, wearing only his pants. Wondered briefly if it was George. Peered through the spyhole. More knocking with some force behind it.

'Gonzales?'

Opening the door, the Mexican detective pushed his way into his room. 'Get dressed, Paul,' he said, the excitable grin sliding from his face as he spotted Van den Bergen's sternum-to-abdomen scarring. He turned away abruptly and began to study the plan of the hotel on the fire escape notice, pinned to the door.

'Are you drunk?' Van den Bergen peered down at the back of his head, trying to work out what the hell was going on.

'No, my friend,' Gonzales said, his attention still fixed on the door. 'I'm sitting in the bar with Baldini and I get emailed anonymously with GPS co-ordinates for a location in the jungle. I figure, maybe it's a hoax or maybe it's real intel about cartel activity, right? It's worth checking out. So, I send the highway patrol guys to take a look. And you'll never guess what.'

'No. I guess I never will.'

'They spotted a huge meth lab and what looks like some accommodation in active use. They're waiting on me and my guys for backup. I thought you'd want to come with us. Baldini is waiting outside.'

Pulling a T-shirt over his upper body, Van den Bergen tugged a pair of jeans from his case and a clean pair of socks. 'You can turn around now,' he said. 'I'm decent.'

'Aren't you hot in jeans, man?' Gonzales asked, raising an eyebrow. 'And *socks*?'

'Malaria.' Van den Bergen did not clarify further.

'You won't get malaria here!'

'Are there mosquitoes?'

'Naturally!'

'Then I'm wearing jeans and socks.' Hastily, he resprayed his arms with strong Deet. It wouldn't do to get bitten. He had heard the test for malaria involved giving a blood sample every day for three days running. No bloody way.

As the police truck bounced along a rutted track that led deep into the nocturnal blackness of the Yucatan jungle, Van den Bergen was irritated to see that he couldn't get a signal on his phone. What if George had been in touch? Marie had finally confessed that she had bought a ticket to Toncontín airport in the Honduran capital of Tegucigalpa on George's behalf. But where was his contrary, absent lover now?

'I can't wait to see if this is the source of the bad meth,' Baldini said, talking over the chatter of Gonzales and his uniformed driver at the front of the truck. 'I sure as hell hope it is. I don't wanna see no more dead kids on the back of it.'

Van den Bergen wrinkled his nose at the smell of beer on the American. He stared in silence into the dense tangle of trees and palms, feeling strongly that they were on a wild-goose chase on which George had persuaded Minks to waste thousands of the department's euros. Even if the meth lab did turn out to be connected to his floaters, he had no jurisdiction over a Mexican cartel. Hell, even the Mexican authorities had little control over the cartel bosses. The problem was endemic throughout Central America. And he had bigger problems in the Rotterdam Silencer being back on the scene in Amsterdam. The very thought made the hole in his hip, left over a decade earlier by a bullet that had been shot from the gun of that drug-dealing morally bankrupt bastard, twitch painfully.

'We're here,' Gonzales said, peering into the darkness through the windscreen. They had pulled up alongside another Policía truck. He tossed two bullet-proof vests into the back. 'Put these on, guys, and stay behind my men.'

Suddenly, it occurred to Van den Bergen that he was placing himself in mortal danger on a continent and in a country that had nothing to do with him or the Dutch police. Hadn't he sworn to his daughter, Tamara, that he would take more care of himself now that he had little Eva in his life? Fastening the clips of the vest, his hands started to shake. He clutched the Kevlar tightly, hoping that, in the poor light, Baldini wouldn't have noticed his weakness.

Pull yourself together, you lanky streak of piss, he admonished himself. *You're more experienced than the lot of these swaggering tits. You have the battle scars to prove it. Now is not the time to lose your nerve.*

Whispering instructions to his uniforms, Gonzales motioned that they should creep forwards alongside him towards the compound.

At first, Van den Bergen could see nothing apart from the strobing light of the torches, held by the uniforms who led the way. Dry stalks crunched underfoot. The heady smell of chlorophyll was everywhere. The jungle rang with the sound of cicadas chirruping and the eerie cries of strange, exotic creatures that called out into the night. Then, he became aware of the shapes of the trees. The pitch black was no longer quite as impenetrable.

'Look!' Baldini whispered.

Van den Bergen squinted beyond the fat leaves of some tropical bush and caught his first glimpse of a clearing that was dimly lit by one or two lights, strung high on tree trunks – no doubt powered by a generator, hidden somewhere on the makeshift cartel complex, judging by the low thrum.

The team of policemen gathered in the treeline in silence, guns drawn. Van den Bergen could feel the adrenalin being pumped around his body. At last, his thoughts had turned from mosquitoes and snake venom to the thrill of a raid. He reached for his service weapon but remembered that he had left it locked in the safe back home. No place for that, here, where he was only a guest.

'*Vámonos!*' Gonzales whispered.

With Van den Bergen and Baldini bringing up the rear, the law enforcers crept into the clearing, working in twos. The set-up resembled a tiny hamlet fashioned from corrugated iron shacks that had been traditionally thatched with giant palm leaves, presumably to prevent them from being spotted by helicopters flying overhead, Van den Bergen assessed.

The Mexican police dipped into each dwelling, guns drawn. Withdrew, shaking their heads at Gonzales, whose weapon was trained more generally on the scene. He directed his men to search the subsequent shacks.

'*Nada,*' they said, approaching and speaking to him in Spanish.

Gonzales sighed and turned to Van den Bergen and Baldini. 'There's nobody here. Let's take a look around.'

Most of the shacks showed signs of having been slept in – mosquito nets, discarded water bottles, makeshift pump-up mattresses and a bucket full of human waste in the corner.

'They've been sleeping two to a shack,' Van den Bergen said. 'And look! This one has handcuffs at the end of heavy chains, welded to the walls.'

'Prisoners?' Baldini said, taking a pen from his pocket and lifting the opened cuffs into the air for closer inspection.

Van den Bergen nodded. 'Poor bastards. It's like a prisoner-of-war camp. Who do you think these were for?'

Gonzales shrugged. 'If they were worth cuffing, they sure as hell weren't cartel gang members. You cuff slaves or a prisoner that has value. So I'd say either women used for sex by the men or specialists, working in the lab, maybe. Who knows?'

Inside the other shacks, there was evidence of a communal area with a rough dining table and benches, where people ate, and a kitchenette, where food had clearly been prepared.

'They're not long gone,' Van den Bergen said, sniffing at a supermarket packet of cheese; rummaging through some salad that had been left inside a beer fridge, powered by an extension cable that had been plugged into the generator outside.

'This place looks like it's been abandoned in a hurry,' Baldini said.

'Maybe it hasn't been abandoned,' Van den Bergen said, stalking into the adjacent shack. 'Look!' He called his counterparts inside and pointed to an old portable television that sat on a wooden crate. It was still on. 'I'd say they're very much planning on coming back!'

Behind a screen of green, the largest of the shacks was a solid-looking prefabricated Portakabin, about four metres long. Its roof had been covered with palm leaves and other foliage, purely for camouflage purposes – that much was clear.

When Van den Bergen stepped inside, he gasped. The sizeable space contained a well-equipped meth lab, the likes of which would not have been out of place in a university science department. 'Jesus.' He whistled low at the sight of the oversized bell jars, test tubes and barrels of chemicals on the floor. 'It's a bit different from what I saw in the Czech Republic. Those guys were amateurs. But this? This is a professional rig-up, if ever I saw one.'

'It's clean, for a start,' Gonzales said, looking around at the spotless white space. 'Money has been spent on this.'

Van den Bergen approached one of the barrels. Examined a label on the side. 'Chinese,' he said, failing to understand what was written in the unfamiliar script. 'But hang on!' He leaned over and examined the far side of the barrel. There was an export label, with the company name, 'InterChem GmbH', written on the side. 'This has been shipped from China to a German company,' he said, frowning. He turned to Baldini. 'Can you give me a hand? Let's see what's on the bottom of this baby.'

'Sure.'

His muscles screamed in complaint as they lifted the heavy barrel onto its side. Van den Bergen gasped as he stood, pain spasming in his hip. Grinding his molars in a bid to quash the agony, he leaned over and scrutinised the base of the barrel. There was another label showing the German company's name. He ran his fingers over it. Smooth and warm – it felt too thick to be just one piece of paper.

Baldini sighed. 'Nothing new there, bud.'

'Have you got a penknife?' Van den Bergen asked Gonzales, sensing that some vital piece of information might be just within his reach.

The Mexican Federale handed him his keyring which doubled as a Swiss Army knife.

'There's another label under here,' Van den Bergen said, gouging at the thick German label. He abandoned the knife in favour of his thumbnail. 'I know it.'

'There's nothing there. I don't see it,' Gonzales said.

'It feels wrong,' Van den Bergen said. Finally, he got a corner of the German sticker to lift cleanly. Carefully, slowly, he peeled it back. Beneath was a second sticker, as he'd anticipated. In black lettering, it showed the name:

Chembedrijf

'I don't believe it,' Van den Bergen said. He stood too quickly so that his hip cracked audibly and the blood rushed from his head. 'A Dutch chemical company is somehow involved.'

CHAPTER 31

Mexico, elsewhere in the Yucatan jungle, at the same time

The camber of the ground changed. They were heading upwards, running to escape the threat of suffocation in a death trap of a tunnel that had miraculously remained intact. He tried to brush the earth off, though it clung to the sweat on his face and in his hair. A long way above them, beyond the uppermost branches of the royal palms and frangipani trees, he could see the deep-blue velvet sky, streaked with the last of the red and scattered with the diamond brilliance of the first stars. 'We made it through to the other side. I don't believe it! I can smell the sea,' he said, pausing to drink in the welcome fresh blast of air. 'It's cooler, isn't it?'

A jab in the ribs from Jorge's balled fist signalled clearly that his hope of a simple, optimistic exchange was a non-starter.

'Shut your fucking trap,' the guard said. He cupped his hand to his ear. With the traffic noise of the highway long behind them now, the lapping water of the Caribbean Sea was suddenly audible. Jorge held his index finger to his lips. 'Silence,' he whispered.

Two whistles came from the scouts who had gone ahead to check that the beach was clear of people. A further three whistles in short succession followed. A code.

'Go!' Jorge said. 'It's safe. Hurry!'

213

The guard kicked him in the back of his right knee so that his legs almost gave way beneath him once again.

At the front of the procession, *el cocodrilo* and Miguel were the first to disappear from the gloom of the jungle. Their muscle followed behind. Then, the sub's trailer rattled down, beyond the treeline and onto the beach, the mules braying as they tugged their heavy twelve-metre load through deep sand.

'Quickly!' Miguel said.

Even in the lavender-grey light of early evening, he could see that Miguel's pistol was drawn and pointed at the scouts who steered the animals. But the beach ... the beach was magnificent. A curve of white sand, lit by the newly woken moon and the glittering stars that danced above them in the blackening sky. The calm waters of the sea washed gently ashore and then slid back out again, teasing the silken ribbon of slowly cooling sand with its foaming warmth. Crabs scuttled across their path, observing the strange procession of men, mules and sub, clicking their claws in some vain warrior's dance. It was the first time he had seen the open sea in years. The first time he had felt a freshening breeze on his soil-encrusted face since he had been kidnapped.

The last time he remembered feeling the wind on his face, he had been hiking in the hills above Tegucigalpa. A lifetime ago, now.

Tears pricked at the backs of his eyes when he realised how close to civilisation they might be. Perhaps within yelling distance of the police officers who patrolled the highway, or some security guards who might be manning an exclusive development on the seafront. Perhaps there were tourists, walking hand in hand by the treeline, further along and out of sight of *el cocodrilo* and his men – tourists who could raise the alarm.

But there were none. At that moment, he felt like his heart might finally break.

So close ... and yet, he was still as powerless to escape *el cocodrilo* and his men as ever.

'Get the sub onto the sand!' he heard *el cocodrilo* say, snapping his fingers.

King of all he surveyed, *el cocodrilo* lit a cigar and started to swig from a brand-new bottle of Scotch as the scouts and three of his gang members heaved the vessel onto the waterline. He watched them toil with apparent amusement – clearly someone who relished the notion that every other man was beneath him and existed merely to service his every whim.

At that moment, the diesel engine of a truck encroached upon the peaceful rhythmic sound of the breaking waves in the distance and the swish of the palms behind them. No headlamps, but he could see a large van approaching along the beach, driving right onto the sand where it had been compacted during the day by the changing tides.

'Get the meth on board as quick as you can and get this thing in the water,' *el cocodrilo* said to the *transportista* who emerged from the truck's cab.

The woman was flanked by two of her female colleagues, who clutched rifles close to their tattooed bodies. Together, they unlocked the shutters at the back to reveal six more armed *transportistas* and a pallet, stacked to the ceiling of the truck, containing blocks fashioned from crystal meth, wrapped in clingfilm. Choreographed perfectly, they worked in unison like a colony of wasps, doing the bidding of their queen, to move the product from the truck into the sub.

'Please ask him not to have them load more than the sub can take,' he said to Jorge. 'It's not physically possible to take ten tonnes. We'll both go down with the thing once we're in open water. It's not like there's room for lifeboats! There's barely room for life jackets. It's a suicide mission, I'm telling you.'

But Jorge merely stood idly by, smoking a Marlboro cigarette; studiously ignoring him. Eventually he said, 'If you're feeling so fucking brave, why don't you tell that to *el cocodrilo*? Because I'm not. *That* would be suicide!' He crossed himself in the moonlight and gazed at the night sky. 'I've got a good feeling, though. If we're successful on this maiden voyage, I get a pay rise and you might get to live to build another sub. Consider yourself lucky.'

Frustrated, he watched the women load the parcels of meth into the sub's hull. Finally, when he could no longer stand, he flopped onto the sandy ground.

The last package had been installed in the sub. The men of the cartel began a macho show of back-slapping and whooping. The fearsome-looking women fell back in line like trained militia, clutching their rifles and awaiting orders.

El cocodrilo was still standing and swigging heartily from his Scotch bottle. His body language had become loose and imprecise. 'Wait! Wait!' he said, interrupting his men's self-congratulatory high-fiving. 'We need to launch this baby in style. Mayan style.'

The young scouts and the cartel muscle turned to their boss wearing puzzled expressions. They lit cigarettes, exhaling plumes of smoke into the perfect night sky.

'We can't hang around, *jefe*,' Miguel said, laying his hand on *el cocodrilo*'s arm. Thinking better of it once he was treated to a terrifying stare. 'We're already taking a big risk loading up on the beach. Look!' He pointed along the coastline towards a floodlit ruin perched on a clifftop in the distance. 'Tulum's only a stone's throw away and you know as well as I do that it's teaming with tourists.'

'Not this time of night,' el *cocodrilo* said. 'These conscientious scouts of yours have been scoping this beach for months. We're good.'

But there was an urgency in Miguel's normally placatory voice. 'Seriously. It's time to get it into the water and wave Jorge and *el mecánico* goodbye before the Federales show up.'

El cocodrilo dropped the glowing stub of his cigar into the dregs at the bottom of the Scotch bottle. The liquor ignited immediately, transforming the bottle into a fiery crucible, which he threw with some force at Miguel's head. The glass smashed, dousing his second-in-command in a deadly flaming cocktail.

When Miguel slumped to the ground, screaming, trying desperately to smother the flames with sand, the other men simply looked on. From his vantage point beside Jorge, he watched the way they stiffened, balling their fists, as though they were poised to do the right thing and run to the man's aid. But nobody did. Apart from one of the *transportistas*, who took a step forward but was dragged back into line by one of her compatriots.

He got to his knees, unable to resist the natural urge to help.

'Stay where you are, *mecánico*,' Jorge whispered, grabbing his shoulder.

It was clear, however that the assault on Miguel had not sated *el cocodrilo*'s desire for violence.

'I tell you what,' he shouted. 'The Mayans would have known how to mark an occasion like the launch of a beautiful feat of engineering in style.' He swayed slightly, seemingly unperturbed by the now sobbing and charred Miguel. 'You know what they used to do? Human sacrifice!' He pointed to the clifftop Tulum ruins along the shoreline. 'They'd take their prisoners to the top of those ancient pyramids, chop off their heads and cut out their fucking hearts. They watered the land with human blood so that it would be fertile and sustain their people. Now that's showmanship. That's how you establish and rule an entire civilisation. No mercy. No compromise.'

Lunging for one of the young scouts, *el cocodrilo* wrapped an arm around the wide-eyed lad's neck before he had a chance to escape. Whistled to one of the cartel gang members, who had been tasked with hacking the way ahead through the jungle with a large machete.

'Hey, you! Give me your blade.'

Transfixed by the gruesome spectacle that was unfolding, *el mecánico* clutched his knees with growing unease. Guessing what would come next. He closed his eyes, wishing he was anywhere but on this beach. Wishing he had never gone to work that fateful morning when the corporate shuttle bus had been hijacked by the tattooed maras. To think, he had been on the cusp of making the decision to stay in bed with a sore throat. But then *el cocodrilo* had hand-selected him months in advance of the kidnapping as the engineer who would build his semi-submersible, according to Jorge. The man who had just beheaded a scout, turning the idyllic perfect Caribbean beach into a bloodbath; the man who was cutting out the heart of that poor youngster – somebody's son – and was squeezing the blood inside the extracted organ onto the keel of the semi-submersible, like some perverse rendition of launching a ship by smashing a bottle of champagne against the side … that monster would have found him, whether had he gone to work that fateful morning or had boarded the first flight back to Europe. Because *el cocodrilo*, rather like the crocodiles he kept fed with the dismembered bodies of his victims, was not the type of cold-blooded monster ever to let go of his prey, once he had it within his sights.

'Hey, *mecánico*!' his blood-soaked captor shouted, swaggering over to him, pointing the tip of the machete at both him and Jorge. 'Get off your knees and get in that fucking sub! I've anointed it with blood from the beating heart of a virile youth.' His speech was languid, his consonants slurred. 'There's no way it's going to sink. Not now. The ancient Mayans are watching over you. So, on your feet! I want to see your bony Spanish arse at the helm of the vessel you built, I paid for and I've aptly named *Ella*.'

He swallowed hard, steeling himself to walk past the decapitated, defiled body of the scout and the howling, charred figure of Miguel, who looked like he might not see out the next hour. Marching through the phalanx of the *transportistas*. As he did so, he was sure one of them purposely bumped into him. He felt a hand slide onto his hip. Dispelled the sensation as the product of an overwrought mind.

Taking one last, lingering look at the beach that had seemed such an idyll only hours earlier, he felt certain that he would never return to those shores again alive. It was his fate to die inside the vessel named after his daughter.

CHAPTER 32

En route from Tegucigalpa, Honduras to Palenque, Mexico via Guatemala, 27 May

'You don't talk much,' Paola said.

'I don't have anything to say.' George was sitting on a wheel arch, intently watching one of the other women stripping down her rifle and cleaning it. Memorising her every move so that she might copy her convincingly if push came to shove. So many bits, though! George knew she would struggle to remember in which order they all went back together. 'I'm just thinking about getting my money back from the slimeball that ripped me off.'

Paola nodded. 'Have you got a guy?'

'Yes,' George said, thinking wistfully of Van den Bergen, who would almost certainly be chewed up by worry and annoyance at the way she had simply disappeared into the crowds of Cancun airport. Perhaps he would never forgive her. Perhaps. 'You?'

'Sort of.' Paola smiled and pulled her vest up to reveal the portrait of a man, skilfully tattooed on her belly. 'This is him. His name is Alejandro. He's in jail back home.' She chuckled. 'Aren't they all?'

'Mine's much older than me,' George said, grinning. 'He's a miserable bastard but he's my miserable bastard.' She sat in silence a while, contemplating her implicit rejection of her lover in favour

219

of her long-lost father, realising she could be left with neither and might also forfeit her own life by the end of this fool's odyssey.

'You got kids?' Paola asked.

George shook her head. Then added, 'A step-grandchild, I suppose. I told you my guy was old. You?'

Paola took out a crumpled photo from one of the pockets in her cargo trousers and showed it to George. 'This is my daughter, Ximena,' she said. 'Isn't she beautiful? She's got her papa's eyes.'

George saw the smiling face of a toddler who sat in an older woman's arms. 'She lives with your mother?'

Nodding, Paola sniffed, her mouth arcing into a downturned smile. 'I work as a *transportista* and send the money home. You know what it's like for young women like us in our shitty villages. What else are we gonna do for money unless we sell our bodies or work in the fields for next to nothing? I don't want to spend my life on my back, getting beaten up, catching diseases and being treated like an animal by some ugly, fat sons of bitches. I don't want my family to starve. And besides, this pays well and we don't get any hassle from men. Way better. I'd sooner risk getting shot and make sure my kid's fed.' She gnawed at fingernails that were already down to the quick. 'What about you? Why are you in this game?'

'Same reasons,' George said. 'I don't like men telling me what to do. In fact, I don't like anyone telling me what to do.' She shot a furtive glance over at Maritza and realised the matriarch of this little band of mercenaries was watching her every move and eavesdropping on every single word that came out of her mouth. The naivety of what she had said wasn't lost on her. Maritza was as fearsome a taskmaster as any mid-level gang boss she had ever met. She could see it in the set of the woman's jaw and in that brutal scar – a terrible wound she had sustained and survived. *What's the bet the other guy came off much, much worse?* George pondered.

It was a tight squeeze in the truck with so many of them perched on crate after crate of guns.

'What happens if the truck gets stopped by the police?' George asked Paola.

The girl paused thoughtfully in the middle of tying her long, black hair into a bun. 'If they can't be bribed, we use our womanly charms on them, of course!' She winked. Pushed George's thigh. 'I thought you said you were experienced at this game?'

During the uncomfortable twenty-hour journey from the Honduran capital to Palenque Chiapas, George felt Maritza watching her regularly. The older woman didn't trust her, she was certain. Every time a bead of sweat rolled down George's neck, she was fearful that her temporary tattoos would peel and wash away. It wouldn't take much to uncover the truth. If they found her phone and the GPS tracker, gaffer-taped into the lining of her rucksack, or her watch, secreted inside her vagina, wrapped in a condom, there would be rather more than just questions.

Just follow their lead, George told herself, trying to keep her ragged breathing steady. *Keep your mouth shut wherever possible. Sleep with one hand on that hunting knife. You can do this. You can, because you believe you can.*

After only three stop-offs to refuel at some gas station in the middle of nowhere, where they bought snacks and used the filthy facilities, which under any other circumstances, she would have refused to do, George began to feel herself drifting off to sleep. An urge that she mustn't allow herself to give in to, while the others were all gathered around her and her bag was vulnerable. Jerking herself awake every time she felt her lids getting heavy, she tried to think about childish songs Letitia and her father used to sing to her at bedtime when she had been a toddler. Silly rituals and rhymes that she had adored and which had made her feel utterly secure in her little world. Hadn't her father recited '*Cinco pequeñas ranitas con lunares*' – 'Five little speckled frogs'? She could still remember the words fondly. Her own fate seemed to mirror that of the rhyme. All the speckled frogs in her life were vanishing into the pool, one by one, never to be seen again. How long before she was the only frog left? The thought was saddening and sobering enough to help her beat sleep.

Where the other women engaged in conversation, talking about their lives, spent juggling mundane family commitments with the insane level of risk and violence associated with gun smuggling, George held her tongue, preferring instead to stare sullenly at a dent in the side of the truck. Perhaps these weren't such fearsome fighters after all. Perhaps it was all tattoos and bluster. Perhaps she was safer than she thought.

She could feel it when they finally began to ascend in earnest. Her ears were popping as they climbed higher and, though she could not see the road ahead, she could tell they were negotiating hairpin bends as they lurched from side to side periodically. The metal box that constituted the cargo area of the ex-army truck was suffocatingly hot under the Central American sun. As dusk snuffed out the sunshine, it was still a sweltering sweatbox, cooped up with all those women.

Several rhythmic thumps from the cab on the other side of the partition shook her out of her complacent torpor.

'Kill the lights!' Maritza said.

All but one nightlight was extinguished instantly, plunging them into near-darkness. Everybody sat bolt upright, waiting for Maritza's pronouncement; prepared for some kind of confrontation, judging by the way they checked the ammo clips on their rifles.

Maritza held her index finger to her lips. 'Guatemalan Polícia Nacional,' she whispered.

In the absolute silence, gripped by abject fear of what might come to pass in the next few moments, George listened hard to the conversation that was taking place outside. Men's voices.

'What are you doing in the mountains at this time of night?' one of the officers asked.

'Going to visit relatives in Palenque,' the driver said. 'My cousin is getting married.'

'And you need a big truck like this to go to a wedding?'

'It's all I've got, Officer. I take produce to the market for a farmer. This truck is my livelihood. Me and my sister here. We're delivery drivers.'

'You're not from Guatemala or Mexico. I'm not stupid. What are two girls like you from across the border really doing this far north? Take off your jackets and show me your arms.'

'You want to see our arms? Not our papers?'

'It's too hot for jackets. We're *policía*. We're not fucking imbeciles. Take them off.'

'No.'

At that moment, George's only thought was that she desperately needed to tell Van den Bergen that she loved him and to give him her exact co-ordinates, so that he could eventually send a search party to retrieve her body. She wanted to tell Aunty Sharon that she baked the best fruitcake in the whole world and gave the very best hugs. And she wished she could thank Sally Wright for taking a chance on her. Without her, the future for Ella Williams-May would have been a dismal life behind bars or stacking supermarket shelves in perpetuity. But to convey those final messages, she would have to fish her phone out of her bag and switch it on. There was no time. It was too risky. Her breath came short. She felt like she might vomit at any moment. But all the while, she tried to visualise her missing father. The man with strong arms who smelled of tobacco and aftershave. *I've got to see this through. Got to get to you. Grow a pair of balls, George, you fucking wimp.*

'Get out of the truck and open the back,' the officer said. His breezy, friendly tone had gone now. All business. 'Keep your hands where I can see them.'

'Suit yourself, Officer.'

Footsteps, as the driver, her passenger and the two officers marched around to the shutters of the truck. Fiddling with the lock.

'Get on with it,' one of the officers said.

'Well I would if you'd shine the torch on the lock instead of in my face.'

'I don't like your attitude. One more word out of you, and I'm throwing you and your friend here in a cell for the night.'

The women inside the cargo area were all poised like jaguars, ready to pounce on their prey. It was clear that Paola's idea of a charm offensive did not involve the fluttering of eyelashes or honeyed words of flattery.

Maritza held her arm out, signalling they should wait for her sign. George clutched at her rifle. Copying Paola's stance and carefully observing how she held her weapon. *Oh my days*, she thought. *I held Danny's gun every now and then, dicking around for laughs, but I never fired one in my life. And now, I'm supposed to shoot some innocent coppers or be arrested or shot myself? Jesus. What the hell am I doing? I must be mental. I'm going to shoot myself in the fucking face by accident and it will be the least I deserve.*

Rattling at the lock, the shutters flicked quickly upwards, allowing the starry moonlit night and the riot of chirruping cicadas to flood into the metal box. The police officers were standing before them, night-blind and unwitting, shining their torches into the truck.

Maritza dropped her arm. The cops' eyes widened with surprise at the sight of the *transportistas*, illuminated by the blisteringly bright flashes of the bullets as they fired their weapons. But the men's visible surprise was as fleeting as a solitary breath. Their black uniforms were punctured with a deadly spray of bullets, sending them flying through the air backwards, crashing to the ground in a cloud of their own blood.

George had aimed her rifle towards the scrub and had pulled the trigger, girding herself to sit tight and not fall over from the recoil. Beset by a horrifying mix of euphoria at having used such a powerful weapon, adrenalin at the potential for her own death and disgust at the broken bodies of the policemen, she swallowed down a lump of rising bile. Willing her hands to stop shaking. Had the driver and her passenger noticed that her bullets had deliberately gone astray? Surely not in the dark.

'Good girls,' Maritza said, as though she were a teacher, pleased that her pupils had completed a maths test satisfactorily. She glanced at her watch as the nightlights were all reignited, attracting opportunistic fluttering moths from outside into their hiding place. 'Let's get this show back on the road, or we'll be late for Nikolay.'

The truck's engine shuddered back to life. The shutters were closed. And all George was left with was a lingering memory of the surprise on the policemen's faces as they had been pumped full of lead, together with the stomach-churning thought that she was heading straight for the lion's den.

CHAPTER 33

Amsterdam, Red-Light District, 30 May

'Come on,' the long-haired man with the bandana said, glancing over his shoulder. 'Pay up.'

He held a trembling hand out to Elvis. A potato peeler in the other. His amber-stained fingers were just the hors d'oeuvres for a main course of filth. His informant had clearly been sleeping rough, of late. A blackened, flaking thumbnail was just visible, suggesting that his kidneys were failing. He had almost certainly been hitting the bottle.

'What's wrong, Sepp? You look like a man who's feeling the heat.'

Sepp pulled his mirror shades off to reveal blurry, bloodshot eyes that were almost hidden behind red swollen flesh, as though some child had been tasked with creating a man from Plasticine and crayons. 'Look, Dirk. I told you what you needed to know. The Rotterdam Silencer is running this place again, now that The Duke is under lock and key.'

'You told me something I already knew, but I *still* gave you some cash, as a gesture of goodwill. Why should I pay you again if you've got nothing?'

'The information I gave you has landed me in a pile of steaming shit and I need to get out of town. Okay?' As if to corroborate

226

what he was saying, he glanced over his shoulder again. Put the glasses back on with an enigmatic air, his hands shaking like a man who needed money for supermarket-brand vodka far more than a train ticket out of town. 'Seriously. These guys don't fuck around.'

Elvis shrugged. 'I don't have any more than the fifty euros I already gave you. Sorry. I can't give you money from my own pocket because I haven't got any.' Eyeing his surrounds, Elvis suddenly realised that meeting his informant down a seedy, grimy back alley where there were no overlooking windows was not the smartest idea he had ever had. 'I've got to go,' he said. 'It's Saturday. I've got personal stuff. I've got to be somewhere.'

Sepp grabbed his arm with a dirt-ingrained claw. His grip was surprisingly strong. 'I've seen you with your fag boyfriend,' he said. 'I've been watching you.'

Elvis felt the blood drain from his face. The prickle of panic in his lips. 'What do you mean, my fag boyfriend? That's not a very nice thing to say. And what the hell do you know about me? Maybe I was working a case. Now, get your hand off me, because you're assaulting a police officer and I can arrest you for that.' He tried to shake the informant off. Started to reach inside his jacket for his service weapon, grappling with anxiety that this might turn nasty and indignation that this washed up old ex-con had been stalking him.

Too late.

'Get your hands in the air, pig!' Aman's voice. Shouting. Standing directly behind him. Elvis felt something cold and sharp dig into his back. 'Or I'll cut your spinal cord.'

The slack-faced terror on Sepp's face told him half of what he needed to know. The reflection of the three man-mountains, standing directly behind Elvis, in his mirror shades told him the rest.

Sepp turned and started to sprint down the alley, leaving Elvis with his hands uselessly in the air, wondering how the hell he could fend off an assailant he couldn't even see.

'Don't even think about it,' his attacker said, as the other two men pelted past him, scrambling to turn left at the end of the alley in pursuit of the surprisingly agile old ex-con.

'Who are you?' Elvis asked, wondering what the nursing staff would think if he didn't show for his evening visit. 'I'm a police officer, you know. If you harm me, it's an arrestable offence.'

'Oh, I fucking know that,' the man said.

There was a scuffling sound as the man shifted position behind him. Without warning, the blade in his back was gone, replaced by a garrotte around his neck.

Elvis gasped for breath, feeling the wire eat into his flesh. He tried to speak but could only struggle, his feet jerking to and fro uselessly as the giant behind him lifted him from the ground. The dank walls of the alleyway seemed to be encroaching, folding inwards in an effort to smother him. He closed his eyes, thinking of nothing but survival and the irony that his mother may yet outlast him. Lights flashing behind his eyelids. Dimly aware of Sepp being dragged under the arms back down the alley by one of the men, his head hanging low; greasy hair sweeping the floor. Clearly out cold.

CHAPTER 34

Mexico, Hotel Bahia Maya, Cancun, 1 June

When he woke at 5 a.m., his head thumped as though he had spent the night drinking on an empty stomach. Van den Bergen wondered briefly if he was about to suffer a fatal embolism brought on by the stress of George being gone. Reaching out, he felt her side of the bed. Nothing but cool white sheets and a pillow that hadn't been slept on. She was supposed to be here by his side. But though the bed was dishevelled, it was merely as a result of him tossing and turning, spending hour after sleepless hour worrying about the woman he loved being lost in the murder capital of the world. The thought that he might never see her again caused tears to well.

'Get a grip of yourself, you old fool,' he said, blinking the tears away. But merely willing the sorrow away was ineffectual against the wracking sobs that assailed him with determination, taking his hard-won stoic poise prisoner and supplanting it with crippling pangs of grief and a distillation of pure fear. For twenty minutes, he hugged the pillow George was meant to be sleeping on and stifled his noise with it, lest the Canadian tourists in the neighbouring room overhear him.

As he hiccupped and the sobbing started to abate, leaving only exhaustion in its wake, the image that lingered in his mind's eye was not one of George slipping through the crowds of Cancun airport but of the shack in the cartel's jungle compound where prisoners were being kept. Might George have been kidnapped by now and cuffed to the wall in some stinking hovel to be used for sex?

'Enough!' he said.

He swung his legs over the side of the bed, staring blankly at the brightly coloured décor. Tiled floor. Bright yellow walls, orange and blue curtains. If his headache didn't kill him, the clashing colours might. Filling his glass on the nightstand with water from the minibar, he pressed several tablets out of their blister packs, swallowed them one by one and then picked up his phone. He switched it on to no avail.

'Shit. No juice in your bloody phone, Van den Bergen. You irresponsible old fart.'

He removed the plug-in mosquito repellent and plugged in his charger.

The phone sprang to life, buzzing with a sudden influx of new messages. The first was a text from Marie.

```
I'm really worried about Elvis.
```

Nothing more. They had had an email exchange about InterChem GmbH and Chembedrijf before he had gone to sleep. She had mentioned Elvis then, too. And now, this …

The second text was from Tamara.

```
Hope you're safe and well in Mexico. Eva
started to walk today! Love you and miss
you. Xxx
```

A video clip had been attached, showing his granddaughter in her sleepsuit taking wobbly steps with bowed unpractised legs, arms outstretched, from his son-in-law, Numb Nuts, to Tamara, who had clearly been holding the camera. Van den Bergen watched the delight and triumph in the little girl's dribbly face. He felt bittersweet longing curdle with his early-morning tablets.

Next, he opened a text from Maarten Minks, demanding an update. Van den Bergen considered telling his boss about the sophisticated meth lab they had discovered in the jungle but decided to hold the information back until Gonzales' technicians had analysed the samples of crystal meth found there.

Finally, an email he had not been anticipating but had long hoped for.

Hello you. It's me. Don't worry. I'm safe. Can only check phone intermittently. Have been travelling north to Palenque with some women, so won't be far from you soon. It's possible Dad was kidnapped and brought to Chiapas in Mexico to work for a cartel. Nikolay Bebchuck is apparently there! Will text more when I can. If I die, know that I loved you with all of my heart and soul, old man. You are The One. I knew it from the moment we met. George. xxx PS: I'll try not to die.

Van den Bergen read and reread the message, noticing that it had been sent three days earlier but had only just reached him. Clasping the phone over his battered, scarred sternum beneath which his heart now beat strong and steadily, he looked up at the rotating fan, thanking whatever god might be watching over his lover for her at least having made it thus far on her father's trail in one piece.

Shaking his head, he allowed himself a smile, though tears started to fall anew. Started to thumb out a reply.

If you die, I refuse to speak to you ever again. This message has taken days to get here. Do not face Nikolay alone! Send me your position so I can get you out of there safely

and get him arrested. Your father wouldn't want you to
risk your life like this. You're an idiot but you're my idiot.
Love always. Paul. X

Ten minutes later, the cop in Van den Bergen had started to
win out over the lover.

If you get close to Nikolay, see if you can get something
with his prints on or an object we can profile for DNA. And
still don't die. Px

They had less than twelve hours before their flight home
departed, whether they were on it or not. He was alive. George was
probably, possibly, hopefully alive. Their quarry was potentially
just within reach. He had to devise some way of tightening the net
around this bastard without jeopardising the case, involving
possibly corrupt Mexican officials and getting them all killed.

After an exceedingly early breakfast, where he had deliberately
asked to be seated on the opposite side of the dining room to the
overly energetic and garrulous Baldini, Van den Bergen was ferried
to the sticky office in the Cancun police station for a debriefing.
There was a lightness to his step now that he had finally heard
from George, but he kept his buoyant mood to himself.

Mexican police officers queued in the overstuffed room to
pour themselves coffee from the percolator machine at the back.
Large floor-mounted fans uselessly blew warm air around. Still
no sign of the air-con engineer. Grappling with handouts, the
men gathered around Gonzales, who had wedged his fleshy
bottom on the corner of a desk like a small king presiding over
his fiefdom. Van den Bergen was the last in line for the coffee
pot. He grimaced at the strong brew that sat treacle-like in the
bottom of the jug, remembering coffee was supposed to be acidic
and therefore bad for his reflux. Turned around to find Gonzales

waiting for him to pay attention like a disapproving teacher. Not quite so friendly and amiable after all.

The debrief was delivered first in Spanish.

Yawning, Van den Bergen squatted against the wall at the back and reread the email that had reached him in the small hours from the workaholic, Marie – only two hours after the discovery of the clandestine cartel jungle complex and before he had hit the sack.

Hello boss.

InterChem GmbH seems to be a shell holding-company with Nikolay Bebchuck listed as the director! There are no company accounts on file but there's an address registered to Stuttgart. When I looked it up on Google maps, it's just a barber's shop. I've done some digging into Chembedrijf. They're a huge multinational with the head office in Groningen's Energy Valley. There is a smaller office in Amsterdam. Company accounts show that they have a turnover of over €1 billion per year, with a fat corporate finger in all sorts of pies, from pharmaceutical research and development to drugs manufacture to cornering the market in household name toiletries and cleaning products. They trade frequently with China, buying chemicals cheaply, sometimes selling them on to dodgy regimes, from what I can tell. I had a scan through the list of employees. Only one name flagged up as being of interest among the thousands on the payroll: Adrianus Karelse. He's working as a junior project manager.

Elvis is missing.

Regards
Marie

Van den Bergen chewed over the two pieces of news that glowed from his phone's screen. Elvis was 'missing'. This was clearly really bothering Marie. Could he not simply be at the hospital because his mother had taken a turn for the worse and he hadn't managed to call in? Yes. That seemed most likely. But Adrianus Karelse. Ad. George's first serious boyfriend and Van den Bergen's love rival for some three long years or more.

'Jesus,' he said aloud, sighing.

Two of the Mexican uniforms turned to look at him, perplexed.

'Not you,' Van den Bergen said, treating them to a judgemental glare.

Would Karelse work for Van den Bergen as an informant, doing a little below-the-radar snooping into whatever shenanigans were going on in Chembedrijf? He knew the spineless little prick wouldn't piss on the man who had stolen his girl if he was on fire. But George … George, he would almost certainly still move heaven and earth for. 'For old times' sake' would be a cynical card to play, but he was prepared to play it – and he knew George would be too – if it meant the hedonistic, drug-taking little idiots on Amsterdam's club scene stopped being poisoned with this Mexican shit.

As Gonzales rattled on to his men in indecipherable Spanish, Van den Bergen Googled Ad. The prick's Facebook account had maximum privacy settings. All that was visible was a generic man's silhouette in white and blue. Did he want to add Karelse as a friend? No he certainly did not! Casting his mind back to conversations with George about her failed long-distance romance with the turd, he remembered Karelse had previously been in a serious relationship with a girl called Astrid. Just a hunch. Van den Bergen searched for Astrid Karelse and there she was – a pink-faced milkmaid of a woman with a completely open profile. He clicked on her 'about' section. Allowed himself a satisfied smile. Astrid Karelse was, of course, married to Ad Karelse. The well-scrubbed, loved-up Mr and Mrs Karelse were parents to blond-haired toddlers of about four and two years old. Well, well, well. How likely then did that make it that Karelse might help George if asked? Would he be missing his little walk on the wild side? Van den Bergen studied Astrid's neat blonde hair, cut into an unsightly short style that was every new mother's dream of easy-to-maintain and every man's sexual anti-fantasy. Yes, Ad would be missing George McKenzie all right. Probably. Then, there was a company profile, showing that Karelse was, in fact, an IT project manager, which might be perfect for gaining access to computerised records of the firm's business transactions. He noted with a derisory snort that Mr Pretty Boy's previously lustrous dark hair was starting to recede in earnest. Ran his hand through his own luxuriant white thatch, just to check it was still present and correct. Instantly felt like a vain arsehole when he noticed the absence of a finger on Karelse's hand and remembered how the boy had come to lose it.

'Chief Inspector Van den Bergen!' Gonzales shouted across the packed office.

Clearly his host had been calling his name for some time. 'Sorry. I was following up ...'

Gonzales folded his arms and raised an eyebrow, expectantly. 'What do you think of that, then?'

'Oh.' He was meant to say something in response to some remark that everybody but him had clearly heard. How long had Gonzales been talking to him exactly, while he had been mentally bitching about some poor fingerless kid in Groningen? 'Yes.' Gonzales was grinning, so there was obviously something to be happy about. 'Absolutely ... the thing.' He nodded, trying to arrange his features into something resembling earnestness.

'Good,' Gonzales said, beaming at his captive audience. 'So, now we know we've got a match between the traces of meth we found in the jungle lab last night and the chemical composition of the meth that killed the victims in Amsterdam and NYC. We know we're looking for the right guys. The plan is, we stake out the lab – and it's not going to be easy to keep an eye on this camp without them spotting us. But I'm stationing a team of men nearby who can pile in as backup if things turn nasty.'

Baldini made a fist and thumped the palm of his left hand. 'I say we take them out right now! Get them in for questioning and hammer the information out of those sons of bitches before they've even finished their *churros* and coffee.'

Sitting only a metre or so away from Baldini, Van den Bergen could almost smell the testosterone coming out of the American's pores. His enthusiasm was exhausting to watch.

'We can't afford to let them slip through our fingers,' Baldini continued, abruptly rising from his chair as if to prove his point further. Shifting from foot to foot. 'That camp was fresh and they were planning on coming back. If they get wind they're being watched, it'll be *adios amigos!*'

Van den Bergen shook his head. Cleared his throat so that he had everybody's attention. 'No, come on, Baldini!' he said, tempted to stand but realising only a dick would use his height to his advantage in an argument such as this. 'I've worked big drugs cases before. We all have, right? If you let the bottom-feeders know you're onto them now, the big fish will swim away. These sorts never buckle easily. They've got too much to lose. Their lives are worth nothing. Their families' lives are worth even less.'

He locked eyes with Gonzales and saw appreciation there. Nikolay or whatever moniker he might use in Mexico was the prize. They both knew it.

'Maybe we wait,' Gonzales said. 'We stake out the camp as best we can. Track their movements. See what we can find out. If there's no sign of a boss after forty-eight hours, we pull them all in.'

'My flight leaves tonight,' Van den Bergen said.

Gonzales shrugged. 'Compromise, then, I guess. We'll watch their movements today and raid the place at sundown. Maybe you'll go home a hero.' He smiled.

'Or maybe you'll go home in a wooden casket,' Baldini said.

CHAPTER 35

Mexico, Palenque town in Chiapas, 28 May

'Okay, girls,' Maritza said. 'We're here.'

George jolted awake, horrified by the realisation that she had nodded off. The other *transportistas* were all yawning and stretching. Some had been sprawled on top of the crates that contained the guns and were now just sitting up. Heart thudding uncontrollably, George looked between her feet and was relieved to see her bag still there – still zipped with its contents apparently still undiscovered.

Scratching at her matted black hair, Maritza dialled a number on her mobile phone. Spoke in rapid-fire Spanish to somebody, nodding. Gouging at her scar with a filthy fingernail.

'Jesus. I've got to pee,' Paola said, swigging from an almost empty water bottle.

'That can wait!' Maritza said, ending her call and shoving her phone into one of the pockets of her cargo trousers. '*El jefe* wants the guns safely stored immediately before sunrise drags the cops out of their beds.'

The shutters were up and George drank in the fresh air, almost cool while the tropical sun was a mere yellow-grey streak on the horizon. With her rucksack safely on her back, she grabbed one handle on a crate of AK-47s as Paola grabbed the other. They clambered gingerly out of the truck. It was the first real glimpse George had had of Mexico apart from the view of the flat green blanket that was the Yucatan jungle from the air on the flight over. That felt like a lifetime ago. Now, in the half-light of dawn, she saw that they had parked on what might normally be a busy street of shops and bars, some built in a faux-colonial style and painted in pale colours. Bunting hung outside one or two places, suggesting a hearty Mexican welcome for whatever tourists might throng the place during wakeful hours. But that early in the morning, the town seemed deserted like an abandoned film set, given authenticity by the tangle of overhead electrical cables that snaked their way towards the green mounds of the mountains in the distance. Under normal circumstances, George would have loved to have visited this place and the nearby ruins she had heard tell of as a tourist. But for now, she was anything but.

'This weighs a tonne,' she said to Paola, lugging the crate through double wooden doors into a courtyard.

'If I don't get to a toilet, I'm going to piss my pants,' Paola said.

They followed their colleagues to a store, the entrance to which was concealed behind a heavy, leafy curtain of cornflower-blue morning glories, which were just opening as the sunlight intensified. A stocky, grubby-looking man held back the climber with one hand to let them through; held a cigarette in the other.

'Hurry up,' he said. 'Get this lot stacked and locked inside fifteen or the boss won't pay your ugly asses. Half in my storeroom. Half to stay on the truck for the hacienda. Those are the orders.'

As she passed him, George could smell a rancid tang of body odour and stale booze and cigarettes on the man. His attention was focused steadfastly on her breasts. He breathed out a plume of smoke contemplatively towards her bosom. If it were possible to see in somebody's eyes a disregard for women as anything other than an easy fuck, she could see it in this man's. Reflexively, she sucked her teeth at him. Remembered she wasn't in Southeast London. Would this guy even realise that she had slighted him? Would he care? No. Bollocks to him, anyway. She waved her pinkie at him. He was oblivious to that, too.

Together, she and Paola heaved the crate onto a pile.

'*El jefe* wants you to gather in the bar,' the man said, gesturing at the glazed doors on the opposite side of the courtyard with his cigarette. 'You'll get paid half what you're owed in there. Half when you get to the hacienda. And when you get there, he's got another job for you.'

Maritza led the way and her *transportistas* followed in an orderly line. George contemplated the prospect of meeting Nikolay – an international trafficker that she was supposed to be on good terms with. *Jesus. I'm going to die. He'll take one look at me, realise I'm full of shit and that will be the end of that. I'll be plugged with bullets like those Guatemalan cops and dumped in the hills. Christ, Letitia. If you're dead and watching over me, now's your chance to make up for being a shitty mother.*

With the rising sun brighter by the minute and her body more charged with adrenalin by the second, George could feel the temperature rising to furnace-like levels. She trooped inside, scanning the surprisingly well-furnished bar for a man who resembled a drug lord. The place seemed empty. The ceiling-to-floor poles in the middle of a dancefloor told George everything she needed to know.

'Well. Where is he?' Maritza asked the grubby man, grabbing him brusquely by his shirt collar and hoisting him with apparent ease off the ground. 'I was told he'd be here to pay me in person. I deal with *el jefe*. Right? Where is he?'

'*El cocodrilo?*'

'Yes, fucking *el cocodrilo*. Or Nikolay. Whatever you want to call him.'

'He was here yesterday, inspecting the new Russian girls that

239

have just come in. But he's had to go on ahead to deal with some other business. He'll meet you at the hacienda. He wants you to go to the landing strip in the mountains.'

Maritza's glare burned with naked aggression. The musculature of her tattooed arms was a match for any man. 'Where's our money? I show up with the guns, as arranged and I get *you*? You sack of shit!' She threw the man onto the floor, sending a bar stool flying. 'I don't do business with some underling who hasn't seen a bar of soap in years.'

Sudden movement and a sharp inhalation of breath in the corner caught George's attention. She squinted through the murk and spotted two Caucasian women, seated in a red leather booth. One blonde. One brunette. Though it was no later than 5.30 a.m., they were already scantily clad in sparkling bikini tops and hot pants. Their platform shoes were visible beneath the table.

'Give us our money!' Maritza yelled at the man, who was back on his feet now, clutching at his head.

'Okay, okay, you crazy bitch,' the man said. 'I was going to pay you anyway. *El cocodrilo* said you should hang out here today, get something to eat and drink and get some rest. Meet him at the airstrip tomorrow for your next job.'

As he reached into a cash tin behind the bar, Maritza pulled a pistol from her waistband. Deftly clicked the safety off. 'That had better be money you're pulling out there, pal, or it will be the last thing you ever do.'

The man treated the *transportista* to a withering glance. 'Jesus. You're not cool, do you know that? Not cool at all.' He withdrew a tight, fat roll of cash and flung it to her.

She grabbed it cleanly from the air. Turned to the other women. 'Use the restroom. Freshen up. Help yourselves to whatever you want from the bar, girls.' Turned back to the grubby barkeeper. 'Bring us some food. We want breakfast. Big. Hot. Fresh. Got it?'

While her fellow *transportistas* barked their orders at the man, George grabbed a Coke and approached the booth where the two

240

women were seated. Close up, she could see that they were no more than eighteen or nineteen, though their heavy make-up suggested they were older.

'Hello,' she said in English, wedging her bottom onto the booth's table. 'Where are you girls from?'

The blonde raised an eyebrow and glanced at the brunette, as though she was seeking guidance.

'You speak English?' the brunette asked. She spoke with a heavy Eastern European accent. Pointed to George's tattoos with a barely concealed grimace. 'But you look like them.'

'I am one of them,' George said. 'But I'm half English and used to work for Nikolay in Europe. What are you doing in a Palenque brothel at the crack of dawn, dressed like you're ready to party?'

The blonde girl spoke quickly to her compatriot in a tongue George was certain was either Russian or Polish. Her bloodshot eyes implied either sleeplessness or tearfulness or both. She was shaking her head, shooting George with a mistrustful glance.

The brunette lit a cigarette, dragged deeply on it, exhaling the smoke over George. She grabbed George's Coke bottle from her, taking a hearty gulp. 'My friend Rozalina here doesn't think we should speak to you.'

'I'm just being friendly,' George said, holding the palms of her hands high. 'You both seem a long way from home. Like me. What's your story?'

Chattering away in the unfamiliar tongue, the blonde mentioned the name Nikolay and followed it seemingly with a stream of abuse, judging by her tone. She pulled the cup of her bikini to the side to reveal a florid bite-mark on her surgically enhanced breast.

The brunette sighed. 'We are from Russia. I am Yana.' Flicked her ash mournfully into the ashtray. 'And we are sitting here because our last customers of the night went only a half-hour ago.'

'You're working girls?' George asked, staring at the cigarette

241

and wondering if it would be morally wrong to cadge a smoke when she was supposed to be giving up.

'No!' Yana said, dolefully staring at the poles in the middle of the dancefloor. 'We met Nikolay's man in Moscow. He told us Nikolay lived in Amsterdam but had enterprises everywhere. We paid him thousands to come to the US in search of a new life. It started out well enough. We ended up on a cargo ship for a month, travelling to the Dominican Republic. At least we had crossed the Atlantic.' She scratched at her crotch area. Sighed again. 'But when we got to Mexico, thinking we would just travel north over the border into the US and get jobs as hairdressers, Nikolay's men took our passports.' She turned to Rozalina and spoke in Russian. There was a brief exchange between the girls. Rozalina started to tremble, then weep silently. Her narrow shoulders heaved with grief.

'They made us start to work in brothels as dancers and hookers. When we said no, they beat us.' She pointed to the ghost of a black eye beneath the heavy foundation and eye make-up. 'They charge the men five hundred dollars a time with all of us Eastern European girls.'

'All of us?'

The girl inclined her head towards the ceiling. 'There are about ten more girls upstairs, sleeping it off. Every day, we start at about 11 a.m. The men come from all over. Tourists. Officials. Men who can afford to pay large sums like that in cash. I listen to the conversations if they speak in English because I studied English back home, thinking I would need it when I got to the US! What a joke.'

'What sort of things do they talk about?' George asked, pushing her Coke bottle towards the girl in a show of solidarity.

'Drugs, mostly. They think we don't understand. But I understand fine. Nikolay himself has occasionally come in here to do business with big shot American drug dealers from New York and Chicago. Places like that. He has a lab in the jungle that makes meth, apparently. But if you're in one of the groups of *transportistas* that he likes to employ, you must know about that.'

'Sure.' George nodded disingenuously. Committed every word to memory, wondering how she could relay this information to Van den Bergen without alerting potentially corrupt local cops to her whereabouts. 'Do you know where the meth lab is?' she asked breezily.

Rozalina shook her head. Lit another cigarette. She smelled of smoke and too much cloying perfume with the underlying but pungent scent of sex evident as she crossed and uncrossed her legs. 'Of course not. We're stuck here in Palenque. We have been for months, now. Our money's gone. Our passports have gone. Our hope of a fresh starts in the States is just a dream. And we have nothing to do with drugs, though I know they sell them behind the bar if you know who to ask and how to ask. The guys smoke weed and meth in the rooms when they're with us girls. It makes them aggressive. It's horrible.'

Again, Yana snapped at her and slapped her own mouth, as if admonishing her friend for speaking out. Rozalina patted the girl's leg reassuringly.

'Anyway, when the drug dealers from the US come, they have a good time with us girls at Nikolay's expense,' she said. 'We are like hospitality. If he says we must go with a man, we go. And the time one of the girls refused, she got thrown to Nikolay's pet crocodiles, apparently.'

'That's why they also call him *el cocodrilo*,' George offered, joining the dots.

'Yes.'

She shuddered visibly, as did Rozalina, who mouthed the words '*el cocodrilo*' in near silence.

'Have you thought about going to the police?' George asked.

The Russian girl shook her head. Tugged fretfully at her long dark locks. 'There are police who come in here as customers. You don't know the straight guys from the crooked.' She frowned. Her

243

mouth seemed to harden. She folded her long, bruised arms. 'You're one of them,' she said. 'How come you're asking me if we're been to the authorities? Are you trying to catch me out? Are you one of Nikolay's spies?'

Yana turned to Rozalina and said something that made Rozalina's blue eyes harden.

'No!' George said, realising she had revealed too much. 'I'm not spying.' Searching for an excuse for her cross-examination. The last thing she needed to do was draw attention to herself in front of Maritza, who was busy about a pile of chocolate-dipped *churros* but who, George reasoned, would instantly swap her breakfast for the thrill of a kill and an extra share of the money. 'It's just that we *transportistas* are independent. You know? We're not slaves or trafficked like you two. We work for Nikolay but, hey! We're all women, aren't we? I don't have to like that you're being exploited.'

Pursing her lips, Yana sized George up. Lit another cigarette with shaking hands. 'You don't have to like it?' she asked. She laughed mirthlessly. Leaned in with a suddenly stern expression, lowering her voice so that she could not be overheard. 'Now I *know* you're lying. Because that pig who runs the bar told us that about ten Salvadoran girls from another of Nikolay's brothels managed to escape and ran into the hills to an airstrip in the middle of nowhere, hoping to get a flight back to El Salvador. But they got caught. He said they've been rounded up and taken prisoner. And you know what?'

George didn't like the expression on the Russian girl's face. It had a fatalistic air of bitter resignation to it. 'What?'

'Before you lot showed up, he said your next job would be to travel to the airstrip to meet Nikolay, where you'll be expected to chop the heads off the escaped girls.'

Opening and closing her mouth, George felt the Coke fizzing unpleasantly in the pit of her stomach. Beheading runaway trafficked women. This was not something she had ever signed up to do in the course of trying to track down her missing father. She swallowed hard. And this Nikolay would definitely be there. Maritza would be expecting her to be on familiar terms with him. *Shit. This is getting worse by the minute*, she thought. *I've got to see this through but if I do, I'm definitely either going to have to kill or get killed. Why did I sign up to this? Why?*

'Oh,' she simply said in answer to the Russian girl.

'Because that's what he does,' Yana continued. 'Nikolay has earned his nicknames because he's a brutal, lying monster. *El cocodrilo. El silenciador*. Human life means nothing to him. He steals everything from you. Your money, your body, your future, your voice.'

Standing, George realised she was attracting attention to herself by talking to the Russian girls. Yana now had her arm around a sobbing Rozalina. Maritza and the other *transportistas* were looking over at them. But something had struck a chord with George.

'Hang on a minute. Did you say one of Nikolay's names was *el silenciador*?' She felt the colour drain from her face. 'And that he lives in Amsterdam?'

'Yes.'

'The Silencer?'

'Yes.' Yana nodded and blew a plume of smoke into the air.

George stumbled backwards as the enormity of what the Russian girl had said hit home. There was only one Silencer. And he would recognise Georgina McKenzie in a single, rotten heartbeat.

CHAPTER 36

The Caribbean Sea, just off the coast of Mexico, 1 June

'Look,' he said to Jorge. 'You can't smoke in here. It's a fire risk.'

The heat on the inside of the sub generated by the engines was already unbearable. Sweat rolled down his face and back, soaking into the uncomfortable 'Captain's chair', which was nothing more than a second-hand typing chair. But Jorge, who was sitting on a mattress, seemed unperturbed.

'Who's the one with the gun, *mecánico*? Me or you?' Jorge waved the pistol towards him like a dismissive flick of his hand.

'You.'

'Exactly. Now, it takes three days and nights to sail to the Dominican. I suggest you worry less about what I'm doing and captain this goddamn tub right. Because if you screw up and we go down, you're dead whichever way you look at it.' He set his pistol down on the mattress, struck a match and lit the foul-smelling cigar, examining the glowing end with a satisfied smile.

Turning back towards the console, he wept inwardly with frustration, considering how the next sixty-odd hours might pan out. If the cigar started a fire, the tonnes and tonnes of meth would start to burn and would kill them both with narcotic fumes. If Jorge insisted upon lighting cigars for the next two and a half days, the ventilation system wouldn't be able to cope with his exhaled smoke – that much was clear. The diesel stink was already overpowering. The bucket that sloshed in the corner with urine was rancid. The conditions were even worse than he had anticipated, and all because that murderous fiend *el cocodrilo* had insisted he set sail before the semi-submersible had been tested properly and any glitches had been ironed out. Mercifully, the thing was staying afloat and watertight, despite it having been overloaded.

'How far have we gone?' Jorge asked.

He checked the navigation display. 'We've been going about nine hours. Seventy-three nautical miles.'

'Go faster.'

'We can't. This thing does eight nautical miles an hour. We've got about six hundred nautical miles to go. Jorge, you're going to have to be patient. This is no speedboat. And please, for the love of God, put your cigar out and stop smoking.' He scrutinised his guard's face for understanding or at least a glimmer of interest, if only motivated by self-preservation. But he saw only indifference and arrogance on that sweaty, heavily stubbled face. 'Well, at least be careful with how you dispose of the smoking materials and try to keep your smoking to a minimum. We can't afford a fire on here. The cargo will be lost, we'd have to abandon the vessel, and the mighty *el cocodrilo* will come after you and maybe use your blood to launch the next sub.'

Finally, Jorge shuffled on the mattress, looking contrite. He stubbed the cigar out on the sole of his flip-flop and lay back with his arms above his head, revealing in all their glory the epic sweat stains around the armpits on his vest.

Go to sleep! he thought. *Please go to sleep. Surely he'll drop off at some point.*

But Jorge crept on his hands and knees over to the bricks of meth that the *transportistas* had loaded onto the semi-submersible. He pulled aside the many layers of clingfilm and pulled out several crystals.

'You never saw this,' the guard said, winking. Crawling back to his mattress, Jorge crushed the crystals on a plate with the butt of his pistol and snorted the resulting powder through a rolled-up fifty-pesos note.

No. The guy would never sleep. Not now.

An hour passed. He stared blankly at the instruments, mesmerised by their glowing displays. Jorge had grown restless and garrulous, talking endlessly about men he had beaten up or killed for the cartel, women he had fucked to within an inch of their lives and time he had spent in prison, caged in overcrowded cells with other gang members.

'This is my life, *mecánico*. My calling. I am totally committed to Coba and *el cocodrilo*.' Jorge thumped his chest and rolled over, facing the wall. But still, he continued to drone on and on in his meth-fuelled eulogy. 'You know what? This makes me proud. This makes my family proud. Because the country … the state offers men like me nothing. No way to feed my wife and kids. No means of looking after my parents now that they're old and can't work. You know what my neighbour's mother does to make money? She goes around the streets in Playa del Carmen collecting empty water bottles from the tourists in a big sack so she can get a few pesos for them. Not my mother.'

Realising that Jorge was utterly absorbed in the telling of his own life story, whether he interjected or not, he started to remember the scene on the beach. The beheading of the scout. The armed *transportistas* who had loaded the meth onto the sub. Hadn't one of them knocked into him as he had stumbled towards the vessel? A young woman, tattooed like the others but not pure Latin American. She had been mixed race. Perhaps originally from one of the islands in the Caribbean, Afro-Salvadoran or Mestiza. The memory sharpened. She had touched his hip. Was it possible that she had slid something into his pocket?

Holding his breath, he nervously glanced over to Jorge and saw that his guard was still jabbering away to the wall, to the

248

ceiling, to anything that wouldn't interrupt his autobiographical flow. Perfect.

Tentatively, he slid his hand inside the pocket of his shorts. His heart thudded inside his chest, feeling like it might explode, for there, at the end of his fingertips, he felt a piece of folded paper. A note. A note! What could it say? Why had that woman slipped him a secret missive? If only there had been a dunny on board the sub. He had no option but to try to read it now.

Withdrawing it with careful, determined fingers, he slid the note out of his left pocket and transferred it to his right side – the side that Jorge could not see from where he lay on his mattress. Unfolded it. It was a handwritten letter of sorts, penned in a very tight hand, and now shaking between his sweaty fingers so violently that he could not read the words. Appearing to examine the clipboard that contained readings of their position, he silently clipped the letter beneath some nautical data. Started to read.

CHAPTER 37

The Netherlands, a warehouse in a dockside location, at the same time

The gaffer tape stung as it was ripped from Elvis' mouth, waking him. Opening his eyes, he realised he was in a warehouse of sorts. Dank and dark with boxes stacked to the double-height ceiling. A well-used fork-lift truck idling unmanned some ten feet away, but otherwise empty. The place smelled of mildew and diesel. Outside, the call of seagulls told him he was by the sea. But where was his abductor? And why did his throat throb so badly? He swallowed and winced. The pain lanced through him. The fear paralysed him.

It was all he could do to swivel his eyes to search for whoever had removed the gag.

To his left, plastic flaps served as a door into some adjacent area. To his right—

'Jesus!'

The water bit into his skin like an ice pick. He could barely see. His breath came in miserly choking gasps. Shaking his head, he tried to shout out but his words emerged no louder than a whisper. 'Who are you?'

A man loomed before him, clutching an empty bucket and wearing a sadistic grin. The giant whom he had last seen as a reflection in the mirrored lenses of his informant's sunglasses. Dressed in all black with a leather jacket, like some B-movie gangster. He even had the buzz cut.

'What are you doing?' Elvis asked, his voice an agonising, hoarse rasp that grated his throat raw with every syllable he managed. 'Let me go. I've got no problem with you. You've got no problem with me. Please. Take my wallet, if it's money you want.' Looking into the giant's expressionless face, Elvis could see that his words were wasted. This was not a man to barter with.

'Shut your mouth,' the man said, planting a right hook on Elvis' left cheekbone that almost knocked him from the chair he was tied to. 'We want you to listen and learn, gay boy.'

Elvis spat blood onto the floor, remembering the alleyway. He had been bickering with his informant Sepp one minute and under attack from these brutes the next. Garrotted. 'Where's Sepp – the old guy with the long hair? What did you do with him?'

Grinning, the man whistled. The engine of the yellow fork-lift cranked up and the vehicle began to reverse towards him. Panting fast with adrenalin, Elvis noticed that it was being driven by one of the other men from the alley – one of the men who had sprinted after his informant. The fork-lift, which had had its sharp forks pointing in the opposite direction to Elvis, spun around. There, impaled on the end of the raised blades, hung the lifeless body of Sepp, transformed from a hoary old biker to a battered rag doll that dripped blood onto the warehouse floor in a trail. The vehicle moved closer and closer, coming to a stop only a couple of feet away. On closer inspection, Elvis could see that the old junkie was missing an eye. Blood dripped from the empty, ruined socket. A fresh kill.

'Oh my God!' Elvis cried. 'Why did you do it?'

'This prick was on our payroll,' the giant said. He folded his arms, looking up at the body and nodding, as though he was admiring an art installation rather than a corpse. 'One of us. His job was to watch you and your little friends – one little friend in particular, goes by the name of Georgina McKenzie.'

'George?' Elvis asked, staring at his abductor's broken nose.

'Yes. My boss has got a hard-on for McKenzie. She's been a naughty girl and cost him a lot of money. So, my boss paid your man here to put the frighteners on McKenzie. Shadow her a bit. Let her know she was under scrutiny. But your little grass got greedy, didn't he? You can't take cash off the Rotterdam Silencer and then go running to some gay-boy pig for another handout in return for information on him. That, my friend, is called shitting where you eat.'

'Why the hell did you cut the poor bastard's eye out?' Elvis whispered. Tears leaked onto his cheeks, betraying his show of bravado as nothing more than that. *They're going to kill me and cut out my eye too. Mum's dying. And here I am, strapped to a fucking chair in some dockside warehouse. I'll never see Arne again. My one shot at happiness and it's over though it never really began.* Then, it dawned on him. 'You!'

'Me what?'

'The eye in the gift-wrapping in Vinkeles restaurant. *You* sent the eye to McKenzie and made her think it was her mother's. But it really belonged to some two-bit dealer that had been killed and dumped on wasteland. Nasser Malik. The pathologist said it was an obvious gang-style execution. You did it!'

The man inside the fork-lift truck started to laugh. 'He's not stupid, is he?' he shouted.

'It might have been me,' the giant said, winking.

'Where's McKenzie's mother?' The pain of his garrotted throat and the blood that seeped from his split cheekbone were the last things on his mind, now. Elvis was feverish with intrigue as he started to piece the puzzle together. Even his mother had receded to the back of the queue of conscious thoughts as his imagination raced away with elaborate theories. 'McKenzie thought it was Gordon Bloom that sent the eye. The Duke. But it wasn't, was it? It was Stijn Pietersen. And you work for him, don't you?'

'Clever boy. I already fucking said that.' The sarcasm was audible in the man's voice.

Elvis struggled in his chair, his nostrils flaring, working overtime to keep his cortisol-flooded body suffused with oxygen. This was it. The end of his life. 'I've got no interest in the Rotterdam Silencer. Tell him that. You must tell him. I heard nothing. I've reported nothing.' Deep inside him, his policeman's honour and principles were intact. But they had been temporarily overridden by survival instincts. 'Please. You've got to believe me.'

'What do you want me to do with this arsehole?' Elvis' pleading was interrupted by the driver of the fork-lift, who manoeuvred the forks up and down for clarification. The sad body of Sepp, the duplicitous informant, flapped around like a listless puppet, showering Elvis with thick droplets of coagulating blood.

Elvis tried to scream but could only emit a half-hearted whimper, clenching his eyes shut. Opening them again, willing himself to face his murderers like a man.

His abductor shrugged. 'Stick him in a body bag for now. I'll take him to the incinerator when I get a minute.' He turned to Elvis. 'Now, there's just the question of you, gay boy.'

He withdrew from his pocket something wrapped in a red-stained rag that had been placed inside a clear plastic lunch bag. Removing the object from the bag and peeling the edges of the rag back, the giant revealed a ratty, staring eyeball between his fingers and thumb.

'Open wide,' he said.

'No! You're fucking mad!' Elvis said.

But the giant pinched Elvis' nostrils together with his left hand, forcing him to gulp air through his mouth. Briefly, Elvis tried to shake his head around enough to evade the man's cannibalistic intentions, but he had a strong grip on Elvis' nose.

'Pop it in your mouth. There you go, gay boy. A fudge-packer like you should have no trouble putting a ball in your gob, should you?'

He rammed the eyeball into Elvis' mouth. Quickly produced a roll of gaffer tape from his jacket's inside pocket and unfurled a strip with deft fingers. Placed it over Elvis' full mouth in one fluid move.

Elvis started to gag immediately. He could feel the vomit rising in his gullet, realising there was no way out for it. This was worse than being garrotted. In five minutes' time, he calculated he would have choked to death in any case. A bullet would have been kinder. *Kill me*, he thought. *I can't take this anymore. This is not what I signed up to. This is not bravery. It's torture.*

'So, gay boy,' the man said, leaning over so that his bowling ball of a head was level with Elvis' face. Gripping his knees with hands like shovels. 'This is the message the Rotterdam Silencer wants to send to Van den Bergen. And you'd better make sure you fucking give it to him, okay?'

Nodding, the tears streamed down Elvis' cheeks. Vomit that had no other exit route sprayed through his nostrils, burning his throat on the way up and his sinuses on the way out.

'Are you listening? I want you to give him and that bitch, McKenzie – especially McKenzie – the message that he's watching them. The Silencer sees everything. But McKenzie in particular owes him big time for taking down The Duke.'

The man smiled and raised his eyebrows as Elvis fixed him with a quizzical look.

'Yeah. That's right,' he said. 'Gordon Bloom was the Rotterdam Silencer's right-hand man. And when you dicks took him out of the picture, you forced the Silencer out of semi-retirement. So, now you're going to pay. An eye for an eye, right? There's a shit storm of biblical proportions brewing. It's coming this way and it's coming for Van den Bergen and McKenzie.'

CHAPTER 38

The Caribbean Sea, off the coast of Mexico, at the same time

Amid the thrum of the semi-sub's engine, he read the letter, digesting every word as thoroughly but as quickly as possible, before Jorge spotted his subterfuge.

Dear Michael,

I don't know even how to start this letter. I can't believe I've found you, more than twenty years after you left. There's so much I want to say to you, but now is not the time. Time is the thing we have the least of. We are both in danger, but for now, I know you're alive and that's the main thing.

When I saw you in the jungle encampment, handcuffed to the wall of the shack you share with their chemist, it was all I could do not to cry with relief. I've travelled halfway across the world to find you, Papa, and don't worry. While there's breath in my body, I won't let you go. Not without a fight. Like Letitia, the one thing I excel at is fighting. I've inherited her stubborn streak, you'll be glad to hear.

So many things to tell you …

Know first, that I have never forgotten you. I realise that Letitia stripped you out of my life and that your departure was not your fault. I remembered all this time the way your voice sounds and the way you smelled when you put me on your shoulders and I hugged your head or when you cuddled me if I had fallen over. I learned Spanish at school to keep the memory of you alive, always quietly hoping that we would be reunited one day but, sadly, never finding time to look you up in those years when I had the chance and you were still safe and living in Spain. I'm so sorry for that. We should never delay the important stuff, like telling the people we love so dearly that they are loved. You never know when that opportunity might be gone forever. Well, I do love you, Papa. I always did. I never stopped.

I will see you on the beach tonight when I load the drugs into the semi-sub that you are supposed to pilot to the Dominican Republic. Travelling undercover with this band of violent transportistas, I am writing this letter from the relative safety of a locked toilet, praying that my true identity is not discovered. I don't know how things will play. But I have a plan to rescue you.

The man you are working for is extremely dangerous. He knows exactly who you are and I have a feeling he kidnapped you specifically to get back at me. That's possibly why he named the sub after me (though my name is now something entirely different). It's a long story that I don't yet fully understand all the twists and turns to. But I'm not afraid, Papa. I'm coming to get you.

All my love always and forever.

Ella xxx

Realising that he had already been staring at the clipboard's contents for too long, George's father wiped away the tears with the back of his hand. Set the clipboard down and thought about the fragment of an old photo concealed inside the back of his watch, showing his beautiful daughter as a tiny 3-year-old. A photo he had kept in his wallet since it was taken almost twenty-five years earlier; a photo he had secreted inside the watch shortly after being snatched from his company's shuttle bus by those

Honduran gangsters. Years ago, now. He silently chastised himself for not taking note of the *transportista* who had bumped into him on the beach. He had no notion of the woman his little girl had turned into. His internet search efforts had revealed nothing under the name Ella Williams-May. It was as though she too had disappeared.

'Hey! What's this you're so damned interested in?' Jorge asked. Unexpectedly on his feet, stooping at his side beneath the low ceiling. His guard picked up the clipboard and leafed through the paperwork.

'Nothing!' Michael said, trying to snatch it back. Suddenly ice-cold in the knowledge that his only chance of rescue was about to be discovered and that his daughter's safety – already more than precarious – was now in jeopardy. 'Give it to me!'

The blow to the head from Jorge's practised fist stung. But it was clear that the guard had happened upon the letter.

'What's this shit, *mecánico*? Eh?' Another stinging punch sent him flying from the chair onto the floor of the sub. 'A letter in English? What the fuck is this, man? Tell me what it says.' Jorge leaped on top of him and started to rain down merciless blows on him.

'I don't know. I can't read English,' Michael lied.

'Where did you get it?' There was meth-fuelled bloodlust in Jorge's eyes.

'The chemist! The guy I share the shack with. He must have put it in my pocket. I haven't got a clue what it says either. I swear.'

Jorge pinned him on the floor painfully, digging his knees into Michael's arms so that they felt like they might snap in two. He took his pistol out of the waistband of his sweat-soaked jeans. 'You're lying. I can see it in your lying Spanish face.'

Clicking a bullet into the chamber of the gun, Jorge bared his teeth like a feral dog, his nostrils flaring. Ears ringing. The end of Michael Carlos Izquierdo Moreno's life decelerating almost to single stills right down now, as though someone had slowed the footage on old film to capture his final moments in slo-mo. Michael's only thought as Jorge pulled the trigger was not of the deafening gunpowder blast or that he was going to die. He thought of his daughter, being discovered and beheaded because of his own stupidity.

And then the bullet found its mark.

CHAPTER 39

Mexico, Hotel Bahia Maya, Cancun, a little later

'When are you coming home, Dad?' Tamara said.

Swallowing hard, Van den Bergen drank in the sight of his daughter on screen, committing her maturing face to memory. Then, his focus turned to his granddaughter, Eva, who was sitting on her mother's knee, pulling chunks out of Tamara's hair. Half of Numb-Nuts' DNA but still the most adorable child in the world. His muscles still held the memory of what the chubby, tiny girl felt like in his arms and the baby smell of her skin. 'I'm just about to start packing,' he said, altering his laptop's screen when he realised the camera was only filming the top of his head. 'My flight leaves tonight. I'll be back before you know it.'

'I hope George has been looking after you,' she said.

Eva made a gurgling noise, lunging forwards and covering the screen in dribbly handprints.

Van den Bergen reached out and touched the screen, thankful for the miracle of Skype and his girls, if nothing else in this godforsaken world was worth an iota of gratitude. 'I'm fine. Look, I've got to go. I'll call when I land at Schiphol, tomorrow. Give my little princess a kiss from her gramps.'

He killed the connection before the pain became too acute.

Wondered if he'd ever make it back in one piece to his little family. Prayed that the woman he loved would make it back in one piece to him.

'Where the hell are you, Georgina McKenzie?' he said, staring at the string of texts from her on his phone, dating back months and months. Van den Bergen liked to keep every single exchange between them as a memento of what he still couldn't believe he had, though he had been loath to agree to it for years.

His finger hovered over the call button, but he realised that dialling George's number was out of the question. If her phone rang and whoever she was with discovered she was speaking to a Dutch cop who was in cahoots with the local Federales, he could get her killed. If she wasn't dead already. Without knowing if his words would ever reach her, he had texted her with that prick Ad Karelse's details, including an explanatory note that Nikolay Bebchuck's holding company, InterChem GmbH, was a client of Karelse's employer. He had been careful to point out that Karelse was working in IT at Chembedrijf, potentially with access to the company's intranet, accounting systems and employees' email accounts. If George had received the text, she would have known immediately what the subtext of his message was: Van den Bergen wanted her to shelve whatever life-threatening activity she was currently preoccupied by in order to contact her ex-boyfriend and engage him in acts of industrial espionage. It was a simple ask, wasn't it?

He sipped his cranberry juice and water, gazing sullenly at the turquoise Caribbean Sea and the cobalt-blue sky that hung above it like a doting lover. His fingers trailed absently in the fine white sand, already warmed by the mid-morning sun. A tropical idyll, trimmed by well-tended royal palms, and here he was, sitting on a sunbed by the sea, on an almost-week-long trip that had been paid for by Maarten Minks, who was practically ejaculating with excitement about the developments. But without George safe and sound at his side, Van den Bergen may as well have been trudging through the torrential rain on the Hoek van Holland dockside, being shat upon by giant seagulls who didn't like the look of lanky, misanthropic, ageing detectives.

Checking his watch, he realised it was time to get on with it. His suitcase wouldn't pack itself.

He was just about to close his laptop and put it into its bag when he noticed that a new email had appeared in his inbox. Sent from an email address he didn't recognise – info@silent-crocodile.com. It was marked as urgent.

'Let me guess. A phishing scam or some middle-class mummy-preneur trying to sell me overpriced toys for Eva made from organic Himalayan yak shit.'

Growling with derision, loud enough that the hotel employee who was raking the beach paused in his task to check him out, Van den Bergen moved to redirect the email straight to junk. Thought better of it and clicked it open.

There was a message, written in English.

I spy with my little eye, something beginning with S ...

The cryptic message was accompanied by a photo of Elvis, strapped to a chair in what appeared to be a loading bay in some sort of warehouse. Elvis' mouth had been gaffer-taped. His battered, bloodied head lolled forwards onto his blood-stained chest. It was impossible to tell if he was dead or alive. But the Sig Sauer handgun that was pressed to his temple by a man who was just out of shot told Van den Bergen that if death hadn't already paid Elvis a visit, it would take very little to entice him over to that loading bay.

'S,' Van den Bergen said, feeling his fingertips start to prickle cold. Light-headed now, his pulse had gone into overdrive. The beach was beginning to spin and fragment, as though his life was nothing more than somebody else's view through a kaleidoscope.

'Pull it together, Paul,' he said, trying to regulate his breathing.

Focusing his attention away from the gruesome photograph and back onto the details of the message.

He reread the email address of the sender. Silent crocodile. I spy … S for Silencer. With a shaky click on his mouse, he revisited the bookmarked Wikipedia page that Gonzales had sent him, giving the unofficial history of the infamous Coba cartel that operated in the Yucatan peninsula and Chiapas regions – almost certainly the originators of the bad meth. Almost certainly the guys they were hunting. And there in amongst the sensationalist reportage was a detail that caused a ball of burning stomach acid to explode back up Van den Bergen's throat like a plume of magma.

A notorious Coba cartel boss is reputed to be the enigmatic el cocodrilo, named after his pet crocodiles, whom he allegedly feeds his enemies to. The Mexican Federal Police has no record of el cocodrilo or idea of his true identity or the whereabouts of the ranch where the crocodiles are kept. It could be that he is nothing more than an urban myth.

But Van den Bergen could guess exactly who the 'silent crocodile' was. His men had either killed or taken Elvis as a hostage on one continent. But there was a strong possibility that if she hadn't already, *if* she was still alive, George was heading right into his jaws on another.

CHAPTER 40

Mexico, Chiapas Mountains, 29 May

'So, it's a simple execution job,' Maritza said, as the truck bounced ever upwards into the Chiapas slopes. 'Nikolay … *el cocodrilo* wants us to behead some girls that ran away from the brothel. Make sure your machetes are sharp. Come to me if you need a whetstone.'

The other women nodded as though their leader had just told a gang of shelf-stackers in the supermarket that they were to load up a new variety of baked beans.

This is ridiculous, George thought, observing her travel companions. *What the hell am I doing? I can't get involved in this shit anymore. These women have lost their moral compasses entirely. I'm going to have to come up with another way of finding out what happened to my dad. I've got to get the fuck back to Van den Bergen somehow.*

But George's musings were interrupted by Paola, who nudged her in the ribs and smiled. 'Hey, Jacinta. We get well paid for executions. This is going to be a good trip.' She rubbed her hands together. 'My family are going to be partying in the streets when I get home with a fat roll of cash.'

Forcing herself to return the enthusiastic smile, George realised there was no way that this adventure was going to end well. She had been lucky thus far, but she was certain her luck was going to run out right about now.

The truck came to a standstill. Rummaging in her bag to check that the secret contents were all still properly concealed, George jumped when she realised Maritza was standing over her, holding a blade that was designed to hack down a mature palm tree with only a few good swings. The woman reached out, tilting George's chin upwards with shining, razor-sharp metal that was only an inch away from her carotid artery.

Steeling herself to show no fear, George treated Maritza to a cocksure glare that she had employed to good effect as a teen on the hardest streets of Southeast London.

'Here. You can borrow my spare,' Maritza said, removing the machete and offering George the handle.

'Thanks.' George ran her finger along the blade lightly and drew blood. Stifled a gasp at the unexpected sting by sucking her finger. The metallic taste was sickening. How she wished she could wash her hands with antibacterial soap and hot water. Despite her revulsion, she never took her eyes from the *transportista*'s. 'Nice and sharp,' she said. 'Good tools do a good job.'

'I'm expecting you to do a good job,' Maritza said.

George felt the weight of the weapon in her hand. 'You can count on me.' Forced a flash of teeth and hung the weapon carefully from her waistband.

After the remainder of the guns was unloaded into an elegant old farmhouse that harked back to the area's heyday of colonial pomp and splendour, George found herself stalking through the boiling-hot plantation. She was surrounded on all sides by tall crops of coffee, cotton and maize. Through the web of stalks, she spotted a woman, picking ripe coffee beans and putting them into a wicker basket. The woman was dressed in a colourful skirt and top; the top, heavily embroidered with flowers, and the skirt, elaborately woven into a rainbow of horizontal stripes, as was the traditional style of the indigenous Zapatistas. A baby was tied to her back in a papoose made from a blanket. When she saw George and her company of gun-running mercenaries, she took her basket and shrank further into the phalanx of coffee plants. The Zapatista insurgents held no sway on this plantation. Neither did the Mexican armed forces. This was a far-flung outpost in the Rotterdam Silencer's empire. Only his word was law. And George was heading to meet him.

She checked her tattoos. She had carefully gone over patches that were prominent and subject to wear during her too-few clandestine trips to the toilet. Still intact, thank God. George said a silent prayer of thanks to the staying power of WHSmith's smudge- and waterproof felt-tipped pens and the elaborate, temporary tattoos that eBay had yielded. She followed that with a prayer to the gods of staying power that the tattoos wouldn't curl, that the remaining ink in her pen would suffice and that the battery in her phone, which was already low, would last long enough for her to maintain contact with Van den Bergen, even if it was only via one brief text each day.

Not that any of that mattered now. For George was about to come face to face with Stijn Pietersen – a man whom she had thought to be behind bars; a man who had stood in a warehouse on the outskirts of Amsterdam some ten or so years earlier, telling her to strap bags full of ecstasy beneath her breasts and to cover the contraband with a nun's habit. A man whom her ex-squeeze, Danny, had worshipped as though he had been a demi-god. If he recognised Jacinta, the inexperienced *transportista*, if he realised who she had once been and who she now was, Stijn Pietersen, the Rotterdam Silencer, would have everything to hate George for. Not only was she the lover of his nemesis, Van den Bergen – a man he had put a bullet in – but she had testified against him in a closed court, producing a faithful and damning sound recording of his criminal activities from the kit that had been concealed on her person by a man she fondly remembered as the Gargoyle. Oh, the bitter irony that fate had led her back to him.

Testifying against Stijn Pietersen had been the start of her new life, but facing him now, she knew, would bring that life to an abrupt and brutal end.

Goodbye, Van den Bergen, my love, she thought. *Goodbye, Letitia. Goodbye, Papa. Goodbye shitty world with all your unanswered questions and unfulfilled dreams. If I'm going out, I'm going out showing not a shred of fucking fear. And I'm taking that murderous bastard, the Silencer, with me.*

She ran her hand over the handle of the machete and smiled grimly at what was to come.

With a pounding heart that made her feel never more alive, though she had reached the end, she emerged into a clearing. The sun beat down on the dusty glare of the landing strip, glinting off the windows and shining fuselage of a light aircraft that was positioned at the far end. George pulled a pair of sunglasses from her cargo trousers and pushed them up her nose. Balked at the sight of about ten women who were arranged in a line in the middle of the strip, kneeling with their hands tied behind them and bags on their heads. The workers from the fields were being roughly shepherded towards them, forming a macabre and silent audience of shuffling, cowed women in clothes that seemed too jaunty for what was about to happen.

'Line up behind the prisoners!' Maritza said to them. 'There are more of us than them, someone will have to duck out and take a hit in pay. Paola. Sit this one out.'

Feeling that she might at any moment bring her breakfast up, George marched over to her allocated victim. A screaming woman on her knees. Jesus. A woman she was supposed to behead. How the hell was she going to wriggle out of this?

'Right,' Maritza said, wiping her face with the hem of her dusty Santa Muerte T-shirt, revealing a tattooed but bulging stomach that belied multiple pregnancies. 'We wait for *el cocodrilo*.'

'Wait!' George said, holding up her hand. She pointed to Paola. Spoke to Maritza, breathing steadily, trying to keep the blind panic out of her voice. 'Let Paola do the job. She's got a kid and a mother to feed. I haven't. Seriously.' She shrugged nonchalantly. 'I'd love to do it, but there'll be other opportunities.'

Approaching in a slow swagger, Maritza stood nose to nose with George. The older woman's breath smelled of chewing tobacco and coffee. She whipped off George's shades and seemed to look straight into George's soul.

Keep breathing. You feel nothing. Everything you've told this woman is the truth. She cannot see what lies deeper.

The tension rippled on the air like heatwaves. The *transportista*'s hand rested ominously on her rifle, slung to the side.

Then, Maritza took a step back, her lips curling upwards just a fraction. 'You're a good girl. Too good for our band of crazy bitches!' The half-smile blossomed into a fully fledged grin. 'You sure you're one of us?!'

George merely raised an eyebrow in response and took a thankful step back. Exchanging a gang hand-sign with a delighted-looking Paola.

'I owe you a beer, Jacinta,' Paola said.

I owe you my soul, George thought.

But she had no more time to reflect on her lucky escape, for *el cocodrilo*, a.k.a. Nikolay, a.k.a. the Rotterdam Silencer, had just emerged from the dense treeline into the clearing. And she was certain he was staring straight at her.

The order was given. In one smooth movement, the *transportistas* all drew their machetes. The screaming of the women as the bags were removed from their heads was gut-wrenching. It was the sound of grim realisation dawning. It was the worst thing George had ever heard in her life. Averting her gaze, she saw fear and shame in the fieldworkers' faces as they were forced to watch. They were all party to this bedlam. Prisoners of the Silencer's whim. Even the *transportistas* who held the blades aloft, poised to behead the runaways, were trapped inside his vortex of violence that they could only escape through death. Behind her sunglasses, she closed her eyes and conjured the sound of Curtis Mayfield. A favourite anthem of manufactured optimism at a time when all hope seemed otherwise to have fled the scene. This was the wet road Mayfield had always sung of that lay ahead. And still, she could not slip. And still, she must bite her lip and dared not cry.

God forgive me for standing by and doing nothing.

The blades fell. The sound of the victims' heads rolling on the compacted dirt of the airstrip had a dull finality to it.

Watching the reaction of his fieldworkers and chatting to a small, deferential man who appeared to be the head of his considerable entourage of vest- and jeans-clad gangsters, the Rotterdam Silencer started to nod. Laughed out loud at something his lackey said. Snapped his fingers and beckoned Maritza over.

He hadn't recognised her. Had he? Surely not!

It was all George could do to stifle a whoop, inappropriately tacked onto the end of her despair and disgust, like a text that delivered bad news being signed off with a winky emoji. Except her relief was short-lived as Maritza ordered them back to the truck.

'We're to follow *el cocodrilo*,' she said to their group, stalking over the decapitated bodies of the dead runaways. Her boots left a red trail in the dust. 'We're going to the Yucatan jungle. He's got work for us there.'

Though the risk of being recognised by the Silencer remained, George told herself that if she had managed to evade detection thus far, the chances were that she might slip beneath his radar, as long as she remained a safe distance away.

But when his Mercedes pulled over by a food stall at the roadside and Maritza turned to her, George felt suddenly certain that old Curtis Mayfield was full of shit.

'*El cocodrilo* wants a *tostada* from the stall,' she said. 'We're his armed escort to the jungle. You know him personally, Jacinta. You go. It'll give you two a chance to catch up.' She winked.

It had to be a test. George silently admonished herself for being so stupid as to believe she could deploy temporary tattoos, A-level Spanish and a couple of months of watching El Salvadoran soaps on YouTube as a means of duping these people? But there was no glimmer of trickery in Maritza's expression. Perhaps George's act *had* been that convincing. And maybe she was the natural linguist and accomplished performer that Sally Wright and Van den Bergen had always said she was. Hadn't she pulled stunts like this before? With Danny and Tonya. With the Silencer himself.

You can do this. Keep going for Papa. Keep going for the dead kids in the canals. Keep it up for those women whose lives were just snuffed out on the airstrip.

Ordering the *tostada* and marching over to the Mercedes, wearing her sunglasses and her best poker face, George was careful not to look directly into the car at the Silencer. Her heartbeat was thunderously fast – so much so that she felt her hands trembling from the rapid blood-flow through her body. Clenching her fists close to her hips so that she would give nothing away. She felt him scanning her breasts; the familiar contours of her face. But the smell of alcohol on his breath was strong. The possibility that he was simply too drunk to respond to any prompts from his subconscious gave her courage.

'Enjoy your snack,' she said.

'How about you come into the air-conditioned cool and enjoy my snack?' he said, grabbing at his crotch. 'I'm *el cocodrilo*. But I promise not to bite.'

Glancing into the truck, she finally saw his face up close. He had aged dramatically since she had last seen him, dressed like an accountant in a sharp grey suit inside that Amsterdam warehouse. A decade later, his tanned face was scored with deep lines, giving him the appearance of overcured leather. Hair that had been greying all those years ago he had now bleached blond, and there was a puffiness to his lower eyelids that put her in mind of drunks she had seen sleeping rough. Though incarceration had clearly not lasted long for Stijn Pietersen, his subsequent self-imposed exile in the sun-drenched inferno that was Central America or the frozen wastes of Eastern Europe had not been kind to him. During that momentary derisory glance, George got a snapshot of a man who had pushed things too far and who had pushed himself right to the edge in doing so.

Don't suck your teeth. Don't suck your fucking teeth. If you do that, you're dead. This isn't Catford or Lewisham. And you're a transportista, *not a Peckham rude girl. Move it. Get to the truck before he changes his mind and drags you into the car. And don't piss yourself.*

She walked away, clenching her pelvic floor for all she was worth.

CHAPTER 41

Groningen, Chembedrijf corporate Head Office, 1 June

'You've got some bloody cheek, getting in touch with me after all this time,' Ad said under his breath to his computer screen. Grinning at the words that shone with adventure and daring in that otherwise drab, grey office.

Feeling the flutter of anticipation in his stomach, he reread her message, rolling his typing chair closer to the monitor, angling his screen away so that his colleagues might not see what he was doing. At that moment, he was glad that telepathy was a figment of somebody's imagination – the sort of bunkum Astrid believed in, along with angels and hellfire.

'Talking to yourself again, Karelse?' Roel said.

Ad glanced to his left to take in the sight of the overweight computer programmer, who was lounging in his chair, chewing on a gooey *stroop wafel*. Wearing a yellow shirt and a green tie, with no discernible spine, judging by his consistently hunched posture, Roel put Ad in mind of an overripe banana.

'Yes,' Ad said. 'It's the only way I can get a sensible answer.' He pointed to the photo by his computer of his two shining baby pearls. A photo of their mother beside them. He put Astrid face down onto the desk. No need for her to know what he was doing. 'That's what kids do for you.'

Banter. He hated office banter. But Roel was snorting with laughter, so perhaps he'd mind his own damned business and leave Ad in peace to read on …

… an international drug- and people-trafficking ring, headed up by a man named Nikolay Bebchuck. It's alleged that he's actually the Rotterdam Silencer, but we need concrete proof … kids dying from a poisonous batch of crystal methamphetamine. I'm here in Mexico, trying to track down my father but I've run into … You always were the best sidekick a girl like me could wish for, Ad. Remember the excitement of your trip to Heidelberg, surrounded by all those sword-wielding, mensur-duelling wankers …? When I realised you were coincidentally working at the very company Nikolay Bebchuck is listed as doing business with, I thought …

You are in my heart.

Be well and please say you'll help.

George x

Though Adrianus, a married man almost 30 years old and father of two, thought this was his difficult ex-girlfriend's cynical attempt to rope him into a police investigation against his will and better judgement, the young Ad who had risked life and limb to help that old bastard Van den Bergen track down a deranged serial killer had to undo the top button of his shirt and loosen his tie. The excitement was almost unbearable. And George had made contact with him. After all these long years.

Fleetingly, he remembered the smell and the feel of her naked body. The taste of her kiss. The sound of her voice as they had spooned in her bed, talking about their hopes and fears and what kind of a life they might build together.

Just memories now. He had chosen to walk away for a reason. George had betrayed him. They had not been so compatible after all. And he had settled for the lovely Astrid, who had always been so very good on paper and who wouldn't harm a fly. Everybody loved Astrid. She was the woman who had given him the two most precious things in his life – his babies. Georgina McKenzie, on the other hand, had broken his heart. She was just using him. She could go fuck herself.

As he clicked the email closed, the phone rang. He picked up.

'Chembedrijf, good morning. Adrianus Karelse speaking.'

'Oh, darling. I'm in the supermarket.' Astrid, of course. The sound of little Lucas and Sofie screaming in the background to the sound of a supermarket jingle. 'We've got Lies Oostendorp and her hubby coming for dinner. You didn't forget, did you? Do you think I should do fish or beef? How about *witlof*?'

'I hate *witlof*,' he said, visualising a steaming dish of snotty endives. He had hated them when his mother used to foist them upon him. He hated them now.

'Great. I'll do *witlof*!' she said, clearly not listening. Jabbering on about Lies' new car, which was Japanese, would you believe it? And Lies' new hair colour, which was a full shade brassier than the blonde she used to have. And Lies' cleaner, who had stolen some money, but then, she was Romanian, after all, so what did she expect? 'I love you, honeybunny!' Astrid's voice rang like Sinterklaas' sleigh bells on a crisp winter morning. Except it was summer and he was too old to believe in Santa Claus, and Zwarte Piet, his black sidekick – almost always represented by some white guy who thought it was funny to black-up and don an afro wig – was just plain racist.

'Yep. Bye!'

'Fish or beef?'

'Chicken.'

He hung up and opened the email from George yet again. Fingers hovering over his keyboard, poised to respond …

273

CHAPTER 42

Mexico, Yucatan jungle, 30 May

'What's in the middle of the jungle that's so important?' George asked Paola.

She could tell by the way they had started to bounce around the now empty truck that their route had shifted from a smooth road to somewhere woefully uneven and undeveloped. Though they were still sitting in the darkness of the cargo area, with no view of the world outside, George was certain they had entered the Yucatan jungle. They had been travelling for a while now, and the terrain had flattened out. Was Van den Bergen close? More to the point, might she find out more about her father?

Paola was busy examining her teeth using the selfie function on her mobile phone. 'Maritza said *el cocodrilo* needs us to load a shipment of meth onto the truck and take it down to the beach. He's had a submarine or some shit specially built to sail the drugs over to the Dominican.'

'Why doesn't he use his own guys?'

Paola shrugged, still staring into the phone's display. Running her little fingertip over her eyebrow. Checking her chin for spots, as if she could actually see anything beneath the camouflage of her facial tattoos.

'I don't think he trusts them with meth that's got a street value of hundreds of millions of dollars. Would you? These low-level guys are always out to con and double-cross each other. *El coco-drilo*'s not stupid. He maybe has a few men he trusts and keeps close like that greasy little asshole, Miguel, but the rest would sell their grandmothers for a new cell phone. And he's used us before, don't forget. All of the cartels use us because we've got the reputation. We don't take sides. We don't take crap. We get the job done. Everyone knows Maritza. Everyone's scared shitless of her too.' She chuckled, popped some chewing gum into her mouth and observed her leader with evident admiration.

'A sub?' George asked.

As the truck lurched its way down whatever dirt track it had taken, she wondered how likely it was that Stijn Pietersen would be cunning enough to kill two birds with one stone – kidnap her father, a skilled engineer, so that he might design an ocean-going smuggling vessel, and simultaneously destroy her family. George didn't believe in coincidences and she was staking her life on the likelihood that those had indeed been the Silencer's intentions all along.

Unexpectedly, the truck came to a halt. A thump on the partition that divided the cab from the cargo area jolted George out of her reverie.

'We're here,' Maritza said. 'We break for lunch first. Then, we load the truck. Delivery after sundown. Back on the road home tonight. Got it?'

The women all nodded, swinging their rifles onto their backs.

Dappled light suffused with a green glow flooded the truck as the shutters rolled up. She was faced with a backdrop of dense, lush jungle, where butterflies fluttered among the exotic flowers that hung in clusters from trees. A dragonfly as large as a man's hand zipped by in staccato bursts, so fast that it left only a notion of its iridescent blue body and diaphanous wings behind before disappearing.

She had arrived in paradise.

George scrambled out, breathing in the fresh air. But the air was baking hot and damp, making her hair and clothes stick to her body. She had not felt clean since leaving Amsterdam. *Now is not the time, arsehole*, she told herself. *You're a transportista. Stinking armpits and bad hair are part of the job description. Don't worry about the filthy fingernails. You can get a scrubbing brush on them if you make it through this alive.*

She had arrived in hell.

'This way!' A tiny barrel of a man had appeared from the thicket and grunted the instruction at them, eyeing them warily. A stained white vest clung to his belly. Jeans that had been cut off at the knee hung from low on his hips. Flip-flops on his feet. He waved an Uzi at them. 'I'll show you to the camp. You sure you weren't followed?'

'We're not stupid,' Maritza said, clicking her fingers so that the rest of the *transportistas* fell into line.

Clutching her gun like a safety blanket, George walked at the back, wondering what the immediate future might hold for her. Would the Silencer be there? Had they been summoned to pack up the lethal batch of meth that was responsible for the floaters back in Amsterdam? Was this search for her father nothing more than a wild-goose chase?

In her peripheral vision, as she trod gingerly over tree roots and the brown giant leaves that had fallen from the palms onto the jungle floor, she caught sight of insects scuttling to safety. She shuddered. Had that been a spider clinging to a tree trunk? Spiders weren't meant to be that big. What if there were snakes …? *Stop this right now, you unutterable wimp. The wildlife is the least of your worries.*

Up ahead, her compatriots came to a halt on the edge of a clearing that was guarded by two men who were similarly armed with Uzis. They engaged in a brief exchange with Maritza, whereupon the men stepped aside. Advancing into the clearing, George shivered as she felt the men watching her.

Her surroundings comprised several small corrugated iron shacks that had been camouflaged with palm leaves and other foliage. At one end of the makeshift complex, there was a solid-looking Portakabin, complete with a door and a properly glazed window. Smoke curled upwards towards the jungle canopy from a flue that poked out of the roof. The stench of sulphur wafted over towards her. She grimaced but steeled herself not to hold her nose or pass comment.

'Food first,' Maritza said, rubbing her hands together in the face of the man who had been their jungle escort, much to his obvious chagrin. 'My girls need a good meal inside them. And you'd better not poison us with that stink coming from your lab. We don't get paid for that.'

As they trooped over to a large shack where men came and went through a curtain of Perspex flaps, George studied the complex's inhabitants. The rough-looking, dark-skinned gang-sters, small in stature and sporting thick black hair, were all locals. That much she could tell. Shabby clothes. Flip-flops on their feet in the main. But there, inside the dining shack at the far end, seated at a long trestle table opposite a guard who was idly toying with the ammo clip on a semi-automatic handgun, was a Caucasian man. Rail-thin, his fair skin singed an angry-looking pink on his nose and cheekbones, with unkempt, curly red hair that clearly hadn't seen a pair of scissors in a year. His wrists were ringed with red scabs. Had he been cuffed? George held her breath. Clearly, this man was not her father, but an outsider, nonetheless. Why else would he be eating with an armed guard watching his every move?

She helped herself to a plate of refried beans, salsa, guacamole and a couple of small tortillas from a buffet table at the end that was manned by a bored-looking old woman who wore a tradi-tional embroidered dress, covered in food stains around the belly. Took a seat next to the European man and his guard, who was now miming shooting at his charge's head.

'Come over here,' Paola said, patting a seat at another table.

'No. I'm good thanks. I've got a headache. I'll just sit tight for a while.'

The European balked at the sight of her. He pulled his plate to the left; shuffled over, putting space between them, and, for the first time, George became aware of how she might appear to others – covered in fearsome tattoos and sharing her lunch with an AK-47.

'Hurry up,' the guard said to him. 'You gotta get back in the lab and finish up, or *el cocodrilo* will wanna know why you screwed up his shipment.' His English was spoken with a heavy Mexican accent. 'You fancy being croc food? Cos I ain't gonna clean your fucking teeth and that weird gringo hair of yours up off the floor when they've finished with you.'

'I'm coming, man,' the chemist said, staring down at his plate which seemed to contain only scraps. He started to shovel what was there into his mouth at speed, speaking with a cheek stuffed with food. 'Give me a break, for Christ's sake. *El mecánico* was snoring all night.' His speech had a Texan twang to it. Or perhaps a flavour of New Mexico.

'He's been ordered to rest. He's sailing to the Dominican tonight with Jorge.'

Locking eyes with George, the guard suddenly leaned over and punched the chemist in the side of the head.

'Ow! What the hell was that for?'

Still searching for some acknowledgement in George's face, the guard waved his pistol at his charge. 'I don't give a fuck about *el mecánico, hombre*. You gotta job to do. Time to go.' He winked at George as he rose from the table. Kicked the heels of the shuffling chemist.

But George wasn't in the slightest bit interested in this show of machismo. She was interested in the mention of a mechanic – or had it been a euphemism for an engineer?

If the chemist shared accommodation with *el mecánico*, it was likely they slept in one of the huts that was positioned around the fringes of the clearing.

'I'm going to stretch my legs,' George shouted over to Paola, who was sitting with the other women. She grabbed her bag and her rifle and headed outside before anybody could object, least of all the steely-eyed Maritza who seemed to miss nothing.

Donning her shades, George stalked around the compound as if she owned that place, despite the incessant flutter in her chest. There was no sign of the Silencer thankfully, but gang members were everywhere, idling away their afternoon, sitting on upturned beer crates, smoking marijuana or meth pipes.

'Hey, *chica*,' one of the men said, amid wolf whistles from the others.

Adrenalin coursed through George's body, heightening her senses. Lewd comments being shouted at her. She could feel sexual threat coming from every direction. These were men who were used to taking women by force or being rewarded for their violent services-rendered by their boss with trafficked girls who had been drafted against their will into sexual slavery. Under normal circumstances, they would surely think nothing of dragging her into a shack and sating themselves. But a *transportista*? Would they really pick a fight with her in this guise?

Turning around, she marched back to the wolf-whistling pack of lustful henchmen. Held her rifle to her shoulder and peered at them down the sights. 'You want to tell me how much you love me, boys? Write me a love note on a bullet. How's about that?'

The men balked visibly. The wolf-whistling stopped. George lowered her weapon and started to walk away towards the shacks.

'Dyke,' one of them said.

Keep going or respond? Keep going. You haven't come here to pick fights. You've come here to find Papa. But George didn't like disrespectful men. She turned back and marched up to the man who had called out. Rifle aimed at his forehead.

'Call me that again,' she said, breathing heavily through her mouth to keep up with her frenzied heartbeat.

The man leaned into the rifle, grinning maniacally at her. High – that much was obvious. His brown eyes shone with malevolence. 'Dyke. I called you a pussy-munching dyke.' He grabbed his crotch. 'You need to be shown how it feels to be fucked by a real man.' He threw his head back and laughed raucously.

George assessed the situation as coolly as her red mist would allow. The others weren't joining in. She lowered the rifle swiftly and shot at the man's feet. He yelped. Then, switched her grip on the AK-47, bringing the butt up in one slick move to make contact with his jaw. It struck him with a nauseating crack. The man fell back off his crate, howling. A well-aimed kick to the balls was all she needed to add a full stop to this particular conversation.

'Jesus!' he said, clasping at his crotch. 'You crazy bitch! I can't believe what you just did.'

Placing a boot on his ribcage, George pointed the rifle anew at his head. Rested the sights on his nose, squashing the cartilage to the side. 'Apologise,' she said.

The man's face had crumpled with obvious shame. Not because he had been disrespectful towards her, but because he had been embarrassed by a woman in full view of his friends. George realised this much.

'I'm sorry! I'm sorry!' he shouted. 'Okay? Leave me alone.'

The other men started to laugh, sensing the shift in power.

As George realised how foolish she had been, she took a step back. Spat at the ground, trying to maintain her hard edge. Turned and walked away quickly. Passing the dining shack, she saw Maritza standing in the doorway, arms folded, smiling wryly at her. The head of the *transportistas* winked and nodded. A show of respect. Good.

Perhaps there was just enough of Letitia in George, after all.

Before matters could take a turn for the deadly, she stalked over to the smallest of the shacks, reasoning that prisoners would hardly be afforded spacious accommodation, no matter how important their work was. The first shack was empty, but for two filthy mattresses and a scattering of pornographic photographs on the floor. The second shack contained a man who sitting on a wooden chair, cleaning the components of a gun. But the third was home to two filthy mattresses. One was empty with dishevelled bedding. A pair of handcuffs hung level with where feet might ordinarily lie, soldered to the corrugated iron walls. The other contained a man who was curled up into a foetal ball. No sheet covered him. His stick-thin arms and legs were tanned almost to the deep mahogany of the local men. His shoulder blades stuck out in sharp triangles that perched like wings above his emaciated torso.

Without warning, the sleeping man rolled over onto his back, snoring loudly. Stretching out with his arms above his head, revealing a rack of prominent ribs beneath a hairy chest. His only clothing was a pair of ragged, washed-out shorts.

Feeling emotions start to engulf her like tsunami moving shoreward from the open sea, George took a step inside to get a better look at the sleeping man's face. But she already knew what he would look like, though given the full slops bucket in the far corner of the shack, it was impossible to ascertain whether or not he still smelled the same as he had smelled when she had been a small child, sitting on his shoulders, clutching at his head.

'Papa,' she whispered, wiping a tear from her eye as she took in the detail of her father's face. He had aged. He was perhaps only half his normal body weight. His black hair was greying and had receded sharply. But she recognised that same nose that she had inherited from him. Ran a finger along her own and smiled wistfully. Those thick eyebrows that she had remembered during childhood as being reminiscent of eagle's wings were unchanged.

'What are you doing in here?' a voice said behind her. A woman's voice.

George spun around to see Maritza standing in the threshold to the shack, hand on the hilt of her machete.

'I wanted to see if this guy is the arsehole who owes me money,' she said, thankful for the sunglasses that concealed a film of tears that threatened to fall and betray her emotional investment in this sleeping man.

'Oh really?' Maritza said.

'Yes.'

'I've been watching you. You're not one of us.'

Stifling the urge to swallow hard and give away her trepidation, George said, 'What do you mean?'

Maritza gestured with her chin toward the clearing. 'Come with me. I want to speak to you.'

CHAPTER 43

Mexico, Cancun airport, 1 June

'Welcome on board, sir!' the air hostess said, smiling at him – all pearly-white teeth and perfect red lips that would look great, wrapped around his cock at an altitude of 50,000 feet. Checking his boarding card with perfectly manicured hands. 'Dr Ackerman.' She sparkled with health and enthusiasm for her job. She was like a well-bred young mare with good long legs and a glossy coat. 'Upper class cabin is this way.' She waved her arm gracefully towards the superior seats.

As he stepped across the threshold into the 747 flight to Gatwick, Stijn Pietersen, or Dr Niels Ackerman, whom the passport he was currently using billed him as, felt optimistic about all he had achieved during his sojourn in Mexico. He smiled at this attractive blonde. These air hostesses were always improved by a week spent in Cancun, sleeping off the jet lag from their outward journey. He wondered if she wore nice red underwear underneath that red uniform. It had been a while since he had fucked anything but trafficked Russian whores. Maybe he could get to grips with this one in the toilets before lunch was served.

Buckling into his seat in the privacy of his own spacious, dedicated area, he checked through his diary engagements on his phone. The shipment of meth wouldn't leave the Dominican for four days and would arrive in Rotterdam weeks later. He knew there was a problem with the chemical composition, but that was down to the barrels of shit he'd bought from China via Chembedrijf. His sources had told him the DEA was aware of six deaths in NYC as a result of his defective product. Six in Amsterdam. The deaths didn't bother him but the damage to his reputation and trade did. He read through the email from his man again.

Dear S
Van den Bergen has undercover cops working the clubs and he's been asking questions about meth production as far afield as Prague. He's out of town for now with McKenzie. Haven't been able to find out where they've gone. We have neutralised old Sepp, like you asked, and sent a message to VdB. Problem is, the kids aren't coming to buy the gear anymore. You need to sort your supply out. We can do damage limitation and repackaging this end.
D

Wanting to thump the window in frustration but realising the upper-class cabin was not the place for a show of raw aggression, he settled for sipping from a flute of perfectly chilled champagne. Proceeded to thumb out an email to Bram Borrink at Chembedrijf, confirming their meeting to discuss the dud chemicals that the Chinese manufacturer was palming off on them. The rendezvous was booked – a lunch at Paradijs, the following day.

Closing his eyes, allowing the thrum of the aircraft's engines to lull him into a semi-slumber, he thought about Ella Williams-May and how he might best proceed to the next stage of ruining her. When her father returned from the Dominican Republic – if he returned at all – he resolved to have him fed to the crocodiles. He'd served his purpose and the maras could always kidnap another engineer to build more subs, after all. There was hardly an easily exhaustible supply of pen-pushers in the world. And then, he would send Ella – or Georgina, as she now liked to call herself, thinking that a name change somehow made her untraceable – the photos. Perhaps he'd even send her Moreno's stupid balding head in a box.

There was also the small question of her mother.

CHAPTER 44

Mexico, Hotel Bahia Maya, Cancun, later

'What do you mean, there's no trace of him?' Van den Bergen said. 'Detectives don't disappear without there being some trail left behind. Check the street CCTV footage around the time he went missing.'

'Don't you think I'm doing all that, boss?' Marie stared sullenly back at him through the screen. Her face was redder than usual. Had she been crying? 'I pulled all the city centre's security footage but there's hours and hours of it to watch and just me to watch it.'

Grinding his molars together, Van den Bergen racked his over-taxed brain to suggest a means of finding Elvis, dead or alive.

'I've asked Minks to put more resources at your disposal,' he said. 'Manpower. Budget. Whatever you need.' He thumped the dressing table in his hotel room. 'Jesus. This is so frustrating. I have no idea where George is. Elvis has been kidnapped. What a goddamn mess.'

'You don't know where George is?' Puzzlement contorted Marie's florid features.

'I need to come back right now, but my flight doesn't leave until this evening. You can't just jump on a plane. Everything's fully booked.' Van den Bergen leaned forwards and grabbed chunks of his white hair. 'This is a waking nightmare.'

'Boss! What do you mean, you don't know where George is? She borrowed money from me to cover her ticket to Honduras. A flying visit, she told me. Has she not showed up yet?'

He glanced at the live Skype image of Marie. She had moved closer to the camera, like some grand inquisitor. He lowered his gaze to the bed. 'Let's focus on Elvis,' he said. 'What were his last movements? What did he have in the diary?'

Marie clicked on her mouse. 'I've got his schedule here. He had blocked out the morning to go and see his mother in hospital. She's on her last legs, apparently. He was due back in in the afternoon but never showed.' She picked at a spot on her chin, frowning. 'He has been behaving oddly of late.'

'Oddly?'

'I think he's got a girlfriend. He's been very secretive. But we know who's taken him, so that's irrelevant. The question is where.'

'Any informants he's been working with lately?'

'Yes. Some old biker. But I don't know the guy's name. Dirk doesn't keep any records on his grasses. But I do remember that he said this guy was one of several who approached him about Pietersen.'

'Do some digging and get back to me. There should be a nationwide manhunt on for a bloody kidnapped cop. This is an appalling lack of commitment from Minks. The sooner I'm back, the better.'

Marie nodded. 'I'm doing what I can this end. I'll keep you posted.' She severed the connection.

His bags were packed. His documentation was in order. But Van den Bergen only had a matter of hours left to help Gonzales catch the bad guys and reunite with George.

He reread the latest message from her.

Ad will help. He says InterChem GmbH is on Chembedrijf's roster as a client. His big boss has a lunch meeting with the Silencer coming up in Amsterdam but he wouldn't say when or where. Just 'leave it to me'. Out of my hands now. You must have worked out that I passed the co-ordinates for the jungle camp onto Gonzales. Couldn't risk him knowing it was from me, in case of bent Mexican cops. I'm deep undercover. Things are tricky. My dad is alive!! I've slipped him a note. I've got one shot at getting him out, so I'm going after him alone. Get Gonzales to raid the jungle camp at 6 p.m. I'll meet you at the airport. Bring my case, something to dissolve stick-on tattoos and permanent marker, wet wipes and anti-bac hand gel.

Love you. I won't get killed if you don't.

George. Xxx

6 p.m. Van den Bergen slammed the laptop shut and growled. 'Jesus, Georgina! The bloody flight leaves at 7.15 p.m.! It's not enough time.'

She had still been alive at the time of sending the message. But would she make it onto the plane in one piece?

CHAPTER 45

The middle of the Caribbean Sea, later

Floating on his back in the hull of the sub, with perhaps no more than six inches between his face and the fibreglass ceiling, Michael realised he was going to drown. After all he had tried to save the vessel, death was still inevitable. His biggest regret was that he would never get to look upon and embrace his fully grown daughter, despite her only being a few nautical miles away on this godforsaken, lawless continent. He would never get to tell her how much he still loved her and how he had thought about her every single day since he had left their unhappy family home in Southeast London. Those were dreams of a reunion that would remain unfulfilled, now, as he allowed his watery grave to embrace him. There was no point struggling any longer. He had all but bled out anyway.

The bullet from Jorge's gun had ripped through Michael's shoulder and into the fabric of the hull. The pain had been intense. He had screamed, clasping at the wound, feeling his blood ooze thickly through his fingers. Then, as if the shock had taken a few seconds to register, Michael had frozen, whimpering with pain and staring in disbelief at the monster that straddled him. There had no longer been any sign of reasoned thought behind his guard's eyes, so high and so feverish with bloodlust had he been because of the meth. But even amid the panic, some calm and analytical part of Michael's brain had noted that Jorge's colour had drained, giving him a sickly pallor.

With nobody at the helm, the sub had lurched downwards abruptly, throwing Jorge off him.

'You stupid, ignorant bastard!' Michael had shouted, scrambling to his knees. His ears had been ringing with the deafening sound of a shot having been fired from a gun in an enclosed space. Though his strength had been no match for the well-nutritioned, drug-fuelled Jorge and though his shoulder had been bleeding freely, he had thrown himself on top of the guard, clasping his gun hand to seize control of the weapon. For the first time in decades, Michael had rediscovered the fire that Letitia had snuffed out of him. 'Drop it! Drop the fucking gun, Jorge! You'll compromise the sub's stability. We'll sink, you prick.'

'I'm going to kill you, *mecánico*. You're a lying, sneaking son of bitch.' Jorge had pulled the trigger a second time, with the bullet embedding itself this time in the fibreglass ceiling. As the sub had lurched ever downwards, water had started to trickle onto the grappling pair.

'We're going to die, anyway!' Michael yelled. 'Drop the gun! We need to plug that hole and get this sub back to the surface fast. We're going down.'

Instruments on the navigational dashboard had started to ping loudly in alarm. Michael had lunged for the gun again, encircling Jorge's wrist with his own bony hand. But though Jorge had tried to throw him off, pistol-whipping him hard on the mouth so that Michael had balked at the unsavoury metallic taste as his mouth had filled with blood, the guard's energy had seemed to dwindle rapidly, like a leaking fuel tank on an old car.

'I don't feel so good,' Jorge had said, suddenly relinquishing the gun. He had rolled over and vomited.

The sea had started to force its way in through the bullet hole in earnest, replacing the trickle with an insistent spurt, which had showered down onto the prone Jorge.

Snatching up the weapon and stuffing it in the waistband of his shorts, Michael had realised that he had three almost insurmountable problems to contend with. If he didn't bind his shoulder immediately, he would bleed to death, perhaps inside five minutes. The sub had been sinking, causing the hull to groan in complaint. The painful pressure in his ears had told him that the descent was too rapid. The vessel would break up. But the main problem had been the water ingress.

He had staggered over to the pile of meth bricks and had unfurled a long piece of clingfilm, binding his shoulder tightly as best he could so that the flow of blood had at least been stemmed. Shooting a glance at Jorge, it had been clear that his guard was out cold, lying in a watery pool of his own vomit and the encroaching sea. Determined that his humanity should not leave him, Michael had knelt by the man, feeling for the pulse in his neck. But there had been none. The grey tinge to Jorge's lips and his unseeing eyes had told Michael that he was now alone. Mercifully still breathing and with his own life still to fight for.

'Come on, for God's sake. You're *el mecánico*. You made this tub. You can fix it. Dear God, don't let me die.' He had rammed a ball of clingfilm into the leaking hole made by the bullet. Had at least stemmed the flow enough to turn it from a spurt back into a trickle, though he had known it was nothing more than a temporary fix.

Saying a prayer silently, he had made for the pinging nautical instruments. The digital displays had been flashing apocalyptically at him, showing that the vessel had dived some twenty-five metres already and had drifted way off course.

'Shit!' He had closed down the sub's computer, feeling his hope and his own energy ebbing away. The blood had still been flowing defiantly from his wounded shoulder, beneath the clingfilm, but he had ignored the increasingly light-headed sensation, knowing there was no time for self-indulgence.

The propellers had fallen silent. The sub had been plunged into darkness.

Flipping the switch, he had prayed that the system would rectify itself automatically. With no laptop to tinker with the on-board computer's programme, it had been his only hope.

Nothing.

He had flipped the switch again, thumping the dash. There had clearly been a fault with the computer's power supply. Had the first bullet that had passed through his shoulder caused damage to the reams of delicate cabling that ran in a fat tangle through a pipe embedded inside the Kevlar? 'Reboot for God's sake!'

A third time, and he had held the button down.

Finally, the lights had come back on and the engines had whirred back into life. The navigational instruments had all been working, except the reboot had wiped the sat nav's memory. The co-ordinates of their destination had disappeared.

'Damn! Damn! Damn!' He had held his fists to his forehead, running through the implications of having a malfunctioning sat nav.

Lost at sea. Great. And Jorge had died, taking the co-ordinates with him.

'Pockets.'

Rifling through Jorge's pockets, gagging from the smell of the dead man's vomit, he had, at first, been hopeful of finding the slip of paper. But his search had revealed nothing. Then, sifting through the ashes from Jorge's smoking materials by his mattress, he had spotted the remnants of a singed slip of paper. They had showed only a fragment of the information he needed. It had not been enough.

'Great. So I'm stranded in the Caribbean Sea,' he had shouted at the ceiling. 'Thanks, God. Thanks for nothing.'

His best bet, he had calculated, would be to bob on the surface and pray that he was picked up by the coast guard. *El cocodrilo* had expressly demanded that no facility for transmitting an SOS signal be incorporated into the design, so that his men would not be captured by the Federales, should they run into trouble. It had always been designed to be a semi-submersible on a semi-suicide mission. It had dawned on Michael then that he had unwittingly colluded in his own demise.

'Shut up! Shut up!' he had shouted. 'This is loser's talk. Enough!'

He had had to try harder.

Having re-programmed the semi-submersible to climb once more, he had realised the vessel was not heading fast enough towards the surface. The water had been starting to come through again in earnest and was now gaining pace, gushing, rather than just spurting. Already, Michael's ankles were submerged. He had pulled off his boots and had studied the tightly packed pallets full of crystal meth, destined for the cargo ship in the Dominican Republic. If he had only been able to jettison the load, he knew he would have been able to bring the sub safely to the surface.

But it had been impossible to open the hatch on such a basic piece of kit without flooding the entire vessel within minutes.

After a while, he had brought the reluctant sub up to fifteen metres below sea level. But it had refused to rise any higher. He had calculated that his only option would be to wait until the sub had filled with water with the intention of opening the hatch at the last minute, once the pressure would have equalised with the outside. Then, he would have to pray that he would be able to hold his breath long enough to swim for the surface without getting the bends. And then, there was the small matter of not drowning in the open sea or being eaten by a shark, mistaking his bony shell of a body for a disappointing dolphin. It had been flawed, but it had been his only plan.

And so, Michael Carlos Izquierdo Moreno had resorted to allowing the sub he had built over the course of two years to fill with water. Lying on his back, he had waited until the water level had been only six inches or so away from the top. At least the water had been warm and Jorge's body had remained somewhere on the bottom, pinned to the floor of the hull in perpetuity beneath the weight of the meth that had killed him.

When he had judged the water level was just high enough to give him sufficient air to breath, he had started to manoeuvre the wheel that allowed him to open the hatch manually. But his arms had been weakened by blood loss and the wheel was jammed. The faster his heart had beaten with rising panic, the more light-headed he had grown, his energy leaching from him entirely.

Eventually, he had accepted that he was not going to escape this watery sarcophagus after all. It had been ordained that this would be the end of him; the end of his hopes for freedom; an end to his aspirations to reforge contact with his long-lost daughter and to make amends for the decades when he had not been there for her.

'Goodbye, Ella,' he said to the darkness.

Consciousness was leaving him. He knew it was over. He had, at least, fought valiantly to stay alive this long. Perhaps Ella would be proud if she ever found out the truth about her papa and his epic tale of trial and redemption.

CHAPTER 46

Mexico, Yucatan jungle, 1 June

Poking her head out from the shack's threshold, George checked the way was clear. Twilight was not far off now. She could smell sundown in the air and hear it in the sounds of the jungle's insects and animals, as the dayshift started to change hands with those that were of a nocturnal disposition. Pulled her rucksack on her back and checked again that the pistol she had conned from Maritza was loaded. It wouldn't do to make a mistake now. This was her last chance.

'Good luck, Jacinta,' Paola said.

George turned around and took one last glance at the woman she had bunked with for a week. Wondered if the girl would ever make it past twenty-five. 'Thanks. You too,' she said.

'I hope you find your guy and get your money back.' Paola dragged on her cigarette and exhaled as the old television with an execrable reception hissed away on the wall, showing some telenovela.

'Oh, I will,' she said. 'Safe journey home. Tell Maritza thanks again. For everything.'

Without looking back, George advanced across the clearing, ducking past the gang members who were all assembled around another television, jeering at some football match, judging by

295

the sounds. She needed to get away from this place without hindrance.

Her run-in with Maritza had been a close call. The leader of the *transportistas* had pulled her to one side and had accused her of being a wild card.

'You're no team player, Jacinta,' she had said, scanning George's face for the truth. Glancing over George's shoulder at her sleeping father. 'I don't think I can have you working in my group of *transportistas* anymore.'

George had been at pains to look as wounded as possible, carefully controlling her breathing so that her abject fear of discovery wouldn't be obvious. She had been well aware that her luck must surely have been due to run out at any minute. 'Oh, but Maritza. Really?! This has been great for me after working in Europe. You guys have made me feel so welcome. I've been the lone wolf for too long. Know what I mean?' She had deliberately strolled as far away from her father as possible, not wanting to put his relative safety in jeopardy. Maritza would have had no compunction about putting a bullet in him as he slept, she had been certain of that much.

'I saw how you handled that guy who disrespected you,' Maritza had said. 'I admire you, Jacinta. You've got balls. You remind me of myself as a younger woman.' The *transportista* had laid her hand on George's shoulder and had squeezed her affectionately. 'But my girls are like a military unit and it's going to be disruptive if you stay. You're too much of a free spirit. You need to go and find the bastard who owes you money, but you and I have to part company here, I'm afraid.'

George had nodded stoically. She had treated Maritza to a warm, appreciative smile. And then, she had got her to agree that she could stay that night, after the semi-submersible had been loaded up, and hang around for most of the following day, leaving with a rifle and a handgun, as well as her pay, as a parting bonus.

With the letter safely stashed in her father's pocket and Van den Bergen informed of an ideal time at which to raid the camp, when George was fairly certain all the major players would be there, watching the second half of the football match between Brazil and Argentina, George had known she must leave and track down her father, before Jorge found her letter or their sub got too far out to sea for her to stand a hope in hell of finding them.

Now, with the inhabitants of the camp ensconced in the same shack, drinking beer and screaming at the injustice of an early goal from Argentina, George slipped into the treeline, knowing she had to put some distance between her and that place before Gonzales and his men descended upon it in approximately one hour's time. She knew instinctively that it would be a bloody battle. As she turned her face towards the canopy of the jungle, spying the ghost of the moon in the early-evening sky, she said a silent prayer that Van den Bergen would emerge from the raid unhurt, and that they would be reunited at the airport. She had less than three hours to find a needle in a haystack.

This is bullshit, she thought, trudging through the tangled thicket, waving away clouds of bloodthirsty mosquitoes that were coming out to play at her expense. *I'll never find my dad. I've timed it all wrong. He's too long gone. What the hell was I thinking? I'm going to get eaten alive by a fucking jaguar or a giant spider and this will all have been for nothing.*

But then, remembering the pitiful sight of her emaciated father, sleeping on the filthy mattress with his legs chained to the shack's wall, George chastised herself inwardly.

I'm not giving up. Enough of this loser's talk. There's a speedboat moored at the far end of that beach where the sub launched from. I've seen it for myself and I'm having it. Hang on in there, Papa. I'm coming to get you.

When she reached the beach, there were some locals having a picnic. A family, by the looks. They shrank away from her as she stepped out from the treeline, the mother hugging her two children and the father putting a territorial arm around all three of them. George remembered how she must look, armed and dressed as a *transportista*. Part of her was horrified that decent family folk should be so intimidated by her. Part of her found the power intoxicating.

'It's okay,' she said, holding her hands aloft. 'Just get on with your picnic.'

Would they call the police? No. Most of the locals would be petrified of retribution from an apparent gang member. This was a culture where crimes went unreported for a reason.

Advancing down the beach, she spotted the speedboat, moored in shallow water only a few metres out.

'What the hell do you know about speedboats, Georgina?' she asked herself, imagining Van den Bergen quizzing her like the curmudgeonly, logical old fart he was. 'Nothing,' George told the lapping waters of the Caribbean Sea. 'Not a sausage. But I've got my provisional licence and I've done the roundabout at Elephant and Castle during rush hour without crashing. How hard can a boat be?'

Wading out, she realised it was bobbing on the surface in water that was deeper than she had anticipated. She held her rifle above her head and threw it into the boat. Tried to jump up to grab the side. Her hands slid uselessly along the fibreglass hull. Tried again.

'Come on, you fat clumsy twat. It's going to be dark in an hour. And you're going to miss your sodding flight. Aunty Sharon will kill you if you miss Skyping during *Bake Off* for another week.'

Hurling herself out of the water, she finally gained a purchase on the edge. Her arms screamed in complaint as she tried to drag herself upwards. Her breasts were painfully flattened against the side. She kicked her legs up, finally managing to hook a foot over the lip of the boat. As she threw her body into the vessel, she heard shouting from the beach.

'Oh shit. Here we go,' she muttered.

'Hey! You! That's my boat!' An American voice. A man was running towards her, coming from the direction of a beautiful white, two-storey villa that was nestled in the treeline. A tourist or ex-pat, no doubt. 'Get out of my fucking boat or I'm calling the police.'

George could see the anger in the man's face. Then she watched his aggression dissolve clean away as she stood and he saw her in all her tattooed, *transportista* glory.

'I need to borrow your boat,' George said in English. She picked up her rifle and clasped it to her body.

The American held his hands up. A change in his attitude once he had heard her speak English. A mixture of surprise, resentment and loathing in his face. 'Okay, you crazy bitch! Take it. But I'm calling the cops. I don't take any shit from you beaners.'

She pointed her rifle towards the man and shot up the sand to the left of him.

He leaped backwards. 'Jesus! What was that for?'

'Beaners,' she said simply. 'Say it again and I'll put the bullets in your racist dick. Now, I need your boat. I'm an undercover cop from England,' she lied. 'Call the coast guard and get them to get a rescue helicopter out to sea. Tell them I'm looking for a semi-submersible that's heading towards Santo Domingo in the Dominican. Tell them it's got drugs and a kidnapped Spanish national on board.'

'You're full of shit,' the boat owner said. 'Get out of my fucking boat, bitch.' His hand was planted firmly on his hip. His face was etched with fury. Was this guy some kind of psychopath that he wasn't cowed by a fearsome-looking woman holding a semi-automatic rifle? Or maybe he just didn't believe a woman could have cojones bigger than a man.

George let off another round right by his feet. 'Fuck you. Give me the keys or I'll kill you.'

This time, the man glared at her, reached inside his shorts …

299

'Easy,' George said. 'Don't try anything stupid.'

… pulled out a bunch of keys and threw them to George. 'Don't wreck it,' he said.

'I'll try not to,' she said, plucking the keys out of the air. 'And don't forget. Call the coast guard and tell them about the semi-sub headed from this beach to Santo Domingo. It can't have got more than a hundred nautical miles, tops. And tell them to go easy with the firepower. There's an innocent man on board.'

The boat owner didn't move.

'Go!' she shouted, raising the rifle to her shoulder and peering down the sights.

As the man sprinted back towards his villa, she took in the array of buttons and dials on the dash of the motorboat in confusion. Started the engine. Noticed there was a sat nav. She programmed in the co-ordinates for Santo Domingo: Latitude – eighteen degrees 30'00' N, Longitude – sixty-nine degrees 59'18' W. Pushing aside naysaying, nagging concerns of her sensible alter ego that she didn't yet even have her driver's licence, George hit the throttle. The boat lurched forwards, ripping its anchor from the seabed. Spun around violently.

'Shit, man!' she shouted, thumping the dash. 'How hard can this be? Come on, McKenzie. You're a fucking PhD for God's sake! Use your loaf.'

Gathering her composure, she pulled up the anchor. A little less throttle this time and soon she was jerking forwards, at least in the right direction. Checking the fuel gauge, she saw that the boat only had half a tank. Not good. Silently, she gazed out to the horizon, calculating that her father's vessel must be travelling around eight nautical miles per hour. Reasoning that this motorboat going at full throttle might hit fifty. She was no mathematician, but she realised that half a tank of gas, travelling at speed, would not get her very far and certainly wouldn't get her back to shore. Still, what option did she have but to try?

'I can do this,' she said. 'Come on!'

Taking fast, shallow breaths, she gunned the boat into open water, checking behind her to see that there was nobody in pursuit. Only the owner of the boat had reappeared on the beach and was now a small speck standing at the far end of a strip of white, fringed with palms. *Good. Hope the arsehole called the coast guard like I asked, else I'm going to be lost at sea myself once the fuel runs dry.*

A mile out and the waves were rapidly becoming tall enough to make the keel of the boat slam into walls of water, sending spray everywhere. She was soaked in brine and parched with thirst in the remains of the day's hot sunshine. But her only option was to plough on through. Darkness was not far off and if she didn't find her father by sunset, her mission would be doomed in any case.

More than an hour passed. Though the seas had mercifully quietened to flat calm and the boat was ripping through the miles at speed, the sinking fuel gauge showed that George's rescue attempt was coming to an end, whether she wanted it to or not. The sun was sinking in the west, its burnished light reflected in the water. Streaks of pink, orange, red in the sky as though somebody had taken a sharp knife and slashed open the belly of the firmament. With no drinking water on board, she touched her salty, cracked lips with melancholy resignation – thoughts of dying only just trumped by wonder at where that damned coast guard was.

'Great. I'm going to be stuck here in the dark,' she told the first star of the night that had appeared low in the sky. 'I'm going to dehydrate and will be dead from sun exposure by this time tomorrow. And I'll have missed my flight home and wasted the rest of my life. Shitting Nora. I've failed.'

Slumping into the driver's seat, George started to weep. Wracking sobs shook her body as she thought of Van den Bergen shuffling round Amsterdam without her like a lost boy in an old man's body. If Letitia was dead, she would soon be joining her in hell or whatever purgatorial replacement was offered for non-believers, though that notion gave her no comfort whatsoever. And her papa would almost certainly meet a brutish end – if not now, then soon, at the hands of the Silencer's crocodiles or the predators that lurked in the depths of the Caribbean Sea.

As if their fates had now been intertwined, the under-fuelled boat ploughed on, burning through diesel with abandon in tandem with George's already dry body, which was haemor-rhaging precious moisture every time a fat tear rolled down her cheek. Pretty soon, they would both be running on empty.

Some fifteen minutes later, the engine started to sputter and lose power. She had no idea where she was or where her father's semi-submersible might be in relation to her, though it surely couldn't be far off by now, surely, given the huge difference in travel speeds. Holding up the high-powered binoculars that she had found in a kit box, she scanned the water on all sides. Not a ripple out of place in the minimal undulations of the sea.

'Well, that's it, isn't it?' George checked the time on her phone. Her flight home would leave in thirty-seven minutes. With maths never having been her strong suit, she had miscalculated the time she had needed to intercept her father's sub. The gate would be closing now, if it hadn't already. 'Game over.' She sucked her teeth. Started to thumb out a farewell message to Van den Bergen, though there was no phone signal this far out at sea. Perhaps one day, when her body was retrieved, they would charge up the phone and the message would find its way to him then. Her voice from the other side.

My darling Paul, she began, wondering how best to express her heartfelt longing to be with him on that plane home and regret that she had ever undertaken this foolhardy adventure. Alter ego George, the naysayer, was fully in charge of the narra-tive now.

Except her missive was interrupted by a whirring sound that cut through the sound of gentle lapping against the sides of the boat. George stuffed her phone into her pocket and scanned the fiery sunset skies for signs of a helicopter. Nothing. Though the rhythmic sound was growing louder. She lifted the binoculars once again and, after several fruitless passes, spotted a black dot coming from the direction of the Mexican coast. Growing larger by the second, though the wind made it seem like the sound was coming from a different direction entirely.

Grabbing at the flare gun she had found together with the binoculars, George aimed the weapon into the air and fired. Nothing but a click. No cartridge. She threw it onto her seat in disgust.

'Tits! I don't believe this!'

Scrambling to the back of the boat, she fumbled in the kit box to find a cartridge. The helicopter was visible with the naked eye, now, though it was impossible to tell if it was making for her specifically or merely flying nearby coincidentally. She prayed silently that it would be the coast guard and not one of the Silencer's men, coming to snuff her out before she caused any more trouble.

'Where's the fucking cartridge?' she shouted, hurling the contents of the kit box onto the deck.

Skimming perhaps only 100 feet above the sea's surface, the black behemoth sliced through the air with a deafening sound. Making right for her, seeming to suck the remaining daylight from the sky as it approached. A giant sinister bug of a thing, suddenly upon her with machine guns pointed downwards like deadly, accusatory fingers. George threw herself flat onto the deck, blasted by the wind from its rotating blades. Surely it had spotted her! But she had glimpsed its livery – Policía Federal. This was no coast guard. This thing was armed. And some of the police were reputed to be in the pay of the cartels. Would this be her end instead?

The beat of its blades remained directly above her boat as it hovered. Daring to look up, George was surprised to glimpse a familiar face peering out of the window. Holding up a large hand in greeting. Pressing his face momentarily to the window. The door of the helicopter slid back and there he was, looking positively green, even in the twilight.

'You are fucking kidding me!' George sprang to her feet, jumping up and down and waving back like an overexcited child. Tears of relief streaming down her face. 'Paul!'

A rope ladder unfurled from the helicopter and dangled just out of reach, being blown hither and thither by the gusting wind.

'Grab the ladder!' she heard Van den Bergen yell above the din of the whirring blades. Just.

'I'm bloody well trying!' George screamed. It was too high above her. She was too short to reach. It was too dangerous to stand on the driver's seat and try to jump. Then, the ladder hit her squarely in the head. But when she tried to grasp a rung, it was wrenched upwards, as the helicopter rose several feet.

'Oh Jesus.' There was nothing for it but to perch on the bow of the boat, risking falling into the water.

Leaving her rifle behind, George donned her rucksack and stuffed the handgun into her waistband. Mounted the slippery bow. After three attempts, she finally grabbed the ladder and clung on.

'Climb up!' Van den Bergen bellowed.

The helicopter rose into the air, leaving her swinging helplessly over the sea. She willed her limbs to respond to her brain's demand that she climb. But not only was her upper body not strong enough, she reluctantly admitted to herself that she was paralysed by fear. Clinging, clinging to the rope and the bottom rungs like an anxiety-ridden koala.

'For God's sake. Climb!'

The helicopter was moving forwards now, leaving her spinning and drifting at an untenable angle.

'I can't!' she shouted. 'Find the sub.'

'What?'

'Find the fucking sub!' She couldn't even bring herself to look up at Van den Bergen who was presumably hanging out of the aircraft, battling with his own demon of motion sickness.

With the light failing in earnest, the helicopter's searchlight came on, probing the darkening waters with its strong beam. George steeled herself to search the surface for any trace of a sub. But the sea was vast and her father could have drifted off course entirely. At that point, as her arms screamed with the effort of holding on, she realised their search was in vain.

A second voice shouted down at her. One she didn't recognise. A Mexican man's voice. 'Dr McKenzie, I'm sorry. We've gotta turn back. Try again tomorrow.' His words, whipped away on the wind, were barely audible.

'No!' George shrieked. 'Five more minutes.'

'It's a waste of time. Try to climb the ladder. You'll not last the journey, hanging on like that.'

In truth, the waves had begun to gain power and momentum, spraying her bottom half with foamy water. George realised the helicopter's blades were not the only thing generating a gust. Bad weather was setting in. But then, just as she was about to attempt to climb to the safety of the helicopter, she spotted something that crested very briefly with a wave some hundred metres away.

I don't believe it, she thought, blinking hard into the murk.

'There!' she shouted, not daring to let go of the ladder to point. Willing the pilot to hear her feeble voice and spot the large object. Had she been mistaken? Had it been a large shark or a whale?

'Climb, Dr McKenzie! We have to go back to shore.'

She could hear the urgency in the man's voice above her but was too intent on trying to spot the object again to listen.

Where is it? Come on, for God's sake! Show yourself, whatever you are.

The waves rose and fell but the helicopter's searchlight had moved.

'George!' Van den Bergen was shouting now.

The searchlight swept to the left and there, in amongst the mounting waves, she saw it. Very definitely. And it was neither a whale nor a shark.

'Down here!' George shouted. 'Look! The sub is there!'

'No! You've got to come up!' Van den Bergen's companion shouted.

The helicopter started to climb and banked away from the object in the water. Looking back from her vantage point some twenty feet higher, George could see the shape clearly now. She had never felt more certain of anything.

This was her father's sub.

The water was inky-black now. The waves were powered by some malevolent energy she could not comprehend. It was a shark-infested sea. What could possibly go wrong?

George let go of the ladder and hit the water with a stinging slap that knocked the breath out of her lungs with a violence she hadn't anticipated. Salty bubbles pressing their way up her nostrils, making her head pound. She surfaced, barely having time to gasp for air before a wave crashed over her and pushed her beneath the water again.

Swim. Get swimming.

The helicopter's searchlight was on her now. A buoyancy ring had been dropped just within reach. George grabbed onto it and started to swim in the direction of the sub. But where had it gone? She was disoriented, looking this way and that, unable to see anything at all in the troughs but whisked upwards when the waves peaked. There! She spotted the distinctive oval shape in the dark. Started to swim towards it, mustering all the strength she had left in her exhausted body. Were the waves carrying her closer or further away from the sub? She couldn't tell at first. But after a minute of frantic, one-armed front crawl, a wave picked her up and threw her against the vessel. The pain in her arm as it bore the brunt of the impact was intense.

Would the sub sink with her weight on it? Hardly daring to

contemplate what she was doing, George scrambled onto the deck and located the hatch. Slipped and slid her way towards it, praying a wave wouldn't crash over her, whisking her back into the water and off in the opposite direction. Grabbing the handles, she used every last ounce of strength she possessed to loosen the heavy lid on this tub. She was vaguely aware of somebody climbing down the ladder from the helicopter, swaying on the rope above her. The searchlight illuminated her quest.

'Come on, you bastard!'

With a final heave of the almost-defeated, George felt the handles on the hatch give. She levered the lid open and discovered in horror that the sub was almost entirely full of water. 'Papa!' she screamed.

Taking a deep breath, she plunged through the hole. Almost utterly black but for the strong shaft of white light that came from the helicopter above. And there, bobbing with its nose and mouth just out of the water, she saw a body. Those eyebrows were unmistakeable.

'Papa! Oh my God. Oh my God. Please don't be dead,' she said, kicking hard to drag him along the tiny air gap that ran the length of the hull towards the hatch. His skin was cold. But there was not enough light to ascertain if his colour was that of a dead man or one who yet lived.

Clasping the edge of the hatch with one trembling arm, she caught her father under his left arm and hoisted him into the pool of dazzling light and the breathtaking wind.

'Here! Let me take him!' The voice of the man who had called to her from the helicopter. George barely registered the first thing about him, other than his being dressed in the black uniform of the Polícia Federale. He was peering into the sub. A kindly face.

She pushed her father upwards, kicking her legs with all the power she could muster to propel herself out of the water. The Federale grabbed him underneath his arms and dragged him onto the flat deck. But George could feel something pulling her back into the sub's belly.

'Hey! Help!' Her foot was caught.

As she felt herself being sucked into the deathly trap of the flooded sub, she noticed Van den Bergen, dangling from the end of the rope ladder. They locked eyes. He let go and fell.

CHAPTER 47

Amsterdam, Paradijs restaurant, Amstel, 2 June

'Would sir like to see the wine menu?' the waiter asked, clasping his hands together deferentially, wearing an enthusiastic shit-eating grin.

'No. I'll just have tap water, I think. Thanks.'

Ad sat at his table for one in the Michelin-starred Paradijs restaurant, feeling rather more like he was in hell, as opposed to paradise. Why on earth was he doing this? It was bullshit. He was a fool.

The waiter seemed unconvinced as Ad's phone pinged yet again with some nagging request or other from Astrid about nappies or a DIY-fail that was all his fault. She had no idea that he had absconded to Amsterdam for the day. It felt like a small victory.

'Actually, yes. I'll see the wine menu. That would be great.'

The grin was back as the immaculately dressed waiter nodded and retreated, the derision and lack of comprehension that Ad should ever have requested tap water in a place like this tacit behind the show of approval.

Glancing at the food menu, he noticed that the starters were more expensive than the mains he might choose in the local eaterie where he took Astrid for the occasional date. *If* one of their parents had agreed to babysit. *If.* He examined the slightly worn cuffs of his striped work shirt and the ghost of a toothpaste stain on his polyester tie. Studied the cool elegance of the clientele in this place, with its plush velvet chairs and quiet ambience of extreme wealth. It was the sort of fine dining that only captains of industry, old money and politicians forked out for. Ad knew he didn't belong here. His clandestine meal was going to cost him two days' pay at least. But he was doing it for George. He blushed at the thought and switched his phone off.

As the waiters drifted to and fro past his table without coming back to take his drink order, Ad realised he was almost invisible in that place. Handy, because he was seated at the table adjacent to that of Bram Borrink, the Chief Executive of Chembedrijf. Borrink, an immaculately dressed man in his fifties, whose perfectly round paunch served as evidence of many a boozy business lunch in similarly luxurious surroundings, was sipping at a glass of red wine. At a glance, he was a grey-haired man, wearing a grey tailored suit with a grey complexion that said he didn't see much of the outdoors apart from through the generous picture windows of places like Paradijs. And yet, Ad could see his incredible wealth shining through the grey veneer of respectability. He was staring through a pair of bifocal glasses at a business broadsheet.

When Borrink glanced back to the entrance, presumably looking for his lunch date, Ad found himself in the Chief Executive's eye line. He felt his cheeks flush bright red and held the menu up hastily to cover his face.

Shit, he thought. *I'm going to get the sack, at best, and get myself killed, at worst. What an idiot I am. The last time I pulled a stunt like this, I lost a finger. Will I never learn that George McKenzie is bad news? Forgive me, Astrid. Sorry Daddy's such an emotionally unfaithful arsehole, kids.*

'Would sir like to order some wine, now?' the waiter asked, having suddenly reappeared at his side.

Lowering the menu, Ad cleared his throat and took a deep breath. 'I'll have a small glass of Chardonnay,' he said, keeping his voice deliberately low, lest he draw attention to himself.

'Sir?'

Too quiet.

'Chardonnay, please.'

The waiter wafted off, leaving him alone once again. Ad's thunderous heartbeat slowed somewhat as he reasoned that, having only ever met the big boss in passing at some IT presentation some two years earlier, it was fair to assume that this man from the top wouldn't afford him a second glance, let alone recognise him.

You can do this. Calm down.

Glancing furtively at the maître d' who stood behind the reception desk by the entrance like a sinister penguin, Ad balked when a man with bleached blond hair and a deep mahogany tan walked through the rotating door. Just as George had described him. This had to be the man he awaited. The enigmatic Rotterdam Silencer.

'Mr Bebchuck?' the maître d' said, all charm and obsequiousness in his tone and body language.

The Silencer nodded, handing him his coat.

'Your table is this way, sir. Mr Borrink is waiting for you.'

At the next table, Borrink rose, hand extended. 'Nikolay,' he said. 'So pleased to see you. Thanks for coming.'

The Silencer stalked past Ad. He was a tall man, though not powerfully built. But he exuded arrogance, and his tan served only to emphasise the white curve of a scar on his cheek, giving him a disconcerting, loutish appearance that was at odds with his immaculate suiting. Even if Ad hadn't heard tell of the Rotterdam Silencer's legendary criminal exploits from George and Van den Bergen, he would have intuited that this was not a man to get on the wrong side of.

'Sit the fuck down, Borrink,' he said. 'I'm not shaking your hand.'

The maître d' backed away rapidly, the smile sliding quickly from his face. 'I'll leave you to it, gentlemen …'

But his politesse went unnoticed. The Silencer threw himself into his seat and barked, 'Bring me a good single malt!' at their waiter. Words that rang with hauteur and a thick Rotterdam accent. 'Lagavulin, if you've got it. No ice.'

Furtively, Ad watched from behind his menu as his own waiter set an ice bucket next to him. Produced a frosty-looking bottle of white wine, removing the cork with some ceremony.

'Would sir like to taste?' the waiter asked.

Ad waved dismissively. 'Just pour,' he said. 'I'm sure it's fine.' Somewhere at the back of his mind, the thought that he had only ordered a small glass of Chardonnay registered with him. Now was not the time to quibble, however. And he was ready for a drink.

Taking a large gulp that might cost him an hour's pay after tax, he pointed absently to a dish on the menu that didn't cost upwards of €30.

'Would sir like some potatoes with that?'

'What? Yes. Yes. Bring me whatever you think.' Ad strained to hear the conversation at the next table and was pleased when his waiter finally left him in peace. He clicked the sound recording app on his phone to 'on'.

'So, my secretary said you sounded agitated on the phone,' Borrink said, studying his menu. Not making eye contact with his lunch companion. If he was intimidated by the Silencer, he certainly didn't show it.

'And why the fuck do you think that is?' The Silencer was glaring straight at Borrink, drumming his fingers impatiently on the table.

Finally, Borrink set the menu down. Took his glasses off and placed them in their case. Steepled his fingers together, clearly wanting to make the other man wait. 'Mr Bebchuck, you are one of several thousand clients that Chembedrijf deals with on a

312

regular basis. We are one of the biggest companies in Europe. I'm sorry that you seem so upset, but there is really no reason why I—'

'You sold me a dud batch,' the Silencer said, spitting with indignation as he spoke.

Their conversation paused while the waiter set a whisky down before him. Ad was momentarily distracted by yet another warm bun being set on his side plate with silver tongs. Then, when the attentive waiters departed, round two began in earnest.

Borrink surveyed the other diners in the restaurant, leaned in and dropped his voice. 'We acted as an intermediary for you,' he said. 'If your product was faulty, that's down to the Chinese. Not us.'

Smacking his lips as he swigged at the whisky, the Silencer leaned back in his chair, as if chewing over Borrink's words which had been neither an apology nor an admission of culpability. Clearly a response he had not been gunning for. 'I pay you through the nose,' he said so quietly, that Ad was certain his voice would not be picked up on the sound recording. 'I pay you to get me precursor chemicals from those Chinese cunts, shipped to Mexico and Prague, using my shell company as the intermediary. I use you, because you're a giant sprawling blue chip that deals in petrochemicals and pharmaceuticals. When you order precursor chemicals, nobody gives a shit. It's your stock in trade. Your job is to get them for me in giant quantities and at a knockdown rate and to ask no nosey questions.'

'And we have never failed you, Mr Bebchuck.' Borrink's smile was a mere show of expensively whitened teeth. 'I value your custom as one of Chembedrijf's ... special clients.'

'Then why are the barrels you got for me last time giving my clients fatal lead poisoning?' The Silencer's scar seemed to glow as he flushed with obvious anger.

Ad's eavesdropping was interrupted by his waiter setting down a large plate containing a small sliver of some sort of meat, stacked high with a lattice of who the hell knew what and drizzled in a pretty pattern with several different colours of sauce. He didn't know whether to weep that it wasn't a nice sandwich or applaud it for its artistic merits. The plate was followed by an inadequate-looking side order of potatoes. At least, he presumed they were potatoes.

'Thank you,' he said, looking wistfully at his buttered bun.

The captain of industry and the international trafficker at the next table were also served their food during a farcical hiatus, where neither spoke except to thank their waiter.

The Silencer shovelled an overloaded forkful of meat into his mouth and poked his knife towards Borrink. 'Get me another supplier,' he said, chewing noisily as he spoke. 'You want to do business with the likes of me so you can bolster your pension fund? You make sure I'm not fobbed off with substandard goods! I'm a businessman, no different from you. Right? I need to put out premium product, or I'm going to end up with a ruined reputation.'

Borrink threw down his napkin. Stood abruptly, almost knocking his chair over. 'I don't have to put up with this from you,' he said. 'You don't get to speak to me like this. I'm not some two-bit hoodlum.'

The other diners had started to turn around to see where the commotion was coming from.

'Sit the fuck down and stop shooting your mouth off, Borrink, or I'll silence you myself,' the Silencer said, clenching his fist so tightly that his tanned knuckles were white. 'You really want to mess with me? You want to try me and see if I'm bluffing? You think I won't get one of my guys to go and pay Mrs Borrink a friendly visit or turn up in the middle of the night to give you a free haircut with an open razor?' His voice remained low and deadly. His blue eyes were ice-cold; the set of his jaw, unyielding.

Gripping the edge of the table, Borrink took his seat again. His mounting colour had blanched suddenly.

'Now, now, Nikolay. There's no need to be like that. I resent—'

'Watch what you say!'

Borrink pursed his lips and examined his nails. Clearly considering his response carefully, lest he provoke the Silencer further. Though Ad realised this man was wittingly colluding with a gangster, causing the deaths of innocent kids by importing chemicals that were only ever intended to be used in the manufacture of crystal meth, part of him felt sorry for the big boss. Even he, the head honcho of Chembedrijf, was susceptible to bullying in the workplace. No different from when Ad had his stapler stolen and hidden by the wankers on his team who thought it was so very bloody funny to goad the stuck-up university boy. Henpecked as hell by his wife. Cockpecked to within an inch of his life by his colleagues.

'I'll have words with our Chinese supplier, Nikolay,' he said, finally meeting the Silencer's questioning gaze. 'I'll get you some compensation and source a new supplier for you. But don't ever threaten me or my wife again.' Not such a grey character after all. 'Do you understand? Because you won't find many legitimate businessmen who will deal with you as loyally and discreetly as I always have. And I don't deserve it. This is not my fault. It's just one of those things.'

The Silencer set down his cutlery and stood. 'I'm going. I want solutions, not bullshit.' He started to peel notes off from the wad in his wallet. 'This isn't a pissing competition or a test. This is business. Sort this out or you're dead. Period.'

Borrink held his hand up. His eye twitched as he spoke. 'This is my treat. Please allow me to made amends and start by getting lunch.'

'Fuck your treat.'

Nikolay Bebchuck, a.k.a. the Rotterdam Silencer, threw a shower of €50 notes onto the table, turned his back and stalked towards the exit of Paradijs restaurant.

Draining his glass of wine. Ad forked some food into his mouth and glanced surreptitiously at his big boss.

For a moment, Borrink sat at the table in stunned silence, his face flushed with embarrassment, perhaps, or indignation. Then, he simply rose and headed off to the restrooms.

Clicking his sound recording app off, Ad sipped again from his refilled wine glass. Feeling all at once thoroughly tipsy and adventurous. Remembering the time he had last put himself in a precarious situation to gather intel for the police. He puffed out his chest, suddenly feeling more like a spy than a father of two.

What should I do? I've got the voices but he didn't say much about drugs. Come on, Ad. Don't make this a wasted trip. How long does it take for a rich man to have a piss?

Eyeing the other diners, Ad calculated that he had no more than three minutes before Borrink returned. But the waiters were glancing in his general direction. Would they come over and retrieve the money?

'The money,' he said under his breath. 'That's it.'

He needed something with fingerprints on for the forensic pathologist. What was she called again? Yes. Marianne de Koninck. Ad remembered vomiting in her office wastepaper basket all those years ago when he had been faced with the photos of a decapitated head. She could turn a €50 note with a good fingerprint or the DNA left on the Silencer's whisky glass into cold, hard evidence, proving that Nikolay Bebchuck and the Rotterdam Silencer were one and the same.

Turn away, you bloody fussing idiots, he thought, willing the waiters to stop gawping over at him to see if he needed topping up. But fortunately the Chardonnay was working. Two-thirds of a bottle down, though he had no idea how that had happened, Ad was now a telepathic ninja or a Jedi master or something of that ilk. As if they had heard his thoughts, the waiters moved to the other side of the restaurant. Swiftly, Ad snatched up two of the euro notes and swiped the Silencer's glass, wrapping it in a napkin and placing it in his worn, canvas man-bag. He shoved what was left of his main course into a buttered bun and wedged the impromptu sandwich into his mouth. Pulled the money from his wallet that he had reluctantly withdrawn from the cashpoint, realising Paradijs would cost rather more than a cheese *boterham* and a cornet of *patats met knoflook*. Momentarily nonplussed as he tried to work out exactly how much his meal might cost. Shit. They had brought him an entire bottle of wine instead of a small glass.

Ad was torn. Technically, he had stolen €100 from the big boss' table and was also probably underpaying for his meal. Feeling the sweat beading on his forehead, he balked when Borrink emerged from the restrooms, staring straight at him. Peering down into his wallet, now empty but for the money he had trousered from the Silencer, he realised his only options would be to run and hope the waiter discovered his accounting error once he was far away enough to be beyond reach, or ask for the bill and use his credit card. But then, they would have a record of Adrianus Karelse having been in the restaurant, rather than the work-worn-looking man who had booked the table in the name of George van den Broek.

'You!' Borrink was approaching. Staring unequivocally at Ad. 'Don't I know you?'

Wide-eyed and fumbling like a bat trapped in a bright conservatory, Ad gathered his belongings. Decided he was drunk and feeling courageous enough just to leg it.

'No.'

'Yes, I do!' Borrink's baffled expression started to morph into a noncommittal smile. Deciding if this was some business contact he ought to know better. Clearly struggling to place Ad with his shabby clothes and crappy old bag. The smile started to wane. 'Where do I know you from?'

Ad cast his mind back to a presentation he had given six months earlier to the board of directors on the implementation of some new accounting software. There had been ten grey men sitting around a grey ash table looking grey-faced and terminally bored as he had mumbled and stumbled his way through a PowerPoint presentation. Bram Borrink had been seated at the head of the table and had spent almost the entire hour thumbing through something apparently riveting on his mobile phone – perhaps a series of texts from an international drugs trafficker. Perhaps porn or spreadsheets or a shopping list from his wife. Either way, Ad had been reasonably confident that Bram Borrink would never, ever remember Ad's face.

Borrink glanced down at the centre of his table to the place where the Silencer's notes had landed. Only two notes now, rather than the four that had been left behind. And now Ad was leaving in a hurry with a bulging bag containing an object the approximate size and shape of a whisky tumbler.

'Ad Karelse,' the big boss said, pointing. It was an accusatory index finger, wagging at him. It would have been no less excruciating if Borrink had been shouting through a loudhailer to the other diners that here was a scruffy interloper who had wrongfully encroached on their exclusivity and had stolen from them.

'No. I'm George van den Broek,' Ad said, trying to suppress the squeak in his voice.

But Borrink had already snapped his fingers to alert the maître d' …

CHAPTER 48

Mexico, Hospital Galenia, Cancun, 2 June

'That was some stunt you pulled, old man,' George said, squeezing Van den Bergen's hand. She shifted her position on the hospital bed, tugging the saline drip that had been plugged into her arm with her. Glad to be lying on a relatively comfortable mattress in Cancun's Hospital Galenia instead of sleeping rough as a *transportista*, wondering when a bullet or the blade of a machete would find her. 'You're like some kind of dyspeptic James Bond.'

'Don't talk to me about stunts,' Van den Bergen said, withdrawing his hand and folding his arms. 'You …' He glared at her. Clearly choosing his words carefully. 'Are incorrigible and irresponsible.'

Rubbing at her skin in an attempt to erase some of the fake tattoos that covered her, George shrugged. She met the cynical expression on her lover's face with a grin. 'Yep. And? Didn't I save my dad? Didn't Gonzales arrest half of Coba cartel's foot soldiers and close down the meth camp that's been churning out poison and killing kids?' She poked herself in the chest. Felt the dried-in salt beneath her finger. Made a mental note to ask for a shower. 'All thanks to me!'

Van den Bergen ran his hands through his hair and rubbed his face, as though trying to wash away his frustrations. He shook his head and took her hand into his again. Stroking her palm. 'You're fearless and headstrong and stubborn as hell, Georgina McKenzie. It's a terrible combination. I worry that one day, this gung-ho crap will get you killed.'

'Stop whingeing and pour me a glass of water, will you? I'm still pissing soy sauce, even with the drip.' Shunting herself up the bed, George started to consider what an enormous gamble she had taken in stealing the motorboat. The alternative turn of events that could have come to pass made her shudder to think of them. 'Good job that dick who owned the boat called the cops.'

'Good job his description of you was reasonably accurate,' Van den Bergen said. '"A lunatic with an afro who says she's an English cop and has a smart mouth on her. Great tits, though."'

'Guilty as charged,' George said. 'I can't help being blessed with an impressive set of swears.'

Van den Bergen's stern expression finally softened with a broad grin and a silent chuckle. 'Anyway, the timing was perfect. Gonzales' men were just about to head off into the jungle to make the rendezvous time you'd suggested. The decision was made that I'd go out to sea with the helicopter to find you, you terrible woman.'

'You were green!'

'I felt sick as a pig. Those things are instruments of torture for people with middle-ear complaints.' He dug a finger into his ear emphatically.

'Nice jump onto the deck, though. You're a bona fide hero, pulling me out of that sub! I'm telling you. That's some proper 007 shit right there. You've still got it, old man,' she said, sticking her foot out from beneath the sheet and scrunching the groin area of his jeans with her naked toes. 'Ugh. You're sweaty. Didn't you bring any shorts or T-shirts?'

Van den Bergen emitted a low growl. Didn't try to remove her foot. 'Damn weather. It's not healthy.' It was hard to see if he was blushing beneath his tan but George preferred to think that he was. He blinked repeatedly. A twinkle in those melancholy eyes.

'I want to see my dad,' she said, poking at the bulge beneath the denim.

'They're keeping him in another day for observation.' He pushed her foot away, gently. 'But both me and Gonzales have managed to take his initial statement. He's fine. Just needs fattening up, a course of antibiotics, some jabs and a decade of therapy.'

'Right. Well I still want to see him.' George swung her legs over the side of her bed and stood, pulling her hospital gown over her exposed bottom. She grabbed her drip stand. 'This is like déjà vu.'

'More like Groundhog Day,' Van den Bergen said. He clutched at his stomach. 'There's not a diet in the world that's alkaline enough to calm the heartburn you give me.'

George linked him, kissing him on his upper arm, since that was as high as she could reach in flip-flop-clad feet. 'Shove your guilt trip. Take me to my long-lost papa.'

When she entered her father's hospital room, she swallowed hard. Gone was the man she had carried a mental image of for decades. He had been replaced by a shadow of the once vibrant Michael Carlos Izquierdo Moreno. Emaciated. Hollow cheeks. Sunken eyes. Tatty greying hair that needed a good cut. But his arms. His olive-skinned arms, covered in black hair, were only thinner, more sinewy versions of the arms that had lifted her as a tiny girl, swinging her onto his shoulders.

'Papa,' she said, letting go of Van den Bergen's hand and wheeling her drip stand to the bedside. Just saying the word aloud unlocked the maelstrom of emotions she had bottled inside her for her entire adult life: Longing for love and approval that he hadn't been there to provide as she was growing up. Nostalgia for her childhood when he had still been a daily presence in her young life. Guilt that this reunion was some kind of a betrayal of Letitia, who had always cried wolf that she had been abandoned, when George knew she had pushed him away.

Her father's eyes opened. The first thing George saw in them was fear.

'Help!' he shouted in Spanish. Focusing on Van den Bergen. 'Get her out of here!' Then, repeated the demand in English.

Taking a step back, George swallowed hard and wiped away her tears in defiance with the back of her hand. Feeling the rejection bite like the venomous sting of a hornet. A flurry of aggressive words jostled their way to the tip of her tongue, but she realised her anger had no place here. He simply hadn't recognised her. She clasped a hand over the fake tattoos. People believed what they had been conditioned to believe. Why should he see her ink as anything but the real deal? 'It's me, Papa,' she said. 'It's Ella. I wrote you a letter. Did you get it?'

His face softened. His consternation in his face was replaced by a broad smile. He held his hand out to her. Spoke in English.

'I did,' he said in a hoarse voice. 'It kept me going, right to what I thought was the very end.'

He squeezed George's hand with a weak grip. His skin was too warm and clammy. George forced herself to maintain the contact, savouring the physical closeness after all these years yet itching to scrub her hands under a scalding hot tap. After all she had witnessed and endured over the past week, she was certain she might never feel clean again. That kind of dirt might be indelible, though the ink on her skin would surely wash off eventually.

Sitting beside her long-lost father, George drank in the detail of his face. Imagined him fatter. Younger. Not so different, after all, on closer inspection.

'I tried to find you when you were a teen,' he said, reaching out to touch her hair. 'Even though your mother asked me not to. I did. I scoured the internet week after week. But I just couldn't track you down.'

'Ella Williams-May disappeared,' she said, wishing he would

322

leave her hair alone. It needed a good wash and some Moroccan oil on it, for a start. 'It's a long story. I'll tell you on the flight home.'

'Home?' He angled his face towards her, frowning inquisitively.

Van den Bergen approached the bed, filling the room with the smell of sport deodorant and oranges. He crouched by the bedside. 'We need you to come to Amsterdam to testify, Mr Moreno.'

'Call me Michael,' her father said.

Nodding, Van den Bergen's mouth remained a grim line. 'The meth you were shipping to the Dominican ... The meth being produced in that jungle lab has killed a number of young people in my city, giving them fatal lead poisoning. Kids in New York too. But my concern is the bodies that have been found floating in my canals. The Dutch police have just got hold of irrefutable forensic evidence ...' He glanced knowingly at George and winked. 'That ties your *el cocodrilo* to Nikolay Bebchuck, otherwise known as the Rotterdam Silencer. These are all the pseudonyms of the man who had you kidnapped – Stijn Pietersen. He's a Dutch national and we have reason to believe that's he's currently on Dutch soil. We know he's been purchasing precursor chemicals from China through a Dutch multinational to service his labs in the Czech Republic and Mexico. Last night, when I'd finished taking your statement, George told me about all the violence. His gun-running and people trafficking.'

'I'm living proof of that,' her father said, patting George's hand as a tear tracked along the contours of his thin face.

George wanted to envelop him in her arms but felt she couldn't. Not yet. She was overwhelmed by a sense that their roles had been reversed, where her father was now the vulnerable one who needed looking after, and she was now his capable guardian. She was aware of tears pooling in her eyes for all that had been lost but willed them to be absorbed back into her body. Van den Bergen was talking about the case. The time to interrupt him with an outburst of mixed feelings about her childhood would come. But that time was not now.

'Pietersen has the monopoly on the crystal meth market and he's long overdue a prison sentence that will put him behind bars for good.' Van den Bergen pulled up a chair from the corner of the room and folded his tall frame into it. Leaned forwards, placing his elbows on his knees. Speaking with the gravitas of the Chief Inspector that he was, rather than something approximating to a son-in-law who was inappropriately too old for a woman in her twenties. 'We're going to need you. If you don't mind.'

Michael turned to George, studying her face. She realised she had no way of knowing what this man was thinking. Though he was her father, they had only just met for the first time in almost twenty-five years. He had no idea that Van den Bergen was her partner in more than just crime. He knew precisely nada about George. She knew absolute zero about him. But she sensed that he had a good soul.

'How's your mother?' he asked, smiling weakly at her. The glimmer of fond reminiscence in his eyes.

'Oh,' George said. 'About that …'

CHAPTER 49

Amsterdam, Schiphol airport, 4 June

As the plane touched down in Amsterdam's Schiphol airport, Van den Bergen undid his seat belt before they had even come to a standstill.

'What's the rush?' George said, tugging at his belt as he pulled on his raincoat.

She was all sleepy from the long flight. Still holding hands with her dad. As if he had time for that kind of oversentimental crap, no matter how valid it may be.

'Elvis is still missing,' he said. 'He's been gone too long.' He checked his watch. The working day had not yet begun. But the time that had elapsed since he had received the email containing the gruesome photo of Elvis did not bode well for the boy's safety. 'If my detective is dead because I wasn't here to supervise the investigation into his disappearance, I'll never forgive myself.' Abruptly, he leaned down and kissed George full on the mouth, clasping her face in his hand.

He sensed that Michael was watching him. An intelligent man like that had worked out quickly enough the nature of his and George's relationship. But at nearly 50, Van den Bergen was not about to make excuses to any man for his romantic commitment to a woman young enough to be his daughter.

The heart wants what it wants. Those had been George's words.

Dropping the keys to his apartment into her lap, he proffered his hand to Michael. Shook it in a businesslike fashion, careful not to crush those starved, fragile fingers inside his oversized shovel. Dark circles under his eyes said he hadn't slept in ten years, but then the doctors had said he was dangerously anaemic as well as generally malnourished and almost certainly likely to suffer from PTSD once he started to process what had happened to him. Poor bastard. It was a miracle he was alive at all. 'Get some rest, Michael,' he said in English. 'George here will take good care of you. But don't let her cook if you want to see your next birthday.'

George thumped him playfully in the thigh. 'Twat!'

'Make your dad comfortable at my place,' he said, ignoring the Tannoy announcement that demanded all passengers should remain in their seat until the aircraft had come to a complete standstill. 'Fill the fridge. It's on me. There's cash in the spaghetti jar. I'll be back when I'm back.'

A flash of his ID card ensured he was first off the plane, no questions asked. Van den Bergen arrived back in Amsterdam Centraal Station, emerging beyond its Renaissance Revival redbrick façade into dank drizzle and a stiff wind that was blowing inland from the North Sea. He inhaled the choking diesel fumes from the sightseeing barges that whipped over to him from the canals like some pollutant greeting, relieved to be back on familiar ground. This was his turf. This was a place where a guy could wear a light jumper and a raincoat and feel comfortable, most of the year round. This was home. But Elvis was missing.

A cab took him to the police headquarters on Elandsgracht.

'Well?' he said to Marie, slamming open the door to her office.

She had been sitting with her back to him, intently poring over what appeared to be programming language on her computer screen. Now, she clasped her hand to her chest. Her normally flushed face blanched.

'God, you gave me a fright, boss.' Her eyes were suddenly glassy. Unexpectedly, she sprang to her feet and embraced Van den Bergen in a bear hug. 'We've got to get him back.'

'And I think I know where we can find him.' A man's voice came from behind the door. 'If you've finished slamming the door onto my knees.'

Van den Bergen detached himself from Marie and pulled the door closed to reveal Ad Karelse's idiotic face smiling at him.

'What the hell are you doing here, Karelse?' he said, eyeing his erstwhile love rival up and down. Noticing the slight paunch that had appeared since they had last met, face to face. He no longer wore glasses, which gave his face an odd imbalance and made his nose look too long. And to think George had once considered him a pretty boy.

'Where's George?'

Hope emanated from every pore in the spineless prick's body. Except Van den Bergen realised that Karelse was anything but a spineless prick, given he had opted to risk his life to spy on the Rotterdam Silencer's clandestine business lunch.

'Busy.' Forcing himself to do the gentlemanly thing, Van den Bergen stuck out his hand. 'Thanks,' he said.

But Karelse returned the gesture only with a sneering, disdainful expression. The old wound ran deep, clearly. 'I didn't do it for you.'

They had reached a social etiquette impasse. There was no point in trying to build any more of that bridge.

'Where do you think Elvis is?' Van den Bergen asked, swiping aside the pile of empty snack wrappers, knick-knacks and stationery that covered Marie's desk to perch on the edge. 'And why haven't you told us this earlier?'

Karelse remained standing with his arms folded. Staring at Van den Bergen, as though he was trying to slice him from top to toe with two beams of pure vitriol. 'I've been up since 4 a.m. I couldn't sleep. I went into the office early and started to trawl through old accounting archives.' He turned to Marie. 'Hacking the system from the inside is easy for me.' Smiling as though Marie would be impressed by his bullshit. 'And I couldn't believe it.'

'Spit it out,' Van den Bergen said, drumming his fingers on the sticky desk. Trying his damnedest not to wrinkle his nose at the smell of stale cabbage and onions in Marie's lair.

'I have a Dutch delivery address for InterChem GmbH that was used several times for chemicals ordered from Chembedrijf back in 2010. In Rotterdam.'

'Why the hell didn't you just phone this information through?' Van den Bergen stood, feeling momentarily woozy. Jet lag, probably. Or possible deep-vein thrombosis thanks to a long-haul flight. Another thing to get checked out for. But that could wait. He took two steps closer to Karelse, looking down at him. There were only thirteen centimetres between them, but each one counted.

'Well, I got the first train out of Groningen. I wanted to deliver the news to George personally. Maybe help her look for Elvis.' Karelse seemed to puff out his chest and broaden his shoulders. He shifted his feet to stand with legs astride like that posing idiot Poldark, whom George made Van den Bergen watch on TV whenever he visited her in England. 'But she's not here.' He could see the Adam's apple in Karelse's throat pinging up and down. Disappointment dulling the shine on his hopeful young man's face.

'No. She's not. So, give me the address, and you can go home.'

'I risked my safety and my job to get you evidence!' Karelse shouted, looking over at Marie for tacit approval that came in the form of the briefest of nods. 'I spent a fortune on a lunch I didn't even enjoy and got you a sound recording, a glass and some money. Bram Borrink recognised me, for God's sake! I had to string him some bullshit about having lunch to celebrate my dad's memory on the first anniversary of his death.'

'Very nice,' Van den Bergen said. 'Congratulations on doing your civic duty. We'll reimburse you for your lunch. Address!' He raised his voice loud enough to make Karelse shrink back. Felt guilt wrapping its fingers around his stomach, squeezing hard until acid erupted upwards into his gullet.

CHAPTER 50

Amsterdam, Van den Bergen's apartment, at the same time

'Come on, Papa,' George said, plumping the cushions on Van den Bergen's sofa. Arranging them so that they were perfect diamond shapes. She tweaked the corners until they stood stiffly to attention. 'Come and get comfy on here. It's nicer than the guest bed. I'll make you some coffee and see what's in Paul's fridge. Sod all, probably, knowing him.'

Her father took her by the forearm and kissed her knuckles. Patted the back of her hand affectionately. Things she remembered him doing all those years ago when she had been a small girl in dungarees, covered in paint, with Plasticine under her fingernails.

'I still can't believe I'm out of there,' he said. 'I can't believe it's you!'

George considered his stooped frame. He seemed so much smaller than she had remembered. She smiled and yawned. 'Believe it. Come on. Sit down. I'm knackered, so you must be dropping. We'll have a bite to eat and then let's both have a good kip.'

Helping her father to the old vintage sofa, George went into Van den Bergen's bedroom, pulled a heavy sweater from his wardrobe and took the just-in-case blanket from the end of the bed. Insisted that her father wrap up warm, given the abrupt change in temperature from the balmy tropical climate of Mexico to the chill of an Amsterdam attempt at summer.

Squatting beside him, she stroked his untidy, wispy hair. Examined that almost unfamiliar face that was so reminiscent of hers and yet so different. Was Michael Carlos Izquierdo Moreno a good man or a bad man? He had seemed like a king to her when she had been but a child. 'It seems strange to be tucking in a grown adult. Not to mention my long-lost papa,' she said, hoping he couldn't sense the emotions that curdled inside her.

'I'm so sorry about Letitia,' he said, closing his eyes. 'I wish I could have seen her.'

'Don't you be sorry for her,' George said, rising and making for the kitchen. Camouflaging with the brisk efficiency of a hostess her deep-seated fears that her mother might be dead. 'Whatever she's doing right now, she won't be feeling a shred of remorse about how she's treated you or me over the years. She won't be worrying her selfish arse about me scouring half of Europe to find her. She'll be shacked up somewhere, reinventing herself and having the time of her life.' She opened the food cupboard doors and found some baked beans she had brought from London. Half a sliced loaf in the freezer. Food of the gods.

'Do you really think she just upped and left?' her father shouted from the living room.

Had she been wrong to string him a line on the plane about Letitia having taken herself off in some rebellious exercise, designed to give the two-fingered salute both to her diagnosed illness and her family? Was keeping the gift-wrapped eyeball and the bogus, threatening emails secret respectful of her father as a grown adult? She had merely wanted to spare him any further anxiety after his horrendous ordeal.

'Yeah,' George said, pleased she wasn't able to make eye contact from the kitchen. 'Knowing her? I'd put money on it!'

Taking out the cream cleanser, George filled the sink with a kettle

331

full of boiling water and started to scrub away at Van den Bergen's already clean worktops. She noted the image of herself reflected in the glazed tiles of the splashback. A portrait of an El Salvadoran *transportista* whose mind was forever sullied by murder and whose skin would be forever blighted by ink. She removed her long-sleeved T-shirt so that she wore only a bra. Took the scrubbing sponge, emptied a large blob of cleaner onto it and started to rub at her skin where the tattoos still told the tale of her collusion in the deaths of those trafficked women on the airstrip. These painted arms had not wielded the machete but she had done nothing to stop the others. Sometimes doing nothing was sin enough.

Scouring while the kettle boiled and the beans simmered on the hob, scrubbing until the pain made her eyes water, George's attempts at expunging her guilt were interrupted only by her phone ringing shrilly on the side.

The display said it was Jan, her former landlord from the Cracked Pot Coffee Shop in the red-light district. His photograph lit up her phone's screen with a dopey hippy grin and frazzled marijuana eyes behind Trotsky glasses.

'Jan,' she said, stifling a jet-lagged yawn. Feeling the kitchen floor rise and fall beneath her. She hoped to fuck he was quick.

'Hey, George. How's tricks?' His greeting was nothing out of the ordinary. His serious tone rang alarm bells.

Clutching the phone to her ear with her hunched shoulder, she wrestled the frozen bread into the toaster. Stirred the beans. Ignored the smarting skin on her arm where the cream cleanser was already drying into a white film. 'Well, actually, Jan, I've just got off a long-haul flight and I'm dying to—'

'You know that guy Stijn Pietersen? The ugly one who was in all the papers when that cop of yours locked him up … Long time ago. I remembered you telling me you'd had a run-in with him once as a kid.'

George turned the hob off and glowered at her reflection in the tiles. 'Yes. Go on.'

'Well, you know how I am about never forgetting a face.' Jan started to wheeze inexplicably with laughter, as was his wont. Always one irrelevant comment away from weed-giggles.

'Come on, Jan. What is it?' George took a cloth, wet it under the tap and started to wipe at her raw skin. 'I'm on tenterhooks here.'

'He looks completely different at a glance, you see. He's got some dumb bleached hair and a face like a keg of Duvel. But it's him. I swear it.'

'Stijn Pietersen? Are you telling me the Rotterdam Silencer is—'

'Yeah, man. On a houseboat in Prinsengracht. I was taking a walk near the Anne Frank museum, watching all the tourists queue around the block. And there he was, on the deck. It's not the first time I've seen him either. But this time, I crossed the road and walked over to him, just to make sure.'

George swapped the phone over from her right to her left ear, her heart beating wildly, speeding cortisol around her body. She was suddenly freezing cold. 'You silly bastard, Jan. What did you say?'

'I wished him a good morning, because it was a very nice morning before the rain set in. He was sitting on a deck chair, reading a paper. I told him I recognised him.'

'Oh you *didn't*!'

She could almost visualise Jan shrugging on the other end of the phone, taking a contemplative toke on his spliff. Could hear him inhaling. A rattling cough as he exhaled. 'He said he had that kind of face. I offered him a smoke. He thanked me and said no. That was it.'

'Are you sure?' George asked, standing on her tiptoes to peer out of the kitchen window to the little copse of trees below. Opening the cutlery drawer slowly and withdrawing the carving knife.

'Well, actually … now you come to mention it, that's not completely all.'

She slammed the drawer shut. 'Jesus, Jan. Out with it!'

'He said I must have that kind of face too, because he was totally sure I was the ex-landlord of a girl he used to know.' He chuckled unconvincingly. 'It was a bit creepy really.'

'Oh shit,' George said, as the toast popped up in the toaster. 'Close the shop and lock all your doors. Now!'

'What?' She could hear voices in the coffee shop. The tinkle of the door as someone opened it. *It's your overactive imagination*, she told herself. *Calm down. Jan's always stoned. He talks a load of verbal diarrhoea at the best of times.*

'Just do as I ask, Jan. Please. For your old pal. Until Van den Bergen has had a chance to speak to you.'

But Jan wasn't listening. Her words hung uselessly in the stale air of the kitchen. Her ex-landlord had already hung up.

CHAPTER 51

Rotterdam, Dockside, the Port of Rotterdam, later

'It's got to be one of these,' Van den Bergen said, squinting through the lenses of his glasses at the address Karelse had scribbled on the piece of paper. 'But they all look the same. Damn it! And I can't read the number he's written here. Is it a one or a seven? Useless prick.'

He scratched at his neck with the muzzle of his service pistol, removing his glasses to regard the dock full of identical grey warehousing that stretched into the distance. The chill sea wind ruffled its briny fingers through his hair and slapped him about his jet-lagged, dehydrated face. At his side, Marie tugged on the piece of paper, trying to decode the scrawl. Behind them, an armed response unit was sitting in an unmarked van. An ambulance had parked just around the corner, awaiting instructions.

'It's a seven, boss. Unit twenty-seven. I'm sure of it.' Marie was shivering, clutching her inadequate fleece closed against the harsh dockland micro-climate. Seagulls wheeling overhead almost drowned out her voice. They splattered the asphalt with guano, as if adding their own exclamation points to her confident assertion.

Beckoning the van to follow discreetly, Van den Bergen stalked along the row of warehouses, bypassing fork-lift trucks and men in overalls who were busy about loading palletised freight into heavy goods vehicles. It was a noisy place. He shoved his gun into his coat pocket, remembering he was no longer in Mexico, where the Gendarmería Nacional toted their weapons as a visual deterrent at all times.

'Do you think we'll find him, boss?' Marie asked. 'After so much time has passed. Is it likely he'll be alive?'

Van den Bergen didn't answer. He merely visualised Elvis, strapped to a chair behind any one of these Identikit industrial frontages. 'How's his mother?'

'She died.'

'Dead?' Van den Bergen came to a standstill. Turned to her. 'Shit. Oh no. That's terrible.'

Marie nodded. 'I know. She passed away the evening after he went missing. I got a call from the hospital. If the Silencer's men haven't killed him, this definitely will. If you know what I mean.'

'Poor bastard.'

'Oh, and he's got a boyfriend.'

Gazing momentarily out to the busy shipping channel of Nieuwe Maas, he saw the overcast sky and the unfathomable grey-brown water. It dawned on him that he knew absolutely nothing about his own place in the universe or the world around him. 'Jesus. How could I have worked with him all these years and not sussed that he was gay?'

Marie patted his arm. 'Don't worry, boss. I spoke to his boyfriend. Dirk didn't know himself until a couple of weeks ago. I think your gaydar's still fully functioning.'

Elvis' mother was dead. Christ. That was a shitty turn of events for both of them – that Elvis, if he was still alive, had been denied the chance to say goodbye after all of his dutiful travails. And for her. To have undertaken the hard, hard work of departing this life on her own in a hospital bed. Nobody to usher her to the end, as Van den Bergen had walked his father to the threshold of death.

336

But Elvis' mother was gone now, and her possibly still-breathing son was Van den Bergen's only concern at that moment.

'Unit twenty-seven,' he said, drawing his gun at the sight of the giant numbers mounted high on the side of the warehouse. He turned back to the van. Beckoned the driver to draw closer.

'Can I help you, mate?' a man said, appearing in the doorway of the warehouse, carrying a box that looked heavy.

Van den Bergen sized him up as he showed his ID. 'Police.' The man was wearing jeans and a fleece. No overalls, though there was a company logo in red displayed on the hoarding above the entrance that said, *1,2,3 Logistiek*. No steel-toecap safety boots on his feet, which the men working in these logistics places tended to wear. Something was off.

The man dropped the box. Retreated back inside at speed.

With a nod from Van den Bergen, the uniformed armed response unit were out of their van, guns drawn.

Sprinting through the warehouse after the man, Van den Bergen had a moment in which to take in his surroundings. Boxes stacked to the ceiling. It was no different than any other dockside warehouse, rammed with produce from Southeast Asia, India and China to be delivered to shops all over Europe. This was Rotterdam, after all. Had his jet lag skewed his reasoning? Had the man simply lost his nerve and run?

Feeling suddenly overwhelmed by dizziness, he shouted out. 'Police! Stop where you are or I'll shoot!'

The man glanced back but did not slow his pace – surprisingly swift for a short, overweight man.

Ignoring the peculiar floating sensation that was turning his long limbs to jelly, Van den Bergen fired a warning shot by the man's head and kept going. But darting around a corner, the warehouse worker disappeared from view.

'Bastard!' Van den Bergen said, bending over and clutching at his knees. That giant unfamiliar space seeming to spin around him. The ground beneath him rose and fell as though he was still standing on the deck of the semi-submersible in the middle of a rough Caribbean Sea.

Some way behind him, he caught sight of Marie, advancing slowly. Gun drawn. Checking behind towers of boxes for ambush potential. 'Check for rear exit point!' she whispered into a walkie-talkie to their backup.

Forcing himself to go on, Van den Bergen stalked towards a secondary storage area off to the left, following black tracks that had presumably been made by fork-lifts coming and going. It was darker in there. The giant fluorescent lights that hung from overhead were switched off. Had the warehouse worker absconded into this vast, shadowy hangar of a place?

Advancing into the murk, it was as though Van den Bergen's jet lag had been switched off, just as the light had failed. He was running on pure adrenalin, now. Breathing faster. Feeling more himself.

'Come on, you piece of shit,' he said softly, holding his pistol in front of him with steady hands. 'Where are you?' He could hear the armed uniforms scampering forwards stealthily. They had clearly gained entry from elsewhere and were now advancing towards him. Surely, they would flush this slippery gatekeeper out.

The blood rushed in his ears. He sensed he was being watched. Marie was several metres behind him. His back was covered. Or was it?

Glancing behind for a fraction of a second, he realised his IT expert was no longer in view. Damn it!

The plank of wood swinging towards him was all he glimpsed before he registered a sharp, stinging blow to his forehead.

Van den Bergen reeled backwards, emitting a muffled cry. But was somehow still on his feet. The warehouse worker had dropped the plank with a clatter and was sprinting towards the back of the space.

'Stop!' Van den Bergen's vision was blurred but he aimed his weapon at the man's legs. Pulled the trigger. The crack of his shot ricocheted around the warehouse, pulsating painfully in his ears.

The warehouse worker screamed. His legs buckled at the knees. He went down hard, with arms flailing uselessly in the air. There was shouting from all around, then, as the armed response unit poured into the place – rifles raised and poised to fire – abandoning stealth in favour of a show of strength and slickly co-ordinated manoeuvres.

'Find Marie!' Van den Bergen bellowed, advancing towards the wounded would-be fugitive.

Shaking his head, poking at his ears. He holstered his weapon. Pounced on the warehouse worker, pinioning his arms together behind his back and cuffing him. 'Who are you, you shifty little shit? Who do you work for?' He grabbed a handful of the man's hair, yanking his head around to make eye contact. 'Where are my detectives? A man called Dirk and the redhead that entered the building with me.'

The man's face was contorted in pain. But behind the grimace, there lurked a dull-eyed insolence. 'Fuck you!' he yelled. 'Get me an ambulance. I'm bleeding to death.'

'We've found Marie, Chief Inspector!' one of the armed response uniforms shouted, appearing from behind a stack of boxes. 'She's out cold. Blow to the head.'

'Christ. Get the paramedics round here, immediately. Make sure they see to Marie before this arsehole.' He kneeled heavily on the buttocks of his captive. 'Now, where's my other detective? Do you know what terrible things can happen in prison to pricks like you who assault police officers?'

The man craned his neck to face Van den Bergen. 'Shove it up your arse, pig.' A glob of sputum hit the Chief Inspector squarely in the belly.

As Van den Bergen stood, he was careful to put all of his weight onto the man's kidney with his knee. The man screamed in agony. 'That's for knocking my detective out and hitting me in the head with a plank.'

'I'm going to sue you for police brutality!'

'Go right ahead, you lump of shit.'

Already, Van den Bergen could feel the endorphin rush of the chase abating, leaving unbearable, crashing fatigue in its stead. 'Get that cadaver dog in here!' he ordered the uniforms. 'Make sure the exits are sealed, then I want you to search every nook and cranny of these premises.'

Striding over to the now ashen-faced Marie, Van den Bergen knelt by her side. Moved a strand of her hair off her forehead. There was a livid bump where she had been struck on the temple. 'Jesus, Marie,' he said. 'I'm so sorry.'

The paramedic jogged over, carrying a large bag, followed by two ambulance drivers. She ushered him out of the way, setting her bag down and removing a blood pressure cuff, a stethoscope and a myriad of other bits of kit. 'We've got this. Okay?' she said, offering a reassuring smile. 'What's her name?'

'Marie. Be careful with her, won't you?'

'Don't worry, Chief Inspector. Marie's in good hands.'

Feeling suddenly lost, Van den Bergen stood in the middle of the warehouse, watching the claustrophobic towers of cardboard boxes and metal shelving spin around him in a tornado of hopelessness and dead ends.

In Cancun, Gonzales had arrested at least twenty low-level cartel members and El Salvadoran *transportistas*, had rescued a chemist from San Diego plus two trafficked Guatemalan girls being used as sex slaves and had closed down the killer meth lab.

But back beneath the overcast skies of the Netherlands, Van den Bergen had nothing. He had worse than nothing, which amounted to one missing detective, one seriously injured detective, and no big prize in the Silencer. Having the evidence to convict Stijn Pietersen felt like an empty victory for those dead kids in the canals without him knowing the whereabouts of the murderous, trafficking bastard. You couldn't arrest a myth and put it behind bars.

'Chief Inspector,' one of the uniforms said, pulling Van den

Bergen out of his downwards trajectory. At the end of a thick leash that he gripped with both hands, a giant of a German shepherd was barking in a near-frenzy and rearing on its hind legs. 'We've found something.'

'Oh no. Don't tell me,' Van den Bergen felt an inferno rising in his throat. His fingertips turned to ice.

'There are two body bags back here, stashed on the prongs of a fork-lift. You'd better come quickly.'

CHAPTER 52

Amsterdam, Van den Bergen's apartment, a short while later

'What do you mean, he's out on confidential urgent police business? This *is* urgent police business. And I'm Dr McKenzie, the criminologist.' George was aware that the pitch of her voice had risen by several notches. 'I work for his damned team as a freelancer.' Feeling her father's inquisitive gaze fixed intently on the side of her face and having this stubborn jobsworth on the end of the phone, dropping the shutters on every word she uttered, George felt the will to live being squeezed out of her, leaving her drained and limp like one of Aunty Sharon's empty piping socks.

'Well, *if* you work for him, call his mobile,' the receptionist from the police HQ said. Not a voice that George recognised. '*If* he's given it to you.'

Sitting on the end of the sofa, watching her father eat lukewarm beans on toast, George tucked the blanket in around his feet so tightly that he emitted a disgruntled yowl and shrank away from her touch. She mouthed, 'Sorry!' at him and winked. Back to the receptionist. 'Don't you think I already tried that? I've tried Marie too. Nobody's picking up. I want you to get word to him somehow that George needs to speak to him urgently.'

'I'm afraid I can't.' The woman on the other end was starting to sound defensive. Perhaps one sentence away from quoting some kind of employee handbook.

'You bloody well must!'

'Please don't speak to me like that. I don't have to take your verbal—'

George ended the call, feeling like she needed to punch or bleach something, fast. She almost opted for the former, but her father had been traumatised enough without having to see his long-lost daughter using Van den Bergen's beanbag as a punchball. The apartment felt oppressive and stale, unsurprising, given it had been locked up for a week.

Flinging open the patio doors and gulping the fresh air hungrily, George considered an alternative course of action. She stood on the balcony, sparked one of her Mexican cigarettes from Cancun's duty free into life and exhaled deeply.

'Those things will kill you,' her father said.

'So I've heard.' George's mind was elsewhere. She yawned absently and her blocked ears popped with an agonising squeak. 'Minks!' she said, snapping her fingers. She turned back to her father and smiled. 'I'll call Minks.'

Five minutes later, she was satisfied that a heavily armed police unit was being sent to the Prinsengracht, as a precautionary measure, to check out the preposterous notion that the infamous Rotterdam Silencer was hiding in plain sight on a slightly shabby, flower-festooned houseboat.

'Good,' she said, ending the call. Feeling like the last thing in the world she wanted to do was to go out. The craving for sleep was already weighting her eyelids down and making her thoughts sluggish. The ground heaved beneath her feet like the Caribbean Sea.

'What's good?' her father asked, smiling benignly.

'Nothing,' she said. 'I've got to nip out. I need to get some bits for the fridge and I've got to check on something. I won't be long.'

Throwing the blanket off, her father swung his legs over the side of the sofa. His shinbones jutted sharply through his skin like long blades, all too visible in Van den Bergen's unworn summer shortie pyjamas that he had tied tight with a dressing-gown cord. 'I'm coming with you,' he said.

'Don't be silly,' George said, trying to usher him back onto the sofa. 'I'll fix you a cup of coffee or a hot chocolate ...' Grinning bashfully. 'Although I don't really know how to make hot chocolate, but I'll fix you one anyway. I won't be more than an hour. I promise.'

Her father had already risen to his feet, however, and was pulling on the jeans he had been given by Gonzales, back in Cancun. 'We've been apart for twenty-five years,' he said. 'I've just lost three years in the Yucatan jungle and escaped death by the skin of my teeth on a daily basis. Do you know how much I yearned for my little girl when I was over there?'

With unsteady bony fingers, he took off his battered old watch. Removed the back, teasing out a thumbnail of colour that had been sandwiched between the watch's time-keeping mechanism and the cover. With a flourish and a proud smile, he showed her a dog-eared, stained photo of her when she had been about 3. All chubby smiling face, brush-like eyelashes and fat bunches on the top of her head, tied with blue bows. It was a head-and-shoulders shot that had been roughly clipped from a larger photo.

'Letitia used to have the full version of this before she burned all the old photos,' she said, handling the tiny image carefully in the palm of her hand. 'London Zoo. The three of us. We were at the zoo. I remember. You and Letitia had had a full-on bust-up by the chimpanzees or some shit. Maybe it was the tigers. I'd been crying – I remember that much. But you cheered me up with an ice cream and the pair of you patched it up long enough to get some posh lady to take the picture of us with your old camera. She acted like she felt sorry for us, the patronising cow. But still ...'

Her father smiled, pocketed the photo, slipping it deftly back inside his watch, as though he were still a prisoner at the mercy of men who had denied him any link with his former life as a free man, lest it gave him rebellious ideas. 'Well, I'm here now. And you're here. And I'm not letting you out of my sight until I'm sure this is all real.'

Standing in the middle of Van den Bergen's eclectic thrift-shop jumble of a living room for some thirty seconds with her hand on her hip, George drank in the sight of her broken father. Mulling over whether to indulge him or draw the boundaries she so desperately needed to demarcate with everyone now – thanks to years and years spent apologising to and appeasing Letitia.

'Come on, then,' she said. 'I'm only nipping to check on a mate in the red-light district. It's a couple of tram stops away. If you think you're up to it. If you feel rough, just let me know and we'll turn back. Right? Is that a deal?' She grinned broadly and fluffed her hair out.

Her father nodded. Seemed to stand a little straighter, then.

As they pulled on raincoats by the front door, her phone rang. Lank hair, a dopey smile and Trotsky glasses appeared on her display. 'Oh, Jan. What do you want, now? For God's sake. I'm on my way.' She pressed accept. 'Hey, what's up, you old hippy? I'm just coming over—'

'Georgina McKenzie?' the voice was familiar but George did not immediately place it. A heavy Rotterdam accent. The gnawing dread in the pit of her stomach told her something her brain was clearly missing. 'Just the girl I'm looking for.'

CHAPTER 53

Amsterdam, a houseboat on Prinsengracht, at the same time

'When I give the signal, knock,' Maarten Minks said into his walkie-talkie, enjoying every terrifying, exquisite moment of this unanticipated foray into hands-on policing. *This is how Van den Bergen must feel*, he thought. *I feel invincible. This beats the hell out of strategy meetings and press conferences. No wonder these hard-boiled old-school guys keep at it long after their marriages fail and their livers start to pack up.*

He breathed in deeply, suddenly aware that his senses were sharper. Even the impressive brick-built Westerkerk opposite seemed statelier and somehow more solid. He imagined that he could hear the conversations between the tourists queuing round the block to gain entry to the Anne Frank museum. He could smell rain in the air.

The crackling message came back to him that the response unit was ready to go at his word, over and out.

At his word. As though he was some kind of demi-god, moving mortals around on the board in some heavenly game. And the mortal he was about to capture and punish was none other than Stijn Pietersen. The Rotterdam Silencer who had managed to beat a life sentence on appeal, thanks to some five-star legal

346

shenanigans and perhaps even the odd greased palm higher up the food chain. The man who had merely assumed the new name of Nikolay Bebchuk and had continued to expand his criminal empire, killing Dutch kids from a safe distance with his shitty crystal meth; lurking several fathoms below the radar.

Until now.

Van den Bergen wasn't going to get the Rotterdam Silencer this time around. He was. Maarten Minks. Excellent.

Minks felt certain that had he been wearing his heart-rate monitor, he would almost certainly be at his maximum 180 beats, now. Had he known that stakeouts would put his body through the paces as effectively as an hour on the treadmill in the gym, he might have opted to spend more time pounding the streets when he had joined the force straight out of university and less time preparing strategies and analysing policing trends for efficacy.

'Hey, young man! What's going on?' an old woman asked, wheeling her bicycle along the Prinsengracht towpath.

Minks eyed her with suspicion. Could she be an accomplice? 'Who let you beyond the cordon?'

'There's a cordon?' She frowned. Her turkey neck wobbled with indignation. 'But I live here.'

He pointed to the houseboat that was barely visible behind the display of pots and hanging baskets that dripped with petunias and geraniums. 'You live here?' Felt his gun surreptitiously. Just in case.

'No, not this one,' she said. 'Next one along.'

Eyeing her sandalled feet and walking shorts, Minks reasoned that perhaps she wasn't involved with an international trafficker, except by accident of geography. In her bicycle's basket, she had a loaf of bread, a carton of caramel *vla* and a bunch of roses from the market. Definitely not the tools of the trafficking trade.

Turning to his men, Minks scowled. Spoke softly into the walkie-talkie. 'I thought I told you to clear the damned area! Get her out of here!'

He focused on the chin of the disconcerted-looking woman, who was now all raised eyebrows and open mouth. Flashed his police ID. 'I'm afraid you'll have to wait further back on Bloemgracht until one of my officers gives you the all clear.'

With frustration mounting inside him, threatening to neutralise the insane, heady buzz, he shooed the old woman away. Took four deep breaths. Gave the word.

'Knock!'

There was a sudden flurry of activity as two teams of five officers swooped down from the adjacent Bloemgracht and the Westermarkt bridge respectively onto Prinsengracht itself. As one co-ordinated organism, the first team approached the entrance to the houseboat on the canal's edge. Swung a giant battering ram against the door, once, twice. Blasting the door almost off its hinges. The other men had the place surrounded; guns trained on the canal in case Pietersen opted to jump or had some other means of escape at the ready.

Minks could hear the search play out on his walkie-talkie. He took confident strides towards the houseboat, imagining what it would be like inside. The defeated expression on Pietersen's face when he read him his rights.

'It's clear, sir,' came the update, crackling along the airwaves.

Hardly bothering to keep his voice down as he spoke into the device, Minks felt suddenly as though his bright, bright morning had been enshrouded in dankest grey, snuffing out all the light and possibility and hope that the phone call from the lovely Georgina McKenzie had offered.

'What the hell do you mean, it's clear?' he shouted. Marching along the gangway and into the houseboat.

It was small inside. Just one bedroom, a living room with a kitchenette at one end and a cramped bathroom. The whole place reeked of cheap floral perfume and cigarettes. On the sofa, there was a pillow with an indentation where a head had rested. A dishevelled blanket. An empty whisky glass. But in the bedroom, there were women's things. Two sets of clothes. An overflowing ashtray. A long, broken nail next to a solitary photo – the only personal thing in the entire houseboat.

'Come and take a look at the windows, sir. If you ask me, they've been glazed with bullet-proof glass,' one of Minks' men said, beckoning him back into the living room. 'And there's a really sophisticated alarm system rigged up. In fact, the bedroom is a zone in itself.' He thumbed deadbolts that had been recessed into the architrave of the bedroom's threshold. 'It looks like whoever sleeps in here gets locked in. Bloody weird.'

But Minks was hardly listening to his uniformed officer's observations. He was too busy staring at the single framed photo on the bedside cabinet. Two women. Both Black. One younger and lighter-skinned. The other, darker-skinned, overweight and clearly older. Both looking miserable as hell in each other's company. Picking up the frame, he ran his thumb over the image of the familiar younger woman.

'George McKenzie.'

CHAPTER 54

Amsterdam, Van den Bergen's apartment, then, the red-light district, at the same time

It was hard to determine to whom the terrified screams in the background belonged, but George was certain they were coming from Jan. The call was from his phone, after all. She was glad that her father couldn't possibly have known the dreadful sound of despair that was filtering into her left ear.

'Come to the Cracked Pot Coffee Shop and come alone,' her caller said. 'If I spot any police, you'll pay in blood.' He hung up.

At that point, it was clear that this was no prank on Jan's part. And it was clear whom she had just received this sinister demand from.

The Rotterdam Silencer. Stijn Pietersen had her friend.

George grabbed her father's arm. 'You've got to stay here, Papa.'

Ignoring his protests, she ran through to the kitchen area and hurriedly grabbed whatever she could fit in her anorak pockets in a kitchen where the homeowner was certainly no avid cook: a vegetable knife, cheese wire and a meat tenderiser. She grabbed an old can of wasp killer for good measure.

'What on earth are you doing?' her father asked, leaning limply against the architrave of the kitchen door.

'I've got to go,' she said, kissing him fleetingly on his stubbly cheek. 'A friend's in trouble. Big trouble.' She glanced at her phone. Low battery. 'Do me a favour. If I'm not back in two hours, call the police and ask them to go to the Cracked Pot Coffee Shop in the red-light district. Tell them it's a matter of life and death.'

Her father's brow wrinkled with lack of comprehension. 'Call them now, then!'

Shaking her head, George pushed past him and hastened to the front door. 'No. It's too dangerous. Seriously, Dad. *Don't* call them now.' With a wave, she slammed the door behind her and headed to the tram. No swift way of getting into town.

'Come on, for fuck's sake,' she said, tapping her foot impatiently as she waited. Repeatedly, she dialled Van den Bergen's number. Straight to voicemail every time. After five attempts, she left a message. 'If anything happens, Paul ... oh, about fucking time. It's here! I've got to go. Love you.'

As she entered the busy front carriage of the tram, she was so preoccupied by thoughts of Jan's safety, she had not caught sight of the man who had surreptitiously slid into the rear carriage, just before the doors had shut.

Willing the driver to go faster, she checked her watch repeatedly. Jan needed her. Jan was at the mercy of the Rotterdam Silencer, who had a hard-on for hurting her, clearly. The strange turns of events since her mother's disappearance all made sense now. The eyeball at Vinkeles and her mother's phone. The threatening yet cryptic emails. Her father's abduction. The sight of the long-haired old biker who had kept appearing in her peripheral vision. And now, Jan. Stijn Pietersen, whom she had testified against all those years ago, hated her. He was hell-bent on revenge. He had in all likelihood killed her poor, annoying mother. He had stolen the liberty of her father. Today was the day. He was finally coming for her.

She wrapped her hand around the handle of the knife in her anorak pocket and acknowledged the mounting fury that mushroomed inside her. Those elderly passengers and mothers with babies in strollers who were giving her the evils as they reacted to her still-visible faux tattoos, shrinking away from her, were within her blast zone, now.

'What are you looking at, you nosey bastards?' she said.

They became suddenly interested in the world outside the tram's windows.

Finally, she alighted on Damrak, walking briskly across the chewing-gum-spattered paving of Dam Square through the hordes of tourists who prevented her from sprinting. Hurried past De Bijenkorf on her left, the white stone spire of the national monument on her right, down to the Grand Hotel Krasnapolsky and left onto Warmoesstraat, where she started to run. Running, though her sullied lungs screamed that they could not keep up with her noble intentions.

'I'm on my way, Jan. Hang tight, you daft old hippy,' she said aloud, gasping for breath; forcing herself to break into a run once more, holding her makeshift weapons close to her body in case they came tumbling out of her pockets.

Feeling like she had been kicked in the chest with a stitch that snatched the breath away from her, George emerged from the warren of backstreets to the canal on which the Cracked Pot was situated. Here, the lights in the shop windows had turned from white to neon red and pink. Flashing displays told her that live sex shows would accept her euros in return for a smorgasbord of erotic delights – some of them, participatory. Fag Butts' Gay Porn offered her a fisting from a rubber forearm or a half-hour in a cubicle where she could watch an extreme hard-core mini-movie and engage in whatever the hell she liked with whomever she desired in relative privacy. But George was interested in none of those things.

As she sprinted the final 100 metres towards the Cracked Pot, she imagined the red light, reflected in the canal's flat, unfathomable waters was Jan's blood. She took out her knife and hid it up her sleeve, praying she didn't slash her own wrist by accident.

The glazed door to the coffee shop above which she had once lived showed the CLOSED sign. No red lights shone in the rooms above, which had once belonged to her neighbours, Inneke and Katja, but which were now normally occupied by a couple of girls from the Ukraine. The windows in her old attic room showed no signs of life within.

With a trembling hand, breathing fast and shallow enough to make her light-headed, George tried the handle. It gave. The bell tinkled. She walked into the dark shop.

'Welcome, Ella. Or should I say, Georgina? Or should I say, Jacinta?' the Rotterdam Silencer said in that sing-song accent of his.

Scanning the space – so eerily unfamiliar without any lights on – George could not see him. Only the wonky-eyed figures of Jimi Hendrix and Bob Marley on the glow-in-the-dark murals seemed to glower at her now. She held her hand behind her back, allowing the handle of the knife to slide down into her palm. Except she had inserted it the wrong way up and could not now turn the blade around inside her sleeve to face downwards. Shit! Where was the Silencer? And why could she no longer hear Jan?

Then, a glint of something shiny. Metallic.

Gun first, Stijn Pietersen emerged from the booth where he had been sitting, patiently waiting for her to appear; watching her enter the shop and looking around. She shuddered at the thought.

As he advanced towards her, he grinned nastily – his teeth appearing overly white and sharp in that mahogany-tanned face. Crocodile's teeth set into brown leather. George realised she was his next meal.

'Come in, dear,' he said, breathing whisky fumes that she could smell from the door. 'I've been waiting a long time for this. Do you have any final words?'

CHAPTER 55

Rotterdam, a dockside warehouse, Port of Rotterdam, a short while later

Kneeling down, Van den Bergen took a deep breath and started to unzip the first body bag. The only noise in the warehouse was coming from the barking cadaver dog.

'Get that thing out of here!' he shouted, never taking his eyes from the zip.

The smell that emerged was that of sweet putrefaction, where the bacteria had already got to work on the mouldering flesh. Intestinal gases, all escaping the body bag in a noxious, invisible cloud that made him gag.

He expected to see Elvis' face staring blankly out at him but saw instead an unfamiliar long tangle of grey hair that framed a wizened face. No eye in the right socket. Only a blackened mess remained. There was extensive scabbing around the man's mouth.

'A junkie,' he said, holding his nose. A nagging feeling of déjà vu whispered to his subconscious that there was something familiar about this dead man's ruined features, though. Scrolling through the records in his memory of past arrests, he happened upon a match. 'This guy was one of my detective's informants,' he told the uniforms. 'Sepp something or other. An ex-con. I remember, because I'd arrested this chump years ago. He was running with the Rotterdam Silencer in the Nineties. Did a couple of years for dealing coke to tourists looking for a little extra sparkle dust to jazz up their long weekend.' As the zip moved downwards, it revealed holes the size of a man's fist in the body's abdomen. 'Jesus! What the hell caused this?'

At his side, one of the uniforms cleared his throat. 'There a fork-lift back there, Chief Inspector, sir. Its blades or prongs or whatever you want to call them are covered in almost-dried-in blood.'

Nodding, Van den Bergen exhaled slowly and turned to the second bag. Knew exactly whom it contained. Or rather, what it would contain, since his young detective had clearly departed this life. The cadaver dog was never wrong.

He sighed. Tugged at the zip and drew it in one smooth movement to the bottom. Best to get it over with. Tears were queueing in their ducts for release. If it were possible for a heart to sink literally, he was sure his just had. He could feel it in his bladder. Or maybe that was just prostate trouble or a urinary tract infection. 'Here we go.'

Pushing the bag's aperture wide, he drank in the grim sight of Elvis' battered body. His mouth had been gaffer-taped. His nostrils were encrusted with what appeared to be stale vomit. Dried blood on his forehead had turned his otherwise ashen face to purple-red. But there was a bulge behind the gaffer tape.

Van den Bergen reached inside his pocket. It was empty. 'Damn it! I forgot my gloves.' He turned around to face the sombre audience. 'Anybody got any latex gloves?'

The paramedic, who had been standing some way behind the investigative gathering, stepped forwards. 'Here,' she said, proffering a pair.

In vain, he tried to snap them onto his hands. 'Too small.' They stretched and split immediately.

'I'll get more from the ambulance,' she said, smiling apologetically.

'No. Don't bother. Sod it,' Van den Bergen said, taking hold of the edge of the gaffer tape between his fingertips. Gently, he peeled the tape away from Elvis' mouth, taking some of his skin with it. He winced. Wondered briefly that Elvis' raw lips started to bleed immediately.

'Er, Chief Inspector,' the paramedic said.

But Van den Bergen wondered what was inside Elvis' mouth. He parted his detective's lips with careful fingers to reveal a bloodshot, dull eyeball that stared blankly at him. 'Christ,' he said, calculating that since Elvis' eyelids were closed tight over eyeballs that were clearly present and correct, this must be the orb that the grey-haired informant was missing. 'Sick bastards.'

'Chief Inspector!' the paramedic said, pulling at the sleeve of his raincoat.

Turning around in irritation, Van den Bergen barked, 'What? What the bloody hell do you want, woman?' Saw the feverish excitement in her eyes. Became aware at that moment that the skin of Elvis' cheek beneath his fingers, though deathly pale, was still relatively warm.

'He's alive!' they said in unison.

CHAPTER 56

Amsterdam, the Cracked Pot Coffee Shop, at the same time

'Get over here,' the Silencer said, staring at her intently down the barrel of his gun. 'Drop the knife.'

'What knife?' George said, sticking out her chin. Her feet were rooted to the ground, both in defiance and simply because her legs had turned to jelly, having run half a mile from the tram stop. *If you can get through a week with the transportistas, you can get through this,* she told herself. *Maritza was way scarier than this wannabe wanker. She would already have put a bullet in you by now. He's not going to kill you straight away. He wants to play with you first.*

'The knife I can see reflected in the fucking glass of the door, you stupid cow.'

He lunged forwards, reached around her torso, grabbing her wrist tightly, forcing her to drop the knife to the floor with a clatter. Pressed the gun to her temple – all in one smooth movement. Practised in the art of pouncing on and pinioning his prey, just like the crocodile that waits in ambush on the muddy riverbed to engage in a death roll with some gazelle that dares to drink by the water's edge.

'Walk, bitch,' he said through gritted teeth. 'Upstairs.'

As they shuffled together to the back of the shop where the light from the street barely penetrated, past Jan's counter with its heady stink of marijuana coming from produce on the shelves behind as well as the bushy, live plants that flourished in every corner, the Silencer reached into George's anorak.

'Get your hand off my tits,' George said, stifling the urge to punch him in light of the cold steel pressed to her head.

The Silencer laughed. Squeezed her breast playfully. Reached beyond it to withdraw the can of wasp killer from her inside pocket. He threw it to the floor. The meat tenderiser followed suit. As did the cheese wire.

'Nice try,' he said. 'Were you expecting to come here and share a nice bit of Leerdammer, you crazy cunt?'

She was completely unarmed. Not good.

Trudging up the creaking back stairs to the rooms above, George bit back regret and disbelief that she should find herself facing death in a building that had always been part-haven, part-Achilles heel. All paths seemed to lead her back to the Cracked Pot Coffee Shop. Here was the place where she had sought cheap sanctuary as a student. Here, beneath this roof, she had found love with Ad. Here was the house her Aunty Sharon and cousins had stayed in when they had fled the murderous intentions of Gordon Bloom's foot soldier. And yet, this was the same haven that had been infiltrated by the Firestarter. And now, the Silencer. The past connected with the present as if some strange wormhole had appeared in the Cracked Pot Coffee Shop, merging the lives of Ella Williams-May and Georgina McKenzie.

'What the fuck do you want with me, you old has-been?' George asked, desperately trying to keep the panic out of her voice. 'I thought you were locked up. Next minute, you're filling the gap that Gordon Bloom left. Fancy yourself as a Duke, do you?'

The Silencer punched her in the small of her back, shoving her up the stairs. 'Gordon Bloom worked for me, you silly little

358

whore! It wasn't enough that you and that lanky bastard Van den Bergen put me in jail. I got out in five, thanks to a great lawyer. So, I was willing to let that go. I couldn't find you at first, and I'd already put a bullet in him. But then, you two took out my top man in northern Europe, you pair of do-gooding shits, meaning I had to come out of my nice semi-retirement abroad. What Bloom started, I had to finish.'

George tried to steal a glance at him over her shoulder but lost her footing, falling up the stairs. She put her hands out to save herself. Felt her wrist almost give way. Stifled the urge to cry out. 'The Duke was your lackey?! Jesus. How high does the pyramid go? Who do you bloody work for, then?'

'Get up!' the Silencer shouted, kicking her in the behind. 'Get in the fucking room before I put a bullet in your head. I've got a nice surprise for you.'

Her mouth was dry. Her head was spinning. Nausea had a grip on her. On the other side of the door, she could hear muffled moaning.

'If you touch one hair on his head, I'll—'

'You'll what, exactly?'

The Silencer reached around her and pushed open the door to Inneke's old room. The curtains were half closed, allowing only a shaft of glum light through from the street. He flipped the switch and the red light came on. There, beneath the devilish glow, George saw the sources of the muffled moaning. Not one, but two people, standing on chairs with nooses around their necks that had been rigged up from large hooks, hanging from an exposed joist in the ceiling. On the right side stood Jan – mouth taped shut, staring at her through the red light. His glasses on the floor by her feet. On the left side stood an overweight, shabbily dressed woman with matted, caramel-coloured hair extensions and puffed-up eyes where she had presumably been punched repeatedly over time.

'Letitia!' George shouted.

Her mother emitted a series of desperate guttural noises that were masked by the tape. Tears rolling from her damaged eyes, splashing onto her bosom and the floor. A glistening rivulet of snot that had poured from her nose to her chin.

The Silencer pressed his gun harder into George's temple and gripped her upper arm behind her with such ferocity that she could feel only pins and needles in her fingertips.

'You! You took my mother? My fucking mother, you bastard. You've had her all this time?' George could feel every emotion vying for supremacy. Relief, disbelief, confusion. But wrath was the alpha, trampling on those other beta-emotions. She balled her free fist, feeling the fire track down her arm from her heart. Saw the pleading in Letitia's eyes. Saw the vulnerability in Jan's unseeing stare. They were the only things that stayed George's hand. 'And my landlord. An invalid and an old hippy, you low, morally bankrupt son of a bitch.'

Beside her, the Silencer laughed, filling the air with the smell of stale whisky and cigars. 'Your landlord sells great weed, but his coffee's fucking poison. He deserves to die just for that. And your mother?!' He spat at Letitia's stockinged feet. 'I've kept that mouthy cunt fed and watered for the best part of a year, waiting for my moment to come. I wanted to torture you good and proper, the way you tortured me.'

'By kidnapping a pain in the arse from Southwark with a chain-smoking habit? Are you mental?' At that moment, all George wanted to do was cut down her obnoxious mother and soap-dodging landlord, smothering the two with grateful embraces and kisses. She opted not to reveal a shred of this weakness to the Silencer. She felt certain it would be their undoing.

But behind her gag, Letitia was clearly shouting abuse at George now, as opposed to begging for release from her captor. The fight in her hadn't entirely gone, George was pleased to see. Not that fight was any use against a well-tied noose and a drunken psychopath with a loaded gun.

'Wasn't my father enough?' George said, no change to her facial expression when she heard the dim tinkle of the door downstairs. Had the Silencer heard it? Or had the whisky and bloodlust dulled his senses?

'Your father will be dead by now,' he said, biting her ear playfully. No change to his behaviour. 'I told Jorge to put a bullet in his head on the journey back from the Dominican. He was worth taking, though. He was more useful than that bitch, your mother.'

The back stairs creaked. *Oh my God. If it's Van den Bergen, will he remember after all this time to step only at the sides of the treads?*

When another of the stairs groaned loudly in complaint beneath the newcomer's weight, George coughed. Had the Silencer noticed? No. He was now sucking on her neck like a starving vampire, intermittently telling her how he was going to kick Letitia's and Jan's chairs away and fuck her while they wriggled and jerked themselves to death. She could feel his erect penis pressing into her right buttock.

'Do what you like,' she said. 'You're the one with the gun, *cocodrilo*. Or should I say, Mr Bebchuck?'

Another stair creaked. Closer this time. The door behind them was ajar. She had to keep this lunatic busy.

Reaching behind her, she felt for the bulge in his trousers and began to massage him through the fabric. 'I worked for the *transportistas*, didn't I?' she said, forcing a lascivious grin. 'What makes you think I wouldn't get off on you killing them two?'

So tempting, just to grab at his penis and try to wrench the damned thing clean off. But George was buying time, and sex was always an acceptable form of payment with this kind of man. If he released her right arm so that he could undo his trousers, she would momentarily have two hands free. Could she possibly disarm him, then? Was the approaching person on the stairs friend, foe or simply a nosey customer, looking for the working girl who normally occupied this room?

361

The room was still but for the heavy breathing of the Silencer. It was as if her world had frozen in this macabre scene of her nearest and dearest, hanging from the ceiling, wearing baffled expressions while their future murderer masturbated himself against her hand.

'Take it out,' George said, surreptitiously winking at Letitia. 'I want you in my mouth.'

'Good girl,' the Silencer said, starting to move rhythmically against George. 'Young Danny always said you were hot stuff.'

Ignoring the searing pang of grief that mention of her dead ex-lover evoked, George bit back her revulsion and waited for the Silencer to move. He had to let go of something. Either her, or the gun. Lying on top of a cabinet next to the bed in the room, she spied a bullwhip, a cat-o'-nine-tails and a giant purple dildo. They would have to do. She felt hope surge inside her. Another creak on the stairs. She coughed again.

In the fraction of a second when George felt the Silencer's hand release its grip on her upper arm, she flung herself across the room. Grabbed the cat-o'-nine tails. Flicked it with all the power she could muster at the Silencer's now-exposed erect penis. He screamed, firing a bullet into the ceiling so that a shower of white plaster and dust fell onto them.

At the same time, a man barrelled headlong into the room, spraying an aerosol into the Silencer's face. Her father.

The Silencer dropped the gun, clasping his hands to his eyes, screaming. Sank to his knees. But George's father stood over him, emptying the can of wasp killer over his nose and mouth.

'Die, *el cocodrilo*!' he shouted in Spanish. 'Die like the vermin you are.'

'Enough Dad, you're gonna kill us all,' George shouted.

She snatched up the giant purple dildo. It whistled as she swung it like an erotic baton onto the back of the Silencer's head – hard enough to knock him onto the floor. Grabbing the bullwhip, she straddled the writhing trafficker. Yanked his arms

362

behind him, while he coughed and spluttered. Tried to bind his hands with the end of the whip. Perhaps she could hog-tie the bastard.

'Go back and find the knife,' George said. 'I dropped it near the door. Cut these two down. Call the police.'

But her father was transfixed, looking up at the struggling Letitia with his hand over his mouth against the stinking chemical fug of insecticide.

'Do it!' she yelled. 'And get a bloody window open before we all asphyxiate.'

He nodded. Clattered back down the stairs. Beneath her, the Silencer began to flex his body back and forth like a crocodile in captivity, trying to free itself from the constraints of its human master.

'I'm going to fucking kill you, bitch!' he yelled, punctuating the sentiment with a coughing fit.

'Keep still, you twat!' she shouted, searching the floor for the discarded gun. She spied it underneath the bed. A judgement call. Shift her weight on this wriggling quarry, or go for the gun? Getting the gun meant she won.

Arching her back, she let go of the whip momentarily. Reached for the gun. Banking on being quick enough. But she no longer had enough purchase on the Silencer's body to keep him pinned down. He flicked his legs out from under him with such force that both chairs beneath Letitia and Jan toppled.

'No!' George screamed, seeing her mother and ex-landlord writhing at the ends of their nooses like butterflies trying to free themselves from their chrysalises. 'Papa!'

The Silencer was trying to get to his knees though his hands were still loosely tied behind his back. She snatched up the pistol and took another hefty swipe at his head with the butt. Drop-kicked him in the groin. He crumpled back to the ground, his eyes unfocused and skewed.

Grabbing the lower legs of both her mother and Jan, using

363

every ounce of strength she could muster, she pushed them back upwards in a bid to loosen the pressure on their necks.

'I'm coming! I'm here!' Her father rushed through the open door, holding the knife.

'Cut them down,' George cried. 'Please don't let it be too late.'

CHAPTER 57

Amsterdam, Onze Lieve Vrouw Hospital, 5 June

'Ah. Here he is,' a familiar, deep rumbling voice said on the other side of the room.

Elvis opened his heavy eyelids and waited patiently until his brain slowly made sense of his surroundings. The room was overly bright and austere. There were several scents on the air. A medicinal smell of cleaning fluid, unwashed skin, oranges and cabbage. The sound of medical machinery in the background, bleeping. A Tannoy announcement somewhere further away that Dr Awaad should report to the paediatric ward.

He was in hospital. Was he with his mother?

Trying to turn, he realised he was in a neck brace. He was the patient. Not her. The muscles in his lower back were on fire. His bottom was almost entirely numb. The tingling in his toes reminded him he was cold. Swallowing was agony.

'I—'

The words wouldn't come. He smacked his lips until a redhead appeared by his side, holding a glass of water, trying to position a straw on his tongue. The smell of cabbage came with her. Her signature scent. Good old Marie.

'Here you go. Have some of this,' she said, smiling. 'I brought you a cake. I know you don't like cake, but I baked it myself. And if you don't like that, I got you a twelve-pack of crisps.'

He took a tentative sip. Realised he was parched. Then, drained the glass, though the water scratched like shards of broken glass on the way down.

'You had us all worried for a minute there,' the rumbling voice said.

A tall figure loomed behind Marie. Long and lean and topped with a shock of white hair. His face came into focus. Unsmiling. Large hooded grey eyes framed by the dark bows of his eyebrows.

Elvis winced by way of greeting. 'It hurts everywhere,' he said, his voice cracking.

'I'll ask the nurse to give you more painkillers, shall I?' Marie asked. She stood, scraping her chair on the vinyl floor. Left the room, reaching up and patting Van den Bergen's shoulder as she did so.

Van den Bergen took a seat, folding his long frame so that he would fit by the bedside. Elvis relished the fatherly presence. Wished his mother was there to comfort him.

'Do you remember anything?' Van den Bergen asked, leaning forwards so that Elvis didn't have to move his head to see him clearly.

'Not really,' he said. 'There were some guys in an alleyway. They went after my informant and then came for me. They knocked me out. Next minute, I'm in a warehouse and …' He allowed the terrible memories to flood through him like fast-acting poison. Wishing he could unthink those thoughts. When the tears came, he had no energy or inclination to stem their flow.

'We'll get you counselling, Dirk,' Van den Bergen said, patting his hand. 'You don't have to talk about it now.' He reached into his cardigan pocket and brought out a blister pack of some medication or other. Popped two bright red pills into his hand and swallowed them down with a gulp of Evian from a vending machine bottle. 'And that bastard Stijn Pietersen has been silenced for good. He's back behind bars, thanks to George and her dad. He'll go down and stay down, this time. Even the most expensive brief in the world won't get him off. But there is something I need to tell you, I'm afraid.'

Almost too weary to listen to his words, Elvis started to drift off to sleep. He registered the mention of his mother but that was all. Opened his eyes again, sensing somebody was in the room apart from Van den Bergen.

'Did you hear any of what I just said?' Van den Bergen asked.

'Eh?' Elvis smiled at the handsome Arne, who was now standing at the end of his bed, bearing a bunch of really horrible orange and yellow flowers.

'Your mother …' his boss began, standing and offering a curt smile to the newcomer. He turned back to Elvis. Opened his mouth to speak. Seemed to think better of it. 'It'll keep,' he finally said. 'Main thing is, we got the bad guy. That's all that matters. Live your life, Dirk. It's spread out before you now like a feast. Eat your fill, son. And savour every mouthful.'

CHAPTER 58

Onze Lieve Vrouw Hospital, moments later

'Why the hell can't I get a frigging decent cuppa tea in this shithole?' Letitia said, pushing the cup back towards George with such unveiled disgust that the contents slopped onto the pristine hospital sheet. Turning to her sister and sucking her teeth slowly, she scratched at her matted hair-extensions. 'Are you hearing this, Shaz? Fucking Liptons, innit? I ain't drinking that pisswater after I've been locked up like some dog what's got rabies with my dodgy pulmonaries and sickle cell anaemics. On a *houseboat*. A boat, like some fucking vagrant. By a man whose name is "stain" but spelled wrong. Stain, I axe you! For a full *year*, though!' She widened her eyes, which was a feat in itself, considering how swollen they still were. 'I get seasick when it bloody rains too hard. That bastard left me on my own for a month at a time with nothing but a freezer full of bread and forty-six tins of ham. Ham! And it was from some shitty bargain bin supermarket like Lidl. I don't even fucking like ham, do I, Shaz?'

Aunty Sharon folded her meaty arms and shook her head so that her super-sleek bobbed wig wobbled with indignation. 'No, love. You said it gives you wind. And that tinned ham's rough as arseholes. I wouldn't have ate it.'

Amid the riotous family reunion that had temporarily seen a

368

truce between Letitia and Aunty Sharon, George helped herself to a blob of antibacterial gel and allowed herself a satisfied smile. Massaging the gel in thoroughly between her fingers and under her nails.

'What you grinning at, girl?' her mother said. Sneering at George's father who was sitting at the side of her bed in a day chair. 'And what's he got to be so happy about, and all? It's like the two of yous is in cahoots.' She wagged her finger between them. No shellac nail extensions on them today.

'We saved your life,' George said. 'Your mate Stijn is banged up for good. Anyway, are you even going to ask about poor Jan?'

'Who the fuck is Jan to me? What do I give a shit about some old hippy white feller?' She grabbed dramatically at her throat. Jabbed her thumb in Michael's direction. 'If it weren't for Julio bleeding Iglesias, here, dicking around with that wasp killer when he should have been cutting me down, I wouldn't have big marks on my sodding neck. I'm gonna have to wear a scarf now! How can I wear a low-cut top to bingo, if I've got a fucking scarf wrapped round my neck? It's diabolical, is what it is.'

'Papa's a bona fide hero,' George said, reaching out to squeeze her father's hand.

Letitia treated her ex-partner to a sour, downturned smile. 'An hero? Maybe you could get a job in pest control killing invisible wasps, darling, but I don't think you'll be getting a call back to audition for the next Batman film. Certainly not with them legs. Know what I mean?'

Aunty Sharon stood with a flourish, all dressed to impress in her Designers at Debenhams Sunday best with her bloated feet stuffed into her favourite Betty Boop shoes. She marched over to Michael and clamped his head into the sort of hug George had craved all the while she had been travelling with the *transportistas*. The sort of hug that made anyone feel safe.

'Take no notice of her, love,' Sharon said, patting his newly cropped hair. 'She's got that PSTD.' She lowered her voice. 'She ain't changed, you know. She still wins Olympic gold at being a cow. But I'm glad she's alive. And you got a diamond of a girl in our George. You should be very proud.'

George's father nodded, blinking fast and blushing. 'I am. I'm the luckiest man in the world.'

'Oi!' Letitia shouted over Tinesha and Patrice's heads to her sister. 'Get out the way, you disrespectful little rarseclarts! I'm trying to have a conversation with your mother, here.' She reached out, swatted her niece and nephew with the hospital lunch menu. 'Did you just call me a cow?'

'Nah.' Aunty Sharon kissed George on the head. She didn't smell of baking or the stale, dry-ice smell of the titty bar today. She smelled of her expensive perfume that Tinesha had bought her for Christmas. 'You got defective ears on top of all the other shit what's wrong with you,' she said, sitting heavily back on her vinyl armchair so that the air in the cushion hissed out noisily like a well-aimed cuss.

'I've only got four years to live!' Letitia said, her bottom lip wavering though there was no sign of tears. Calculating her next move.

George cleared her throat, drinking in with no small degree of satisfaction the sight of her entire family, gathered together at short notice in that cramped hospital room. Relieved that Jan was down the hallway, already complaining that the doctors were trying to poison him with untested pharmaceuticals. And there was Van den Bergen, visible through the window, chatting to one of the doctors in the corridor about Elvis' condition, no doubt.

'Well,' George said. She rose from her seat, ushering Aunty Sharon, Patrice and Tinesha to their feet. 'If you've only got four years to live, Mother Dearest, how about you spend five minutes talking to your long-lost baby-father. We've all got some place we need to be, haven't we, Aunty Shaz?'

'Yeah,' Sharon said, linking her by the arm. 'I need a smoke and I'm having cake withdrawals. We're going to the caff. I'll bring you back a slab of chocolate-flavoured arsenic, if you behave.' Chuckling mischievously. They walked in unison to the door.

'Smuggle me some cigs in, will you, Shaz?' Letitia called out. 'The doctors said I mustn't get stressed, innit? And get your face scrubbed, girl!' A comment clearly intended for George. 'You look like a bleeding mental case with that magic marker all over your mush. They're gonna take the piss out of you something rotten when you get home.'

'Bye, Letitia,' George said, grinning at her mother; turning to wink at her father.

He smiled back at her and raised a thick, black eyebrow, exactly as he had done when she had been a child.

In the middle of a busy hospital corridor, surrounded by her family, standing by the side of Van den Bergen, George considered the journey she had embarked upon. Reflected on where she was now, in relation to where she had been some fourteen months earlier – a girl in a restaurant who had lost everything and had gained only an eye and a bellyful of blind panic. She had followed a trail that had led her halfway across the world in pursuit of the truth and in pursuit of justice, under the guise of investigating the mysterious deaths of six young people. There, high in the peaks of Honduras and Chiapas, deep in the jungle of the Yucatan and lost in the middle of the Caribbean Sea, she had faced her worst nightmare. Her only real fear. Not anxiety about dying, but the fear of being utterly on her own.

There, in the midst of that bustling hospital ward, George McKenzie, the consummate loner, realised that she was anything *but* alone. For now, at least, there was nothing left to be afraid of.

Acknowledgements

The Girl Who Had No Fear sprang from three sources. The first was my bez, Louise Owen, who insisted there was a story in city canals that mysteriously claim lives. You nagged the fuck out of me, Weez, but you got there in the end! Well done. The second was my friend, Max Barber, who told me all about the risks men take at gay chem-sex parties in pursuit of hedonistic fun. I hope I've done your observations justice, Max. The third was my ex-husband, Christian, with whom I've shared wonderful trips to Mexico and continue to share a great love of all things Central American. Thanks to those three friends for their inspiration.

As ever, the people who make my writing possible are as follows:

My children, Natalie and Adam, who make me want to be a better woman and write better stories, which, one day, they will be old enough to read.

My wonderful partner in crime, Caspian Dennis. Where I'm the bullshit, he's the business, but more importantly, he regularly fixes my head when the going gets tough with words of wisdom, huge laughs and medicinal gin. If it weren't for him, you wouldn't be reading any of this. Thanks also to the other folks at Abner Stein – world's best literary agency, especially Sandy, Ben, Laura and Felicity.

My editor Phoebe and the outstanding team at Avon, HarperCollins – Oli, Helen, Helena, Natashas H & W, Hannah, Ellie and Louis. It is their forward-thinking and excellent taste that has brought you a series starring a character quite as kickass, unapologetic and savvy as George McKenzie. I salute them.

The amazing book-bloggers, who are so giving of their time in reading and reviewing my novels.

The online book clubs, whose members are such passionate and discerning readers.

Those who have stuck with the George McKenzie series from the beginning and those who are just discovering it for the first time with *The Girl Who Had No Fear*. You are definitely the best readers ever, and I owe you a huge debt of gratitude. I promise to write bigger, better, faster and importantly, more George stories just for you!

The cockblankets, who improve life immeasurably. And no, these aren't unusual pets or erotic toys.

My writing buddies, Wendy Storer and Steph Williams, for ongoing support and tremendousness.

Enjoyed *The Girl Who* series? Get your hands on the fifth gripping thriller in the George McKenzie series.

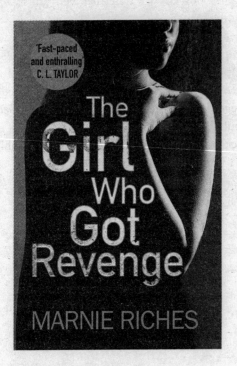

Find out how it all began in *Born Bad*, the first in the gritty Manchester crime series

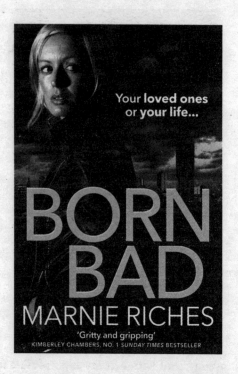

'A leading light in Mancunian noir' Guardian

How far would you go to protect your empire?

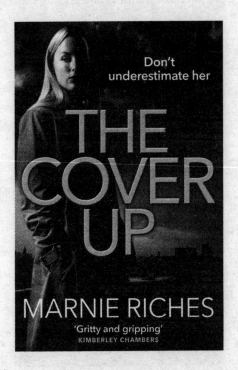

Don't
underestimate her

THE
COVER
UP

MARNIE RICHES

'Gritty and gripping'
KIMBERLEY CHAMBERS

A heart-stopping read with a gritty edge, perfect for fans of Martina Cole and Kimberley Chambers.